Triggs
Triggs, Bob
Tumble : the andaman event

$25.95
ocn952446726

WITHDRAWN

TUMBLE
the andaman event

BOOK ONE OF THE TUMBLE PENTALOGY

TUMBLE

THE ANDAMAN EVENT

BOB TRIGGS

TUMBLE
THE ANDAMAN EVENT

Copyright © 2016 Bob Triggs.

All rights reserved. No part of this book may be used or reproduced by any means, graphic, electronic, or mechanical, including photocopying, recording, taping or by any information storage retrieval system without the written permission of the author except in the case of brief quotations embodied in critical articles and reviews.

This is a work of fiction. All of the characters, names, incidents, organizations, and dialogue in this novel are either the products of the author's imagination or are used fictitiously.

iUniverse books may be ordered through booksellers or by contacting:

iUniverse
1663 Liberty Drive
Bloomington, IN 47403
www.iuniverse.com
1-800-Authors (1-800-288-4677)

Because of the dynamic nature of the Internet, any web addresses or links contained in this book may have changed since publication and may no longer be valid. The views expressed in this work are solely those of the author and do not necessarily reflect the views of the publisher, and the publisher hereby disclaims any responsibility for them.

Any people depicted in stock imagery provided by Thinkstock are models, and such images are being used for illustrative purposes only. Certain stock imagery © Thinkstock.

ISBN: 978-1-4917-9506-4 (sc)
ISBN: 978-1-4917-9507-1 (hc)

Library of Congress Control Number: 2016908543

Print information available on the last page.

iUniverse rev. date: 06/17/2016

This book is for my daughter and my son-in-law,
Sarah and Alan Durbin.

The Tumble series is dedicated to my wonderful wife,
Dongyan.

CONTENTS

PART ONE

Wednesday, December 25, 2019

1: *Khaolak Golden Palace Hotel, Khao Lak, Thailand; 1725h* 3
2: *Mehganinagar, Sector 28, Gandhinagar, Gujarat, India; 2004h* 20

Thursday, December 26, 2019

3: *Khao Lak Beach, Khao Lak, Thailand; 0600h* 44
4: *Fortune Resort Bay Island, Port Blair, South Andaman Island; 1009h* 51
5: *Institute of Seismological Research, Gandhinagar, Gujarat, India; 1031h* 60
6: *Khao Lak Beach, Khao Lak, Thailand; 1033h* 77
7: *Rashtrapati Bhavan, New Delhi, India; 1217h* 96
8: *Institute of Seismological Research, Gandhinagar, Gujarat, India; 1609h* 117
9: *97-20 57th Avenue, Corona, New York, USA; 1759h* 133

Part Two

Sunday, June 21, 2020

10: *Davis Street, Stanley, Falkland Islands; 1540h*.............................143
11: *97-20 57th Avenue, Corona, New York, USA; 1907h*................... 156

Monday, June 22, 2020

12: *Infinity Meteorological Database Systems, Palo Alto, California; 0815h*..166
13: *Met Office, Stanley, Falkland Islands; 0959h* 176
14: *Infinity Meteorological Database Systems, Palo Alto, California; 1417h*... 184
15: *M/V Akademik Knipovich II, South Atlantic Ocean; 2104h* 191

Tuesday, June 23, 2020

16: *Met Office, Stanley, Falkland Islands; 0916h*............................... 207
17: *Infinity Meteorological Database Systems, Palo Alto, California; 1022h*..216
18: *Infinity Meteorological Database Systems, Palo Alto, California; 1347h*.. 227

Wednesday, June 24, 2020

19: *National Weather Center, Buenos Aires, Argentina; 0811h*........ 241
20: *Infinity Meteorological Database Systems, Palo Alto, California; 0827h*..252
21: *Dover Heights, Sydney, Australia; 1347h* 272
22: *Infinity Meteorological Database Systems, Palo Alto, California; 1506h*.. 282

23: *The Oval Office, The White House, Washington, DC; 1559h* 292
24: *Infinity Meteorological Database Systems, Palo Alto, California; 1637h* 301
25: *CPC Central Headquarters, Zhongnanhai, Beijing, China; 1800h* 307

Thursday, June 25, 2020

26: *Infinity Meteorological Database Systems, Palo Alto, California; 0758h* 314
27: *National Weather Center, Buenos Aires, Argentina; 0823h* 320
28: *Infinity Meteorological Database Systems, Palo Alto, California; 0902h* 328
29: *The Oval Office, The White House, Washington, DC; 2104h* 344

Friday, June 26, 2020

30: *Infinity Meteorological Database Systems, Palo Alto, California; 0814h* 355
31: *The President's Private Study, The White House, Washington, DC; 1123h* 360
32: *Infinity Meteorological Database Systems, Palo Alto, California; 1242h* 367
33: *Bir Lehlou, Western Sahara; 1317h* 375
34: *Infinity Meteorological Database Systems, Palo Alto, California; 1446h* 384

Saturday, June 27, 2020

35: *Los Robles Avenue, Barron Park, Palo Alto, California; 0601h* .. 394
36: *The President's Private Study, The White House, Washington, DC; 1017h* 404

37: *Petro Santa Nella Service Station & Diner, Gustine, California, USA; 1114h* 408
38: *LAX International Airport, Los Angeles, California, USA; 1326h* 413
39: *The Oval Office, The White House, Washington, DC; 1434h* 419
40: *Arland Avenue, South San Gabriel, California; 1647h* 447
41: *The President's Private Study, The White House, Washington, DC; 1812h* 455
42: *Arland Avenue, South San Gabriel, California; 1903h* 463
43: *The President's Private Study, The White House, Washington, DC; 2101h* 473

Acknowledgments 483

PART ONE

1

Khaolak Golden Palace Hotel
Khao Lak, Thailand
Coordinates: 08° 37' 48.4" N, 98° 14' 40.2" E
Wednesday, December 25, 2019, 1725h

A blue-and-red taxi sweeps through the entrance of the Khaolak Golden Palace Hotel and comes to an abrupt halt on the red herringbone forecourt with a screech of underinflated tires. The driver's door swings open, and a small, aging Thai who couldn't be a day under seventy leaps out with surprising sprightliness. As he hurries around to remove a suitcase from the trunk, the passenger door opens.

Peter Hutchins, a forty-seven-year-old computer software engineer from London, climbs out and faces the five-story hotel with a distant expression in his blue eyes. He is six feet tall, slim, muscular and his dark brown hair is turning gray, but he's still handsome and an attractive catch for any woman. Casually dressed in a white golf shirt and loose gray flannel trousers, he takes a moment of pause to swallow back an emotional lump as mental images of the disastrous trip fifteen years earlier remind him that he's not here on vacation. For too long, he has wallowed in a stagnant pool of guilt, self-pity, and grief. This is supposed to be a therapeutic journey intended to kick-start his life, but as the horror comes racing back, he begins to wonder if this might be a huge mistake.

He senses the ghostly presence of his wife standing happy and content beside him as the kids run ahead toward the entrance. His eyes rove over the front of the structure, and he's overwhelmed with disenchantment. *Has anything changed at all?* Even the facade has been rebuilt to its original design. *Yes, very little has changed, yet nothing is the same.*

His ruminations are interrupted by the taxi driver, who places the suitcase on the ground at his side. The visions of his family vanish as Peter snaps back to the present. He removes a wallet from his pocket and counts five hundred Thai baht into the cabbie's hand.

Peter turns his head in the direction of the ocean as the old man stuffs the money into a pocket and climbs back into his car. The beach is hidden from view behind a tall hedge and a line of palm trees, but he doesn't need to see the sand and water to know where it is. How could he forget? It's been the bane of his miserable existence for the past one and a half decades.

The click of hurried footsteps on the Omega block paving disrupts his thoughts for a second time, and he swings around to see a porter rushing across the forecourt. Peter has only one suitcase, and as it isn't heavy, he declines assistance from the bellhop. He picks up the case and heads for the main entrance. A concierge opens the door as he approaches, allowing him to pass unimpeded into the spacious lobby.

Inside the hotel, the floor is covered with blue carpeting overprinted with golden designs of the Ratchaphruek tree in full bloom. It represents a combination of the national flower and Thai monarchy. A large pine tree adorned with twinkling lights, colored balls, and garland stands in one corner while the back walls are beautified with bright, multihued paper decorations. The soft sound of Christmas music drifts around the atrium, and a subtle aroma of cinnamon has a soothing effect on Peter's senses as he walks over to the reception desk.

The young clerk smiles pleasantly before addressing him in perfect English. "Good afternoon, sir. How may I help you?"

"I have a reservation for the next three nights," he replies wearily. "My name is Peter Hutchins."

The receptionist turns to a computer and checks the files with a few swift strokes on the keypad. "I see you've flown in from London, Mr. Hutchins," she remarks, turning her head to look at him as she speaks. "Are you here for the memorial service tomorrow?"

"Yes."

The young girl takes a few moments to validate the key card for his room before laying it on the countertop in front of him. She pushes an open registration book in his direction and places a pen on the facing page. "Please sign here, Mr. Hutchins. Your room number is 304." Peter picks up the ballpoint and signs the register while she continues to talk. "Did you know someone who died in the tsunami?"

"My wife and two daughters."

Perhaps the blunt response makes her feel she is being too

intrusive because her cheerful expression switches to one of embarrassment. She stammers a hasty apology. *"Oh ... I-I'm sorry."*

Peter replaces the pen back on the open page with a wistful sigh and makes an attempt to dispel her unease by sounding more upbeat. "That's okay, love. What's done is done. No one can go back to change it."

She slides a pamphlet and a coupon across the countertop. "People will be congregating on the beach for prayer around the time the tsunami came ashore. This is a list of various religious groups and churches who will be holding memorial services throughout the day. The tsunami warning sirens will sound a three-minute accolade beginning at ten twenty-seven." She taps the face of the voucher with her forefinger. "This is for a special service open to hotel residents and guests in our banqueting suite. It starts at one o'clock and will be followed by a free buffet, compliments of the manager."

Peter manages a weak smile as he picks the pamphlet and ticket up from the countertop. "Is there somewhere nearby where I can buy flowers?"

The receptionist nods and points toward a wide passageway leading out of the lobby to his left. "You'll find a florist at the end of the shopping hall, but I think they're closed for the day. They'll be opening early tomorrow morning though—around six o'clock, I believe."

"Tomorrow morning will be fine," he replies. "Thank you."

"You're welcome, sir."

Peter picks up the suitcase and walks across to an alcove on the right where the elevators are located. He pushes the call button and, feeling more relaxed, begins humming to the strains of "Silent Night" while he waits for the car to arrive. The shopping hall is a new feature that's been added to the hotel since his last stay, but everything else appears identical to how it was fifteen years ago.

Once in his room, he opens the suitcase to get at the toiletries. He's desperate for a long, hot shower to wash away the dried perspiration and grime that have accumulated on his body over the last twenty hours. Thirty minutes later, he emerges from the bathroom wearing a maroon bathrobe and begins to unpack. He hangs a dark suit, a neatly pressed white shirt, and a black tie in the closet and then transfers the socks, underwear, and casual clothes into a drawer unit. After he's finished, he decides to take ten minutes to unwind before going down to the restaurant for supper.

Peter flops onto the bed and lies on his back with his hands clasped behind his head. He stares insipidly at the ceiling, sifting through the events that bind him eternally to this place. Fifteen years ago, he was thirty-two and an affectionate husband to a beautiful twenty-nine-year-old wife, Beverly. They were the epitome of a perfect couple and the caring parents of two daughters—Kathleen, eleven, and an energetic six-year-old, Angela. They could not have been happier.

During the summer of 2004, cold, wet, and windy weather swept across the United Kingdom with relentless fortitude. It prompted the idea to vacate the damp climate for a fortnight in the sun, and one evening in October, they sat down to flip through some holiday brochures.

Peter used to be an avid wildlife photographer, and a visit to the rainforests of Kaeng Krung National Park in the northwestern Surat Thani Province of Thailand was at the top of his bucket list. The two mountain ranges of protected forestation included creatures such as tigers, tapirs, gaurs, and numerous bird genera. In addition to the faunas, they would see some of the most spectacular scenery the world had to offer, but he knew it would be an uphill battle to get Beverly interested. She never shared his enthusiasm for "uncivilization," a word of her own creation, but then he wouldn't be a worthy husband if he didn't understand these little verities after eleven years of marriage. He knew she would come up with myriad excuses not to embark on a camping adventure, but not least of all, she wouldn't hesitate to use the children if it suited her schema. Beverley's summarization of a perfect break was to laze around on a beach with a margarita. Bearing this in mind, Peter worked on a solution to accommodate both desires, but first he gave her the opportunity to go to Kaeng Krung. As expected, she didn't hesitate to decry the proposition by pointing out how uncomfortable and exhaustive it would be.

"Honestly, I have no aspirations to gad about in a foreign country on the back of an elephant," she said firmly. "I don't know how anyone can construe that as a relaxing holiday."

Peter picked up a brochure with pictures of an idyllic beach at Khao Lak. Golden sand. Blue waters. Sunny skies.

"How about here?" He waited in anticipation for several minutes as she leafed through the pamphlet.

"Can we afford a holiday in Thailand?"

"I don't see why not. Our finances are in good shape."

She took a few moments to answer. "Okay then."

Peter was unable to contain the excitement in his voice. "Khao Lak is a hundred and fifteen miles from Kaeng Krung. I can book a three-day elephant safari for Kathleen and myself while you hang out at the seaside with Angela."

She hesitated, probably to grasp the fact that he'd outflanked her, but there wasn't a good reason for her not to compromise. "Why do you want to take Kathleen?"

"Well, she's developed strong inclinations against the exploitation of animals since we encouraged her to join the junior branch of the World Wildlife Association," Peter explained. "This will be the perfect opportunity to introduce her to some of the creatures in their natural habitat and experience the rawness of the wild firsthand."

Later that night he went online and made reservations for an elephant safari. He expected Kathleen to be excited, but when he revealed the plan to his eldest daughter on the following evening, he was stunned when she rejected the idea. She proclaimed it would be too scary to sleep in a tent with tigers and other creatures roaming around in the darkness.

"There's nothing to be afraid of, sweetie," he said in an attempt to sway her mind. "We're not going to get attacked while we sleep."

"But what if we are?"

"It's not going to happen, babe. We'll be sharing the same tent."

"That won't stop them."

"Yes it will. I'll be there to protect you."

She inclined her head to one side. "And who's going to save *me* after *you* get eaten, Daddy?"

Despite his best efforts, she remained resolute. "Once I cancel your proviso, I may not be able to rebook it," he warned, disappointed at his inability to influence a change of heart in his own daughter.

"That's okay," she replied offhandedly.

However, he clung to the hope that she'd change her mind, and waited for a couple of days before he finally canceled her place on the safari.

Their flight landed at Phuket International Airport late on the morning of Christmas Eve. They had hired a car in advance, but a mix-up in the rental company's booking department meant they were unable to furnish him with their preferred vehicle choice. He expressed his dissatisfaction but had a change of heart when his eyes fell on the LR2 substitute. He liked it inside and out, and after a few minutes behind the wheel, he couldn't deny that he'd fallen in love with the off-roader.

Peter turns to lie on his side and gazes at the pastel-yellow wall through a film of moisture. He'd been optimistic that a pilgrimage would bring some closure. He'd vowed to make this crusade more than a decade ago, but as the date drew near each year, he was filled with dread and postponed the trip until the next year. Now that he has made it this far, he's determined to face the demons. Whatever happens tomorrow, and over the next couple of days, is in the hands of providence.

He begins to evoke happier memories.

Kathleen and Angela would come charging into the bedroom on Christmas morning. Even before he had a chance to focus, the two high-spirited youngsters would be bouncing on the bed, pleading for them to wake up so they could go downstairs to open their presents. The gleam of elation in their eyes, the surprised expressions on their faces, and the happy squeals of delight as they unwrapped their gifts always brought pleasure. In 2004, the parents allowed the girls to unwrap one present each before they left, and the rest would be opened when they got back home. Fifteen years later, the same gifts remain unopened, stored in the attic at the home of his in-laws with the name tags still attached.

His mind drifts back to Boxing Day. The flight to Kaeng Krung was scheduled to depart Phuket at ten-thirty, and he asked Beverly to drive him to the airport. She refused, citing her inexperience at driving on the "wrong" side of the road, and suggested he should drive himself. This arrangement was unsatisfactory because it would leave her without transportation, but Beverly was adamant, emphasizing that she'd never get behind the wheel regardless of the situation. At nine o'clock, Peter accompanied his wife and two daughters to the seaside.

He waited for Beverly to spread a colorful beach towel on the sand before speaking. "I wish you would keep the car … just in case."

"Seriously, Pete, the girls and I are going to be fine," she replied, trying to reassure him there was no reason to fret. "All you've got to do is forget we exist for the next few days; otherwise, you're not going to enjoy the trip."

He watched Angela and Kathleen playing tag on the beach, laughing, and giggling boisterously as they chased each other around in circles. "I have my mobile, so make sure you call me if there's a problem, all right?"

She gently cupped the palm of her left hand over his cheek. "Like you can do *what*, darling? You won't even get a signal in the jungle. Just have fun because that's exactly what we are going to do."

Peter put his hands on her hips and pulled her close to him. "I love you."

Beverly laughed and responded by wrapping her arms around his neck. "I love you too." She pressed her lips against his and began to give him a lingering kiss, but seconds later, Angela's voice interrupted the moment of bliss.

"Oooo … look at Mummy and Daddy kissing." This was followed by a hand-over-the-mouth titter.

Beverly giggled and pulled away. "Go *on*, you silly human being. You've got a plane to catch." She raised her voice. "*Angela! Kathleen! Daddy's leaving now. Come and give him a hug before he goes.*"

Kathleen ran up to him, raised herself on tiptoe, and gave him a brief cuddle. "I love you, Daddy. I hope you have a good time ... and I *really* don't mind if you bring me back one of those cute little monkeys from the jungle."

Peter looked into his daughter's eyes and laughed. "I've got monkeys enough with you two. Why would I want to punish myself even more?"

She giggled and gave him a gentle slap on the arm before stepping aside as Angela, who had been farther away, scampered across the sand toward him. She leapt into his arms in a single bound, clinging to him with her legs wrapped around his waist and her hands clasped behind his neck. Her brow was beaded with perspiration, and panting hard from exertion, she pressed a clammy cheek against his.

"I *love* you, Daddy," she told him between gasps of air, still breathless from running around. She gave him a sloppy kiss on the cheek before leaning back in his arms to gaze at him with a mischievous sparkle in her blue eyes. "I want one of those cute little monkeys too."

Before he had a chance to respond, the energized youngster chuckled and pushed herself out of his arms to land square on her feet. She spun on her heels and cast a glance over her shoulder at Kathleen. With an excited giggle, she ran toward the water. After she'd given herself a decent lead, she yelled out to her sister, "*Last one in is a dork!*"

Peter shook his head in amazement. "That girl's got *far* too much energy."

Beverly laughed before replying. "Well, if I'm lucky, she'll sleep well tonight."

He bade farewell and walked away to recover the Land Rover

from the resort's parking structure. As he reached the beachhead, he threw a final backward glance. Beverly was sitting on the towel, rubbing sunscreen on her arms, and the girls were splashing around at the edge of the water.

It took an hour to drive to the airport. After checking in, Peter discovered he would be flying on an old 1950s DC-3 owned by a small company affiliated with the national parks of Thailand. The first thing he noted on boarding was the well-worn cabin furnishings and fading decor. It was a little disconcerting because it caused him worry about the Dakota's mechanical condition and whether it could fly the seventy-five-minute journey to Kaeng Krung without falling from the sky. Despite a bumpy flight, the pilot landed the seventy-year-old ex-military aircraft safely on a grassy strip that served as an airfield.

After three exhilarating days that exceeded his expectations, Peter arrived back at base camp on the morning of December 30 with two hours to kill before the return flight was scheduled to leave. He was surprised to see hundreds of people surrounding the small building that doubled as a ticket office and departure lounge. Everyone appeared disheveled and weary, but he never read anything into it because after three days in the jungle, his own image left a lot to be desired. What he failed to detect was a heavy cloud of despondency that hung over the crowd.

A middle-aged man with a European countenance sauntered past, and Peter took a step in his direction. "Excuse me, do you speak English?"

"I *am* English."

"Why are there so many people here?"

The man stared back with disbelief on his face. "You haven't *heard*, then?"

"Heard what? I've been out in the jungle for the last few days. I only got back about thirty minutes ago."

"A tsunami hit the west coast on Boxing Day. Phuket International is closed to nonessential domestic flights, and only planes carrying emergency supplies, equipment, and international aid are allowed in."

Peter was aghast. "You're joking, right?"

"Nope. I've been stuck here for three bloody days, and as you can see, a lot of people are waiting to get out."

"Bloody hell. I need to get to Khao Lak. Do you know if they're putting on buses or something as an alternative?"

"Nothing like that, mate. From what I understand, most of the roads and resorts have been swept away, and hundreds of thousands are dead."

The last sentence had a sobering effect on Peter. The enormity of the tragedy the man described suddenly sunk in, and a wave of fear swept through him. *Boxing Day? But that's when I left Beverly and the girls on the beach.* The euphoria of the last three days was killed in an instant.

"What time did it happen?"

"Around ten-thirty."

"At night?"

"In the morning."

In a state of panic, Peter shed the backpack from his shoulders and fumbled inside for his iPhone. It had slipped somewhere to the bottom of the bag, and several seconds passed before his fingers curled around the slim-bodied device. He was relieved to see the green signal symbol flashing, and his hands trembled as he dialed Beverly's number. It went straight to voice mail. *Damn! She's turned the phone off!* He left a short message asking her to call back.

The Englishman spoke. "If you're trying to contact anyone on the west coast, you won't get through. I flattened my bloody batteries trying to get through to my uncle."

"Are there any public telephones here?"

The man nodded toward the small airline building. "Over in the departure lounge, but good luck with *that*. Landline services have been disrupted too."

Peter picked the backpack up by one strap and was on his way at a half run before the man had finished talking. He pushed his way into the packed ticket hall with a tightening band of fear encircling his chest. A flat-screen on the far wall was switched to a news channel, but as the broadcast was in Thai, he ignored it. The long line of people waiting to use the public telephone only served to increase his anxiety. The urge to push through to the front and demand to be next was irresistible, but their urgency was no less than his own. Peter joined the end of the line, and as he shuffled forward a few paces at a time, he expected his phone to ring. It never did.

Forty minutes later, he dropped several fifty-satang coins into the slot and dialed the number to the hotel. An animated message spoken in Thai greeted his ears, and in a state of agitation, he beckoned to a young Asian woman who was next in the queue.

"Do you speak English?"

She hesitated before responding. "A little."

That was good enough for Peter, and he held the handset out toward her. "Can you translate for me ... please?"

"I try," she replied, stepping forward to take the receiver. She listened for a few moments before looking up at him with a puzzled expression in her eyes. "Here is no one."

He snatched the handset back and raised it to his ear. Silence.

The automated exchange had either disconnected or sent him through to voice mail. Peter pulled more coins from his pocket and dialed the number again. This time he handed the receiver straight over to her, and she listened for about twenty seconds.

"The lady says the telephone cannot connect. Where do you call?"

"My hotel in Khao Lak."

"No call Khao Lak. No one can speak to this place."

Peter grabbed the handset from her and slammed it on the hook in exasperation. Tears of panic welled up in fear-filled eyes. "*Why?*"

She pointed to the TV screen on the opposite wall. "Khao Lak *very*, very bad."

Blinded by terror, he pushed his way through the crowd toward the television. The footage was salvaged from security cameras, and the huge volume of water washing ashore needed no translation.

"*Bloody Norah!*" he whispered. Desolation and helplessness wrenched at his stomach as he watched death rise from the ocean, sweeping hundreds of people from their feet. The powerful wave surged inland at incredible speed, crashing through the resort with devastating consequences.

The next couple of days almost drove him crazy. Flights into Phuket resumed but were restricted to a couple of trips daily. Repeated calls to Beverley's iPhone went straight to voice mail, but she'd always had a habit of misplacing it. He was convinced this was more plausible than being swept off in a giant tsunami. Peter tried in desperation to get a seat on the DC3, but with such a huge backlog of passengers, he was forced to wait his turn. He tortured himself by repeatedly watching the agonizing images on the television, scrutinizing each distressing scene to see if he could identify his family among the people struggling for their lives.

More than three hundred people were still stranded at Kaeng Krung for the New Year. Instead of celebrating the transition into 2005 with champagne, cheers, and laughter, they held a prayer vigil on the grassy airstrip. It was a solemn, poignant service that lasted several hours, and a rare occasion where a vast diversification of religions including Buddhism, Taoism, Confucianism, Islamism, Catholicism, Judaism, and Christianity came together with mutual respect for each other's faiths. There were no ordained ministers, clerics, or other religious leaders among the group; otherwise, this historic occasion would likely never have happened, yet its acknowledgment never extended beyond the halo of light on the edge of a rainforest. The spiritual ambiance that hovered over the assembly was electric, and the experience gave Peter comfort, strength, and renewed hope.

His name came up for a seat on the DC3 on the following morning. The seventy-five-minute flight took an eternity, and he couldn't relax as the cumbersome machine lumbered through the sky. At Phuket International, he was one of the first to disembark. Close to physical and mental exhaustion, he pushed his way through the enormous throngs of distraught, tired, and angry travelers in the main terminal. They had probably spent days at the airport waiting to escape the disaster-stricken country, but Peter didn't care. His only mission was to find his family.

The drive to Khao Lak was long and slow. There was no reprieve from the appalling devastation, and it grew worse as he got closer to the coast. Despite the tsunami's horrifying aftermath, his mindset was positive as he pressed forward. He was certain he'd be reunited with his family at the resort, and he never *dared* to think otherwise.

He drove past groups of locals who were clearing a route to outlying villages, but their interest in him was ephemeral. No one cast a second glance at the foreigner passing through their midst, and he wished his own recollections could be as evanescent. Close to the resort, the road disappeared beneath a foot-deep mire. The wheels stirred up an abhorrent combination of sea salt and decayed marine life that was fermenting in the lower layers, releasing the obnoxious odor into the air. It took four hours to reach the Khaolak Golden Palace Hotel, and he stared in horror at the ruins of the edifice as he rolled to a stop two hundred feet from the structure. The northeast corner had collapsed, the facade and framework were skewed, and every window was broken. The structure looked as if it could have been derelict for years.

This was the point when the full veracity of the disaster sank in. He stumbled toward the dilapidated building in despair and stepped through a gaping hole in the wall. What was once a warm, convivial lobby had been transformed into a cold, malevolent chamber. The stench inside was overpowering, and his eyes stung from the fumes as they pierced the gloom. A watermark ran around the foyer two feet beneath the ceiling cornice molding, recording the depth at the peak of the flooding. The walls were covered in huge, dark water stains, drying mud, and a green algae slime. Stachybotrys spores had begun to reproduce in the damp, murky corners.

Peter booked into a motel close to Khao Lak and began a desperate search for his family. Every day, he visited the hospitals where the medical staff worked frenetically to treat the dozens of seriously injured victims. Extra mattresses were laid out on the floors to cope with the crushing number of casualties.

After walking through the overcrowded wards, he turned his attention to the emergency shelters where the authorities made the task easier by posting the names of the refugees registered in each facility on a notice board beside the main gate. Peter was sure it helped thousands of family members, relatives, and friends to be reunited, but the three names he was anxious to see were never on the list. His day ended with a visit to the airport, where he spent hours wandering through the ticket halls and departure lounge.

Two days after he returned from Kaeng Krung, the telephone company reestablished international communications. It filled him with renewed optimism. Beverly was close to her parents, and she would have contacted them at the first opportunity. He even began to think that perhaps she was already back in the UK. His premature sanguinity was dashed when they told him they hadn't heard from her.

A grief-stricken Peter returned to England, where his life became mundane and robotic. He spent most of the time in seclusion with a friendly whiskey bottle and sat for hours staring in abject misery at the unopened gifts beneath the Christmas tree.

Peter sighs, and wipes another tear from his eye. There aren't any bodies to mourn over or headstones to visit. Until he gets irrefutable proof that their lives were claimed by the deadliest tsunami in modern history, he can't find the finality he desperately needs. With no desire left to eat, he closes his eyes and continues to sob quietly. It's taken years of procrastination to get this far, and on the morrow, he'll stand on the spot where he kissed his wife and daughters good-bye for the last time exactly fifteen years earlier. He tries to envisage how they might look like now. Kathleen would be twenty-six. Perhaps she'd even be married with her own children. And Angela? They would have celebrated her twenty-first birthday three weeks earlier.

But as he drifts into a deep slumber, the only images he can conjure up are those frozen in his memory: two young girls of six and eleven who stopped growing on Boxing Day in 2004.

2

Mehganinagar, Sector 28
Gandhinagar, Gujarat, India
Coordinates: 23° 14' 40.4" N, 72° 39' 26.6" E
Wednesday, December 25, 2019, 2004h

Robert Andrews was born to an affluent family from Scotland and was a bonnie one-year-old when the British Financial Foundation appointed his father to supervise a five-year transition of their Asian assets over to the Indian Investment Bank in Mumbai. He has no recollection of life in the United Kingdom, and his older brother, who was six when they migrated, has told him that his own memories are contained to a few flash images of their nanny and a large house that could have been either their Scottish home near Edinburgh or their English home in Kent.

His father's financial management skills didn't go unnoticed by the government of Gujarat, though, who viewed him as a valuable asset. When the reassignment was drawing to a close, they seized an opportunity to poach him by waving a golden package in his direction. The proposal included huge starting and annual bonuses, a large house on 320 acres of prime land, full citizenship rights for the family, and other incentives that were so good the offer was impossible to turn down.

Now forty-five, Robert has youthful features enhanced by deep, brown eyes and a full head of sandy-brown hair with no sign of graying. His broad shoulders and strong, square-set jaw project an air of confidence. He's mild-mannered and is probably the most eligible bachelor in Gandhinagar, but his career takes primacy over relationships. He once came close to getting married, until his fiancée got tired of the inattentiveness and felt the long hours he spent at the institute, often working late into the night, were unacceptable. It gave her the foresight as to the direction their marriage would go, so it was no real surprise to her friends when she moved on.

Robert developed a fascination for geoscience when he was about ten. He spent hours viewing educational documentaries and reading every textbook he could acquire on the subject. After attending secondary school, he went on to college, graduating with a degree, full honors, and a certificate of achievement. This qualified him for a place at the University of New Delhi, where he dedicated the next eight years to earning a doctorate of philosophy in geophysics and a master of science. He studied for both papers concurrently, making many personal sacrifices along the way, but his devotion paid dividends. Now he's head of the Institute of Seismological Research, which was set up by the government of Gujarat in 2003, and under his guidance, the facility rose up as one of the world's leading foundations on seismological and geological research.

Seth hasn't aged quite as gracefully, though, and his appearance is close to that of their father prior to his death. At fifty-one, his graying hair is receding fast, and a developing pot-belly is getting harder to hide. Their mother was a renowned cardiologist with a thriving practice in London's exclusive Harley Street and another office in Gandhinagar, so she was elated when Seth made the decision to attend medical school. Now he's emerged as one of the world's leading neuroscientists, and when he's not absorbed in a research project or involved in a complex surgical procedure in front of a study group, he can be found in a packed auditorium delivering one of his notable lectures to dozens of hopeful students.

A double tragedy struck in 2007, which began with the death of his mother in February. She succumbed to a rare parasitic meningitis caused by the *Naegleria fowleri* amoeba, and health investigators connected the source of her ailment to a recent camping trip she'd taken with acquaintances in the Nallamala Hills, Telangana. She went for a daily swim in a nearby lake, and even though her friends swam in the same stretch of water, she was the only one who caught the parasite.

Seven months after her untimely death, the front tire of a rental car driven by his father blew out and the vehicle careened out of control. It flipped several times, leaving him critically injured, and he lay in a coma for two days before passing on without regaining consciousness.

Robert's hands are thrust deep into his pockets as he saunters behind his older brother. Seth opens the door to his private study and steps aside to allow him to pass through. As it's not unusual for their respective careers to keep them apart for months at a time, Robert always makes a special effort to visit his sibling on

Christmas Day. He never fails to bring expensive gifts for his two nephews, one niece, and his brother's Indian wife of eighteen years, Serita. She is an excellent cook and always produces a gratifying feast fit for royalty. Now they've reached the part of the day where the teenagers are quick to escape the adult world to do their own thing, and the two brothers retire to the study, where they catch up on a year's worth of news about each other, condensed into a couple of hours. Serita usually joins them after she's cleaned up, washed the dishes, and taken a shower.

Nonchalantly, Robert wanders into the middle of the genuine early nineteenth century study. Much of the large colonial era house has been modernized, but this is the one room his brother restored to its original décor; it has become his retreat from family and society when he needs solitude. At one end, a thick rug with a handwoven red floral design is spread out on the floor in front of a hefty walnut desk, and bookcases with an extensive library of medical manuals line the walls to each side. A large open fireplace is located centrally in the west wall behind the desk, with long chiffoniers on both sides that were custom-built to a design of the period. The display cabinets above are filled with sculptures of Indian culture; photograph frames holding fading pictures of Seth, his parents, and himself; and other mementos of the past. An oversize coffee table is set in the center of the room with comfortable armchairs upholstered in rich burgundy leather angled inward on each corner, and a full-size snooker table at the far end. The study exudes a laid-back ambiance of age, history, and knowledge, as well as a unique air of calmness. It's no wonder his brother claimed this room as his piece of tranquility away from the uproar of the twenty-first century.

Robert's eyes follow his brother as he walks over to the chiffonier on the left and picks up a whiskey decanter.

"On the rocks?" Seth asks.

"Is there any other way?"

Robert hears the chink as his sibling drops ice cubes from a small bucket into a couple of glasses and pours two generous shots. He returns to the center of the room with a big smile on his face.

"Season's greetings, brother," he says, handing a whiskey to Robert. "I've been looking forward to this all day."

He taps the lip of the glass against Seth's with a soft clink. "Merry Christmas, and a toast to Serita for such a formidable spread, as always." He takes a sip and smacks his lips. "Mmm. This *is* palatable."

"Johnnie Walker Blue," Seth replies, and he gestures toward one of the armchairs.

"God *darn*, that's the expensive stuff!" he exclaims as he accepts the invitation to sit down. After taking another nip, Robert leans back in the chair and rolls his eyes toward the ceiling as he savors the balanced flavor. "How are things at the hospital?"

"Good, most of the time."

Robert's level of astuteness is high, and he senses that his brother's attentiveness is unusually distant. "I know we only see each other once a year, but I can still tell when something bothers you."

The neurosurgeon sighs before responding. "I was forced to suspend a two-year house resident last week. I need to decide his fate at a tribunal hearing tomorrow, and I'm not looking forward to it."

"Give him a warning, and tell him he'll be sacked if he gets into any more trouble," Robert suggests.

"I wish it were as simple as that."

He knows his brother doesn't enjoy canning his staffers at the best of times, let alone at Christmas. "Then why don't you extend his suspension and give him some time out to see if he'll respond to recuperation or discipline?"

"I can't. I'll need to give assurances to the board that punishment will be effective, and I'm not willing to take that risk. He disrupted a patient's treatment by replacing his medication with a sugar tablet, so who knows what he might do next?"

Robert turns his eyes toward his brother. "Is he a Jehovah's Witness, or belong to some other religious organization that believes God heals all?"

"Not at all. Anyone against medicine isn't going to study the practice," Seth points out.

"Why do you think he did it, then?"

"He came in one morning, and quite out of the blue, renounced the treatment of schizophrenia."

Robert frowns. "I thought you were a neurologist?"

"I am."

"Why are you treating a psychiatric patient, then?"

"I study the brain, don't forget, and my research isn't limited. I'm not treating him, but he still needs medications while he's under my supervision."

The geophysicist falls silent for several moments. "This houseguest … did he explain the reasoning behind his actions?"

"House resident," Seth corrects, and he hesitates. "He has some wild theory that medications are interrupting a natural evolutionary process of the brain, and he believes we're impeding the progression of humans to develop into a superrace."

"*Wow!*" Robert exclaims. "*That's* pretty damn *heavy*. It sounds like he's in need of psychiatric help himself."

"It didn't end there," Seth continues. "A couple of days later, he disrupted a lecture I was giving on the subject by proclaiming that our interference with nature is changing the path of man's destiny, and that the ultimate price for our own vanity will be self-extinction. Switching the patient's medication was the final straw."

"I'm no medical expert, but I'd say he's cracking up under pressure. Does he have examinations coming up?"

"Exams or not, the safety of the patients is my first priority, and while he poses a threat to them, I can't see how I can keep him on."

"*Huh!* The mad scientist syndrome," Robert muses aloud. "I never considered a brain surgeon could be two pence short of a shilling before, but I guess doctors are no different to the average person. I had this stupid notion that you guys could self-diagnose and self-medicate."

"He's not a neurologist yet—and not likely to be if I terminate him," Seth says. "His career will be cut short, and I hate to be the person responsible for such a drastic transformation to *anyone's* future."

Robert stares toward the ceiling while he reflects for a few moments. "I'm curious. How did he support this theory?"

"He gave an imaginative rationalization that would make a good premise for a science fiction story; but in reality, it's invalid."

The remains of an ice cube chinks against the side of the glass as Robert swirls the whiskey around before taking another sip. "You're beginning to intrigue me, brother. Tell me more."

"He has this *crazy* notion, and I use the term with reservation, that schizophrenia is a mental discord produced by the early stages of telepathic resonance."

"What a strange hypothesis," Robert remarks. "I thought it was a confirmed illness."

"It is."

"I think the houseguest would make a good research subject instead."

"House *resident*," Seth corrects for a second time. "I need a patient's permission to do that. I have to admit I was astounded at his principle. We already know that high levels of emotion, whether negative or positive, can result in significant increases of electrical activity in the brain, and he claims the voices in a schizophrenic's head are emissions from an emotionally elevated source in close proximity."

"Could it be possible that's the reason patients with the illness can hear angry voices?"

Seth shakes his head slowly. "There are many classifications of schizophrenia. A person who claims to have prodromal abilities has a basic, but harmless, form of the disease. Some have visions, others hear people talking to them … the list goes on. And there's a lot of unfounded stigma associated with the disorder. Less than one percent of the populace suffer from the condition—certainly far too few to validate his proclamation. I will concur that anger manifestation is a common emotion, but there are innumerable reasons why a person can be in a high state of anxiety."

"I would say that's a fair statement," Robert replies, "but there needs to be a trigger to prompt an evolutionary change to develop."

Seth gives a derisive snort. "He gave me a copy of his thesis. Most of it rambles on, but essentially he lays the blame on increasing ambient noise across the planet that didn't exist a century ago. Cars, airplanes, and machinery are good examples of things that interfere with our ability to communicate effectively. Our primal instincts rely on sight, smell, and sound for basic survival, and these senses are being stifled. The utilization of mobile phones and other electronic devices is forcing our brains to rewire in an attempt to resist a threat of our own creation, making us an endangerment to our own existence. He goes on to conclude that it's still in the early stages and hasn't developed the capacity to filter incoming signals yet. He makes a comparison to tuning a radio receiver to a specific frequency, and he says medications are inhibiting the process. He thinks they might compel the brain's evolution to mutate along a more dangerous path."

"Good *Lord!* What a *concept!* That means that if you terminate him tomorrow, there's a chance he might wish you were dead; and if a schizophrenic is within range, he'll believe he's getting a message from God to kill you."

"That's *not* a nice thing to say, brother."

"It's pretty much what he means, though, isn't it?" Robert knows the correlation has made his sibling uncomfortable.

"I suppose it is."

"Then don't you think there's a *slight* possibility he might be onto something?"

Seth laughs. "Not a chance, brother. Schizophrenia is indisputably an illness. I had another student last year who tried to convince me that homosexuality is induced by reincarnation. She proclaimed that people who lived multiple lives as a female and returned as a male inherited an attraction to men, and vice versa."

Robert loves getting involved in theoretical debates, especially open-ended ones that reside in a gray area, and his brother has a unique ability to open doors for him. "You've got to remember that we've persecuted many good people over the centuries because others didn't agree with, or refused to accept, their theories. Some were deemed as sorcerers or witches and committed to an asylum. Others were imprisoned, or executed in some dreadful manner. Such things occur until one day a scholar arrives on the doorstep, waving in his hands scientific evidence proving that a particular supposition, once considered absurd, is right."

"I agree, but we're discussing unsubstantiated theories, and schizophrenia is an illness unequivocally established by medical science, period," Seth replies.

Robert's eyes flash mischievously. "A good example is Galileo Galilei. Look at how *he* was pursued by the Catholic Church because he defended Copernicanism and the theory of heliocentrism. He faced a Roman inquisition, and they sentenced him to imprisonment, yet there's no mention that he was diagnosed with mental issues."

"He was never incarcerated, though." There's a twinge of uncertainty in his eyes as he adds, " ...or was he?"

"No, he didn't end up in a pit beneath a basilica somewhere in Rome *only* because they commuted his sentence to house arrest for the rest of his life. But house arrest, dungeon, whatever—he's still a prisoner, and his freedom was curtailed. The publication of his existing works, and any he wrote afterward, was prohibited by the church all because he *dared* to contradict the Holy Scripture with a theory they couldn't accept. Could you be persecuting your student by attaching a label to him too?"

"That's an invalid argument, brother," Seth replies. "Galileo is considered the father of modern physics and even hailed as such by Einstein. There's a big difference between one of the greatest astronomers that ever lived and the house resident."

"But that's my point precisely," Robert persists. "Galilei's theories weren't verified until after his death, yet his conjectures *were* accurate. What's to say your bloke won't be proven correct in time too?"

Seth shrugs. "That's something we will *never* know. The

evolutionary process is far too slow, and thousands of generations will pass before humans develop telepathic skills, *if* it ever happens at all."

"Perhaps, but his essence will still be valid even if he doesn't get the credit."

"Schizophrenia is an *illness*," his brother repeats heatedly. "If telepathy ever *does* evolve, it *won't* be attributed to patients with schizophrenia."

A smile forms on Robert's lips, and moments later he begins to laugh hard.

Seth has an inquisitive look in his eyes. "What's so funny?"

"Your last sentence was so unambiguous it reminded me of Mum's favorite yarn."

Robert can see by the embarrassed expression spreading across Seth's face that he's stirred up some uncomfortable memories. His head falls back against the soft padding of the chair's headrest with a gentle thud, and he slaps the palm of his hand across his forehead with a loud groan.

"*Oh, no!* Thanks for the recall."

"No, thank *you* for the memory," Robert replies. He's relentless and continues to remind his brother of the details, even though they are well embedded in his head. "You were playing doctors and nurses with Cousin Annie, and you were so *sure* her favorite doll had suffered a cardiac arrest that you decided to carry out a transplant. She tried to tell you it was only a toy, and didn't have a heart, but you told her"—unable to contain himself, he begins to chuckle as he talks—"not to be so *stupid* …" Hilarity prevails, and he's unable to complete the sentence.

Seth begins to chortle along with him, and picks up the narrative. "Yeah, I know. I performed the surgery with a steak knife from the kitchen drawer."

Robert roars in laughter, and slaps the outside of his right thigh with a loud crack. "After you sliced through the plastic breast to discover the doll was hollow, you sat on the floor bawling your head off because someone had stolen her heart. Mother said it took more than an hour to console you."

"I made one mistake when I was eight and I've been paying the piper ever since," Seth says as he gets to his feet. He picks up Robert's empty glass and walks across to the chiffonier.

"So what's been happening in your world, brother?" he asks, pouring a good measure of whiskey from the decanter into both glasses as he speaks. "You said something over dinner about hoping to get funding for a special expedition?"

Robert has calmed down after the outburst of mirth, and a more disconcerted expression erases the smile from his lips. "A small ridge was discovered on the ocean floor in the Bay of Bengal in 2014, but funding for major projects was still restricted because the economy was still recovering from the global downturn of '08, so I discounted the importance of the find and put it on the backburner. I made a mistake by not pursuing it further at the time."

Despite Seth's being one of the most successful neurosurgeons on the planet, Robert has a sense that there are times when his sibling regrets the career he's chosen. He's remarked on several occasions how geology intrigues him more now than it did when he went to school, and he seems to prefer to talk about Robert's work rather than his own profession.

"I wouldn't regard that as a mistake," Seth says. "It's a decision you were forced to make because the circumstances weren't in your favor."

"I think I would have still dismissed it anyway because the focus of my attention was on an unusual distension in the tectonic plate that was found at the same time. I failed to connect an association between the two incongruities until we had enough funds to carry out a sonar sweep in 2017. The new data took me by complete surprise. Over the three-year period, the swelling *and* the ridge had grown significantly."

"This is happening in the Bay of Bengal right now?"

"Yes. The ridge is 320 kilometers west of the Andaman and Nicobar Islands in the northernmost lobe of the Australian plate. It runs north–south for about two hundred kilometers and is forty kilometers wide along most of its length before tapering at each end."

There's a clink of crystal as Seth replaces the stopper in the decanter. "Hmm, if I understand it right, growth in geological time would amount to nothing more than one or two millimeters per annum."

"Generally, that would be true, but not in this case. The swelling appears to be the result of an abnormal concentration of pressure beneath the plate, and between '14 and '17, the increase was one hundred sixty-four point nine centimeters."

Seth turns away from the sideboard with a replenished glass in each hand and walks back across the floor toward him. "That still doesn't sound like a big deal to me."

"On the contrary, it isn't only irregular, but also downright scary. That's about five hundred years of growth condensed into three years. What's *more* alarming is the ridge, which grew three hundred meters. Geologically, that's *extraordinary*."

"It wouldn't be the first time an island has risen out of the ocean without warning," Seth says, handing him the whiskey. "Is it possible you've chanced on something like that in progress?"

Robert sighs as he accepts the refilled glass from his brother and responds in an exasperated tone. "No, no, *no*. Islands are formed by oceanic volcanic eruptions and, on rare occasions, earthquakes, but there's a difference between the two. Islands produced by a volcano are made up of lava, and of course there would be a crater to expel the molten rock from the magma chamber below. An island that results from an earthquake consists of superheated mud spewing out of a vent, most of which will be dispersed by ocean currents long before it reaches the surface. Both types of islands might be fashioned differently, but there's an analogous feature between them that's fairly prominent—they are circular, not long and narrow like the ridge."

"Have you been back there since '17?"

"Earlier this year we were able to build a three-dimensional chart of the ridge's geological structure by transmitting ultrasonic pulses into the lithosphere from a specialized scientific vessel."

"Lithosphere?"

"That's the rigid outer layer of the planet. The tectonic plate, crust, and pedosphere are all subdivisions of the lithosphere. The data revealed that the ridge formation is solid rock, and there were no traces of lava, which eliminates the probability that it's volcanic in nature. We, as humans, are naturally curious about the unknown, but this is something we should fear and treat with respect until we know more about it."

"You're making it sound like a disaster could be imminent," Seth remarks.

Robert takes a moment to consider whether he should expound on his brother's comment. "Well, I *can't* exclude the possibility, but what could happen?" He shrugs, leaving the question unanswered. "To be truthful, there's insufficient data to be conclusive."

The neurosurgeon continues to quiz him. "You're a scientist. You *must* have a theory?"

"I do, but it isn't anything I can substantiate. You're a scientist, so you know that only the facts are relevant, and unless I can produce solid evidence, it's best to keep my mouth shut."

Seth looks at him with a big grin on his face. "Tell me more. Let's see if I consider you crazy enough to be certified."

"That's *your* forte, and privilege, dear brother." Robert hesitates. He has a yearning to talk about his hypothesis to someone, and now his brother wants to share his thoughts.

He sits up and moves forward to the front of the chair. The whiskey is giving him a pleasant buzz, and the alcohol is encouraging him to impart his suppositions. His sibling has no association with the geological society, and besides, he's confident that once approval is obtained to drill core samples from the oceanic ridge, they'll be rewriting the history books.

"It's my belief that the Pangaean plate took longer to break up than planetologists are saying," he blurts.

Seth gazes back at him with a puzzled frown. "What relevance does that have to do with the ridge, or did I miss the point?"

"I don't know, yet," Robert says distractedly, and he takes a moment to reflect before speaking again. "Sonar mapping shows the ridge is sitting over a huge V-shaped fissure that penetrates about two thirds of the way into the tectonic plate. The rift *and* the ridge mirror each other in terms of length and width. As regards the swelling beneath the lithosphere, the data suggests an immense buildup of pressure is taking place in the asthenosphere, and while it's prominent to the east and west of the ridge, there's no significant displacement to the north or south." He catches the blank expression on his brother's face. "That's the viscous, malleable layer of the upper mantle directly beneath the tectonic plates," Robert explains. He raises the glass to his lips and takes a sip of whiskey before continuing. "We collected enough information to produce a startling image of the chasm."

"So there's an actual *hole* in the plate?"

"It's not a hole per se. It's filled with a mix of mineral deposits that have equivalent properties to the earth's crust *and* anomalous quantities of nickel-iron, olivine, and carbonaceous chondrite, which are materials brought to earth by bolides."

An almost imperceptible smile appears on Seth's lips. "So *you* think a meteorite crashed into the Bay of Bengal? I'm disappointed, dear brother! *That* isn't anything I can commit you on. There are thousands of impact points around the globe where the same materials are found in abundance."

Robert sits back in the chair again and shakes his head with a solemn expression on his face. "The amount of celestial deposits in the chasm exceed the combined total of all bolide material discovered across the planet. Neither does a meteorite have the capacity to penetrate the lithosphere *and* survive, let alone damage the tectonic plate too. Only something of majestic size traveling at an incredible velocity could penetrate the crust to such a depth and *still* have enough impetus to rupture the plate in that manner."

Seth's eyes open wide in astonishment. "An asteroid?"

Robert answers the question with a nod.

His brother continues to probe for more information. "Are you trying to tell me it was something like the one that annihilated the dinosaurs?"

"It was the same one," the geophysicist replies, "except it was much *larger* than scientists estimate." Robert can see the bewilderment in his brother's eyes as he takes a moment to absorb the implications of his words.

"Everyone knows that the extinction of the dinosaurs was caused by the asteroid that created the Chicxulub crater."

Robert lowers his voice, and his voice takes on an ominous tone. "Can you be sure?"

A shroud of doubt drops across his brother's eyes, but moments later he throws his head back and goes into hysterics. Robert remains unsmiling, but he's not angered by the reaction. Fifteen seconds later, Seth wipes the tears of mirth from his eyes.

"*Now* you're getting close to certification. There's never been a mention of an asteroid smashing into the Bay of Bengal … at least not one associated with the demise of the lizards that I can recall."

The geophysicist's face remains pan. "Then let me *give* you a reason to sign the certificate yourself. There were *two* impacts. The first one slammed into the Bay of Bengal, and the second one crashed into the Yucatán Peninsula a couple of seconds later."

Seth begins laughing hard again and rolls his eyes upward. "Oh, pu-*leeease*, brother. I do *love* the theory, and it would sure cause a furor *if* it were true. Excuse the pun, but wouldn't the odds of a collision by *two* huge asteroids seconds apart be astronomical?" The expression on Robert's face remains staid, and his laughter fades. "You're … you're serious, aren't you?"

"Deadly serious."

"I … I'm sorry," he stammers. "I didn't intend to be demeaning. I thought you were, uh, spinning me along."

"I'm not offended," Robert replies, "but you are right. It's been sixty-five million years since the last asteroid with the ability to wipe out an entire species smashed into the earth, so the odds of more than one striking the planet a few seconds apart is highly improbable. I never suggested there were two, though. I'm telling you that it was the *same* asteroid, except it was much larger than originally estimated."

A confounded expression drops over Seth's face like a shutter. "If there was only one, then how did it smash into the Bay of Bengal *and* the Gulf of Mexico? Did it bounce like a ball?"

It's Robert's turn to laugh. "Asteroids aren't made of rubber." He can tell his brother has been drawn in and is eager to hear how this new twist in the story can be explained. "It was shaped something like a dumbbell—two gigantic boulders connected by a narrow bridge of rock—except one was at *least* ten times larger than the other. When it entered the earth's atmosphere, the friction broke them apart at the weakest point."

Seth's eyes light up. "*Ah*, I'm guessing that would be somewhere along the bridge linking the two bodies together."

"*Now* you're starting to get the picture," Robert replies. "The heavier section took a direct trajectory to the surface, crashing into the Bay of Bengal. The smaller and significantly lighter piece flew off on a tangent and struck the Yucatán Peninsula a second or two later." Robert chooses his words carefully, but the excitement in his voice is tangible as he continues to reveal his theory. "The larger portion of the asteroid burrowed into the lithosphere, slammed into the Pangaean plate, and fractured it, creating what we now identify as the Australian, Indian, and Eurasian plates. It happened in a matter of seconds, and the gigantic seismic upheavals that swept across the planet broke the plate up further at the weakest points, giving us the faults that exist today."

There's an inquisitive glint in Seth's eyes. "I thought Pangaea broke up about two hundred million years ago?"

Robert nods his head. "According to planetologists, yes, but I wonder how much it *had* broken up at the time of the collision."

"Is this the Pangaean plate theory you mentioned earlier?"

"Yes. There's no doubt it was in the process of breaking up when the planetoid crashed to earth, but besides fracturing the plate, it caused an exponential acceleration in continental drift that continued for several millennia before slowing down. I think this has misled the planetologists because the equations they use to calculate the drift rate doesn't take into consideration the accelerated period, so their results show the breakup occurring long before it did."

"If you look at a map, I guess the Bay of Bengal is the right shape to be the remnant of an ancient impact crater," Seth remarks.

"I think the bay was a massive low-lying region of flat, swampy land with a synonymity to Bangladesh and Myanmar. The sheer size of the asteroid and the force of the collision allowed the Panthalassa Ocean to flow in, submerging the impact zone."

"Can't you submit this theory to your peers as a work in progress?"

Robert laughs and shakes his head. "If I make a controversial claim like that without infallible corroboration, I'll end up like Galilei. I'll be happy to take credit for the double-impact premise and let someone else go for the subtheories."

"How could you go about proving such a presupposition, though?"

"Once I get my hands on some cores, I can use forensics to analyze the porosity, permeability, and, more important, the mineral extracts to determine the geological age. Then I can compare them to samples taken from the Yucatán Peninsula. If my theory holds water, the fingerprint left at both locations will be identical despite the difference in depths, and that will be all the proof I'll require."

Seth is silent for a moment. "Okay, so how do the V-shaped fissure, the ridge, and the swelling beneath the plate tie into all of this?"

"*That* is the true impact point of the planetoid. The velocity compressed the tectonic plate so deep into the asthenosphere that it rebounded violently with the reflexive pressure, and the result was a two-hundred-kilometer fracture in the plate. The lower lithosphere is a membrane separating the crust and upper mantle, and it began to vibrate fiercely like a gigantic diaphragm, shaking crust material and the remains of the asteroid into the abyss, wedging it open before it could close again."

Seth swishes the remainder of the whiskey in his glass over the ice cube. "So if it's been lodged open for the past sixty-five million years, what's the sudden concern?"

"You need to comprehend things on a geological time scale to understand the ramifications. One of the experiments carried out by the research vessel was to simulate a small seismic event using explosives so the alacrity of the shockwaves could be measured as they passed through the distensions." Robert sits forward in the chair with a frown on his face. "They slowed down so fast that we know they are filled with a thick fluid."

"Magma?"

Robert nods. "Yes. Magma is the planet's hydraulic fluid, and the puissance must be *incredibly* intense to distort the tectonic plate in this manner. It's a dangerous time bomb because the pressure isn't being distributed evenly in the upper asthenosphere and the magma is getting trapped into a bubble. The only way it can redistribute itself to regain equilibrium is by closing the chasm. It's taken sixty-five million years for the crust and the planetoid material that forms the wedge to be compressed into a solid block as the tensile tension at each end of the rupture has increased. Unfortunately the different mineral properties between the wedge and plate rock are so diverse they've failed to bond. It's nothing more than a poor weld."

"I'm trying to fathom the importance of the ridge and what part it plays in all of this."

"The wedge is pushing its way up and creating the oceanic ridge." Robert can tell by Seth's expression that he's finding it difficult to grasp the full picture.

"Wouldn't it be easier to push out tons of loose rubble sixty-five million years ago than one solid block today?"

Robert understands the logic in his brother's reasoning, but of course, that's not the way the physics involved are working. "The walls of the abyss are forty kilometers apart now, but when the fissure was created, the separation would have been more like one hundred twenty kilometers, if not more. Over millions of years, the buildup of pressure on each side has moved them closer together, a millimeter at a time. The plug has been held in place by a limiting friction seal, but it's now beginning to fail, and the only way to go is up."

"Do you think we'll see an island emerge in our lifetime?"

"Without a doubt, but it's something I'd rather not witness," Robert replies. "The walls are well defined in the sonar image, and owing to its triangular shape, two hundred thousand cubic kilometers of rock are getting ejected at an accelerated rate. Unless I've missed something, the one thing it's *not* going to do is stop."

"You're making it sound pretty ominous," Seth mutters.

"That's because it is," Robert replies in a matter-of-fact voice. "It *may* continue to squeeze the plug out of the chasm at a steady rate until the gap is closed again, but that scenario is the least likely to happen. The result would be a new island rising out of the ocean to the west of the Andaman and Nicobar Islands within a decade. It'll be a geological gold mine because it will be the first landmass known to form during the Quaternary Period that *isn't* the result of volcanic activity."

"What can be so bad about that?"

"If the plug doesn't break up as it's ejected, it will be ten times taller than Mount Everest."

Seth gasps. "*Jeee*-zus, Robert. That'll take the summit into space. Is that even possible?"

"The answer to that question is beyond my field of expertise. I've got no idea of what the consequences might be; nor do I want to take a guess. As the plug's profile resembles an upside-down pyramid, it'll probably get top-heavy and topple over. The trouble is, it could be at least two thirds out before it's unable to support itself."

"*Wow!* That's going to be a spectacular sight when it does."

"A very dangerous one," Robert replies. "It will have the potential to generate a tsunami unlike anything you could ever dream about."

Seth is silent as he leans back in the chair and stares up at the ceiling. Robert can see by his expression that he's in deep contemplation, so he waits several seconds before interrupting his cogitations.

"Penny for your thoughts."

His brother sits forward and shakes his head with a bewildered look on his face. "I was trying to visualize a mountain rising out of the Bay of Bengal with a stature that dwarfs Everest."

"Not an easy thing to imagine, is it?"

Seth doesn't answer. The geophysicist leans back in the chair and reflects on the alternate, but more probable, way the plug will get expelled.

"I think it will release every ounce of stored tensile energy *and* the pressure beneath the plate simultaneously. The corollary will be explosive, but less likely to have global consequences, and keep it contained within the Bay of Bengal. I think it will cause a lot of damage to the lithosphere, though, because the Australian plate will drag against the boundaries of the Indian and Eurasian plates, forcing them to buckle upward and turn the region into a hotbed for reoccurring earthquake activity for generations."

"The area is already a seismically active zone, isn't it?"

"Yes, but nothing like it's going to be. It's possible that the government may even have to evacuate the Andamans." Robert scratches the side of his head. "We *should* be recording seismic activity as the ridge formation pushes upward, but there isn't anything ... not even a whisper—and that bothers me. Nor can I get *any* of the models on the institute's computers to enact a feasible scenario. That means something vital is missing from the equation, and I *can't* figure out what it is."

"Perhaps that's because something similar has never happened before."

"To say it's *never* happened would be a false statement because we don't know that with unequivocal certainty," the geologist replies. "The correct perspicacity would be to say that evidence of a prior similar event has not been uncovered; otherwise, the parameters would be in our computers. The truth is, we are venturing into uncharted territory."

"Can't you extract some core samples from within the rift itself and do what we in the medical field call a biopsy?"

Robert shakes his head. "We don't have the technology to penetrate that deep into the earth's crust. The pressure is simply too great."

The study door opens, and Serita enters carrying a silver tea tray and a plate of home-baked biscuits.

"A fresh pot of tea," she says. Robert drains the remainder of the whiskey from his glass as Serita places the refreshments down on the coffee table.

"I thought you'd be playing chess instead of sitting around like two sloths."

Seth laughs. *"Nah!* We're too hyped up. There isn't enough intellect in chess to stimulate minds like ours."

Her eyes open wide in mock astonishment. "Who are *you* trying to kid?"

Robert glances at his wristwatch. "Why don't you grab another cup and join us? I need to be at work early tomorrow morning, so I can't stay too late."

Serita smiles at her brother-in-law and walks back toward the door. "Thank you for the invite. I'll be right back."

Three more hours of banter and small talk follows before Robert thanks them for a wonderful day and, much later than he intended, bids farewell.

3

Khao Lak Beach
Khao Lak, Thailand
Coordinates: 08° 37' 49.4" N, 98° 14' 37.2" E
Thursday, December 26, 2019, 0600h

Peter opens his eyes and glances at the digital clock. The time is 6:00 a.m. Without hesitation, he swings his legs out and sits on the side of the bed. Surprised at how calm and settled he's feeling, he doesn't want to lie in bed dwelling on what the day ahead may hold. As he shakes the cobwebs of sleep from his head, a strange sense of excitement courses through his body. It doesn't mean that his fears and apprehensions have abandoned him, because there's still an underlying flow of anxiety, and it could alter his mood in an instant if he allows it to surface. The best way to keep his current mindset in a positive field is to stay busy, so he slips his feet into a pair of sandals and shuffles toward the bathroom.

After taking a shower, Peter comes back into the room with a bath towel wrapped around his waist. He pulls on a pair of black socks and boxer shorts before crossing the room to open the closet door. Still in an upbeat frame of mind, he lifts the lid to the suitcase, removes a shoe box that contains a pair of highly polished black leather shoes, and inspects them for any blemishes that might need to be buffed out. Satisfied that he can't improve on the shine, he sets them on the floor. He then brushes the suit down, taking meticulous care to eliminate every white speck that shouldn't be there. His apparel doesn't conform to what people would expect to see someone wearing on a beach, but it doesn't bother him. Today he has a special engagement to keep, and he suspects he won't be alone.

By seven o'clock he's ready to tackle the day head on. After a final pause in front of the mirror to run a comb through his hair, he takes the elevator down to the lobby and heads for the shopping hall. His intention is to find the florist, but the smell of freshly brewed coffee and toasted breakfast bagels is tempting. There's plenty of time before he needs to be on the beach, so he goes on a diversion to hunt down the source of the irresistible aroma. It leads him to a small café halfway along the mall. Peter sits down at an outside table and flicks through the breakfast menu. He doesn't feel hungry despite having missed tea on the previous evening, but that's probably a result of the strange mix of emotions going on inside of him. *Excitement? Apprehension?* He can't pin a label to it, but somewhere beneath the butterflies in his stomach he still needs nourishment, and an egg sandwich with a mug of coffee should hit the spot.

Twenty minutes later, Peter drops a tip to the waitress and heads off in search of the florist. The tiny flower shop is at the far end of the shopping hall, and the musky perfume from a wide variety of freshly cut flowers permeates the air around the entrance. After several minutes, he leaves the store clutching three hand-selected roses—one red and two white. His heart is pounding hard as he walks across the hotel lobby toward the exit because the next stop is the beach.

Retracing the same path he took with his family on this day in 2004, he steps on the sand and pauses to gain his bearings. A long time has passed, and everything appears a little different to how he remembers. After a couple of seconds, he walks over to a spot halfway between the beachhead and the edge of the water. He's pretty certain he's at the place where he saw his wife laying the beach towel on the sand.

Peter looks out across the ocean and squints his eyes against the brightness of the sun as it glints off the surface of the Andaman Sea. A light but fresh offshore breeze ruffles his hair, and the semblance is so tranquil that it's hard to imagine the terror that reigned here fifteen years earlier. The golden sands of Khao Lak stretch to either side, and with the exception of an elderly couple standing a hundred yards to his right, the seashore is empty. It was his intention to get here early because he wanted some alone time to reminisce before the mourners started to arrive. The beach is still open to vacationers who aren't there for the memorial services, but signs are placed along the beachhead asking them to respect the people who will be gathering to grieve in remembrance throughout the day.

He sniffs the air. His nose twitches as the sweet aroma from the roses in his hand wafts upward on a light eddy of wind. They are large, beautiful flowers with flawless petals that were harvested at the peak of their bloom hours before he bought them.

A lump swells in his throat, and he swallows hard. This is the rendezvous he's postponed many times, and Peter hopes he will be able to accept that this is where his family died. A sadness builds up inside, and his chest tightens, but it doesn't engulf him like it did when he arrived yesterday. He brushes a tear from the corner of an eye with an index finger.

Another minute passes before he eases himself down to kneel on one leg. He perceives the graininess of the sand shifting through the material of his trousers as his knee creates an indentation to nestle into. It's hard to stay focused as he unwraps the gift paper from around the flowers, and taking care not to prick himself on the sharp thorns, he pushes the long stem of the red rose deep into the sand. He repeats the same process with the white roses, placing them about a foot to each side of the first bloom. By the time he's finished planting the last flower, he's fighting to prevent the tears from welling up in his eyes, but as always, emotion wins. A film of moisture blurs his vision, and he pulls a handkerchief from his pocket to wipe it away.

Peter pauses to recover his equanimity before removing a small plastic container from one of his pockets. He opens the hinged lid to reveal three thumb tacks and places the tiny receptacle on the sand beside his foot. Next he pulls an envelope from his inside jacket pocket and unseals the flap; three photographs slide out. Another tear rolls down the right side of his face, and it drops from his chin to land on the left cheek of the face smiling up at him from the top picture. He stares at the seductive deep blue eyes of his wife and begins to immerse himself in memories that stretch from the first time he laid eyes on her: their first date, their wedding day, the births of their daughters ... too many to count. He could have knelt there for hours and not known how long he'd spent lost in thought.

With a shudder, Peter pulls himself back to the present. He flips the exposure over to read the message that he'd penned on the reverse before leaving England. "To my beloved wife. God called you to Him far too early. I love you, and I miss you." In the bottom right corner he had added "Beverly Hutchins, age twenty-nine."

He leans forward, props the picture against the red rose, and pushes a thumb tack from the box through the top of the photo, fixing it securely to the stem. *That should prevent the breeze from blowing it away.*

Peter takes the second image and holds it in a light grip between his fingers, gazing at the face of a young girl with a huge, cheeky grin so wide that it reveals a gap where two upper milk teeth are missing from the front. She has a mischievous sparkle in her eyes, as she always did, and a small cluster of tiny freckles adorn her childish cheeks. He smiles with fondness, recalling how he used to tease her about them by telling her they were beauty spots. Their GP said they would fade as she grew older, but now he'll never know if the doctor was right. On the back of the photograph he had scribed a simple message similar to the one he had written for Beverly: "Daddy will miss my little cherub always." And as with his wife's photo, he identifies who she is by name in the bottom corner: "Angela Hutchins, age six." He pins it to one of the white roses.

He repeats the ritual with the exposure of eleven-year old Kathleen and studies it with distant contemplation in his eyes. *If only she hadn't turned down the opportunity to accompany me to Kaeng Krung ...* But he's lived in a world of ifs since that day. He pins her picture to the stem of the last white rose. Still on one knee, he hangs his head in anguish, and his shoulders shake as he begins to sob to himself. "Please forgive me ... I'm so, so sorry I wasn't there for you all ... I'm so sorry ..."

He begins to say a pray for each of them. Suddenly the guilt seems to lift away. Peter has a strange sensation that his family are standing beside him, but they seem to be exuding an unusual sentiment he can't identify. It's neither happy nor sad, yet he feels they are wrapped in a shroud of contentment. Are they trying to tell him something, or is his imagination making excuses for the years of remorse? Whatever it is, he's filled with a surreal calmness.

Because of the extended period of kneeling on one leg, he's getting an ache in his lower back, so he stands. Lost in his own private ceremony, he had been oblivious to time, and with a glance at his wristwatch, Peter is surprised to see that more than an hour has passed since he came down to the seaside. He looks along the beach to his left. People are filtering down a few at a time, and it's clear they are here for the memorial, or to say a prayer for loved ones. The thought elevates his mood a little and for the first time he can see that he's not alone with the pain, suffering, and grief; he's among people who are on the same emotional level. He doesn't know a single person, yet there's an awareness that seems to be drawing them together, spiritually uniting them through a common tragedy, and it takes him back to the impromptu prayer service on New Year's Eve fifteen years earlier.

He turns his head and gazes across the sand in the opposite direction. His eyes fall on a small, slim woman about five feet four inches tall who is standing about ten feet away. She's dressed in typical apparel worn by many of the local women in the poorer communities, and until now he'd been unaware of her presence. He doesn't know how long she's been there, and while she's one of many solitary figures dotted along the beach, there's something about her that seizes his attention. She's holding her head up almost in proud defiance as she stares out over the Andaman Sea, her dark, waist-length hair billowing out behind her in gentle puffs on the light breeze.

He's surprised to see she's clutching a Bible in her left hand because about 90 percent of Thais are Buddhist, with the remaining 10 percent spread out among other religions. His eyes roam over her profile in a nonchalant manner. He's a little curious because her countenance is not archetypal of a native Thai, and he deduces that the probability she might have Western genes somewhere in her bloodline is pretty high.

Peter pulls himself out of the reverie and is about to look back out to sea when she turns her head, and her bright blue eyes lock on his. Now that he can see her face, he's overwhelmed with shame. She's much younger than he first estimated, no more than a kid, perhaps in her late teens. An uncomfortable vision flashes into his head as he views himself through her eyes. He may still be handsome, and women around his age might find him attractive, but to her he's nothing more than a creepy old man.

A frown forms across her forehead as she continues to return his gaze without turning away, and his face begins to burn with embarrassment. He realizes his own stare must be disconcerting to her, and even his presence could be making her uncomfortable.

"I ... I'm sorry," he stammers, trying to find a way to explain himself. "I didn't mean to gawk at you like that."

She remains silent.

Peter turns his eyes away and stares out across the calm sea, ashamed to let something like this happen on such a sacred spot. A voice speaks to him in his head. *Something like what? Why should you feel ashamed?* He never had nefarious intentions; nor did any reprehensible thoughts invade his mind.

But she doesn't know that, he tells himself.

4

Fortune Resort Bay Island
Port Blair, South Andaman Island
Coordinates: 11° 40' 35.7" N, 92° 44' 24.7" E
Thursday, December 26, 2019, 1009h

A stone's throw from Aberdeen Bazaar in Port Blair, and overlooking the pristine waters of the Bay of Bengal, lies the picturesque Fortune Resort Bay Island. Constructed in multiple levels from padouk, a red timber found only in the Andaman and Nicobar Islands, the design of the structure holds a resemblance to typical Nicobari huts. This is one of the more reserved resorts on the island, and an air of sophistication, calmness, and serenity emanates from the buildings and grounds.

The same can't be said for the three Australian guests from Darwin who checked in at the beginning of the week. Twenty-six-year-old Lloyd Franklin, and two friends, Sam and Bert, came for what was supposed to be a seven-day fishing trip. With more partying going on, and barely a sober moment, they still need to cast a line between them.

Determined to go on at least one expedition before returning home, the trio made their way to the docks on the previous afternoon. Most of the boats are prebooked days in advance, so they were lucky to find a local boat owner who was prepared to take them out to fish for black marlin, and yellowfin tuna. He required an immediate nonrefundable cash payment in full, which included the rental of deep-sea tackle. Lloyd knew they were being gouged on the price, but an attempt to barter with the skipper was a total failure.

Bearing that in mind, the three friends promised to forego another night out and bunk down early, but the deal was hard to keep. With the fall of darkness, the itch to party grew stronger.

Lloyd opens his eyes, and lies on top of the bed for several moments, trying to recall the events of the previous night. Once again, he and his friends consumed too much local hooch, and his recollections are vague. Much is lost in an alcoholic haze, but with a little persuasion, he begins to evoke little snippets that aren't necessarily in the order of occurrence.

The three young men had gathered in Sam's room around eight o'clock and made a unanimous decision to amend their pact from one of no drinking and an early night to one of a three drink maximum and in bed before midnight. Happy with the revision, they set out for a popular bar not far from the resort. That part is easy to remember because he was still sober, but somewhere along the line, something clearly went wrong.

Didn't we get into a fight with some foreigners?

He digs deeper and extracts a hazy vision of the brawl.

Ah, yes, they were German.

He's unable to recall what, how, or why the fracas started, but as his memory becomes more transpicuous, he secretly admits that they were worthy opponents and deserving of respect. He smiles. They were having a damn good scrap until the flatfoots appeared on the scene and ruined all the fun, and that's when the order of events became jumbled.

He remembers Sam delivering a perfect uppercut that connected with the jaw of a police officer and sent him sprawling along the floor. It was amazing how fast his colleagues reacted. Even before their associate hit the tiles, about a dozen cops jumped his friend and tackled him to the ground. He never stood a chance, and within minutes the Australian was hauled off to jail on the booze bus, yelling and kicking in protest.

Now he remembers. The fight started over an attractive German chick Bert was trying to whore with, but what happened to him after that? He's got *no* idea what his fate was. *Did he end up in the pokey as well?*

Lloyd's recollection of decking a cop himself must be nothing more than an erroneous memory of a past event that got mixed in somewhere. The Old Bill had swarmed the tavern like blue honeybees, and after witnessing the speed with which Sam was taken down, he felt he would've woken up in a jail cell for sure. But how did he get back to the hotel?

The young man throws the coverlets from his naked body, swings his legs over the side of the bed, and sits up. Apart from being a little tired and suffering some minor aching in his muscles, he's grateful that the severity of his hangover isn't as bad as he deserves. Lloyd makes a quick check of his body, but a large bruise on his right thigh and another one on his shoulder appear to be the extent of his injuries.

With a yawn, he rubs his eyes and looks around the room. An

empty liquor bottle and several squashed beer cans are on the top of a small table in one corner. A once elegant table lantern lies on its side. The base was broken after it had somehow fallen to the floor.

He glances at the time. He's supposed to be on the dock with his friends in less than an hour. He decides that if the cops haven't released Sam yet and he's unable to track Bert down, he will go fishing on his own. He has no intention of forfeiting the trip. The best place to start looking, he determines, is in their rooms.

Lloyd picks up the telephone and stares at the handset in awe. The plastic earpiece and mouthpiece covers, including the tiny speaker and microphone that should be behind them, are gone, and a bunch of wires are left hanging out at each end of the housing.

Fuck me! When did that happen?

He replaces the destroyed piece of equipment back on its cradle and deliberates for a moment. The batteries on his iPhone need to be recharged, so the only thing he can do is go to their rooms and knock on their doors.

The young Australian gets to his feet and stretches his limbs before reaching out for a white bathrobe that's lying in a crumpled heap on the foot of the bed. Still half asleep, he slips his arms into the sleeves of the garment and stumbles toward the french windows. He slides them open and steps onto the wooden balcony, where a cool but refreshing breeze swirls around his body. The sky is clear, the surface of the ocean is rippled with tiny whitecaps, and the tang of sea salt in his nostrils is exhilarating. To the east, the tree-covered hills on the northern part of Ross Island peek around the headland, and the waves coming in from the Andaman Sea lap on the shore only yards from the loggia.

He begins to exercise, starting with shoulder and arm stretches, and progresses on to a series of squats, gulping in one deep lungful of ocean air after another. In less than a minute, the blood is surging through his veins, oxygenating his body and reenergizing him from head to toe. Without any facilities to carry out anaerobic exercises, he completes the routine with push-ups. After fifteen minutes, Lloyd is feeling pumped and his bones are telling him that today is going to be a *great* day.

His chest heaves from the exertion of the vigorous workout as he steps back into the room. Beads of perspiration are dotted along the tanned skin of his forehead, and the sweat runs down the side of his face in tiny rivulets as he ambles across the floor in the direction of the shower. Without stopping, he snatches a bath towel from the back of a chair, where he had thrown it the previous day.

Christ, I am a slob, he thinks with some pride. A loud creak emanates from the heavy timbers that form the frame of the hotel, immediately followed by an explosive crack as the ceiling rips apart, revealing the blue morning sky. Before Lloyd's brain can evaluate the dangerous status of his predicament, a tremendous upward jolt strikes the ground beneath his feet, and a searing pain tears through his lower body. The viciousness of the shock he feels is akin to jumping off a three-story building and landing on his feet. The knuckles of his knees grind and crunch together, and the incredible force dislocates both hip joints. A fraction of a second later, the floor buckles upward with so much ferocity that it launches the Australian up through the gaping hole where the roof had been less than a second earlier.

Lloyd's heart thumps hard, pumping vast quantities of adrenaline into his brain. It accelerates his cognitive senses to such a high rate that the world around him flips into super-slow motion. Numb with shock, he tries to rationalize the ludicrous situation he finds himself in. The towel lifts up from his shoulder and hangs suspended about two feet from his head for a brief moment before an updraft whips it away. With a profound expression on his face, Lloyd's eyes follow the path of the rectangular piece of bath linen as it flutters down and away from him like a white butterfly.

Terrified, and oblivious to the pain in his damaged lower joints, Lloyd flails his arms frantically as he tries to find something solid to grab on to. The earth below is dotted with blue-white flashes as electrical transformers explode, and fireballs ignited by ruptured gas lines flare up briefly before they are extinguished. The island has become a living, breathing monster with the resemblance of a thick but fluid paste being churned around by a giant liquidizer. Buildings are instantly sucked down and out of sight before his eyes, swallowed whole by the earth. The world below has become a massive, seething whirlpool of mangled rock, engorging whatever is on the surface. The resort and the bustling city of Port Blair that had been going about its business ten seconds earlier are gone.

Christ! What the fuck did I drink last night? he asks himself, but the pain in his lower body is too excruciatingly real for this to be a hallucination. He begins to scream at the top of his voice: "Heavenly Father, if you're doing this to scare the shit outta me, you've done a good fucking job, so you can feel free to stop now!"

The desperate plea is lost in the earsplitting clamor resounding all around. The deafening cracks and huge explosions are barely audible over a loud, persistent low-frequency rumble that vibrates through his body with so much power it's whisking his stomach contents into a jelly. Every muscle in his being is clenched tight with fear; this is probably the only reason he hasn't defecated.

Lloyd has been flung so high there is little chance he'll survive the plummet back to earth. He claws at the air in terror as he begins the downward journey. Even if some incredible miracle does happen and he's not killed the instant he strikes the ground, is he going to be pulled beneath the surface like everything else?

The bathrobe begins to crawl up his legs, and the garment billows out around his body like a balloon as the air rushes inside. It does nothing to impede his fall, though, and he's powerless to do anything to save himself. In a few more seconds, his existence is going to be snuffed out.

Lloyd's consciousness is still in slow motion with seconds ticking by like minutes, giving him plenty of time to absorb every frightening detail. A thick pall of dust is rising up from the island, but his attention is caught by the strangest thing he's ever witnessed. The earth has stopped swirling around, but now the ground is bubbling like a gigantic cauldron, and the world is going through an incredible geological transformation. Rocky structures that usually take millions of years to form are growing and then eroding again at an astonishing rate. Huge rocky columns shoot up from beneath the surface, spewing steam and shedding debris as they rocket high into the sky before blowing apart in spectacular explosions, collapsing, and being recycled back into the planet again.

The Andaman Sea has disappeared, replaced by a grayscale kaleidoscope of alien landscapes that are being created and destroyed in seconds. Billions of tons of igneous, sedimentary, and metamorphic rock are forged into strange formations by the deadly earthquake, and as surreal as it is, Lloyd is petrified in terror.

Unexpectedly, a huge abyss snaps open beneath him with a sharp, thunderous crack. An enormous blast of scorching air is expelled from its depths amid clouds of dust and rock. The strength of the upsurge arrests his fall so fast that it knocks the breath from his lungs, and he feels as if his internal organs are being ripped out.

By now his nerve endings are so overloaded with the pain radiating from every point in his body that he isn't even aware that the skin on his back, legs, and arms is peeling off in large strips, blackened by the blistering temperatures. He hangs stationary in midair for about five seconds, expecting to be flung back into the sky, before the sizzling updraft dies an abrupt death.

Lloyd begins to fall again, paralyzed in sheer terror as the gaping mouth of the chasm swallows him up. The strip of blue sky above is moving farther away as he drops deeper into the bowels of the planet. Within the dimness of the fissure, his eyes detect perpendicular ripples of reflected light and shadows that intertwine, sway, and dance with each other. They are moving in his direction, and it takes a moment for him to realize what it is. Channeled by the walls of the gigantic aperture, a prodigious wall of water thousands of feet tall is roaring toward him.

He braces himself for the impact, but the deadly surge doesn't reach him.

A gargantuan explosion resounds throughout the enormous rift, and his body is in torturous agony as it quivers from the violent vibrations of the massive sound waves reverberating back and forth between the vertical walls of the chasm. His eardrums explode with the sudden expansion of air, and a powerful jet of blood spurts from his ruptured ears.

Amid thick clouds of scalding steam, boiling mud, and debris, an enormous pillar of rock careens up from out of the murky depths at an astonishing speed and smashes into his spine. The sickening crack is insignificant, lost in the thunderous commotion raging all around, and Mother Nature is the only witness as his body folds backward at an impossible angle a split second before it explodes with the force of the impact. Limbs, flesh, blood, and guts splatter in all directions. The bloody pulp is drawn beneath unimaginable trillions of tons of rock that's rolling over with the fluidity of a giant surf.

Moments later, every living cell that had been a happy, carefree Lloyd Franklin heading to take a shower ninety seconds earlier is buried unceremoniously deep within the earth's crust.

5

Institute of Seismological Research
Gandhinagar, Gujarat, India
Coordinates: 23° 12' 52.7" N, 72° 39' 35.5" E
Thursday, December 26, 2019, 1031h

Dr. Robert Andrews is browsing through the seismic report for the previous day. Thousands of minor quakes were scattered across the globe, but nothing momentous is listed except for a larger-than-average cluster around the northern Sumatran coast. As this is one of the most active regions on any given day, he doesn't feel concerned.

A double-glazed, toughened glass partition separates his office from the main control center. It gives him an unobstructed view of the huge, ninety-by-sixty-meter high-definition LED monitor on the back wall, which has a map of the world on permanent display. The mainframe is linked to thousands of geological entities around the planet who share data in real time via a network of satellite and cable connections. The computer gathers intelligence from a string of sensors that enable it to triangulate the location of the epicenter and hypocenter, measure the magnitude, and collect other important information. It can take anything from a few seconds to several minutes to compile, the time being dependent on a number of factors. A strong earthquake produces an increased amount of data that takes more time to analyze because the intelligence is often contaminated by man-made surface noise. Underground detonations to extract ore and other minerals from the earth by mining companies, fracking, and even pile drivers on construction sites are some examples of the clutter that can mimic seismic waves. The computer can recognize specific markers in such emulations, which it filters away from those produced by a real earthquake.

Special software converts the magnitude of a seismic event into color gradients, and a visual marker shaded to the appropriate magnitude is projected onto the map at the epicenter. As the shockwaves move farther away from the point of origin, concentric rings radiate outward, with pings at five-second intervals, shifting down through the color spectrum to indicate the weakening intensity. This allows the seismologists to determine at a glance what the magnitude is at any given point within the earthquake's range. The mainframe is able to anticipate the level of damage that might occur to populated areas within the radii, and it prioritizes triage levels where immediate help might be needed. It has proved effective on many occasions in directing rescue services and facilitating rapid assistance to isolated regions since being implemented in 2007.

The gamut starts at light yellow for the weakest, at point one, and graduates in one-tenth increments to orange at three point oh, red at six point oh, and purple at the rare level of nine point oh. A Klaxon emits loud two-second pulses for quakes with an intensity of six or greater to alert on-duty seismologists that a major event is in progress.

A knock on the door disrupts the doctor's attention. He looks up to see the tall, skinny figure of the institute's finance minister, Daksha Bhatnagar, through the glass, and invites him to enter with a hand signal.

"Good morning, Dr. Andrews. How did Christmas Day go for you?" he asks as he enters the office.

Robert greets the visitor with the same cordiality. "Good morning, Mr. Bhatnagar. I had a good time, thank you. I spent the day with my brother whom I rarely get to see, so we had a lot to catch up on." He leans back in the chair, and clasps his hands around the back of his head. "How was your time off?"

"Yes, I had a good time too," Daksha replies. He is Hindu, so for him Christmas is a secular holiday that happens to fall on the last day of Pancha Ganapati, a five-day celebration in honor of Lord Ganesha he observes each year with his own family. He walks across the floor and places a manila folder on top of the doctor's desk with a smile. "Your application to finance the rift project has been approved."

Robert's eyes light up as he reaches eagerly for the file. This is for the research of the distension beneath the plates in the Bay of Bengal, and to monitor the unusual growth of the ridge.

"Any restrictions?" he asks, opening the cover.

"They acknowledge that the idiosyncrasies of the swelling and ridge are related, but they want the aggrandizement of the moraine to be the chief focus of the project. That's the only real stipulation I can find in the agreement."

"I can live with that," the geologist replies. "It won't hinder the operation in the slightest."

"I didn't think it would. The full amount you requested is approved, and further funds may be available if necessary."

A relaxed silence descends over the two men while Dr. Andrews glances through the documentation. "I think they're as concerned as we are," he says, turning his attention back to the minister after a few moments with a satisfied smile. "Excellent work, Daksha. We can't afford to delay this project. I'll go through the paperwork and finalize the agreement before the end of the day."

"I need to negotiate the insurance policies, and I can make a start on that once you tell me who you're going to appoint as the expedition principal."

Robert contemplates for a moment. "I will be the principal where the project is concerned, but the role of field leader will be assigned to Mahesh Pawar."

Daksha appears surprised by the geologist's choice. "Mahesh? Do you think he's ready for the responsibility?"

The doctor's reply is confident. "Yes, I do. He might be young and adventurous, but he shows a lot of integrity, and he has strong leadership skills. His other attributes are responsibility, discipline, and safety awareness, and above all, he follows instructions. We've had in-depth discussions on the type of research that needs to be carried out, and he's shown far more interest in the Bay of Bengal than any of the other geologists. In my view, that makes him an ideal candidate."

"That may be so, but I still need to convince the underwriters. They'll be concerned about his lack of field experience and how he'll react in an emergency situation, especially when lives are in danger. I'm not so sure he'll be capable of making fast, calculated decisions under that kind of pressure."

Robert's demeanor remains calm as he defends his nominee. "I'm sorry, but I disagree with your assessment. His candidacy is better than anyone else's, and I think you know me well enough to understand that I would never recommend him if there were any doubts in my mind about his aptitude. I should also point out that the captain of the research vessel is responsible for the safety of the crew and everyone on board. Mahesh would be accountable only if they carried out a manned submersible or off-ship mission, but the nature of this operation will not necessitate the employment of outboard control."

Daksha shrugs. "Okay, I'll see what I can do to push him through for you, but if he's accepted, they may set the premium at a higher rate. I also need a list of the scientists who'll be under his supervision and the agencies they'll represent."

Dr. Andrews gives a nod of approval. "I'll discuss that with Mahesh later. As leader of the expedition, I'll give him the opportunity to select the team he's most comfortable with."

Robert is overwhelmed with elation as Daksha leaves the office. There had always been little doubt in his mind that the project would be approved, but he's exceptionally pleased because this is the first time in thirteen years that a venture has been left openended. He places the file to one side and is about to call Mahesh into the office when a violent jolt hits the center. The floor begins to roll like a ship on an ocean swell, and a loud rumble echoes through the building. A split second later, the Klaxon begins to pulse out a warning that, for once, isn't necessary.

Robert looks out through the glass to see a couple of his staff getting back to their feet after the unexpected jerk threw them to the ground. Hampered by the shaking, which seems to have settled down to a steady rhythm, the doctor gets up from the chair and makes his way unsteadily toward the door. With the exception of the initial shock, the disturbance isn't strong enough to throw him off balance, but the vibration is sufficient for lighter objects like computer monitors, telephones, and documents to slowly bounce across the desks and other flat surfaces.

Dr. Andrews stops in the doorway and holds onto the frame with one hand for support while his eyes sweep around the control center, seeking out dangers that might be a threat to the health or safety of his staff.

The institute was constructed to higher-than-average standards and ranks among one of the top ten safest structures in the world. It's guaranteed to withstand a steady eight point oh for a minimum of ninety seconds, but a sixth sense warns the doctor that this is no ordinary trembler. The rolling motion is an indication that they are on the outer fringes, and making a quick mental calculation based on field experience, he estimates that the magnitude is around a five point four, which means the center shouldn't collapse.

Because of his familiarity with the mineral properties and the geological structure across this part of the continent, the sheer strength of the shaker puzzles him. The nearest location where an earthquake is likely to occur is along the boundaries of the Indian and Eurasian plates, but that's a minimum distance of 630 kilometers to the northwest. There are no known faults close enough to give them a quake of this magnitude, and he wonders if a previously undiscovered fault line has revealed itself.

Robert glances up at the rows of fluorescent lights suspended from the ceiling. The way they swing wildly on their chains is scary to see, but they aren't posing a threat to the people below. He drops his eyes to a row of fifteen printers lined up on a counter beneath the monitor. The machines are secured to prevent involuntary movement, and satisfied that they aren't going anywhere, he continues to look around the room. Reference manuals dislodged from a bookcase are falling into an untidy stack on the floor, while the staff are busy trying to prevent desktop equipment from sliding to the ground.

The lights flicker as the shaking reaches the one-minute mark, and a voice close by yells out in Hindi, "We've switched to emergency power!"

Robert breathes a sigh of relief. The emergency power system was installed when the institute was built, and though a simulation test is carried out every month, this is the first time the fail-safe technology has been utilized during an actual earthquake. Sensors placed around the building measure the intensity of the seismic waves against time and calculate the probability factor for a failure in the national grid. Once the threat level reaches 70 percent, their own generators kick in. A complete outage would be catastrophic for the scientists because they would lose trillions of megabytes of data during the blackout that could never be recovered.

Nawal Tambe is standing close to Robert. She's the youngest junior he recommended for advance training about a fortnight before Christmas, and this is her first day. Something in her eyes as they dart around the control center concerns him. She looks terrified. Worried that the young woman might panic, he staggers over to her and, placing his lips close to her ear, speaks in a loud voice so she can hear him.

"It'll be over in a few more seconds. Stay here. It's safer to remain in the building than to go outside."

The first sentence couldn't be further from the truth. The earthquake continues to rumble on with no sign of abatement, and the seconds tick by into minutes. The earthquake is in its fourth minute, and the blare of the Klaxon mixed with the rumbling is beginning to irritate him. He doesn't want to leave Nawal's side, so he beckons to Mahesh.

"Can you get someone to turn that damn alarm off?"

As the young scientist heads back to the control panel, the quaking comes to an abrupt stop with a jolt far heavier than the initial shock, and caught off guard, Dr. Andrews is thrown to the floor. He makes an unsuccessful attempt to arrest his fall but slams an arm against the corner of a desk on the way down instead. The jar sends computer monitors, keyboards, and other desktop equipment crashing to the floor. Robert quickly gets back up, and his first concern is for the staff. It looks like almost everyone met the same fate, and they're pulling themselves up from the ground with a few grunts and groans.

"Anyone hurt?"

His voice sounds loud in the sudden quietness, but no one answers him. The atmosphere is electrified with anticipation, and moments later, all of them are back on their feet, standing around in a statue-like stupor. The hypnotic silence is broken by a loud whir, and more than a dozen printers kick into life. Without waiting for instructions, the juniors leap into action and start to pick up equipment that's scattered across the floor, and they reposition desks, chairs, and other furniture that was displaced by the shaking. The seniors scramble to their terminals so they can begin to interpret the reams of data disseminated by the mainframe. In all that time, no one speaks.

The Klaxon starts up again.

"We have another one!" a technician yells in an excited voice, but this time the seismic waves aren't strong enough for them to feel.

It's probably an aftershock, Robert thinks as he walks into the center of the room.

Someone turns the alarm off.

"Anyone hurt?" the doctor calls out for a second time. He wants to be satisfied that no one was injured, and this time, a series of nos echo back at him.

The Klaxon begins to pulsate yet again, and he walks over to Mahesh. "Mute that damn thing. Everyone's on full vigilance anyway, so we don't need it screaming at us every ten seconds."

With the scientists back at their terminals, Robert keeps his eyes on the giant monitor. He's growing impatient to see where the epicenter is, but the processors are taking longer than usual to evaluate the data. While he's waiting, twenty-year-old Hiranmaya Singh walks over to the main printer bank and begins to relay the data from a document that's still printing up, in a slow, precise voice.

"The epicenter is located at eleven degrees, twenty-nine minutes, and twenty-seven point two six eight three arcseconds north; ninety degrees, twenty-six minutes, and twenty-two point seven two seven four arcseconds east." She pauses before reading the next line. "Energy release at the hypocenter is four hundred and fifty gigatons."

Dr. Andrews throws a sharp glance in her direction. "Megatons," he corrects, and he makes a quick calculation in his head. "That's close to a magnitude nine."

Hiranmaya hesitates before contradicting him in a firm voice. "No, four hundred and fifty *gigatons*. The epicenter is in the Bay of Bengal, two hundred forty-nine kilometers west of the Andaman Islands."

The marker he's waiting for with increasing impatience appears on the screen. A dark purple indicator begins to ripple outward in concentric circles at the location Hiranmaya read off moments earlier. Robert stares in disbelief as the mauve waves expand across the bay. They don't even start to graduate into the red spectrum until they reach the Indian subcontinent to the west, north through Bangladesh, Bhutan, Nepal, and Western China, and east and northeast across Thailand, Cambodia, Laos, Vietnam, and Southern China. Gandhinagar lies to the northwest, and the waves have barely shifted into the orange scale as they roll across it. It isn't until they traverse Pakistan into Afghanistan and Iran that they drop into the yellow band.

"Impossible!" the geophysicist exclaims, and he takes a few steps toward the giant screen with his eyes fixed on the huge waves radiating out from the epicenter. He's trying to comprehend the enormity of what he's looking at. "That's more than two thousand kilometers from here. We shouldn't even feel a *small* tremor at this distance."

Hiranmaya's voice drifts across the center as she continues to read from the chart, which is still printing. "Richter scale, magnitude eleven point four."

A hush falls over the operations center, and everyone turns to stare at her in astonishment. Robert, who dismissed her reiteration of "gigaton" as a mispronunciation in the heat of excitement, spins on his heels and strides across to the printer. He tears the report off, and his mouth drops open in bewilderment as he reads it. He's beginning to distrust the computer's evaluation and looks back up at the marker on the map. *Is it possible that the extended shaking has caused it to malfunction?*

Mahesh walks over to stand beside the doctor and whispers to him in quiet disbelief, "*That's* the location of the rift."

Robert doesn't respond but continues to gape at the screen in silence. A purple marker pops up in Pakistan, and Hiranmaya reads aloud from another printer.

"A nine point seven has just been recorded east of Lahore."

All fifteen printers chatter away, spitting out reams of information as the computers attempt to publish more data than can be handled at once. An intern is busy moving along the line of machines, loading vellum into one after the other.

"I need someone to go down to the stockroom and bring more paper up," she calls out over her shoulder. "*Lots* of paper."

Five purple and one red marker appear on the map in rapid succession.

"What the fuck is happening?" Robert whispers to himself in bewilderment.

Hiranmaya continues to give a running commentary. "There are three more earthquakes in Indonesia. A nine point seven, nine point four, and *another* nine point seven. Bandar Abbus in Iran has registered an eight point nine, and there's a nine point three out in the Arabian Sea …" She trails off for a moment before adding, in a reflective tone, "Hmm. There are still more."

The intern who is keeping the printers loaded with paper calls out again. "I need a new ink cartridge on printer seven."

Robert is mesmerized by the purple and red markers that continue to ripple out across the map. Two large quakes register almost simultaneously to the south and northeast of Japan, followed seconds later by more across the Philippines. Whatever is happening isn't realistic, and he needs to confirm whether this is really happening. The movie *War Games* comes to mind. He wonders if someone could have hacked into their system and planted malware that simulates seismic events. A dubious shadow hangs over that notion. The shaker was real enough. *Perhaps the sensors are reporting conflicting data statements that the mainframe is unable to process correctly.*

He's about to turn away when an amazing streak of more than forty earthquakes with an average magnitude of between eight and nine curves down through the African rift valley in a time span of five seconds. They start to the east of Addis Ababa in Ethiopia, run down through the borders of Uganda, the Democratic Republic of the Congo, Rwanda, Burundi, Tanzania, Zambia, Malawi, and Mozambique before moving into the Southern Ocean toward Antarctica.

The doctor's jaw sags open. A pattern is emerging, and it fills the geologist with fear. He recalls an infamous debate he had with his brother years earlier, and something he said could never happen might actually be occurring. It's only speculation at this point, but whatever happened in the Bay of Bengal has unleashed an inconceivable amount of energy deep in the lithosphere and dislodged the Australian plate, smashing it into the Indian and Eurasian plates. The rebound has forced the continental and oceanic tectonics to nudge into each other, triggering a sequential reaction along the convergent boundaries as it expands outwards in ever widening circles from the initial event. What's more disquieting is the dynamism of such a feat. The intensity required would be more realistic in the Archaean eon, when titanic events of this stature were commonplace.

He turns to Hiranmaya. "Miss Singh, do we need to issue a tsunami warning?"

An alert would normally flash in large red letters along the top of the map if one were detected, and it doesn't feel right to Robert that nothing has come up. He waits patiently while she pulls some data up from the computer.

"There's no signal, Dr. Andrews. Records are showing that the oceanic flow sensors went dead at ten thirty-two."

The probability that an earthquake of this magnitude spawned a deadly surge of water racing across the Bay of Bengal is too high for him to ignore, and he glances at Mahesh. "Issue an *immediate* tsunami warning for every coastline around the bay. This is going to make the one back in 2004 look like a mere ripple."

Robert turns his eyes back to the screen as the young scientist walks away, and he is horrified to see that massive earthquakes are still spreading out across the globe. He calls out to Mahesh, who is about to exit the control room.

"Amend my last instruction and issue a worldwide alert."

The young scientist nods his head in affirmation and disappears through the door. Mahesh will confirm the magnitude and location to the press when he delivers the tsunami notice, but they'll want to know more about the anomalous dynamics of such an abnormal earthquake, and they don't have the answers right now. Under normal circumstances, Robert would be downstairs making a statement to the media and impressing reporters with his knowledge, but it may be weeks, months, or even years before they know what happened out there.

He's still holding the first report in his hand, and he glances down at it before looking back up at the map. The screen is lit like a Christmas tree with red and purple markers. He can't see a single ripple that isn't overlapped by others, and this brings a different set of unknown values into play. Seismic shockwaves are traveling through the earth and colliding into each other from all directions at speeds of up to 28,800 kilometers per hour. The geologist can't even begin to imagine the severity of the surface damage at the impact points, but he feels sure it will be far more devastating than the earthquake itself. What is happening is unprecedented.

Robert's eyes settle on the purple marker to the west of the

Andamans that set everything in motion, and he whispers to himself, "What have you done, baby? What is your secret?" But he already has a good idea.

A telephone chirps and is answered by a lab intern. She calls across to Robert. "Phone for you, Dr. Andrews."

"Take a name and number, and tell them I'll call back at the first chance I get."

She places the palm of her hand over the mouthpiece and lowers her voice. "It's Prime Minister Sengupta."

The doctor sighs and steps over to take the handset from her. "Good morning, sir."

Runjit has no time for civilities and gets straight to the point. "What can you tell me?"

"There's not much I *can* tell you at the moment, except that an earthquake of magnitude eleven point four has struck the Bay of Bengal two hundred forty nine kilometers west of the Andaman and Nicobar Islands."

"Eleven point four? Are you *sure*?"

Robert responds with dry cynicism. "Of *course* I'm sure. The data shows that it was felt within a fifty-six hundred kilometer radius of the epicenter. This is as far north as central southern Russia, east across China *and* the Koreas, and even Western Australia and parts of the Northern Territory didn't escape."

A long silence on the other end of the line ensues before the prime minister speaks in a subdued voice. "How bad is it, doctor?"

"I can't even begin to speculate, sir, but there's little doubt that anywhere within a proximity of a thousand kilometers will not have fared well. The Andaman and Nicobar Islands are almost on top of it, so that may be a good place to start. The damage there will be colossal, and I'll be surprised if there aren't any deaths."

"I think we're lucky it happened out in the bay and not on the mainland."

"I'm not so sure," Robert replies dubiously. "I think a dangerous tsunami is going to hit the coast during the next couple of hours."

"What's *that* supposed to mean?" Runjit asks, raising his voice once again. "We've spent *millions* placing current-flow sensors across the bay, so I'd much prefer to hear you confirm that with more positivity than 'I think.'"

Robert rolls his eyes at the prime minister's outburst. "Sir, while I understand your frustration, it's plausible that an earthquake of this scale has taken the cables out. For now we should concern ourselves with minimizing the risks before it's too late; we can figure out what caused the failure afterward. A tsunami alert has been sent out, and you can help by spreading the word. Everyone along the eastern seaboard needs to evacuate to higher elevations. The higher, the better; this one is going to be huge. I can't be more positive than that."

Runjit grunts. It's clear he's not happy. "Communications with government facilities on the Andaman and Nicobar Islands are down, and the telecom company is trying to restore connections. Can you at *least* advise me whether I should order the air force to fly a reconnaissance mission down there?"

"I would consider that to be an excellent idea given the circumstances, but that's not my call to make." Why the prime minister would ask such a question is beyond him. *Perhaps he's getting confused about whom he is talking to?* "If you do send a plane, can you get someone to call me with an eyewitness report?"

Runjit's reply is blunt. "I can ask, but that decision is up to the pilot."

"You're quick to demand information, yet you seem unwilling

to help me to obtain anything that might help. We have tons of data coming in. I'll call you back when we've had a chance to analyze some of it, Mr. Sengupta."

Runjit disconnects without saying another word. Unperturbed by the premier's rudeness, the doctor speaks to a senior technician as he replaces the handset. "Kumar, I need you to set up a satellite flyover the Bay of Bengal. I want all-spectrum exposures of the Andaman and Nicobar group through to the coordinates of the epicenter."

Robert turns his attention back to the wall monitor. There are so many red and purple ripples on the map that it's impossible to distinguish one seismic event from another. Multiple earthquakes have been triggered from Turkey to Fiji, Papua New Guinea, the Solomon Islands, and New Zealand, moving out across the Pacific and North and South Atlantic Oceans, and into western Russia with varying magnitudes ranging from seven point five to eight point nine. The US West Coast and South America are going to be next.

Hiranmaya calls out again. "We're registering strong aftershocks of between eight point six and nine point seven in the Bay of Bengal, Dr. Andrews, but they're kind of weird."

"How so?" the geologist asks.

"They're continuous and merging into one another. The computer is unable to separate one from the other is and responding with inconclusive reports."

"You're doing a good job, Hiranmaya," the doctor says. "Just continue to collate the data, and log everything like you've always done. I'll take a look at it as soon as I can."

Mahesh walks back into the main center, and Robert can see a baffled expression on his face. He stops beside the doctor and makes a gesture toward the screen with one hand.

"Is it even *possible* for the plates to jostle into each like that?"

"Do you think that's what is happening?"

Mahesh hesitates. "Objectively, nothing else makes sense, but …"

"Yes?"

"Well, only a tectonic collision could manufacture such a huge event like this in the first place, yet …"

Robert understands why he's being cautious and encourages him to share his thoughts. "Yes?"

"There are no plate boundaries at that location."

The doctor is quick to warn the young seismologist to err on the side of caution. "Mahesh, don't share *any* conjectures or wild guesses with your associates. It's best to keep all speculations to yourself unless you can back them up with hard data."

"Including you, Dr. Andrews?"

Robert flashes a brief smile. "I'm the exception."

He turns away and raises his voice to address the rest of the staff in a loud voice. "May I have your attention for a moment?" He pauses while everyone stops what he or she is doing and looks at him. "Until we know what's going on, *no* one talks to the media. All press releases will be approved by me and will be delivered through an authorized spokesperson for the institute. Is that understood?"

A few okays and yeses affirm his instructions.

"Good," Robert says. "Now return to your tasks. This is going to keep us busy for the foreseeable future. If you come across anything exceptional, unusual, or equal to what we've experienced, skip protocols and alert me immediately."

Without saying another word, he spins around and heads for his office.

6

Khao Lak Beach
Khao Lak, Thailand
Coordinates: 08° 37' 49.4" N, 98° 14' 37.2" E
Thursday, December 26, 2019, 1033h

Peter stares out across the Andaman Sea with a vacant expression. He's trying to visualize a giant wave bearing in toward the coast, pondering how terrifying it must have been. *Did Beverly see it and understand its significance? Did she gather the girls together in a panic and try to escape, or was she mesmerized by the spectacle without apprehending the danger until it was too late? Perhaps she had been lying on the sand, enjoying the warmth of the sun on her body, oblivious of the peril they were in ...*

Without warning, a terrific jolt hits Khao Lak. The beach is tugged from beneath Peter's feet in one sharp movement, and he is thrown backward. He lands hard on his backside about two meters from where he was standing and rolls across the sandy terrain, coming to a stop one meter before the paving that runs along the beachhead. Stunned and disoriented, his first thought is that a huge bomb blast occurred, but this notion is quickly dispelled. The beach continues to shake violently, tossing him around like a rag doll, and a thunderous rumble unlike anything he's heard before is coming at him from all directions. The quaking is vicious. Confused, he's engulfed with panic. It's an impossible task for him to get back on his feet. He's being pitched around with no effort, and his body is rebounding up to sixty centimeters from the surface. It's about all he can do to prevent himself from being flung sideways each time the ground slams into his bottom.

The sensation that the beach is sliding and taking him along with it is unsettling. His legs are spread apart, and he's powerless to do anything. Panting hard from a combination of exertion and fright, he takes a moment to assess the situation. This is his first experience of an earthquake, and the intensity alarms him. The palm trees lining the beachhead are swaying with so much aggression that he expects them to snap like matchsticks. As scared as he is, logic tells him that the open seashore is the safest place to be.

He turns his eyes toward the young girl he had spoken to earlier. She's been propelled up the beach too, but unlike him, she's not attempting to stand. Peter wonders why people live where they are under the constant threat of huge seismic events such as this. He assumes she must have been through countless earthquakes, yet she still looks terrified. It's written all over her face.

The feeling that the seashore is being pulled toward the west still persists. The fierce bouncing starts to make him nauseated, and several times he swallows the acrid taste of bile back down his throat. *How long is this going to last?* He locks eyes with the young girl again, but neither makes an attempt to speak. The noise is far too loud to hold any kind of a tête-à-tête.

A shadowy movement in the corner of his eye draws his attention, and he swings his head around in time to witness several trees toppling, but the deafening rumble drowns the sound as they crash to the ground. There isn't a single person on the sandy stretch of coast left on his or her feet, and most of the people within the scope of his vision appear to have abandoned all attempts to get back up.

Peter has no idea how long he's been at Mother Nature's mercy, but it comes to an end with a massive jolt—heavier than the first. This time he slides on his derriere toward the water. More by reflexive response than a conscious decision, he digs his shoe heels into the sand, which causes his legs to act like vaulting poles. Carried by the forward momentum, his body rolls up, over, and forward, landing facedown before sliding to a stop. The silence that follows is surreal, and he lies motionless for several moments. A female voice speaks to him in English but in an accent typical of Thai's in this region.

"Are you hurt?"

Peter rolls onto his back and sits up. The young girl is kneeling close to him with a concerned expression in her eyes.

"No, I don't think so," he replies, although his posterior is burning from the constant slapping he received from the seism. "What about you? Are you okay?"

"I'm good," she says, and she clambers to her feet still clutching the Bible.

Peter stands up and dusts the sand from his jacket and trousers. "I've never felt an earthquake before, and I'll be happy if I don't feel another one for the rest of my life."

The girl brushes the golden-brown grains from her long dress. "I never feel one so hard like this before. Soon I think there will be another."

The inference alarms Peter. "I hope you're wrong."

"When we get a big one like this, there are always more, but they're not so bad most of the time. They have a special name, but I don't know it in English."

"Aftershock?"

She shrugs. "I don't know if this is it or not."

Peter has finished brushing the sand from his suit and is straightening his tie when she points toward the water's edge.

"Oh, it falls."

The tiny memorial is about thirty meters from where he's standing. The roses and photographs are lying on the sand, but something else puzzles him. The waves are lapping less than a meter from the shrine, yet when he set it up, they were at least 180 meters away.

Peter's hips are sore from the pounding they received by the earthquake, and he limps over to the desecrated memorial. He goes on one knee to rebuild it, and as he picks up the red rose and Beverley's picture, he's conscious of the young girl kneeling down in the sand next to him. Her presence is making him feel uneasy, but he refrains from saying anything for now.

"They are beautiful," she says softly.

"Yes, they are."

"I help you."

Without waiting for his consent, she places the Bible on the sand and leans forward. She shows complete respect and sensitivity to the symbolic value of the shrine as she lifts one of the white roses and the photograph of Kathleen gently from the sand. Peter feels a twinge of possessiveness. It's not one of his common traits, but this is a sacred moment, and he doesn't want to share it with anyone, regardless of how gracious his or her intentions might be.

Peter turns his head toward her with the purpose of asking for some personal space. He intends to choose his words carefully because he doesn't want to come across as brash or offensive, or to make her feel embarrassed, but this is a special plot of sand, and he's prepared to protect its inviolability from everyone until the next tide washes it away.

Peter opens his mouth to speak, but an odd expression on her face makes him hesitate. She is staring at the image of his eldest daughter, and he remains silent as she turns the exposure over to read the dedication on the reverse. A moment later, she lays the white rose and Kathleen's photo on top of the Bible with deliberate tenderness and reaches out to pick up the photograph of Angela. A tiny smile appears on her lips as she scrutinizes the face of his youngest for a few seconds before leaning forward to look at the picture of Beverly, which is still in his hand.

She emits a loud gasp and twists her body around until she's facing him. Her eyes move back and forth as if she's taking in every detail of his features. It begins to make him feel self-conscious, yet he perceives a profound sadness deep behind her blue eyes. They are filled with the innocence of a young child, and he can only speculate that she's here because she lost her own family. Peter swallows on an uncomfortable swelling in the back of his throat and resists the urge to push her away. An intuitive inner sense is warning him not to say or do anything but allow her to speak first.

Her eyes lock onto his, and she raises her right hand, softly placing the tips of her fingers on his cheek below his left eye. She draws them gently over his skin, down past the corner of his mouth to his chin before Peter reacts. He reaches up with one hand, curls his fingers around her small wrist, and pulls her hand away in a firm but temperate manner. He's searching for an appropriate nonintimate response that won't sound offensive when she speaks to him in a timid voice, almost as if she's afraid to talk.

"I see your face, and I think I know you from somewhere."

Peter stares at her with a blank expression in his eyes. It's obvious that she's getting him confused with someone else, and whatever he intended to say is gone.

"We've *never* met before," he replies softly. "I didn't arrive in Thailand until yesterday."

Her eyes darken with disappointment, and she glances back down at Beverley's photograph. "I see this picture, and I know this woman." She gestures with one hand toward the photograph of Kathleen sitting on top of the Bible. "And I know this woman too."

"You *do?*" He realizes how stupid the question must sound right after he utters it, but her unexpected declaration has taken him by surprise. "These are pictures of my wife and daughters."

She reaches out, and there's a lot of tenderness in her touch as she cups both hands over his cheeks. She moves her face closer to his and lowers her voice to an almost inaudible whisper. "Daddy."

The hair on the nape of his neck stands up, and a chill sweeps through his body. She continues to gaze into his eyes without wavering, and he stares back at the girl, paralyzed with bewilderment. He can see her lips and the facial muscles around her mouth quivering, and she's clearly making an effort to control her emotions. Her eyes glaze, and a moment later, a single tear rolls out of the corner of her eye. She holds his face firmly to keep him from turning his head away, and barely able to speak between choking sobs, she stresses each word individually.

"I … am … Angela."

Her declaration leaves him speechless, and it's almost impossible for him to control the sudden rush of emotion, but there are doubts spinning in his head. Here is a young girl who could have been no more than a baby in 2004, searching for her parents, whom she probably can't remember with clarity. *Is she taking advantage of my vulnerability after seeing the photographs of my family?* Angela was six when the tragedy took his family away, and this girl doesn't look old enough to be his daughter.

"How old are you?"

"Twenty-one. My birthday is December sixth," she whispers back.

Peter's throat constricts again, and the muscles in his body are frozen rigid. *She couldn't know that unless ...*

Despite everything he's been through, there has never been an instant in Peter's life when every emotion a human body can experience converges into a single moment of time. The familiarity in her appearance that captured his curiosity earlier, and the family resemblance that had eluded him, leap out at him. The blue eyes—that alone should have raised suspicions about her origins because the dominant color for an Asian is usually a dark pigment of brown. But how *could* he be expected to recognize her? She'd gone through the transformation from childhood into adulthood, and while he'd always refused to believe they had perished in the tsunami, he never expected to meet them again in the same spot where he left them.

His shoulders slump as years of pent-up tension drains from his body, leaving him feeling numb. Unable to focus, he leans forward, wraps his arms around the young girl, and pulls her close to him. Tears well up in his eyes, blurring his vision as he stares out over her shoulder. Her head is buried into his chest, but he can feel her fragile body trembling against his, and seconds later, he's crying with uncontrolled passion. They sit on the beach, clinging to each other, father and daughter weeping shamelessly, and the moment is far too profound for words.

Five minutes pass before Peter sits back and studies her face through a veil of tears. How is it the authorities never identified her and made efforts to reunite them? He admits that the first couple of weeks following the tsunami were chaotic, but what happened after things began to normalize again? There are questions that need to be answered because she was old enough to tell them her name, which country she was from, and plenty of other pertinent information.

As he stares at her tear-strewn face, a spark of optimism ignites.

"Mum … and Kathleen?"

Peter reads the response in her eyes, and the brief glimmer of hope drains away before she answers. Angela is still sobbing, and he waits patiently while she takes a moment to recompose herself.

"Mummy and my sister are only alive with God; this I know. I remember you and Mummy and Kathleen's face as a picture in my head. I think you are in heaven too, until I see your face today, and only in this moment did I know the big water never took you."

"I wasn't here when it happened," he tells her, trying to jog her memory. "Don't you remember? I went to the rainforest at Kaeng Krung."

Angela hesitates before shaking her head. "I don't know. I can only see you on the beach with Mummy." A tiny smile forms on her lips. "You kiss her. I think you love Mummy very much."

A wave of grief sweeps through Peter as he recalls the kiss she's talking about. "Yes, I did. I love you and Kathleen too, and I've missed you all more than you can ever imagine." Angela takes hold of his hands as he continues to explain. "I was on the plane when the tsunami hit, and I didn't know about it for three days."

"What's a tsunami?"

"That's what the big water is called."

"Oh!" and she repeats the word. "Tsunami!"

He pauses for a moment. "Why didn't you say something to me when you came onto the beach?"

"I don't know for sure." She motions with one hand toward the photographs and roses lying on the sand beside them. "I still doubt if you are my real father, but when I look at the pictures, I understand. I come here every year and say a prayer to God for you, Mummy, and my sister." Angela places a hand over her heart. "It makes me feel good to do this."

She falls silent for a moment, and he can see some uncertainty on her face. "My Thai mother and father always bring me here until I am older to come by myself."

He's never been subject to jealousy before, so the sudden rush of this new emotion at the mention of her Thai parents scares him. It takes a few moments of guilty rationalization to calm himself down. If he'd raised the courage to come back one year after the catastrophe, it's likely he would have been reunited with his daughter. Instead, he chose to wallow in self-pity, and it denied him a reunion that should have taken place years earlier. He has only himself to blame for the direction their lives have taken.

He noticed Angela chose her words carefully, referring to her adoptive parents in an alternative fashion, but he also knows he needs to understand that they're a major part of her life whether he likes it or not. Logic dictates that he should feel indebted to a young couple who assumed a paternal role. This part of the world is rife with child exploitation and human trafficking, and she could have met with a less favorable fate. The fact that they kept her biological family alive in her memory and never allowed her to forget them is an honorable sacrifice.

"Your Thai mother and father …" he starts, but he trails off.

Naturally, he wants to bring her back to England with him, but she's twenty-one, and her guardianship is no longer under anyone's jurisdiction other than her own. Peter is afraid that her roots may have grown so deep in Thailand that she might not want leave, and he's not sure how well he'll be able to handle the rejection.

"My Thai parents are good to me," Angela explains in a soothing voice. "Chai Charoen was their daughter, and she was six when her auntie bring her to another beach. They were sad when the big water take her away, but they still look for her. They found me instead. I was hurt, and they helped me get better again. They say Siddhārtha Gautama could not bring Chai Charoen back, but he listen to their prayers, and deliver me so I can give them pleasure to heal their grief." She gives one of his hands a reassuring squeeze in the same manner as Beverly used to do. "They give me much aid for my life, and teach me not to forget my real mummy and daddy."

Peter swallows back on the anger rising up inside his chest. He can't deny his role in this mess, because essentially, he's the one who has kept them separated for so long. *This is going to be so fucked up*, he thinks to himself.

Angela continues. "When I am finished with my prayers on the beach, I take my lunch and eat with Mummy. I always bring her flowers on this day."

He's puzzled by her remark. "What do you mean?"

"She is in the ground behind my church," she tells him. "My Thai parents made her a special box to sleep in."

"Is it a Buddhist temple?"

"No. *They* pray to Buddha but tell me my God is different to theirs and I should always revere my own deity." She raises the Bible up in her hand. "They bought this for me because they thought it would help to heal my spiritual wounds."

Peter is amazed. *Buddhists who still brought her up to be a Christian instead of converting her?* His respect for the couple deepens even further.

She inclines her head. "Would you like to come with me to see Mummy?"

"Of *course*," he replies, choking back his tears at the knowledge that Beverly has a proper burial place. He had worried so much how today would play out, but this is beyond anything he could ever have envisaged. He clears his throat.

"Does Kathleen have a grave?"

"What is a grave?"

"It's where Mummy is, the place where you take her flowers."

She bites at her lower lip, and her eyes grow distant and watery. "I like to think Kathleen is alive somewhere like me."

An awkward silence follows, but he thinks quickly and places a hand over hers. "We'll ask the church to put a memorial in her name beside Mummy's grave so we have a special place to bring her flowers too."

She gives him a weak smile. "That would be nice."

Peter falls silent for a few seconds, and his heart starts to thump a little harder. He decides to test the waters and figure out what his position is, but he makes a vow that if she doesn't give him the reply he wants to hear, he won't get dramatic. He will accept her decision with grace no matter how much it hurts. A bout of insensitivity might drive her away from him forever, yet he feels optimistic that she'll go back home with him.

"Tomorrow, we'll go to the British Embassy and make arrangements to get you a passport so you can come back to England with me."

A tear forms in the corner of her eye, and she shakes her head. "This I cannot do, but I will come one day soon, I promise."

That's the response Peter didn't want to hear, and his voice sharpens. "Why?"

"I'm married," she tells him. "I have a husband"—a pleasant smile breaks across her tear-strewn face—"and you have a grandson. I can't leave my family."

Peter's mouth drops open. This is a dynamic he hadn't factored into the equation, and it leaves him speechless. His life has shot off on a surrealistic tangent, and his head is reeling at the discovery that his carefree, giggly, six-year-old daughter has been transformed into an adult *and* a mother at the snap of a finger.

"Why didn't you bring them here with you?" he asks after getting over the initial surprise.

"He's only three months old. My husband says he is too young this year, so he stay home to be with our son while I come alone. I take you back to my home when we finish on the beach, and you can meet them. Would you like to?"

"Of course ... of *course!*" he stammers. "What is, uh ... my grandson's name?"

"Chatri," she replies. "In English it is meaning 'brave knight.'"

Peter's mind begins to drift. He still wants to ask her how she survived when Beverly and Kathleen didn't, but he doesn't want to probe too deep for fear of exposing traumatic memories she'd rather forget.

The ground begins to rumble and shake again, although it's much less violent than before. It's difficult for him to keep his balance, but he doesn't get thrown to the ground this time. He glances at his daughter in alarm, but she only smiles back at him. This time it's considerably shorter than the first quake, and after forty-five seconds it comes to a stop.

"I tell you another will come," Angela says.

"I think that's what they call an aftershock," Peter replies, but he's not an expert on seismology, so he can't be certain.

"There will be more. There always is."

Peter doesn't like the way she says that with so much confidence. He turns his attention back to the shrine, and going down on one knee, he reattaches Beverly's picture to the stem of the red rose while Angela affixes her sister's photo to the peduncle of the white flower. This time he has no objection to her involvement.

After completing the task, she sits back on her haunches and looks up at her father. "I tell you now, and I hope you don't mind," she says, pointing to the two pictures. "When I finish my prayers, I will take the picture of Mummy and Kathleen when I leave."

"I would like you to keep them," Peter replies. *This is probably the first time she's had any real validation of her family since the day of the tragedy.* She picks up her own picture and, holding it rather awkwardly, begins to giggle. It is the same childish chuckle he heard so many times in the past.

"What to do?" she asks. "I am not with God."

Peter picks the last white rose up from where she had placed it on top of the Bible and hands it to her. "This is yours." He studies her face. The family doctor *had* been right. All those tiny little freckles that used to titivate her jowls are gone. "The picture is for you too. You need to show your husband the beauty spots that used to be on your cheeks."

The reference to beauty spots jogs something embedded deep in her memory, and her eyes open wide in astonishment. "I *remember* it so! You laugh too much at me and tell me it make me look so beautiful." The fact that she remembers something he considered insignificant not only surprises him but also fills him with pride. He's already made the decision to change his return flight to spend more time with his daughter. They have a lot to talk about.

Peter stands up and brushes the sand from his trousers again while Angela slips the photograph of herself between the pages of the Bible. He then reaches down and offers her a hand. After assisting her back to her feet, he turns his eyes toward the water edge, which has receded again by more than a hundred meters.

"Do you mind if I ask you some questions about, uh …" He stops, thinking perhaps he shouldn't dwell on past events but should just be grateful that God has reunited him with Angela. But he's forgotten that her awareness is sharper than he gives credit for.

"Daddy, today is a sad day in every year of my life," she tells him. "We are here to remember and pray for Mummy and Kathleen. It is special for us to talk about them so we don't forget."

Peter is surprised but relieved at her idealistic response. "It's just that I don't want to invoke any bad memories that make you too unhappy, so tell me if you want to stop. I'll understand."

Angela reacts by nodding her head several times. A brief but awkward silence follows. This is going to be as hard for him to hear as it will be for her to tell him, but he needs to know.

"Do you remember if there was an earthquake before the tsunami came?"

She pauses for a moment, and a frown forms across her forehead. "I can't be sure, but I don't think so. Only the big water come." She casts her eyes to the ground and falls silent for several moments before turning to face the ocean. Angela points to where the sand meets the sea. "I was standing in the water, maybe to here." She uses a hand to indicate a level about two inches below her knees. "Kathleen is farther out where it's deeper, and swims far away from me."

She falls silent for several seconds, but Peter remains patient, waiting for his daughter to tell him in her own time. "I hear a strange sound …" She hesitates, and he realizes that she's searching for a way to elaborate further. "I listen to this sometimes when I eat noodles."

He offers a prompt to help her find the correct description. "Like a slurp, or a sucking noise, maybe?"

She appears to be uncertain whether any of the hints are the right words. "If this is how you say it, I don't know, but the water went away very, very fast."

Peter recalls an article he read about tsunamis when he wanted to learn more about the incredible phenomenon that snatched his family away. Some claimed to hear a slurping, while others said something representative of a heavy sigh was preceded by a rapid waning of the tide as the water was sucked out to feed the incoming wave.

"How far out did it go?"

Angela's reply is emphatic. "A *very* long away. I think it was for *many* kilometers."

He realizes that the description is exaggerated from the perception of a six-year-old child, but he doesn't correct her. "Kathleen was screaming, and reaching out toward me with her arms, but the water still takes her away from me."

"You must have been *terrified*."

Angela turns and looks into his eyes. "Not at first. I run to catch up with the water, but everybody on the beach start to shout and scream. *This* is what makes me frightened so much, and I stop." She pauses, and her eyes start to water up. "Mummy is running to me, and she is screaming too. I think she is angry with me." The tear rolls out of her eye and runs down her right cheek as she chokes back a sob. "I think everyone is mad at me, so I run toward her."

Peter removes a hankie from his pocket, and begins to dab the tears from her cheeks. After a few moments, she takes the white square of silk from him and blows her nose into it. Without any additional prompting, she continues with the painful story.

"Mummy takes me up in her arms and holds me so tight it was hard to breathe. She is running and crying and screaming for Kathleen, and I was scared."

He takes her hands in his. "Did you see the big water coming?"

"No," Angela tells him, and she pauses before placing the open palm of her right hand against her upper chest. "Mummy pushes my face here, and I can't see anything."

She falls silent again, and the lull lasts so long that Peter is unsure if she's going to say anything else. Almost thirty seconds pass before the young woman draws herself up and begins talking again.

"Too many people scream, and there was a loud noise like a big earthquake before I am wet. The water is too cold, and it come inside of my nose, and mouth, and I can't breathe. This scare me much more. Mummy was squeezing me so hard it hurt, and I want her to let me go, but she still hold me. Together we are going around too fast." She turns her back toward the shoreline, and points inland. "I can't remember what happened next. I think maybe I am asleep because I wake up a long way over there on the hill." She pauses and sobs again. "My head hurt so bad it make me cry too much. I am wet and dirty, and my body is sore when I move, but I sit up, and I can see Mummy." Her shoulders shake as she chokes back another sob. "Her face is white, and I called to her, but she doesn't answer me. I think she's sleeping too. My legs hurt, and I can't stand, so I crawl through the mud with my arms and tummy." She chokes on another sob. "Mummy was asleep with her eyes open, and she is so cold. I ask her to wake up because my head hurts, but she didn't." More tears roll down her cheek. "I cuddled her because that's all I wanted to do."

She stares at the tree-covered hill where her mother died, and her lips quiver. Seconds later she hangs her head and begins to weep uncontrollably. Peter is suddenly overwhelmed with guilt for allowing her to relive the horrifying experience to satisfy his own curiosity, and he puts his arms around her shoulders. He draws her closer with tears rolling down his own cheeks, and she leans forward into him, burying her face into his right shoulder. Her body shakes against his as she cries harder, and he suspects that this is the first time she's spoken to anyone about the horror of those final moments with her mother.

Peter has no idea how long they have been standing in the sand, drawing comfort in each other's arms, when their grieving is interrupted by a low-pitched drone as the sirens start, rising to an ear-splitting crescendo that obliterates all other sound beneath its bloodcurdling wail. This is the three-minute tribute that the hotel receptionist told him about.

Angela pulls away from him and wipes the tears from her eyes with the handkerchief. She gives him a weak smile before turning to face the sea. Clutching the Bible in front of her in both hands, she closes her eyes and bows her head.

Peter takes a moment to admire the way her long hair and dress flow out behind her in the stiff but steady onshore breeze. His grief for Beverly and Kathleen isn't less easy to accept than before, but the incredible reunion with Angela has counteracted the anguish he expected to feel.

He glances at his wristwatch. The time is ten twenty-two. He clasps his hands in front of his stomach, hangs his head, and closes his eyes. He becomes absorbed in prayer, and even the sirens aren't interfering with his thoughts as he thanks God for bringing him and Angela together again and makes a promise to his wife that he'll ensure her life is filled with the happiness she deserves. He makes a tentative vow to return as often as he can, but he also asks her to forgive him if he's unable to make it every year.

Peter can't even begin to describe the strange sensation of tranquility and peace that's flowing through his body, and for the first time in fifteen years, he acknowledges a spiritual fulfillment within himself. Lost in prayer, he's oblivious to the passing of time, but eventually the chilling, mournful cry of the sirens begins to get intrusive. The early warning system was installed after the 2004 tsunami, and he's certain that if it had been in operation back then, his wife and daughter would still be alive today.

After a while, he opens his eyes and glances at Angela. She's still standing with her head hung, her lips moving in silent prayer. He smiles in contentment and glances at his Timex once again before lowering his head to pray some more, but something bothers him as he closes his eyes. The time is now ten thirty-three, and his mind drifts to what the hotel receptionist said as she slid the pamphlet and ticket over the counter on the previous evening. "… *and the tsunami warning sirens will sound a three-minute accolade beginning at ten twenty-seven.*"

Something doesn't compute. *Ten twenty-seven, and three minutes?* The machines began their banshee-like wailing at ten twenty-two, which means eleven minutes have gone by. Yet the unnerving moan is still in his ears.

Peter's heart skips a beat, his head jerks up, and his eyes snap open. There's a momentary pause as his brain processes the changing vista in front of him. A huge wall of water stretching from the North to the southern horizon is rising from the ocean, growing taller as it races in toward the shore at an incredible speed. His jaw sags and his eyes widen in horror The howl of the sirens drown out any noise that's being generated by the massive tsunami sweeping into the shallow beach waters. As Peter stands paralyzed in terror, a rapid vibration beneath his feet begins, and it grows stronger with every passing second.

He glances along the seashore. A few mourners are running inshore, but it's nothing more than a feeble gesture. It will be impossible to escape the monstrous wave. There are still far too many people facing the sea with their eyes closed, oblivious of the peril they're in. Perhaps these are the lucky ones. Death will be swift and merciless.

He glances back at the enormous wave that's grown to more than two hundred meters in height and tilts his head back, his eyes trying to seek the crest. It's hanging high above him, poised like a giant cobra about to strike, and while Peter is mesmerized by the terrifyingly beautiful but deadly creation of nature, tears stream down his cheeks. He looks at Angela, and the sight of her head still hung in prayer breaks the hypnotic spell. He leaps toward her with outstretched arms, but his long, drawn-out scream of desperation is lost in the noise of the sirens.

"Noooooo!"

The largest tsunami ever recorded breaks down over them with the crushing force of billions of tons of concrete.

7

Rashtrapati Bhavan
New Delhi, India
Coordinates: 28° 36' 51.6" N, 77° 11' 59.3" E
Thursday, December 26, 2019, 1217h

A tense atmosphere hangs over the majestic mansion of Rashtrapati Bhavan as the fifty-six-year-old President Abdul Prasad strides through the corridor connecting the residence to the administrative offices and halls. It's been an hour and three quarters since a strong earthquake rocked New Delhi, and dissatisfied at the sluggish rate at which information is trickling in, he decides to take command of the situation. It's rare for an Indian president to intervene at this level because it's the duty of the prime minister to assume authoritative control over localized affairs, but Abdul likes to get involved early when an event has the potential to turn into a large-scale disaster.

His reputation for getting things done is one of the distinctions responsible for his popularity among the working class and poorer communities. He kept a campaign promise to improve education, living standards, work conditions, and easier access to health and medical care, but his empathy for the less fortunate and his blitz against antecedence and corruption have not been met with the same enthusiasm among the wealthy and elite. His policies threaten the lifestyle they enjoy, and influential immunity from the law is fading. It had been necessary to sack several appointees to the solicitor general's office before the definition of zero tolerance began to sink in. Magistrates no longer dare to accept bribes in exchange for repudiation of serious criminal charges against those who can afford to buy their way out.

The earthquake was hefty and prolonged, and the first damage reports began to filter in at nine fifty-five. Nerves are rattled, but local casualties were minimized to products being shaken off store shelves and similar noncritical incidents. Abdul is relieved that no injuries, deaths, or structural collapses have been declared yet, but he feels the denouement will be different in the poorer communities. Information is slow coming out of these areas, and he can guarantee that the seism was strong enough to destroy many of the shanty homes.

At ten o'clock, the prime minister calls him. "We need to declare a national disaster. Dr. Andrews of the Institute of Seismology tells me that the epicenter is more than two thousand two hundred kilometers south of New Delhi, close to the Andaman and Nicobar Islands."

Abdul raises his eyebrows in surprise. "How big was it?"

"Eleven point four, sir."

"Surely he's made a mistake?"

"He says not. A tsunami alert is active for the Bay of Bengal, but he advises that a worldwide eagre is also in effect." He pauses momentarily before adding "The armed forces are mobilized to assist with the evacuation of coastal towns and cities, but there's no confirmation that our admonitions are reaching the eastern seaboard."

"Why not?" Abdul asked sharply.

"All lines of communications south of Kolkata in West Bengal are dead," Runjit said. "I'm waiting to hear back from the telephone companies, but in the meantime, I've endeavored to get warnings relayed through the commercial broadcasting services."

"An effort is *not* good enough," the prime minister said. "I want it done. The last thing I need is unnecessary deaths because someone neglected to do what he or she was supposed to do." He has no desire to deal with a repeat scenario of 2004 if it can be avoided. "How close to the Andamans is the epicenter?"

"Two hundred forty-nine kilometers west."

"Do we know what the damage is down there?"

"No, sir. Communications with the islands are out. I've ordered an air force P81 from Hyderabad to carry out a surveillance flight over the region."

A dark scowl formed on Abdul's face. "Why didn't you send a jet from the Eastern Naval Command? They're closer."

"We've been unable to establish communications with Visakhapatnam," Runjit explained. "As the aircraft was out over the bay on an unrelated mission, I diverted it to avoid delays."

Abdul grunts. He still doesn't have anything worthwhile to go on. "Do we know when the tsunami will hit the east coast?"

"We don't even know if there *is* one. Dr. Andrews suspects a fatal malfunction with the oceanic sensors is preventing the center from tracking its progress if it exists," the prime minister replies. "The wave spawned by the Sumatran earthquake fifteen years ago took about two hours to reach the eastern seaboard, so using this as a paradigm, somewhere between ninety to one hundred five minutes from the time of the quake is a good estimate."

Abdul glances at the clock and makes a quick calculation. "So we have about an hour left."

"Yes, sir."

The president takes a few seconds to reassess the limited information. "I'm going to redirect all national disaster and military communications through the operations command center. In the meantime, I want you to contact Admiral Padawiya, General Nadarajah, and Air Chief Marshall Appapillai, and I want to see you all in the North Drawing Room in an hour and a quarter. Mobilize police escorts if you need to, but make sure everyone gets here on time."

Without waiting for the prime minister to confirm, Abdul breaks the connection and dials another number.

"Ashan Shanmukhan speaking."

The president is abrupt. "Tell Commander Cariappa to switch up to modus operandi with immediate effect. You are both required in operations control at eleven twenty."

The Communications Command Center is the brain child of his predecessor, and no expense was spared to turn the facility into one of the most secure places in the world. It's constructed two levels beneath Rashtrapati Bhavan, designed to withstand multiple nuclear blasts, and is purportedly impervious to enemy incursion.

The complex is a prodigious underground technological city with more than five thousand employees sitting at their terminals at any given time. Rows of huge flat-screen LCD arrays are suspended from the ceiling, one for each terminal, displaying images of drone surveillance along the borders, or of one of many special operations going on in different sectors around the country. The security of the nation and safety of its citizens rely on the men and women who work here. In general, the center is on midlevel operations, but when a heightened threat to the homeland is detected, or a natural disaster occurs, it takes three minutes to step up to full efficiency. With a few clicks of a computer mouse, the functionality of a town, a city, or a state can be controlled from here, and if necessary, the whole country can be put on lockdown in less than thirty minutes. Communications between all branches of the armed forces are diverted through the command center, while civilian operations, such as buses, railway lines, trains, air traffic, emergency services, radar installations, satellite systems, and contracted agencies essential to the resolution of a crisis can be monitored—and commandeered if necessary.

A security aide opens the door, and Abdul sweeps into the North Drawing Room, where three top-ranking military officers are waiting for him with the prime minister. He continues to walk through the room, toward an exit at the far end, without slowing down.

"If any of you have plans for Boxing Day, they've changed," he says brusquely. The four men fall into step behind him. "We have a crisis that's changing by the second, but we need an update before we can discuss a necessary course of action."

He leads the way through a corridor to an alcove where two armed guards are on duty beside an elevator door. The president lays his hand on a glass panel for his finger and palm prints to be read by a laser before the car, which sits between floors when it's idle, comes up to their level. A few seconds later, the doors slide open, and the small group steps into the elevator. There are no buttons to push, because technically there are only two floors, and the computer knows what level the car is at.

They ride down to the hub in silence, and twenty seconds later, the doors glide open. The president sets off at a brisk pace along a flagstone pathway, circumnavigating a series of consoles, to a large soundproof chamber constructed from glass. This is the high-tech war room where the central communications commander, Dinesh Cariappa, and the head of security, Ashan Shanmukhan, are waiting for him to arrive.

Abdul barely glances at the two men as he breezes in and heads for a long glass-topped operations table in the center of the room. A line of chairs on one side faces a giant monitor—larger than the one at the Institute of Seismology. The president sits in a chair central to the big screen, which displays a satellite image of the Bay of Bengal, including the Indian subcontinent and the coastal regions of Bangladesh, Myanmar, Thailand, and northern Malaysia. Sri Lanka, the Andamans, Aceh, and North Sumatra are also visible. Runjit, Gihan, Rasheed, and Isuru take their respective places at the table, while Shanmukhan sits at one end. Dinesh, who has a wireless device inserted in one ear so he can keep in direct contact with the main center while he's in conference, remains standing close to the side of the monitor.

Abdul gets straight down to business. "Commander Cariappa, what's the latest update from the Institute of Seismic Research?"

"I spoke to Dr. Andrews about ten minutes ago. The only information he is able to provide are the coordinates of the epicenter, magnitude, and duration of the established earthquake. The first aftershock registered one minute nine seconds later, and since then, a continual roll of overlapping shocks with intensities of up to a magnitude nine have been persistent." He motions with his left hand toward the screen. "Satellites are snapping new images, which I expect to receive in a few minutes."

"Damage reports?" the president inquires.

Dinesh shakes his head. "Very few details on subsequent aftermath effects are known because of a widespread failure in communications affecting every province on the subcontinent." He reaches down and picks a document up from the top of the table. "These are the facts we do know. An abnormal earthquake struck this morning at 0933 hours 16 seconds. The hypocenter is beneath the ocean floor in the Bay of Bengal, and the location of the epicenter is 11 degrees, 29 minutes, 27.2683 arcseconds north; 90 degrees, 26 minutes, 22.7274 arcseconds east; and 248.9 kilometers west of the Andaman's. The duration was 4 minutes, 49 seconds, at a sustained magnitude of 11.4 on the Richter scale. The aftershocks vary from 6.9 to 9.8 along a 200-kilometer longitudinal path from 10 degrees, 35 minutes, 57.1993 arcseconds north and passes through the epicenter to 12 degrees, 23 minutes, 44.0748 arcseconds."

Abdul raises a hand and speaks in a gruff voice. "Can you mark the epicenter on the map so I can see where it is."

Dinesh takes a few moments to punch some instructions into his keypad, and a few seconds later, a red line along the 200-kilometer stretch where the aftershocks are occurring, with an X in the center, pops up on the screen. "An average of six to ten overlapping aftershocks are occurring concurrently at any given time along this line, but periodically, there are as many as twenty to thirty simultaneous quakes being recorded. To anyone within the shock zone—in particular the residents of the Andamans—it's a never ending fluctuating seism that hasn't stopped in almost two hours."

"We must evacuate the islands," Abdul says authoritatively.

"There are four hundred thousand inhabitants, so the burden needs to be shared between air, naval, and army commands."

"Dr. Andrews predicts that the damage will be extensive," Dinesh confirms, "and warns that we won't find any structures left standing. Based on statistics, the number of casualties will be high, so hospitals on the mainland will be told to prepare for an influx of patients." He replaces the document on the table and makes direct eye contact with Abdul. "He's advised that due to the large number of high-magnitude aftershocks, we must be prepared for multiple tsunamis that will be every bit as dangerous as the one in 2004, and warnings must not be scaled back until the seismic activity stops."

The commander types some instructions into the computer, and an animation of the eagre's projected path as it spreads out from the epicenter appears on the screen.

"This simulation is based on the data collected from the 2004 tsunami," Dinesh explains. "You can see the west coast of Thailand has already been hit, and the wave is still sweeping up the Myanmar shoreline from the southwest. It's going to reach the eastern seaboard and the southern coastline of Bangladesh at any time. There has been no response to the advisories we sent out to the coast guards and government agencies from Kolkata in West Bengal through the states of Odisha, Andhra Pradesh, and Tamil Nadu, and around the cape to Thiruvananthapuram in the state of Kerala."

"We don't know whether it *did* spawn a tsunami, though," Rasheed interjects.

"Dr. Andrews told me that the odds are ninety-nine point nine percent that a tsunami exists, so we must assume at least one is in progress," Dinesh replies. "Presupposition isn't a mistake, and there won't be any complaints if we are wrong."

Other issues are beginning to worry the president. "Commander, are we still able to secure control over the east coast utilities from here?"

"No, sir," Dinesh replies. He types into the keypad again, and a straight line from Kolkata to Mumbai in the state of Maharashtra is superimposed on the map. "We can manage anywhere to the north of that line, but satellite and landline communications to the south are in failure mode."

Abdul takes a few moments to absorb the information. "I assume you've declared the bay as a critical zone?"

"Including the coastline of the eastern seaboard," the commander confirms.

"I want it extended to encompass the entire subcontinent ... western seaboard inclusive," the president orders.

"That's a *huge* region to cover, sir."

Abdul is far from happy too, but until communications are reestablished, he doesn't see any other alternative. "We do need to reduce the size of the critical zone," he agrees, and he takes a moment to deliberate. "The surveillance drones are controlled from here by satellite, so why don't we have any pictures yet?"

"The signals are relayed through two remote sensing centers," Dinesh reminds him. "One is in Balanagar, and the other is in Shadnagar. Both locations are in the critical zone, and every drone that was airborne when they all went dead is either flying pilotless or has crashed by now."

Abdul glowers at the commander. "Then divert the drones patrolling the Pakistani border into the south."

"We *can't*, sir. Communications to our entire fleet goes through one of the two remote stations, and until they come back online, there's absolutely nothing we can do. Each facility has its own generator, and it seems odd that both have failed. This would suggest that another problem exists, and we need to identify what it is. While the technicians are trying to resolve the problem, I've ordered our air force bases in the North to carry out reconnaissance missions across the subcontinent, and I'm waiting for the first reports to come in." He jabs a thumb over his shoulder toward the command center. "Our guys behind the consoles are in touch with the crews."

The president's simmering frustration boils over, and he goes on a rant. "This is *bullshit*. You mean to tell me we have a multibillion system that's useless in a time of crisis?" Abdul is uncomfortable at the incredible lack of information and fidgets angrily in his chair. He intends to launch an investigation once normality is restored—not so much with the intent to point a finger at a specific department, or individual, but to prevent a future reoccurrence of the same adversity. If an inquiry reveals that the problem is the result of gross negligence, he will personally preside over the discipline proceedings. "Continue with the briefing, commander."

Dinesh appears unfazed by the president's rant and picks up from where he left off. "Communications with the Andaman and Nicobar Islands was lost at the precise time the first seismic shock was recorded. Contact with the Eastern Naval Command in Visakhapatnam failed three minutes two seconds later. We know this because we were halfway through a sensitive data download from headquarters when they went dead."

President Prasad regains control over his composure and speaks with much more calmness than before. "Is that a cable or satellite link?"

"We use cable with satellite backup, and both failed."

Runjit sits forward. "Do you think the loss of communications could be a result of the tsunami?"

"No," Dinesh replies. "The earthquake was still in progress when they went down, so we know a tsunami isn't the source of the failures. Sri Lanka is another place where we've lost contact."

"Is there *anywhere* on the subcontinent that's unaffected by the earthquake?" General Nadarajah asks.

Commander Cariappa shrugs. "No. Dr. Andrews explained that the abnormality and unusual characteristics of this seism sets it apart from everything known about the manufacture of an earthquake, which is why he's dubbed it the Andaman Event. The oddity he refers to is the magnitude, and the unusual characteristics are that it didn't occur on a fault or along a plate boundary. The factor that launched its precipitation is unknown, but the incredible amount of energy unleashed is the origin of a seismic ripple that's moving concentrically across the globe."

"Did the doctor indicate how much energy was released?" Rasheed asks.

"Yes." Dinesh takes a few seconds to refer back to his notes. "Four hundred fifty gigatons. That's in excess of twenty-five million Hiroshimas."

An awkward silence follows, which is broken by President Prasad. "We are not concerned with the global consequences. Our focus must be on the critical zone. The rest of the world can handle its own problems."

The six men agree with a silent but solemn head nod.

Commander Cariappa continues with the update. "Military resources in the North are on full alert and will be mobilized into the regions where they are needed as soon as we start receiving the air surveillance reports." He turns to address Admiral Padawiya directly. "I've mobilized the Western Naval Command. If Visakhapatnam was hit by a tsunami, they could be paralyzed."

"It'll take them several days to sail around the cape," Rasheed replies.

The commander cups a hand over his earpiece and indicates with one finger that he's listening to someone. A few seconds later, he speaks into the microphone. "Switch both sides of the conversation to my earpiece."

Dinesh glances around the table with an odd expression on his face. "Did any of you reroute a P81 to the Andaman Islands?"

The prime minister raises a hand. "I did. Are you in communication with him?"

"Yes, I'm monitoring the conversation on this earpiece. He's gone into a holding pattern pending further instructions."

"*Where?*" Runjit asks, puzzled.

The tension in the commander's voice is palpable. "He's over Port Blair ... or where Port Blair should be."

A puzzled frown forms on the President's face. "What's *that* supposed to mean?"

"The plane has flown the length of the Andamans from the north, and he's seen nothing but ocean. He says there's no sign of land."

Isuru snorts and glances at Gihan. "*What?* Did you send a damn rookie down there? I think you should send him back to flight school to hone his navigational skills."

Dinesh speaks to the operator on the other end. "Confirm his coordinates with a satellite ping."

Gihan, whose eyes are burning with anger at the general's contemptuous remark, removes a lap-top from his briefcase. "Commander, can you give me the pilot's name?"

"Wing Commander Akshat Sarraf."

The air chief marshal begins to tap on the keyboard and throws something representative of a smug glance at Isuru. "I've accessed Sarraf's personnel file. He has given us nineteen years of exemplary service and is up for promotion."

Dinesh presses a finger against his earpiece to indicate he's trying to listen to the operator again. After a few moments, he casts a quick glance at Isuru before looking at Gihan. "The satellite has pinged the aircraft, and they are exactly where the wing commander says he is ... over Port Blair."

President Prasad stares at the commander in disbelief. The information is incogitable, and he can't come up with an appropriate comment. Another ten seconds elapse before a dark glare flashes across Isuru's eyes.

"Someone's playing silly buggers with us."

Abdul sits back in the chair and folds his arms across his chest. "Let me make sure I understand this correctly. You are telling us that the entire Andaman chain is gone ... completely erased from the face of the planet?"

"I am relaying to you what Wing Commander Sarraf is reporting, sir," the commander responds.

Abdul takes a moment to recover from the shocking revelation that the Andaman and Nicobar Islands may be no more, and it's not an easy concept for him to perceive. "The Emerald Isles is a pretty large expanse of land to vanish just like that, don't you think?"

Dinesh stares at the president with a blank expression in his eyes. "I'm equally as taken aback as you are. I wish I had an answer, but at this point I'm left without words."

"Something *must* be visible to show where they are ... uh, were?" Admiral Padawiya says. "It doesn't seem logical for *every* trace of the islands to be obliterated in an eyeblink. I mean ...

mankind isn't exactly at the top of the chain when it comes to environmental cleanliness. Four hundred thousand citizens can't dematerialize without leaving *something* behind, like thousands of tons of garbage floating on the surface."

"I'm still monitoring the wing commander's conversation," the commander says. "He's utilized radar and sonar equipment to conduct a search, but so far he hasn't found anything, not even an oil slick."

General Nadarajah scratches the side of his head with an expression of immense incredulity on his face. "Are we to conclude that the entire population of the island group is dead?"

President Prasad's response is emphatic. "Absolutely *not*. We need to know what happened before we can come to such an appalling determination."

A tiny beep attracts Dinesh's attention to a small monitor beneath the transparent tabletop. "Okay, the first satellite image of the critical zone is in, so give me a moment to redirect it to the big screen."

Abdul watches the commander's fingers flit over the touch-sensitive pad, and a few seconds later, the picture on the big screen is replaced by a new one. Almost immediately, Shanmukhan points to a land mass in the Bay of Bengal.

"What *is* the pilot talking about? The islands are still there."

An uncomfortable silence descends over the small group while they study the outline of the Andaman and Nicobar Islands taken from high in space, but the shoreline is superimposed by an infrared layer because the land is obscured from a regular lens by a large white veil.

A puzzled frown forms across Abdul's face. Something doesn't have a natural conformation. "The entire picture is vapor-free except for a few wisps over Myanmar and parts of southwest India," he mutters, "so why is there a huge cloud hanging over the Andamans when there's no moisture within a radius of one thousand kilometers?"

"Give me a moment," Dinesh replies. He punches some more commands into the keyboard, and as he waits for the computer to process his request, he explains his intentions. "I'm going to overlay the contour of the coast from yesterday's image on top of this new one, but before I do, I'm using the moisture-dispensing tool to remove the cloud cover so we can see the islands with more clarity."

While the process is taking place, he speaks into his headset. "Wing commander, what are the current weather conditions at your location?" A few seconds pass, and he nods his head. "Clear blue sky. Visibility is excellent … thank you."

The mystery deepens, and the officers throw puzzled glances among themselves. The pilot's report of a cloudless sky is in direct contradiction to the satellite image, but something else piques the president's interest.

"How did you get the satellite pictures if you have no communications to the remote sensing centers?"

"These are weather satellite images courtesy of Infinity Meteorological Database Systems," Dinesh replies.

Abdul doesn't respond and remains deep in thought until a loud gasp echoes around the table. The semitransparent contour of the previous map appears over the new one, and he needs to take a moment to process the differences. The islands are in both pictures, but they are not in the same location. The gray outline that indicates where the Andamans *should* be is over open ocean, about three hundred kilometers east of where they are now. In addition, the land mass is larger in length and width than it should be.

Runjit Sengupta is the first to break the quiescence in a hoarse whisper. "It's ... *moved?*"

With the exception of the president, everyone is focused on the islands, and they are all missing details of equal importance that dichotomize the two images. Abdul's voice is hushed in awe as he redirects their focus to other serious aberrations.

"The Andamans aren't the only place that's moved. Look at the coastline all the way up the eastern seaboard. It's not the same shape and has shifted to the east by a significant distance."

Dinesh walks out in front of the screen with a long pointer stick in his hand and circles the tip around Sri Lanka. The island is about forty kilometers east of the previous location shown on the original map contour, and the distance from mainland India has increased by more than thirty kilometers. Though somewhat distorted, it still retains the distinctive teardrop semblance, except that the southern half of the republic is skewed around in an east-by-north direction, and the northern section is narrower and more elongated. The southern tip of the Indian subcontinent has moved east by at least fifty kilometers and twisted at the same angle as Sri Lanka. The massive torque across the mainland has ripped a sixty-five-kilometer-wide tear into the west coast south of Mangalore, where the Netravati River flows into the Arabian Sea and narrows as it runs inland for more than a hundred kilometers.

Abdul's eyes explore the outline of the eastern seaboard, following the coast northwards in awe. It's easy to see a gradual change in the direction of movement, and by the time his gaze reaches Chennai, the pull is due east. A few kilometers beyond Visakhapatnam, the shoreline has been dragged on an east-by-south bearing, which becomes more prominent by the time it reaches the Bhitarkanika National Park region in the Kendrapara

District of Odisha. That's where the distortion stops, and the topography for the rest of the Indian coast remains unchanged. Close to two thousand kilometers of shoreline has gone through an extensive metamorphosis, with new headlands, inlets, and bays where none existed before.

A symmetrical change has taken place on the opposite side of the bay. The coast of Myanmar from Sittwe down to Mawlamyine is more than 40 kilometers southwest of its original position, but about 150 kilometers further south, near the Thai border, the shift swings around to the west. The president's mouth drops open in bewilderment as he tries to envisage the unimaginable force that's ripped southern Thailand away from the mainland. The analogous event has pulled a huge landmass, starting at the southern tip of the Myanmar border, out of alignment with the main Asian continent by 170 kilometers. In the south, it has sliced across 100 kilometers of countryside from Songkhla to Thung Wa, splitting it away from Malaysia. The result is a 460-kilometer-wide passage between the Asian mainland and Malaysia, which connects the Gulf of Thailand to the Andaman Sea—and a huge island that was part of southern Asia when they got up this morning.

Admiral Padawiya's voice is raspy. *"Look* at the *pattern*. The entire bay has been sucked in toward the epicenter from *all* directions. How can this *be*?"

Abdul is in total disbelief, and no matter how hard he tries, he can't comprehend the scale and scope of the devastation. Without taking his eyes away from the screen, he speaks to Dinesh. "Commander, we need to set some boundaries and enforce an operational protocol within the critical zone. We can start by rerouting scheduled commercial flights to destinations inside of the controlled region to airports in the north." He pauses to evaluate the impact his orders are going to have. The president wants to cause as little disruption to travel as possible, but it's not going to be an easy objective to achieve. "Airliners that depart on a path that brings them over the exclusion zone must attain a minimum altitude of seven thousand six hundred twenty meters, or twenty-five thousand feet. Aircraft unable to meet these demands must be rerouted around the restricted area. The same precepts apply to all inbound and through flights."

Commander Cariappa is making notes in a pad as the president gives him the instructions. "What about surface vessels, sir?"

"Submersibles will remain on the surface at all times. Ships, and all watercraft *not* involved with search and rescue, aid relief, or medical evacuations will proceed south *with caution* until they are out of the exclusion zone. Indian registered merchantmen are not exempt from this order."

Admiral Padawiya interrupts the president with an indomitable protest. "Excuse me, sir, but we can't do that. These are international waters and airspace, and we have *no* jurisdiction beyond our own territorial limits, not even in the Bay of Bengal."

Abdul gives the maritime commander a dark scowl. "I am not stupid. These terms apply to normal conditions, but this is a major disaster zone. Hundreds of military and naval aircraft will be airborne, performing emergency relief operations. We *must* reduce the risk of an air collision to an absolute minimum." He pauses to see if Rasheed is going to continue protesting, but he remains silent. "There's another cause for concern. You can all see in the satellite image that major geographical changes have taken place throughout the bay, but what about the changes that aren't visible? I don't want the coast guard tied up rescuing crews and passengers from ships, especially foreign vessels, that have their hulls ripped open on submerged rocks that weren't there before. The bay must be cartographically revised, and new oceanographic charts must be published before surface vessels can reenter. Boats bringing aid from abroad will be required to wait outside the red district for an escort once a safe channel has been plotted."

Rasheed agrees, although he appears reluctant to do so. "Point taken. We can *ask* international entities to honor our appeal, but it will be impossible to enforce the order if it gets challenged."

Abdul glowers at the Admiral but doesn't respond. The president knows he is right, and there would be little they could do except lodge a formal protest if anyone chooses to ignore the request.

He goes over the instructions in his head to make sure he hasn't left anything important out. Dinesh, who had been speaking into his headset in an almost inaudible voice, breaks his train of thought.

"National air traffic control has received and confirmed our instructions. Alerts are being passed through international media, governing agencies, and port authorities across the globe, with a request to divert all aircraft and vessels en route for destinations within the critical zone."

Abdul releases a long, heavy sigh. "Those restrictions will remain in operation until they are emended. We must be judicious in the way we utilize our resources, and execute our actions to the best advantages."

"I'm concerned about how compromised our ability to launch an efficient search, rescue and recovery missions might be," Runjit mutters.

"I want every effort made to reestablish communications with Visakhapatnam," the president says. "The Eastern Naval Command is a major nerve center critical to any operation we'll need to implement. Without them, we will be in some serious shit."

"Are you going to accept international aid?" Ashan asks.

Abdul hesitates before answering. "I won't turn down offers of assistance. The safety and well-being of our citizens is paramount, but we can't forget that the number of major earthquakes across the globe today has been exceptional. Reliance on countries who would normally donate or send physical aid could be premature. They may need help themselves."

"This will attract hordes of media from around the globe," Runjit replies. "They'll only interfere with our efforts."

"*Hmm.* I agree; they're going to be a nuisance," President Prasad admits. "How do you think we should handle them?"

"I think we should set up an official press center somewhere and herd them all into one place."

Abdul cocks an eyebrow at the prime minister. "I like the idea, but I don't want them crawling all over our doorstep every minute of the day. Make sure they're as far away from New Delhi as you can."

Runjit smiles. "I'll direct them to Ahmedabad."

"One other thing. Travel into the critical zone is prohibited, and anyone who enters without authorization will be deported. Indian nationals who disobey these instructions are to be temporarily interned until these orders are relaxed."

"Mr. President?"

Abdul turns his head to look at Dinesh. "Yes?"

The commander's expression is placid, and though his voice is calm, the glint of horror in his eyes is unmistakable. "The first reports by reconnaissance flights over Visakhapatnam are coming in, and they're not good. The city and large portions of the surrounding countryside are submerged beneath the water."

Abdul is unprepared for this unexpected turn of events and

gazes back at Cariappa with a stunned expression on his face. "Tsunami?"

"He can't be sure, but he says the city is twenty-seven point two kilometers east of where it should be, and it looks more like ... uh, everything has slid into the ocean. Only the top floors of the tallest buildings are protruding up through the surface, and it's low tide right now."

President Prasad is quiet, and his eyes sweep around the table at the six men with a dark look in them. In the relatively short time they've been down here, this has rocketed into an incomprehensible disaster, and it's going to test their resources beyond their limits.

"I want you all at your terminals," he orders as he gets to his feet. "Admiral Padawiya, I want a full update regarding the status of the Eastern Naval Command within the hour. I need to know what the damage is because if they are compromised ..." He trails off, leaving the sentence unfinished.

8

Institute of Seismological Research
Gandhinagar, Gujarat, India
Coordinates: 23° 12' 52.7" N, 72° 39' 35.5" E
Thursday, December 26, 2019, 1609h

Dr. Andrews is talking to the prime minister on the telephone, and despite a heightened level of ebullience, he's able to keep the excitement out of his voice. "Yes, sir, I have the satellite images in front of me, and the geological damage is sui generis. It's truly spectacular."

"Can you tell me what happened?"

"I can give you a preliminary assessment, but these pictures only show the aftermath." Robert shuffles through the exposures with one hand as he speaks. "The tsunami was secondary after the fact and isn't responsible for the submergence of the towns and cities along the coast. I will send a team of geologists to Visakhapatnam tomorrow, but I think investigations will reveal that the entire eastern seaboard slipped into the ocean as a result of the seismological disturbance."

"*Christ!*" The tone in Runjit's voice indicates his frustration, and the geologist is far from envious of the horrendous task the minister must be facing. "Is there a danger of another slip? Search and rescue teams are being sent in from the north, and I don't want to put boots on the ground if it's going to place more lives at risk."

"I can't corroborate the stability of the subcontinent from a few aerial pictures, but another slide should be considered as an imminent threat. A full geological survey needs to be carried out across the bay before it can be declared safe again, and that isn't going to happen overnight. Until then, you should be cautious. I understand the dilemma, but I have no other advice to offer."

Robert's eyes flit over one of the images while he's talking, and he frowns. "Mr. Sengupta, why didn't you send me pictures of the west coast?"

"I did—"

Dr. Andrews cuts him off. "I have one that shows the damage from the cape up to the Netravati River, but I don't see anything north of Mangalore."

Runjit hesitates. "I didn't think you would need them. The rest of the coastline didn't move."

An alarm goes off in the geologist's head. His primary supposition was that the Indian subcontinent had been displaced in its entirety, but what if this didn't happen?

"Sir, do you have any photos of the interior?"

"I've sent you everything that's come in so far."

"I need pictures further inland."

Anger seeps into the prime minister's tone. "How far in do you want us to go, for Christ's sake? Our focus is along the coastal regions, where the devastation occurred."

"Did you receive reports of landslides?"

"Communications throughout all the southern states are ..." He trails off midsentence. "What do you mean by 'landslides'?"

"Mr. Sengupta, if the east coast moved but the west didn't, then the subcontinent never shifted. It was stretched, and it's probable that landslides have occurred on a scale you can't even begin to imagine."

"I'm ... not sure I understand."

"The shoreline of the eastern seaboard is out of position by up to fifty kilometers, *excluding* the strip that slipped into the ocean," Robert says, "but the western shore never moved at *all*? That means the subcontinent has widened by more than fifty kilometers, and the fill needs to come from somewhere."

Runjit's voice sounds strained. "Are you *sure?*"

"Nothing would make me happier than if I am wrong, sir ... and I hope I am, but ..." The geologist leaves the sentence unfinished.

"Where would the landslides happen?"

"I know this sounds rather broad, but they could be anywhere," Robert replies. "Low-lying areas would be more vulnerable to sinkholes, and hilly or mountainous regions are likely to have slid into them. Get me a wide-angle satellite image of the subcontinent, Mr. Sengupta. The slides will be easy to identify because they will show up as a distinct longitudinal scar that *could* run for up to two thousand kilometers and will be at least fifty kilometers wide."

"*Good God,*" the prime minister whispers hoarsely.

The door to Robert's office opens, and Mahesh steps in.

"I can offer no other advice until I review the images, sir."

"I will get the pictures for you, Dr. Andrews."

The prime minister terminates the call, and as Robert places the handset back on the main telephone unit, he gives the young scientist an inquiring look.

"A Dr. Boris Medvedev wishes to speak with you, sir," Mahesh says. "He's holding on line four."

Robert has never had the pleasure of meeting his Russian counterpart in person, but he's held video conferences with the renowned astrophysicist on several occasions. He is always pleasant, and the two men often exchange data. He lifts the telephone receiver as Mahesh leaves the office, and he pushes the button to connect the extension.

The geologist greets the Russian cordially. "Boris, how are you doing?"

"I am fine, my friend. Listen, I will not waste your time with small talk, as I suspect you are busy, no?"

"You've got *no* idea!" he exclaims. " I imagine this call is related to the satellite images I sent you?"

"They're in front of me, and things are not looking good. I think you are still gathering surface data, but I want to go deeper. I fear damage to the internal structure of the asthenosphere may have occurred, and my research lies in this direction."

Robert frowns. "You might find more than you bargain for. The main geological shifts are to the east and west of the epicenter, and they funnel in from both directions at angles of plus or minus ten degrees. An even more interesting aspect is that the movement to the north and south appears minimal, *if* there was any shift at all."

Boris takes several moments to respond, and Robert knows he's looking at the satellite images again. "How curious. I've never seen anything like this before."

"You and I both," Robert replies.

"I know this is early hours, but do you have anything you can share with me yet?"

"I wish I did, but lack of data prevents me from making a

contribution." He hesitates. "I *do* have a strong theory, though. I'm trying to build a computer model, but there are too many unknown values. I'm drawing on my experience, knowledge, and educated conjectures to fill them in, but it's going to be pretty much hit-and-miss."

Boris laughs. "Well, if your luck is as good as mine, it will be more of a miss than a hit. But you are a clever man, Dr. Andrews."

The geologist gives a short chuckle. "You flatter me, Dr. Medvedev, but the work I do is nothing in comparison to your research."

"Don't be so modest," the Russian astrophysicist replies. "One word of advice, though. Don't allow yourself to become fixated in one direction because of a presumption you wish to prove. This is a serious problem with me. My habit of wasting time because I try to match the results to the data, and not the other way around, gives me a big headache."

"That trait isn't unique to you alone, Boris. *Everyone* makes the same mistake."

"I understand, my friend. Can you keep me updated as you go along?"

"Yes, of course. I will authorize Dr. Pawar to share the data with you. He's young but knowledgeable, and you'll find him responsive."

"Thank you, Robert. It was good talking to you again."

"Likewise, Boris."

The doctor terminates the call and turns back to the computer. He's attempting to reconstruct a geological duplication of the Andaman Event on the limited data available. The magnitude, energy release, and depth of the hypocenter are known, but he needs to formulate a satisfactory working equation that won't impede the computer's capacity to produce an acceptable scenario.

If he didn't have knowledge of the chasm, formation of the oceanic ridge, and the swelling in the lower lithosphere, he would have been scratching his head for the rest of his life. But this is a first-time event, and without any data he can use as a comparison, Robert inputs grossly overexaggerated theoretical ones into the empty fields. He doesn't expect success on the first run, and he'll need to play with the equations, but all he's looking for at this level are indications that he's on the right path.

The doctor types a few more commands, but he's feeling pessimistic about the results as he sits back and waits for the animation wizard to build the model.

Forty minutes later, the computer manages to finish building the graphics without crashing, which is a good start, and Robert sets the model running. His expression changes to one of incredulity as the animation unfolds in real time. Four minutes forty one seconds later, the last frame of the sequence is left frozen on the screen, and he stares at it in utter bewilderment. The simulation enacts a succession of inconceivable titanic events, and he grows more dubious of the progression, but it's the final thirty seconds that sends an icy chill through his body. After the computer compares the contour of the new coastlines around the Bay of Bengal with the one produced by the animation, it calculates a duplication success of 90.4 percent. Even southern Thailand has broken away from the mainland and Malaysia at close to the same place. It's not an exact match with the shorelines, but the shifting and torquing are identical, and even the Andaman Islands are in a new location to the west.

Robert is elated and slows the sequence down so he can study the mechanics of the abnormal earthquake more closely. He views the animation several times, and while he understands what happened, it's almost impossible for him to wrap his mind around the amount of energy required to trigger a disaster of this scale.

It's time to share the data with the scientists in the lab, and after sending the sequence to the mainframe, he walks into the main control room.

"Ladies and gentlemen, I want your attention for a few minutes." He strides over to a terminal and brings up the most recent satellite picture of the Bay of Bengal. All eyes turn to the screen. "A military aircraft was dispatched to the Andamans and reported that the islands are no more. Then this satellite image came in showing a puffy white cloud to the west of where the islands were. Image processing technologies used a moisture removal tool, and revealed the presence of an island that wasn't there before. The plane was diverted to the new location, and the crew identified the cloud as a huge plume of steam rising to an altitude of ten thousand five hundred fifty meters."

A puzzled expression crosses Mahesh's face. "A steam plume should condense *long* before it reaches that height."

"Not if the object creating the steam is just beneath the surface."

"*Eh?*"

"Infrared exposures confirm that the island is mountainous, and the highest peak is ten thousand five hundred forty-two meters. That's almost one thousand seven hundred meters taller than Mount Everest, but the rock is so hot it's turning the cold air around it to steam."

A loud gasp resounds around the laboratory, but he can see reservation written in the eyes of the skeptics. The senior geologists hold degrees and doctorates, so Robert knows they have good reason to be doubtful. He needs to convince the jury otherwise.

"Sensors on the Infinity weather satellites show the temperature of the steam to be around four hundred degrees centigrade, which tells us something significant." Dr. Andrews points to the image on the screen. "Those are *not* the Andaman and Nicobar Islands."

Everyone gawps at him, and for several seconds the whirring of printers is the only sound that echoes through the control center.

"How can you tell, sir?" Hiranmaya asks. She started off as an intern six years ago and is close to obtaining a degree in physics and geology, so her question surprises the doctor.

"Why do *you* think so much steam is present?"

"I … er, I'm not sure."

She's a smart woman, and Robert suspects that a good thesis has formed in her head but she doesn't want to embarrass herself in front of her peers by giving an answer she can't explain.

A young intern raises his hand. "Lava?"

The doctor shakes his head. "No. Although it *is* close to a molten state, the data indicates that the rock is nonvolcanic. The ocean around the island is boiling, resulting in a concentrated column of steam rising into the upper atmosphere. The colder air is condensing the moisture, and it's falling back to the ground as a torrential rainstorm. There the cycle repeats itself. For the rock to generate that much heat, it can only have been extracted from deep within the planet."

The image on the screen is replaced with the first frame of the simulation, which is a cross-sectional model showing the environmental spheres of the Bay of Bengal. The different strata are defined by a basic color key. The asthenosphere is painted in a hot orange, with a solid black layer representing the tectonic plate over the top. The next level is brown, peppered with gray dots to signify a mix of materials in the earth's crust, and the top layers are blue for water or green to connote land masses.

On the left, the Indian subcontinent slopes into the ocean and levels out along the seabed. It rises above the surface at the Andaman and Nicobar Islands, and again as Thailand's coastline on the right. Robert has inserted a scale model of the ridge and the V-shaped rift beneath it penetrating down into the tectonic plate. The attribute is to the west of the Andamans, and the triangular feature is shaded in the same color as the crust to denote the material that's keeping it wedged open.

Robert picks up a laser pointer and speaks in a slow, clear voice as he circles the fissure. "I want to concentrate on this aperture for a moment. The crust is fifteen kilometers deep, and the thickness of the plate is three hundred thirty-five kilometers. The chasm extends for two hundred twenty-five kilometers into the lower lithosphere, and close to three point six million cubic kilometers of crust fell into it at the time it was created, preventing the fracture from closing again. Over millions of years, pressure built up on each side here"—he circles a portion of the asthenosphere beneath the plate to the east and west of the rift with the red beam of light—"and here, compressing the material to about two million cubic kilometers. During the last decade, it attained a limit where it couldn't be compressed any further, and the exchange forces between the chasm wall and the wedge began to break down. The path of least resistance was upward, so the plug began to eject, creating the ridge we discovered on the ocean floor."

Hiranmaya raises her hand. "Dr. Andrews, do you know what caused the abyss to open up?"

Robert hesitates. He doesn't want to disclose any of the theories he exposed to his brother on the previous evening, so he makes sure to choose his words with care. "The ultrasound scans revealed that the tapered block is thirty-five percent crust, but the other sixty-five percent is made up from minerals not natural to the planet. The amount of bolide material suggests an asteroid collision occurred sometime in the past and buried itself into the lithosphere. The time period of the impact and the size of the object is open for debate, but it *is* the catalyst for what happened this morning."

Hiranmaya continues to question him. "Why didn't it eject the rock and close up right away?"

The doctor draws a circle over the rift between the plate and the ocean floor. "The weight of fifteen kilometers of crust was enough to keep the material from spilling back out as the chasm walls tried move back together. By the time the load became irrelevant, the crust and bolide material had compressed enough for a limiting friction seal to form." He pauses. The seniors know what he's talking about, but he explicates for the benefit of the interns. "Imagine the wedge as a cork in a champagne bottle held in place by a metallic cap that's wired to the neck. Once the magnum is chilled, remove the cap and stand it in a warm room. The cap is no longer germane, because the cork is secured by limiting friction that's stronger than the pressure beneath the base."

Dr. Andrews pauses for breath, and sweeps his eyes around the room. He finds the fascination on the faces of the junior assistants and interns gratifying. "An increase in temperature heats the bottle, causing the glass to expand at the collar, and the grip on the plug tightens. But the gas in the magnum also expands, until the augmentation beneath the stopper is greater than the exchange forces around the neck, and *pop* … the cork ejects."

Robert sets the computer animation in motion. The first sixty seconds is an elapsed time replication of the last six years, showing the wedge pushing up beneath the crust. A ridge starts growing up from the seabed, and the doctor can feel the mounting tension in the room. Almost everyone flinches as the triangular block suddenly shoots upward, and in less than ten seconds it has cleared the chasm. He then stops the concatenation.

"*What* the *fuck?*" Mahesh's awed whisper is loud in the still, quiet vacuum that follows the ejection.

"I'm going to show the sequence again at a reduced speed of fifteen seconds per second," Robert says. "The energy required to blast two million cubic kilometers of solid rock through fifteen kilometers of crust at a velocity of forty-five kilometers per second is incomprehensible, but that's what happened."

He restarts the animation. As the enormous slab pushes upward, gigantic boulders erupt from the seabed. Driven by a force that appears to defy all the laws of physics, they roll across the seafloor in all directions for hundreds of kilometers, impervious to the pressure and friction at that depth. The crust crumbles and spreads outward. With a violent explosion, the top of the wedge bursts through the seabed, and the geologists get the full visual impact of the massive shockwave as the substratum mushrooms out across the ocean floor for more than 600 kilometers to each side. The humongous mound of stone and sludge expands until it emerges through the surface as a landmass more than 1,200 kilometers wide that merges into the Andaman Islands. The wedge continues to surge upward, exploding with titanic ferocity as it climbs higher into the sky. Huge chunks of rock are blasted through the air for a distance of 300 kilometers before crashing back down on the newly exposed land. Robert pauses the sequence as the bottom of the block clears the chasm, and he picks up the narrative.

"The wedge was compressed to such an extent that there was room for it to expand once the pressure was released. Because the discharge was instantaneous, the expansion happened too fast, and two million cubic kilometers of rock blew itself apart in a series of explosions more powerful than all of the nuclear devices in existence combined. It was probably louder than the Krakatoa eruption in 1883."

Mahesh looks at him. "Excuse me, doctor, but the island in the satellite image is smaller than the landmass in this model."

"Yes, but when I restart the simulation, you will see it only existed for about two minutes." He sets the model in motion again, and for more than four and a half minutes, no one speaks as the bizarre sequence of events unfolds. The succession is multifarious, and they will need to view it several times to grasp the full complexity, but Dr. Andrews draws their attention to some of the key elements.

With the plug free of the fissure, nothing holds it open anymore. The tensile energy stored in the plate at each end of the rift, in conjunction with the immense pressure applied by the swelling beneath the lithosphere, the chasm begins to close. Two humongous cliff faces race toward each other across forty kilometers of open space with increasing velocity. As the fissure closes, the tectonic plate to the west begins dragging the crust above it toward the east. The same thing is happening on the opposite side, except the crust is being hauled westward. The earth meets at the epicenter, and crumples upward beneath the remnants of the shattered plug. Robert uses the laser pointer to bring attention to an anomaly within the crust that stretches down to the plate and for three hundred kilometers to each side of the rift. It would not have been visible had he not peppered the brown with gray.

"Look at the way the earth gets churned around, like it's inside a giant blender," he says. "I have *never* seen anything like that before, and what is even more amazing is the double subsidence you're about to witness."

He can see the awe on their faces as the green that represents the Andamans gets caught up in an incongruous rotation and breaks up as the islands collapse into a huge depression scooped out beneath to feed the uplift. The color enables them to track what was once the surface as it is dragged to a depth of ten kilometers and pulled to the west in a fluid concurrent motion. He can hear Mahesh inhale deeply, and his horrified expression relays the thoughts going through his head.

"*Jeee-zus ...*"

About 50 percent of the rock is forced up to construct the new island, while the surplus spills out to each side and rolls back down into an ever-deepening depression, only to get caught up in the spin cycle once again.

Two minutes pass before Dr. Andrews speaks. "This is where it gets *more* interesting. While the earth's crust is being pulled toward the epicenter, an insufficient quantity of stone is falling back into the craters to replenish the amount of rock scooped out. They continue to grow until there are two impressive excavations that have reached a depth of fifteen kilometers, and extend for eight hundred kilometers. The tectonic plate is even exposed to the ocean for a brief period, but the pressure at that depth is insuperable, and it triggers an underwater landslide that may be the largest to have *ever* occurred on the planet. I want you to focus on the subsidence to the west."

Another loud gasp resounds around the center as the ocean floor slides into the massive void, dragging trillions of tons of rock and silt with it. The dangerous flow extends back for a distance of two thousand kilometers, undermining the Indian subcontinent, and the entire eastern seaboard slips into the sea as a result. To the east, there is enough undermining and traction to pull a huge chunk of Thailand away from the Asian continent. The presence of the Andaman and Nicobar Islands is the only thing that saves it from being pulled beneath the surface.

"Because of their proximity, the Andamans suffered the brunt of the disaster," Robert says. "Thousands of Thai citizens were probably killed, but those who survived don't know how lucky they are. If the chasm had been one or two kilometers wider, this chunk of Thailand would have been sucked down too."

Mahesh shakes his head. "There's far too much happening to absorb everything in one viewing."

Dr. Andrews smiles at the young scientist. "That's why I'm going to leave the animation on the mainframe. This is only an overview, and I'm sure I've missed a lot of important details too."

He's getting close to the conclusion of the colloquium, and he pauses before addressing the seismologists again. "Now we are coming up to the grand finale. The two sides of the chasm haven't seen each other in sixty-five million years and are about to greet one other with enthusiasm."

Hiranmaya raises her hand, and Robert pauses. "Yes, Miss Singh?"

"How do you know it's been sixty-five million years, sir?"

The doctor hesitates, realizing his mistake. He's amazed at how fast she picked up on it, but retains his composure. "I don't, but it's been at least that long because the last known asteroid that had devastating consequences on the planet was the one thought to be responsible for the extinction of the dinosaurs."

The answer appears to satisfy her curiosity for now. "Thank you, Mr. Andrews."

Robert brings everybody's attention back to the screen as his narrative comes to a conclusion. "Two sheer cliff faces with a combined surface area of ninety thousand square kilometers are about to slam together."

The animation reaches the last frame, and Robert glances around at the gaping mouths of his team. He's never felt such a thick, suspenseful atmosphere before.

"What about the inhabitants of the Andaman Islands?" Hiranmaya asks.

Robert hesitates. "It took four minutes and forty-one seconds to change the entire geography in the Bay of Bengal. The event was so sudden and violent, I doubt if anyone survived longer than the first few seconds. Mother Nature has sanitized the region, eradicating the islands and eliminating all traces of civilization. Once we've collected more data, and we're able to conduct an extensive study on the phenomenon, we're going to find the Andaman and Nicobar Islands are buried beneath the new island close to where it's depicted in the simulation."

"Dr. Andrews, what makes you so certain that the replication is true to what really happened?" a voice calls out.

"I'm not," Robert answers. "I'm confident I am on the right track because the geographical results are too close to be coincidental."

Daksha raises a hand. "What about the aftershocks, then?"

"The Andaman Event displaced googols of tons of crust material, and the aftershocks are the result of one hundred twenty-six million cubic kilometers of rock shifting as it begins to settle into a permanent position. This explains why there are so many concurrent shocks. It will take years before they stop." He takes a deep breath. "The government will officially name the island, but until they do, we will refer to it as Rift Ridge Island."

Hiranmaya claps her hands, and moments later everyone in the control room joins in the applause. Robert signals with his hands for them to quiet down.

"Now we have *some* idea as to what happened this morning, you all need to be aware that this is only the tip of the iceberg. It will be a geological gold mine once the temperature drops enough to allow an expedition to land on Rift Ridge Island." He smiles. "Thank you for your attention."

A low drone fills the laboratory as the men and women begin to speak in excited voices among themselves. Dr. Andrews walks at a brisk pace toward his office with plans to e-mail a copy of the simulation to Dr. Boris Medvedev. The staff will talk about this for several minutes before they settle back into their routine again, but this isn't necessarily a bad thing. He likes to promote debates, discussions, and exchanges of opinions among the employees, and today's events are doing just that.

9

97-20 57th Avenue
Corona, New York, USA
Coordinates: 40° 44' 12.9" N, 73° 51' 48.2" W
Thursday, December 26, 2019, 1759h

Cobra Dickens, a construction worker with a naturally serious expression, walks through the car park toward a tower block. The six-foot African American keeps his head shaved and walks with an air of confidence; that being combined with a formidable muscular structure, it's easy to see why people might feel intimidated by his presence.

At fourteen, he went through a rebellious phase and had symbols of persecuted minorities tattooed on his body. The most visible design is the Star of David, which is inked over the part of his skull that would be covered by a yarmulke, and his entire back is a canvas to an amazing full-color portrait of an Indian chief in full headdress. There are other tattoos on his arms and legs, but the biggest representation is the color of his skin.

Despite his visual appearance, he abhors unnecessary violence, but he isn't hesitant to protect family, friends, and sometimes strangers in the street if the circumstances warrants. He's intelligent with strong leadership skills and a unique ability to assess adverse situations with uncanny accuracy. Also, he reacts to danger with deadly, panther-like speed. Although he's not a gang member, he has many acquaintances who are affiliated with various street teams. He never preaches to them about the lifestyle they've chosen, though. What they get up to when they aren't in his presence isn't any of his business, but he knows he can call on them for help if a situation arises that he's unable to handle on his own.

He inherited a spacious apartment from his grandmother, who passed away two years prior. He now shares it with his twenty-six-year-old girlfriend, Thelma Carpenter. She is a slim but well-proportioned pretty brown-skinned girl who stands five feet four inches tall with wavy shoulder-length black hair. They met through a mutual friend not long after his grandmother's funeral, and after a year of courtship, she moved in with him.

The dim lighting casts long, eerie shadows across the ground, and a cold wind blows around the corners. Cobra hunches his shoulders against a bitter wind and a flurry of snowflakes swirl around him as he reaches the first flight of steps. The stairs and passages are cold, damp, and poorly lit, the walls are covered in graffiti, and a strong stench of urine drifts around the ground-floor stairwell. It isn't like he can't afford a home in an elite neighborhood. He earns a good paycheck, and is never short of cash, but the apartment will be difficult to sell. The grounds are controlled by an estate management group who charge high annual fees and have a poor reputation for safety and security. They make no effort to expel the drunks and drug addicts who hang around in the shadows, despite complaints from the residents.

Cobra slips the key into the dead-bolt lock and steps into the hallway. The warmth inside is welcoming, and his nose captures the inviting aroma of cooking that drifts through from the kitchen. Thelma is an excellent cook, and the spicy bouquet tells him that she's prepared some Italian cuisine for dinner.

Thelma is sitting at the computer situated in the far corner of a large living room. The young woman swivels around on her chair to greet him with a cheerful smile as he enters.

"Hi, honey."

He walks across the floor and bends down to give her a kiss.

"You're lips are *freezing!*"

"They aren't the only thing that's frozen," he replies. "Working outside in this arctic weather isn't any fun."

"The weathermen are predicting a heavy fall of snow tonight."

He grunts in response. Besides keeping the huge apartment clean, dinner is always ready for him when he gets home, and she prepares everything from scratch using fresh ingredients.

"What're you cooking? It smells good."

"Lasagna. I invited Mrs. O'Grady over for dinner, but she declined, so I'm going to take some for her to eat. The poor thing was mugged down on the corner this afternoon."

Ada O'Grady is an elderly Irish lady who lives on the same floor. She was a close friend to Cobra's grandmother for as long as he can recall. Her husband spent several weeks in a coma after an industrial accident years earlier, and he'll never forget the dreadful day when she made the heartbreaking decision to take him off life support. Thelma calls in twice daily to make sure she isn't in distress and to see if she needs anything from the store.

"Is she okay?"

"The scum left her with an ugly bruise on the right temple and blackened one of her eyes, and she needed ten stitches in the top of her head where she was clubbed. They made off with her handbag, with the last of this month's pension inside. She said they got away with about seventy-five dollars."

A dark scowl appears on Cobra's face. "There were more than one?"

"She said three of them jumped her."

"*Three?*" he echoes vehemently. "And they used a fucking *club* on an eighty-five-year-old lady?"

Anger burns in his chest. There are many types of people that repulse him, but the top two are cowards who mug the elderly, and pedophiles, and he isn't afraid to hunt them down.

"Her medical, Social Security, and other personal identification were in the bag, so I made some telephone calls on her behalf to cancel them. I'm going to take her down to social services tomorrow morning and help her with their crappy paperwork."

"Fuckin' cowards," he mutters. "I don't suppose they caught them, eh?"

Thelma stands up and wraps her arms around his neck. "What do *you* think?"

"Of *course* they didn't. They never do. Muggings are low on their list of priorities. The cops are too busy dishing out traffic tickets and gunning down unarmed black kids to do anything of *real* value. I'm surprised they didn't keep her in the hospital for overnight observations. She could have concussion after a whack like that."

"You know how obstinate Ada is," she replies. "I promised the doctors I would keep an eye on her."

Thelma pulls his face down toward hers, and their lips make contact. For the next fifteen seconds, he responds to her searching tongue before she pulls back.

"Dinner will be ready by the time you finish your shower."

He slides a hand into a pocket and pulls out a thick roll of cash. It's not unusual for him to carry up to $5,000 on his person, but he has an overwhelming distrust in financial institutions and credit card companies. He has a healthy savings account with City Investment Banks, but only because his parents opened it when he was a toddler. He made a promise to them that he would keep it up, and being a person of honor, he makes a monthly contribution. Cobra told Thelma at the outset of their relationship that credit would never be an option, but he always made sure she had plenty of money each week.

He peels five one-hundred-dollar bills from the roll. "Give this to Ada when you take the food over to her."

"You *know* she's going to refuse it."

"Yeah, she's a proud bitch for sure, but tell her to take it or she'll have me to deal with."

Cobra walks toward the bedroom door. Midway across the living room, he stops and turns around. "Hey, did you feel the earthquake earlier today?"

She gives a pleasant little chortle. "*Everyone* in New York felt it, honey. It was a four point five."

Cobra glances at the computer monitor and smiles. He should know better. Whenever something happens, especially if it's a political scandal or a natural disaster, she goes on an information-gathering quest to acquire every sordid detail.

She inclines her head with a sparkle in her eyes. "Did you know it was caused by an earthquake near the Emerald Isles?"

"Emerald Isles?"

"Yes, the Andaman and Nicobar Islands."

"In the Bay of Bengal?" Cobra is astounded.

"Yes, a magnitude eleven point four," she replies. "It was strong enough to trigger more than two thousand five hundred major earthquakes, and thousands of smaller ones, around the globe. There were some pretty big quakes along the San Andreas Fault from Point Delgada all the way to San Diego."

Cobra's eyes open wide. "*Wow! Eleven point four?* Are you *sure?*"

"I'm sure as far as the news goes," she replies. "The doomsayers are declaring that this is the start of a catastrophic global disaster."

The construction worker laughs. "What kind of a disaster do they think we're in for?"

"No one knows," she admits with a shrug. "There's a whisper that the earthquake has changed the geography in the Bay of Bengal although there's been no official confirmation yet."

He studies her with a curious expression in his eyes. "A *whisper?*" Her use of this word means only one thing. "Have you been hacking again?"

"What makes you think I would do something like *that?*" she asks, her eyes full of innocence.

"Because I know you."

Thelma is as good as any hacker around—or at least good enough to avoid detection when she goes into data systems. He knows that she keeps her activities to a minimum and never uses her talent to commit fraud or theft, or execute any kind of nefarious operation. The breaches are only to quench a personal thirst for information. But hacking is still a criminal act in itself. Cobra turns and heads for the shower once again.

"Oh, by the way, Jacko called."

He pauses with his hand on the bedroom doorknob. Jacko is a twenty-six-year-old, dark-skinned leader of a biker gang. The New York Harlequins have earned notoriety among rival chapters over the years, and while they never have a deliberate intent to hunt for trouble, they won't turn their backs when it comes looking for them. Cobra's unusual friendship with the biker began in junior high, and even though they branched off into distinctly different lifestyles, the pair still kept in touch. He's five inches shorter than the construction worker, with a physique to match, but unlike Cobra, he sports a head of long black hair and a thick moustache.

The biker is secretive about his descent and is reticent about his ethnicity to most people—even to his friends. His countenance suggests he could be from somewhere in Central America, but the truth is that Jacko doesn't know who his parents are; nor does he have any knowledge of his ancestry. He grew up in foster care, moving from one home to another, and even now he suppresses an intense rage when people talk about their parents and siblings. These are things he can't relate to, and it makes him feel anonymous. He carries a concealed firearm for security, but it's not his weapon of choice. The biker is lethal with the six-foot length of half-inch stainless steel chain that hangs from his right hip in two and a half loops. He can pull it free with a single tug and have it in action faster than most people can draw a gun. To his rivals, he is cold-blooded, ruthless, and uncompassionate, but he honors friendship as an inviolability and is loyal to his friends down to a fault. He isn't afraid to step forward to take care of a situation when they are in trouble, often without their knowledge. He never wants anyone to feel indebted to him, and to this day, Cobra is unaware that the biker avenged the death of his parents almost seven years earlier.

"What did he want?"

"He's invited us to a New Year's party."

The construction worker throws his head back and laughs. "Can you imagine how wild *that's* going to be?"

"I'm not sure I want to."

Without saying another word, Cobra steps into the bedroom and closes the door.

Thelma turns back to the computer to see new information on the day's big story was posted while her back was turned. The Indian government has released an official satellite image of the Bay of Bengal with a preliminary overview of the damage. Her jaw drops open in astonishment as she studies it.

PART TWO

10

Davis Street
Stanley, Falkland Islands
Coordinates: 51° 41' 42.4" S, 57° 51' 33.6" W
Sunday, June 21, 2020, 1540h

Stanley is a quaint little town situated on the side of a north-facing hill. It overlooks a semisheltered harbor over five miles long from east to west, and three quarters of a mile at its widest point. Prior to the opening of the Panama Canal, it was a busy port that offered a welcome haven to the sailing and early steam ships of the era that sought shelter from violent storms or entered for repairs after getting battered by heavy seas as they rounded Cape Horn. Remnants of the many hulks condemned as unseaworthy still litter the rocky shores, mere skeletons of their former glory now ravaged by weather and time.

John Starker pauses at the garden gate and shivers in the subzero temperature. The atmosphere exudes an eerie feeling, and he glances around with a quizzical expression. Not a single sound pervades the odd tranquility. There are no signs of movement. There are no cars, no people, and, more unusual, no birds.

From his vantage point on top of the hill, he looks out over the bright colors of the corrugated tin roofs. The atypical calmness of the harbor is mesmerizing. The water resembles a huge mirror, a natural canvas that duplicates the low-lying hills of the Camber along the northern shore with sharp clarity. Not a single ripple interrupts the sublime reflection.

It's surreal. John feels as if he's been plucked from reality and plunged into a mysterious yet wondrous dimension hidden from humanity—an inaccessible temple savored only by the gods, unspoiled, untouched, and unseen by creatures of the mortal world. The sky is 99 percent obscured by a layer of altostratus undulatus, deeply scarred by a strong east-west wind shear. He turns his eyes to the west, where the only portion of blue sky is exposed in the cradle between the twin peaks of Two Sisters Mountain. The sun is about to take one last peek at the small town before plunging the world into darkness for the next sixteen and a half hours.

John's chest rises up and down in expectant exhilaration. Each time he exhales, a cloud of condensation is left suspended in the frosty air for several seconds before it slowly dissipates.

"Psst."

He swings around. A prickly chill runs down his spine. He could have sworn that someone uttered an interjection behind him, yet no one is in sight. The meteorologist feels stupid, but he is relieved that nobody is in the vicinity to bear witness to his strange behavior. He turns his attention back to the gap of blue and watches as the bottom rim of the sun slides into view.

Someone giggles. John pivots around in a full circle, but no one is there. Feeling a little uncomfortable, he looks up at the sky.

The sun drops further, and the rays begin to beam up beneath the base of the cloud, flowing through the valleys and over the peaks of the formations created by the wind shear. From west to east, it weaves in and out of the shadows until the sky is illuminated in a blaze of breathtaking color. John is entranced by the way the clouds come alive with bright hues of red and orange that blend into pastel shades of pinks, soft tones of purple, and indigo. The incandescent radiation of the dying sun wriggles gently in and out, snaking through the undulations in a wavy flow. The spectacular display is impressive, and he forgets about the strange hiss in his ear moments earlier.

The vivid and pastel colors merge from one hue to another and back again as they dance and weave through the base of the clouds. He catches a movement in the corner of his eyes, and his jaw drops open as they fall on the vibrant reflection of the skies skating across the glassy waters of the harbor. Nature is painting a three-dimensional picture of magnificence that surpasses even the most creative imagination. The sky and water become two fervent living creatures that interweave and entwine in a slow, pulsating tango of exquisite passion until the entire world is emblazoned in breathing color. There are so many different shades of reds, oranges, pinks, and purples, creating a scene he never thought possible.

John's state of mind is so rapturous that he doesn't heed the soft snicker close to his right ear. Another minute passes.

"Isn't it beautiful, man person?"

The voice is soft, soothing, but has a strange crystalline timbre that induces a vision of tiny ice chips tinkling together like wind chimes on a cold, imperceptible breeze. He snaps his head around. No one is in sight, even though the voice that spoke to him sounded as if it were no farther than a few inches from his ear. But John is too caught up in nature's performance and turns his attention back to the extraordinary extravaganza.

"Enjoy my beauty while you can, man person."

Is it his imagination, or did he feel an icy breath so gentle it might be nothing more than a slight disturbance of air brushing against his earlobe? Somewhat distracted by the compelling light show that's rippling above his head, John frowns. He's unable to discern whether the voice is male or female.

Bemused, but still in a dreamlike state, his eyes alternate between the sky and the surface of the harbor. Soon the sun will slide down behind the ridge and the intense exhibition will fade. John hears the same tinkling voice again, except it's moved to the other side. It speaks into his left ear.

"Tonight I bare my soul to you, man person. Drink deep of my beauty, and take pleasure in what you see. Remember me this way, for when you are consumed by the cold and loneliness, my compassion will forever elude you." The voice pauses for a few moments, perhaps to give him time to absorb the semicryptic words, before it continues. "This moment is for you, and for you alone. This is my greatest creation. The next time such beauty will bring you pleasure and warmth will be when the sun rises from whence it dies tonight."

John is uncomfortable, and he glances around for the source of the words while they are being spoken, but there is no one. He begins to wonder if he's gone crazy, become psychotic, or even slipped through a crack in the pavement into some strange dimension, but he feels compelled to respond.

"Where are you?"

The voice switches back to his right ear, and the invisible entity answers him in a relaxed, unhurried manner. "You are looking at me, man person. I am all around you. I am the beauteous pleasure that fills your soul with bliss in our last moments together. Enjoy the elation while you can, for soon I must depart, and your final journey will not be a pleasant one."

The sun is sinking further behind the cradle of Two Sisters, and only a third of it remains in view. The brilliant shades of color in the sky are starting to fade, and John's intoxicating exhilaration is crumbling with it. Another short interlude ensues before the mysterious voice tinkles once again, except this time it has a melancholic ring.

"My strength is sapped, and I fear my sister has grown much stronger than I. You must beware, man person, for she is evil by far. Her definition of beauty can be found in a sinister, hellish world that no mortal should ever venture to adumbrate. Every soul has a dark side, and mine is beginning to emerge—a millstone I shall bear for eternity. She will undo the splendor I knit for the enjoyment of every creature, but now I am too weak to contain her. Soon this world will not be as you know it."

"Who *are* you?" John asks, somewhat surprised at how calm he is given the bizarre circumstances.

The voice is getting distant, as if the invisible being is moving away from him. "It's time for me to go, man person. Remember this moment when the cold malevolence wraps her arms around you. It may be the only thing that keeps you sane."

The voice continues to fade. The amazing display of natural beauty he's been witnessing and the strange quintessence are somehow synchronized because they're growing fainter together. He begins to feel nervous. *What do I have to fear? The cold? The dark? Loneliness?* A small portion of the sun's upper rim is left, and the colors that danced seductively across the heavens are nearly gone. The voice is almost inaudible, but he can still discern the final words.

"Good-bye, man person ... good-bye ..."

The sun is gone, and the clouds assume a deathly gray tint. A cold, stony silence descends over the town, and a foreboding dread claws at John's heart. He turns his eyes to the east. A huge black cloud is racing in from the horizon like a crazed demon, twisting, expanding, and engulfing the earth beneath it in a darkness more frightening than death. Like a rampant cancer, it spreads out across the sky, consuming everything in its path. Dark tentacles stretch out from the dark mass, lashing back and forth across the skies in a wild frenzy. Bloodcurdling laughter echoes around inside the forty-one-year-old meteorologist's head. It's so loud and intense that the spine-chilling sound locks every muscle in his body, and John drops to his knees in terror.

"And now you are *mine*, man person ... *aaaallll mine*."

Like a fearsome carnivore hunting down its prey, tentacles whip around in a frenzied circular motion and dive down from the sky toward him at an incredible speed.

John sits up in bed with his heart thumping wildly and his forehead heavily beaded with droplets of sweat. He's usually aware that he's had a dream on awakening, and sometimes a fleeting glimpse of something might flit through his consciousness like a gray shadow, but he's never remembered one with such lucidity after waking up before. He can recall every word the invisible entity spoke to him and can still see the bright hues and shades of the spectacle with extraordinary clarity. He swings his legs over and sits on the side of the bed. Something about the dream has unnerved him.

John was born into a dysfunctional family in Coventry,

England. Despite an aimless, troubled childhood, he passed his GCE A-level examinations with high commendation, which was good enough to net a college scholarship. A fascination for climatology- and weather-related phenomena encouraged him to become a meteorologist, but advancing through the ranks was a slow process.

He got married at twenty-two, but it ended up in a divorce court less than a year later. A growing addiction to alcohol began to inhibit his personal and professional life, and he slipped further away from society. He had drinking pals at his local with whom he would share gossip, but because of his eccentricity, he never developed a real friendship with anyone.

Several days after his thirty-ninth birthday, an associate drew his attention to an opening for a chief meteorologist in the Falkland Islands. He made some inquiries and discovered that the post came with a rent-free house and a vehicle, but best of all, he would be in an authoritative position. That would be a favorable credit on his résumé, so he applied for the three-year indenture.

John is eighteen months into the term and anxious to get the other half behind him. He enjoyed being a solitaire in the UK, but there were times when he craved company in a bizarre way. He would go to shopping centers or busy train stations, or walk down Oxford Street on a Saturday afternoon—anywhere there were crowds. He was an anonymous singularity among the masses, but here? With less than three thousand inhabitants on the islands, everyone knew his face, name, and more details about him than he did. The only collectives were sheep and penguins.

John glances at the clock. He's slept through the daylight hours of the shortest day of the year, and it's almost four. The winter solstice is celebrated by the islanders with a costume dance in the community hall, but the observance of Sunday as a pious day is upheld by Falklands law. It prohibits festivities of a nonreligious nature to begin on the Sabbath, despite the significance of the day, so it was brought forward to Saturday. To the amusement of the locals, he kept his costume amazingly simple. He strapped a four-cup anemometer on his head and went as "the weatherman."

John's head is pounding, and feeling crappy in general, he contemplates whether he needs to go into the office. Gavin Fletcher is the only employee under his supervision, and he's responsible for the tutorship of the twenty-two-year-old apprentice. The practice of allowing a trainee to do unsupervised shifts during the first four years is prohibited under the contractual agreement, but with less than a year left before he graduates, John advanced the budding meteorologist to alternating Saturday and Sunday shifts every fortnight. Gavin is more than capable of operating the station on his own, and it gives him some weekend time to himself. He's still accountable if anything goes wrong, though, and for this reason, he goes into the office at four o'clock. He waits for the apprentice to draw up localized forecasts for the islands, and any shipping that might be around, and he then helps him to shut the station down before going home.

Gavin is eager to learn his trade and unafraid to ask questions. He listens with attentiveness to the answers. He respects authority, and John has faith in his capability to deliver an accurate forecast—more so since the British Antarctic Survey program looped them into the Infinity satellite network. The American company's advanced intelligent weather system has destroyed the art of meteorology to such a point that a two-year-old child can deliver an accurate forecast at the push of a button.

He reaches for the telephone and calls the office. "Hey, lad,

I'm a wee bit poorly after last night's bash. How do you feel about drawing up the final daily forecast on your own?"

"I'd like to say yes, but I'm not sure if I can."

John isn't prepared for Gavin's response. "Why?"

"There's something *weird* going on, and you need to take a look."

The meteorologist is disappointed but doesn't make any attempt to persuade the youngster. "Okay, lad, I'll be there in a few."

Ten minutes later, John walks into the office. Their desks are placed front-to-front, which means they are always facing each other, but that makes it easier to communicate when the young man is under instruction. Gavin is sitting at his desk, studying a weather map on the monitor. He turns his head to speak.

"Hold that thought," John says gruffly. "Let me get comfortable, and then you can enlighten me as to what's going on."

He pulls the gloves off his hands, stuffs them into a pocket in his jacket, and hangs the garment on a coat peg close to the exit before walking across the office. The meteorologist slumps into the chair behind his desk, fires up his computer, and puts on a pair of reading glasses. A moment later, he looks across to the young man.

"So what's going on, lad?"

The trainee peers over the monitor at John. "You've got to see these satellite pictures, sir."

Sixteen images are spread out across the top of Gavin's desk, and he shuffles them into a small stack. He begins to explain what's bothering him as he gets to his feet and walks around the side of the two desks with the pictures in his hand.

"There's an unusual weather system developing in the Weddell Sea." He stops behind the meteorologist and places the first exposure on the desk in front of his boss. "These were taken at thirty-minute intervals since eight o'clock this morning. This is the first one."

The image shows a clear satellite view of the Weddell Sea. The Antarctic Peninsula is on the west, Coats Land is to the east, and a section of the vast Ronne Ice Shelf is at the bottom. Surface temperature, wind speed, and barometric pressures are overprinted on the image in different colors. To the untrained eye, they appear random and meaningless, but to meteorologists it's a comprehensive report.

The apprentice drops a second print on top of the first. "Thirty minutes later."

This one shows a few wispy clouds over the Weddell Sea about 165 miles east of the peninsula, but nothing out of the ordinary jumps out at him.

Gavin places a third image on the desk. "Nine o'clock."

John notes a decrease in barometric pressure, which suggests a low depression is forming. A tiny band of thin cloud spirals clockwise toward the center, but there's still nothing abnormal about it.

Gavin drops another image on the desk. "Nine-thirty."

A significant thickening of the cloud has taken place over the thirty-minute interval, and a second band is wrapping around on the outer side of the first. Another drop in pressure implies that a winter storm might be developing.

John speaks without looking up. "It's not unusual for this to happen at any time of year, and after all, it *is* winter."

With perfect timing aimed to maximize the impact, Gavin slides the last picture from the bottom of the stack and drops it in front of the meteorologist.

"This one came in about ten minutes ago."

The image shows a full-blown storm raging in the Weddell Sea. It's expanded to seven hundred miles in diameter, and the Antarctic Peninsula, Elephant Island, and the South Orkneys are obscured by the growing bands of thick cloud.

"*Christ Almighty!*" John exclaims, and he pivots around on his chair. He snatches the rest of the prints from Gavin's hand and glances through them one after the other. "You're pulling my pisser, right? A cold-core *cyclone*?"

"I wasn't sure if I should call you or not, but it seemed pretty bizarre to me," Gavin says.

"Bizarre? I've never seen anything like this in my entire life." He flips between the first and last images. "It's taken eight hours for the barometric pressure to drop by a hundred five millibars and the wind speed to increase from less than three miles an hour to more than a hundred."

"It only took twenty-four hours for Hurricane Patricia to develop from a tropical depression into a category five back in 2015," the trainee reminds him.

"Hurricanes are formed under different circumstances," John replies. "They can't exist in the cold waters of Antarctica." He goes through the images from the first to the last in silence before looking back up at the young islander. "It hasn't moved in one direction or another."

"The outer band was fifty miles south of Elephant Island at two o'clock, so out of curiosity, I ran a prediction for the region, including the Orkneys," Gavin says.

"And?"

The apprentice walks back to his desk and shuffles through some papers before reading some notations he'd scribbled down. "Wind speed less than three miles an hour, skies clear, humidity at thirty-five percent, temperature minus twelve centigrade. Outlook for the next twenty-four hours: no change. Cloud less than point oh one percent, barometric pressure stable."

John is disdainful of the satellite's apparent inability to predict a storm that's only fifty miles out, although he's never known the Infinity system to come up with a misleading prediction before.

Gavin looks across the desk at his boss. "I ran a second forecast for the same location an hour later, after the outer band moved across the island, and it invalidates the previous one. The wind speed is forty-five miles per hour, barometric pressure has dropped significantly, and the cloud cover and humidity are at 100 percent. The Doppler shows that heavy snow is falling, and the temperature was at minus twenty-three centigrade. Outlook: unpredictable."

John throws his head back and laughs. "Unpredictable? I've *never* seen a computer admit defeat before."

"That's why I don't feel confident about drawing up a forecast for the radio and the Russians. I didn't want to get it wrong the first time I do it by myself."

"Aye, I don't blame you, lad, but I think you'll be safe to issue a standard prediction for tonight. Even if the storm begins to move straight for us, we'll still be safe for at least forty-eight hours. We'll reevaluate tomorrow morning."

John goes through the images again. "I can't see what's keeping it anchored in one spot." He pauses. "Did you run a spaghetti chart to see what course it might take?"

"Yes. I received a negative result."

John's wrinkles his forehead, puzzled by the apprentice's reply. "What do you mean by *that*?"

"The satellite is unable to compute a probable path, owing to insufficient data."

"A spaghetti model is created by the surface temperature of the ocean," John says, astounded. "Did you switch over to manual and try to force it?"

"Yep, but it only swings back in on itself no matter what direction I push it in."

"*Hmm.* That's rather odd. Perhaps it doesn't intend to move," the meteorologist asserts. "I think it will be safe to assume that if it *does*, it will go anywhere within a radial arc of three hundred fifteen degrees through to forty-five degrees."

"How do you figure that out when the billion-pound satellite can't?" Gavin asks.

John smiles at him before he replies. "How many storms have formed in the Weddell Sea that you've seen go south?"

The young man hesitates before answering. "Well, never, I guess, but like anything else"—he points to the stack of exposures in John's hand with a big smile—"there's a first time for everything."

The meteorologist drops the pictures on top of his desk and nods his head in quiet defeat. "I'll make you right, mate."

Gavin folds his arms and gazes back at his boss. "So I should issue a forecast without focusing on this?"

"Yes. What's happening that far south won't have an influence on the islands or the Russians in the immediate short term. It's over fifteen hundred miles away, and it still might surprise us by shooting across Antarctica."

John continues to stare at the last image with a distant expression in his eyes. It's already a full-blown storm, but now he's curious to see what it's going to do.

11

97-20 57th Avenue
Corona, New York, USA
Coordinates: 40° 44' 12.9" N, 73° 51' 48.2" W
Sunday, June 21, 2020, 1907h

Thelma is reading an article on the Internet when the doorbell chimes. She glances up at the wall clock. *That'll be Jacko.* The muffled gush of water comes from the bathroom via the open door of the bedroom. Cobra is still in the shower, so she gets to her feet and heads for the hallway to let their visitor in.

The biker greets her with a warm hug and a kiss on the cheek. "Thelma. How're ya doin', gal?" He thrusts a bouquet of flowers and a box of chocolates into her hands.

Her eyes open wide in delight. "Aww, thank you, Jacko. That's so *sweet* of you." She sniffs at the inflorescence as she leads the way into the living room. "Cobra told me you were going to stop by this evening, but he also said I shouldn't hold my breath."

The biker laughs. "Oh ye of little faith." He extends his arms out to each side and tilts his head back. "Ahh, it's so pleasant to be in an air-conditioned room."

Thelma walks through to the dining room. "I don't intend to leave this apartment until the weather gets cooler. The last four days have been over one hundred degrees. The meteorologists are claiming it's the hottest summer ever recorded."

"They play the same fiddle every year," the biker replies, sauntering behind her. "It's the damn humidity that makes everything so vexatious, but you'll know all about that. Aren't you into that kind of shit?"

She lays the bouquet and box of chocolates on top of a large dining table that can comfortably seat five people along each side and one at each end. There isn't a single scratch or blemish on the polished oak surface and intricately hand carved legs. Twelve matching chairs complete the well-cared-for suite that's steeped in antiquity.

Thelma laughs and walks into the kitchen. "I know a fair bit, I suppose," she calls out over her shoulder. "What would you like to know?"

"I suppose greenhouse gases are getting the blame for the heat wave?"

"Of *course!*" she replies. "Bikers who roar around on their CO_2-spewing Harleys are the main problem."

The young woman smiles as his laughter drifts in through the door. She picks up an unusual vase depicting a view across a lake. The water is cleverly pixilated with shades of blue to create the illusion that ripples are moving across the surface. She runs some water into it from the faucet and calls out to the biker.

"Would you like a beer?"

"Are you going to force me to answer the obvious?"

Thelma giggles and places the vase on top of the dishwasher to open the fridge door. She pulls a bottle of Corona from the top shelf, and after popping the cap, she picks up a glass from the rack.

"Sorry, I forgot to put the glasses in the icebox," she says, walking into the dining room.

"Thanks, darling," he replies as she hands him the bottle and glass. Jacko continues to speak while pouring the cold amber liquid. "I'm happy to guzzle straight from the bottle like a *real* man, but for you I'll be dainty."

Thelma is on her way back to the kitchen to retrieve the vase. "You would. You're a biker. You'd drink from a chamber pot if there wasn't anything else around."

"C'mon, gal, even *I* have limitations ... but I'm sad to say that's not one of them."

She returns, laughing hard at his confession, and sets the vase on top of a large coaster to prevent a water stain from accidentally being deposited on the polished surface of the table.

"I can't get over the size of this apartment," Jacko mutters.

Thelma sighs as she unwraps the protective paper from the bouquet. "I've tried to persuade Cobra it's time to move. The management doesn't give a crap about security. They scam us for a high fee to pay for services they're not even providing."

"It's not as if you guys can't *afford* to live in an upscale part of town," Jacko replies, and a smile flits across his lips. "I don't think Cobra wants to upset the residents by introducing his rough-and-ready street friends into a decent hood."

Thelma laughs. "Don't be silly, Jacko. He doesn't want to move because this is where he's lived most of his life. He inherited the other house from his parents when they were killed by that hit-and-run driver a few years back, but he sold it and moved into this one instead."

The biker recalls the incident as if it happened yesterday. The car flew through the red lights of a pedestrian walkway and struck them at high speed while they were halfway across. Cobra's mother died at the scene, and his father passed away hours later. The cops failed to track down and apprehend the offender, but Jacko wasn't convinced they were making a concerted effort. He conducted his own investigation and discovered that the reprobate was an off-duty police officer. The biker flipped when he learned that the lead investigator assigned to the case was the perpetrator. The cop was in a position to cover his own tracks, so late one night, Jacko visited the detective's home. The punishment befitted the transgression, and in his view, justice was served for his friend, but he's never told Cobra.

"That happened before he met you, gal," Jacko tells her. "He tried to get his grandmother to move into the other house, but she was an obstinate old lady. This is where all her memories were, and there was no way she would allow *anyone* to persuade her to leave, not even her own grandson. He ended up selling the house and moved in here with her so she wouldn't be on her own."

Jacko doesn't talk about Cobra's parents to anyone. Thelma is intelligent, with an uncanny knack for extracting information from people without intent; fearful that she might ask some awkward questions, the biker changes the topic. "This table is quite fascinating. It used to belong to his grandmother."

"Yes, Cobra told me it was her pride and joy; you can tell by its immaculate condition. I did some research on it, and the set is a genuine antique. Three handmade suites were built by her great-grandfather in 1900 as wedding gifts for his children."

"*Jesus!*" he exclaims. "Can I be the first to carve my initials into it?"

Thelma bursts out laughing. "As long as I can whittle mine into your wooden stumps after Cobra breaks your legs."

Jacko's eyes fall on the lake design glazed into the side of the porcelain vase and rubs his eyes before taking a second look. "*What the fuck ...?* The vase—"

"Cool, isn't it?"

"Jesus, woman, the water's moving!"

"Yep. You don't need to eat 'shrooms, or drop an acid tab in this household."

Cobra comes out of the bedroom wearing a pair of khaki shorts. "Hey, bud!"

While the two friends greet each other with a punch and a grapple, Thelma arranges the flowering blooms to her satisfaction.

"Flowers? Are you spoiling her now, Jacko?" Cobra exclaims.

The young woman looks across to her boyfriend. "That's what *real* gentlemen do. When was the last time *you* bought me a bouquet or a box of chocolates?"

Cobra wavers for a moment before responding hesitantly. "On our first date?"

Thelma laughs. "*Ooh, how* you *lie*, mister. You've never given me as much as a dead daisy."

"I *did* buy you an expensive dinner, though." He grins.

Thelma laughs and walks back into the kitchen to get him a beer from the fridge. They move into the living room, and the two men collapse into a pair of comfortable armchairs while she goes over to the computer. Jacko calls out as she sits at the desk.

"Who're you hacking up tonight, gal?"

"Everyone and anyone I can."

The two men laugh and start talking. She half-listens to the conversation as she picks up the research she'd been doing before the biker rang the doorbell.

"So what have you been up to, bro?" Cobra asks.

"The usual, you know! I spent the night in the can last Saturday."

"I guess that's par for the course for you. Another bar fight?"

"Yeah. I got into a scrap with a spaghetto who thought he was the bear's tits. I was having fun 'til the fuckin' cops turned up and collared me. *Christ*, I only blackened an eye and gave him a bloody nose. I didn't even *break* it. Hendrickson paid my bond, but I'm up before the judge on an assault charge next month."

"What's a spaghetto?" Thelma asks without turning away from the computer.

"It's derogatory for an Italian who acts like he's black."

"Hmm, I've never heard the expression before," she says. "Have you ever killed anyone, Jacko?"

She doesn't see the skin tighten on his face. "Yeah, I topped a cop once."

"How come you're not doing life?"

"I never got caught."

Something on the Internet catches her attention, and she falls silent. The two men begin talking to each other again.

"*Sweet Jesus!*" Thelma exclaims in a loud voice after several moments.

"What's up, honey?"

"I'm reading the latest updates on Rift Ridge Island. Come over here. You need to see this."

The two men stand up and cross the room.

"Why the hell did they give it a name like that?" Jacko asks.

"It's apt if you know the history behind it," she replies. "The scientists call it that for referral purposes, but the Indian government will be giving it an official name soon. The whisper is in favor of 'New Andaman Island.'"

"There she goes with those damn whispers again," Cobra

remarks. "Why don't you say straight up you hacked into their records?"

"That would be an admission of guilt," she answers coldly.

The two men peer over her shoulders at the monitor. A satellite picture released by the Indians a month earlier is on the display.

"No one's been on the island yet," Thelma tells them. "They've been waiting for the surface to cool down. The Institute of Seismic Research is planning its first expedition next week. It can't be approached by sea or air because the Indian Navy has a tight cordon around it. They were saying that the region is still unstable, but it now seems there might be another reason for the high security."

A curious expression spreads over Jacko's face. "Didn't the Indian Navy lose most of their ships in the tsunami?"

"They lost ninety-five percent of the vessels stationed at the Eastern Naval Command," Thelma replies. "Didn't you see those amazing pictures of their aircraft carrier *Vikrant*? She was commissioned in late 2018, and now she's perched on a hill twenty kilometers from the ocean."

"My perception of distance on the metric scale is minimal," Jacko mutters. "I only understand imperial measurements. What's that in miles?"

"About twelve."

"*Fuck*, that's a long way in!"

Cobra enters the conversation. "Most of the ships that were in port ended up on dry land once the water drained back into the sea."

"Are they still there?" Jacko asks.

"The navy salvaged sensitive onboard equipment and then allowed the stranded vessels to be used as shelters for the homeless."

"I heard that the tsunami destroyed a couple of coastal towns," Jacko remarks.

Thelma gives a short laugh. "You really *don't* follow the news, do you? The entire eastern seaboard of the Indian subcontinent slid into the ocean and took every city, town, and village with it. Cartographers are remapping the Bay of Bengal so they can open up shipping channels and all the rest of it. But getting back to the original subject"—she points at the picture on the monitor—"this is one of the images published by the Indian government. But now it seems that they were doctored."

She can see that Cobra's interest is growing. "Why would they do that?"

"Because they're hiding something they don't want the world to know about," Thelma replies. "Google took a series of images with their own satellite to incorporate the geographical changes into their online maps. " She depresses the Alt and Tab keys in a simultaneous action and flips to a second image. "Can you spot the difference?"

The two men study the screen in silence for fifteen seconds before Thelma switches back to the first one again.

Cobra shakes his head. "I've got no idea what I'm supposed to be looking for."

Thelma points to a cluster of blurred whitish patches scattered around the center of the island. "All those white blotches."

She returns to the picture released by the Indian government. There isn't any sign of the white blemishes. Thelma goes back to the previous picture and zooms in. The objects are pretty large but appear to be reflecting the light. That might account for the blurriness, though it's hard to be certain.

Jacko breaks the silence. "They look like big rocks to me."

"Damn *right* they are, mister," Thelma replies, her voice full of excitement. "Listen to this statement that was released today."

Scrolling down, she reads the report. "'Google were mystified by clusters of large reflective objects scattered around in the center of the island. While most range from the size of a small family car to that of an SUV, there are some larger than tractor-trailer units. The pictures were passed to scientists, who confirmed that these are the largest diamonds ever disgorged by the planet.'"

Jacko emits a low whistle. "*Jeee*-zus ... no wonder the Indians have put a heavy guard around the island. I bet every criminal in the world will try to get their hands on them."

Thelma raises a hand in a signal for the pair to keep quiet. "*Shush!* I haven't finished yet. 'Analysts are baffled because the precious jewels are formed in the upper mantle at a depth of between ninety and a hundred twenty miles. This is the first known event that's not volcanic in nature to extract a wealth of diamonds from the earth, and it's spawned renewed concerns over the extent of the internal damage caused by the Andaman Event.'"

"That happened six months ago," Cobra says, "so why are they only finding them now?"

"Google couldn't get a clear picture before," Thelma replies. "The island was obscured by clouds and steam for several months. The Indians used special equipment on their military satellites to get their exposures."

"They probably intended to keep it a secret until the island cooled down enough that a team could land and camouflage the rocks against aerial observation," Cobra says.

Jacko laughs. "They've got to be the most secure jewels in the world. Thieves would need to bring in heavy construction equipment to shift them."

Thelma isn't joining in with the banter, and a serious expression remains on her face. "That's not what concerns me. I follow every major earthquake, volcanic eruption, and weather phenomenon that happens on this planet. There's a lot I don't understand about geology and all the rest of it, but I know enough to be concerned. I think the Andaman Event has brought us more than diamonds."

Cobra scowls at her. "Oh, *c'mon,* Thelma. The earthquake happened six months ago. If something was going to happen, we would know about it by now."

Without any facts to support an argument, Thelma admits silent defeat and turns back to the computer. She needs to do more research.

12

Infinity Meteorological Database Systems, Inc.
Hamilton Ave, Palo Alto, California
Coordinates: 37° 26' 40.3" N, 122° 09' 36.2" W
Monday, June 22, 2020, 0815h

With a briefcase in one hand, and looking relaxed, Steve Jaeger steps out of the elevator and onto the top floor of Infinity Meteorological Database Systems, Inc. He strides along the passageway toward his office with a light swish of material as his trouser legs brush against each other. The thick carpet dampens the pad of feet, masking the sound of his friend and partner approaching from behind.

"Boy, am I glad to see you, Steve."

He turns his head and looks at the source of the voice without changing pace. "Good morning, BB."

Brad Bentley, known as BB to friends and colleagues since middle school, is a portly man of five feet ten inches and is fast approaching his fiftieth birthday. Their friendship began in nursery school, and by the time they moved up to kindergarten, the pair were already inseparable.

They were born days apart, but Steve has aged with more grace than his partner. He still has a full head of brown hair, although gray threads are starting to weave through it, while Brad's hairline has receded, and what hair he has over the top is thinning. He's a bit shorter at five foot six, and his body hasn't developed a middle-age spread like his friend's, giving him a more youthful appearance. Brad was the first to get married, and it came as no surprise to anyone that Steve was the best man. Eighteen months later, it was BB's turn to stand beside him at the altar.

As a teenager, Steve was interested in weather phenomena, and that led to a career in meteorology. He spent a couple of years as a forecaster for a local television channel, but it wasn't enough to quell the ambitious aspirations churning inside him. He wanted to get into investigative research, but fate had other plans for him.

One inconspicuous Sunday afternoon late in the summer of 1994, Steve and his new bride stopped by to visit Brad and Janice. The two men fired up the barbeque, and after eating, they relaxed in deck chairs beside the pool. The early evening air was pleasant, and they made small talk over a beer as the sun sank behind the palm trees.

"I overheard Shirley refer to you as her dust devil," Brad said.

"She calls me that because she says I'm hyperactive."

"*Ahh*, weather man ... whirling around ... I get it." He started laughing.

That was when Steve made an offhand remark that would set them on the road toward a remarkable and successful future. "We should go into business."

Brad was a software developer in the gaming industry. "What do you have in mind?"

"Anything. I'm getting fed up reciting the weather in front of TV cameras."

His friend grunted. "Yeah, I know what you mean. I'm running out of new ways to blast virtual characters into blood-gory oblivion. To be honest, I'm bored with it. I need something more challenging."

"Why don't we combine our skills to do something innovative."

"Like what?"

Steve slid a finger up the bridge of his nose to adjust his sunglasses before answering. "I don't know, but we're a pair of smartasses. I'm sure we can come up with something revolutionary that's out of this world."

Brad yawned. "Well, give me a holler if you come up with a good idea."

"We could design a computer system capable of predicting accurate weather patterns *before* they develop."

BB gave a short satirical laugh. "I don't think it'll be as popular as iPhones and such. Even if we *did* invent something inspiring, what are we going to do with it?"

"Install it in a satellite and sell it."

"You weren't joking when you said *something out of this world*. Meteorologists are going to love us when they end up going the way of the Dodo."

"Which is?"

"They'll become extinct."

Steve grinned. "Not quite ... I'll still be here."

The discussion ended there, and it did not enter his head again until Brad reignited the subject about a month later. "Do you remember when you said we should invent new technology for predicting the weather?"

Steve gazed at his friend in amazement. "I was only joking."

"Perhaps you were, but I'm not. In fact, I'm dead serious. I've been giving the idea some thought. It'll be exigent, but I think it's achievable."

His curiosity was aroused. "What would be our ultimate goal?"

"To make loads of money."

Steve laughed. "Well, that's a given."

"How about a satellite network that can accurately predict the weather weeks in advance for specified coordinates anywhere on the planet. Sensors can collect the temperatures, pressures, formulation of weather patterns, and a whole bunch of data that can be fed into a central nervous system and processed into a forecast."

"It needs to be different from anything else out there, though."

"It *will* be!" He couldn't miss the confidence and enthusiasm in Brad's voice. "I've been doing some research, and we can sweep existing systems off the grid. You'll need to educate me on the data it will need to gather, and other meteorological stuff, though."

Despite his skepticism, Brad had captured his interest, and it was worth a question or two. "When I brought it up, I wasn't being serious, but what makes you think we need a satellite network?"

"Let's not cut corners," Brad said. "I think I can design an artificial intelligence that can learn and teach itself from the data it collects. It will be able to predict the weather with incredible accuracy days before stuff develops—you know, depressions, hurricanes, heat waves, and so on. If we allow enough space for memory expansion, it will never go obsolete."

"*Christ*, BB, slow *down!* Don't you think that might be a bit overambitious?"

"Maybe, maybe not," Brad replied, "but the technology is

available. All we've got to do is apply it properly. We don't need to restrict ourselves to meteorology, either. We'll give it the capacity to gather other data, such as greenhouse gas emissions, ocean levels, polar ice melt, measurements of the earth's magnetic field, and more."

Steve was dubious about BB's aspirations. "What would we do with the data that isn't weather-related?"

"Sell it to scientists!"

Steve mulled the scheme over for several minutes. He didn't understand enough about software development to know if BB was right, but their years of friendship had instilled an inherent trust between them. *If he says the technology is available to bring this to life ...*

"BB, we must be realistic. The cost of one satellite will run into the millions of dollars, much less a fleet. Have you thought how we're going to finance a project like this?" Steve had always been the businessman, and everything must work on paper before he contemplated practicality, but this didn't seem to dampen Brad's enthusiasm.

"Don't you think I've thought of that?" Brad retorted passionately. "We'll start off with baby steps. Let's develop the software and come up with a viable product first. Once all the crinkles are chipped off, it'll be easier to capture the interest of investors."

Steve didn't have the same confidence but decided to humor his friend. Brad built a shed behind his house and placed a crude hand-painted sign over the door that read "BS Weather Management." This later gave way to the more appropriate name of Infinity Meteorological Database Systems.

The pair devoted eight years to the venture and suffered many setbacks along the way, but their perseverance began to pay off.

With perfect timing, the Palo Alto city administrators moved their offices, and the police department that backed up against them, to a new building, and Palo Alto City Hall went up for sale. The design was ideal because the tower would become their executive suite, and the old law enforcement station was perfect to transform into a maintenance area, research laboratory, and service subdivisions. Steve came up with a strong business plan, and it wasn't long before they had a line of investors waiting in the wings. However, the bank was still hesitant to grant a loan so they could acquire their first asset, and they went through the proposals with a fine-tooth comb. They took so long to make a decision that several financiers dropped out, and the two entrepreneurs almost lost the purchase to a construction company who wanted to redevelop the land.

Infinity was one of the first successful businesses to rise up from the ashes of the 2008 financial disaster. Potential investors looked on with interest when the first rocket carrying the designated MD1000 satellite system was launched by a pioneering space exploration company in November of 2009. It took every cent the pair could muster, at a time when people were cautious where their investments were going, so there was no room for failure. Eight months later, their order books were backed up as governments and private enterprises across the planet realized the benefits of the Infinity network.

Brad wanted to keep a hands-on position in the company so he could remain involved with the software development and maintenance. It made sense because he was the only one qualified to take up the CTO's post, and Steve was happy to slip in on the business end as the CEO. The pair held an equal-share majority, and a board of investors was formed that comprised them and the top eleven financiers.

This is the eleventh year since the launch of the first satellite, and now there are sixty units positioned around the globe. Fifty-three are subscribed, but seven still remain open. The remaining seven are over the oceans in the Northern Hemisphere and are not a direct benefit to anyone yet, but they're necessary for the overall function of the network. Ten more satellites are needed to close up the black spots that still exist over the southern oceans, and this is an argument the two friends have to justify at a special investor's meeting scheduled for Tuesday afternoon. Steve is expecting the proposal to meet fierce resistance from at least one board member. Subscriptions make up a large portion of the profits, and it won't be easy to convey the significant benefits the additional satellites will bring. The ten units aren't going to be beneficial to the short-term financier, but it will be a win-win for the long-term investor. Once the network is complete, they can open up the unsubscribed satellites to shipping companies across the globe, which will give their vessels unlimited access to the seventeen units over the oceans.

Revenue is also generated from the massive amount of scientific data downloaded and stored in the laboratory databanks. The information covers a huge spectrum that isn't related exclusively to meteorology; this is purchased by researchers, universities, and scientists all over the world, including NASA.

The two men reach Steve's office door. Steve turns the knob and pushes it open.

"We have a problem," Brad says, with a disquieting timbre infused in his voice.

The CEO walks across the floor and places the briefcase on the desk before sinking into a large leather chair. His partner pulls another seat forward and sits in it. Steve leans back and clasps his hands around the back of his head.

"I'm sure it isn't anything you can't handle."

He observes a deep consternation on the CTO's face. "One of our satellites has malfunctioned. I got a call around three-thirty this morning to advise me of a failure in the unit subscribed by the Australian Antarctic Division."

Steve raises his eyebrows. Infinity has high standards when it comes to maintenance, and they invested heavily in a proficient technical agenda that gave the customer a platform with guaranteed reliability and support. Routine maintenance schedules are performed with clockwork regularity, and this is the first time there's been a malfunction of their equipment since the launch of the first satellite eleven years ago.

"How serious is it?"

"Bad enough to shut down the onboard equipment."

Brad's demeanor is beginning to unsettle the CEO. "You've established the cause, though … yes?"

BB shakes his head. "No. The techs are trying to trace the source of the failure, but at the moment, we're drawing a blank. I came straight in after I took the call, and ran some preliminary tests. Nothing showed up, so I reset everything to the default values and rebooted the satellite. It came back online long enough to return an error message before shutting down again."

"What was the error message?"

"'Invalid input command: data out of range.'"

Steve is getting nervous and begins to twiddle his thumbs. "What does that mean, BB?"

Brad shrugs. "To be honest, I don't know. I haven't been able to locate the source event or even determine at what level it's being invoked. Neither can I find a reference to any such error message in the troubleshooting manual, which means the code was never assigned in the first place."

Steve is perplexed. He'd been involved in the development of the software, and he'd watched Brad calibrate everything with meticulous assiduousness to ensure it would operate within the parameters of the meteorological data he provided. Yet if he *had* left something out, why would it wait eleven years to reveal itself? "Did you run *all* the diagnostic tests?"

"Twice," Brad replies. "I ran a quick scan, and when that didn't disclose any anomalies, I did a comprehensive test. Everything came back normal and showed the equipment to be fully functional. I even accessed the command interface via a manual override, but all I keep getting is the 'data out of range' message."

"Have you done a complete shutdown and restart of the onboard computers?" Steve asks.

"That's what the techs are doing right now, but it will take some time because there are specific procedural steps that need to be followed." His partner shakes his head with a mystified expression in his eyes. "I only hope to God it resolves the problem; otherwise, we could be in deep shit."

"Even if the shutdown works, we still need to find the cause. The odds of a repeat occurrence are too great if we let it ride."

"I concur. I'll download an operations report. Whatever the origins are, a record will be saved somewhere in the codex."

"Can't you do a comprehensive analysis scan now?"

"I hope that's an option we won't have to resort to," Brad replies. "I'll need to analyze billions of bytes of information to establish the source, and that could take weeks if we're lucky—and months if we're not. I'd prefer it if the shutdown gives us a temporary reprieve for the interim. That will give us time to examine the data streams in depth."

Brad's iPhone rings, and he answers it. His conversation is short, and when he's finished, he stands up with a sigh.

"That was Danny," he says, referring to the senior technician. "The shutdown failed."

"Call me when you make progress. I need to clear this paperwork from my desk, and I'll come down to the lab a little later."

Brad leaves the office. Steve is feeling far from relaxed and sits forward with an anxious shadow on his face.

13

Met Office
Stanley, Falkland Islands
Coordinates: 51° 41' 54.9" S, 57° 50' 58.8" W
Monday, June 22, 2020, 0959h

Gavin's attention is drawn from the computer monitor by the muffled sound of an engine. The young man looks out of the window and squints his eyes against the fierce glare of sunlight reflecting off the heavy overnight frost. The town council's injudicious decision to abolish daylight saving time in 2011 means that in midwinter the sun doesn't rise until nine fifteen. With little strength at this time of the year, the layer of white will linger for a couple of hours.

John's Land Rover is pulling up outside. The trainee can't deny that he's a good boss and an excellent tutor despite his eccentricity, but it never took long for him to realize how contemptuous the meteorologist is of the Infinity system. John made him draw up the forecasts manually, reciting, "Something catastrophic will happen one day, and no one is going to know how to do anything anymore." Yet Gavin was born into the electronic age and can't imagine how people used to live without it.

John steps into the office and removes his gloves. He usually starts at nine o'clock, but today he had to take the Land Rover down to the maintenance yard for a scheduled fluid change.

"What time did you get here?"

"Eight."

He emits an obnoxious snort as he removes his jacket. "Something told me you'd be in early this morning. I used to have the same passion at one time, but you can see where I've ended up."

The meteorologist's grunt of the day seems to fall on deaf ears. "The storm has grown into a *monstrosity*," Gavin says.

John removes his boots and slides his feet into a pair of bedroom slippers. "Is it on the mooch yet?"

"No, but it's one thousand eight hundred ninety miles in diameter and has an eye like a hurricane's. The ten o'clock image should be coming through at any moment." As he finishes the sentence, the printer clacks as the feed draws paper into the print channel.

"There it is now," the meteorologist mutters, and he walks across to retrieve it from the tray. He stares at the document in bewilderment. *"Holy Toledo!"*

"Rather impressive, eh?" Gavin remarks.

John saunters back to the desk with his eyes locked on the image. "I think it's finally on the move. Run a spaghetti and see if it'll map a path this time."

The meteorologist studies the chart in silence. He's never seen a high-pressure system collapse like this before, and he's hard-pressed for a logical interpretation. The barometer has dropped to an impressive 874 millibars, which is only four millibars higher than the lowest on record. The eye of Typhoon Tip was about three hundred miles west of Guam on October 12, 1979, when it fell to 870 millibars, but that was a tropical storm. The air temperature in the outer extremities of this tempest is minus five degrees centigrade, and that decreases incrementally to minus seventeen at the storm's nucleus. When the wind chill is factored into the equation, it's a bone-chilling minus forty-three.

He turns his attention to the wind indicators. The isobars are tightly packed together, and a sustained speed of 105 miles per hour spins around the outer extremities. At the hub, it's a terrifying 198. He wonders what kind of freaky elements have come together to create a hurricane in the Antarctic because that's exactly what it looks like. It's been anchored in one spot for twenty-four hours, and he hopes it will break down just as quickly once it moves out of the Weddell Sea.

"*Christ*, I hope this fellow stays out to sea."

Gavin looks across the desk. "Why? It's about time we got a decent storm."

"You'd best be careful what you wish for, lad," he warns. "Besides, it's *always* stormy here."

"High winds are normal, yes, but not *storm* stormy."

The meteorologist grunts before refuting the trainee's characterization. "Your definition and *my* interpretation of 'stormy' are on different planes. Trust me, son, *this* is something you don't want to get caught in."

Gavin's computer emits a loud beep, and his eyes turn to the monitor. "*Ah ha*, the computer's finished boiling the spaghetti."

"It took its time, didn't it?" John replies. "Send it to my computer, lad."

Moments later, the meteorologist is scratching his head again. There are only three strands that intertwine with each other as they follow the same basic course, and at no point do they stray for more than a mile apart. The chart shows the storm moving northeast toward the South Sandwich Islands, where it uses the eastern contour of the archipelago like a slingshot to sweep around to the northwest. The eye is expected to pass a couple of miles south of South Georgia, and twenty miles north of the Falklands. There are no indications that it will disintegrate as it heads toward the Argentinean coast.

He speaks to Gavin in a disgruntled voice. "I think you're going to get your wish."

The apprentice has been studying the chart too, and he speaks with a disappointed expression in his voice. "The eye is going to miss us."

"If it stays true to the predicted path, it'll miss us by twenty miles," John says, "but don't forget, it's almost two thousand miles across. We're still going to get hit with two-hundred-mile-plus winds, no question about it."

The smile on Gavin's face dissipates. "That strong?"

"All of a sudden you don't sound so enthusiastic," John replies with a little sarcasm, and for the next ten minutes he examines the data in silence. The sporadic clicking of keyboard keys and the occasional rustle of paper pervades the room from Gavin's side of the desk.

"Is the *Akademik Knipovich II* the only ship out there?" Gavin asks eventually.

The meteorologist sits back and rubs his eyes before answering.

"I doubt if she's alone out there, but it's the only one we know about. The Russians never tell us how many ships are in the region, but you can guarantee there are at least a dozen trawlers with her."

"I don't understand why they're like that. I mean, they're only fishing boats, for God's sake. What's the big secret in that?"

"The cold-war-era mentality hasn't changed, even after all these years. You won't know much about that because it was before you were born, but the Russians still haven't gotten over it. Putin revived all the paranoia when he was in office."

The *Akademik Knipovich II* is a huge factory ship stationed permanently in the Southern Ocean. The captain is responsible for a fleet of trawlers who rendezvous with the giant vessel at regular intervals to off-load their catch and pick up oil, food, and general provisions. It's a tough, thankless existence for the crews on the smaller vessels who are forced to work under treacherous conditions for up to twenty hours per shift without a break. Fatigue and sleep deprivation is an occupational hazard often leading to serious accidents, and life-altering injuries and death aren't uncommon.

After the catch has been transferred to the mother ship, a conveyor carries the fish and other marine creatures, such as squid, krill, and shrimp, into the main factory line, where they're sorted, cleaned, and gutted. Some are cooked prior to being canned or bottled, packed into cases, and sent to a cold storage hold. The *Akademik Knipovich II* is regularly serviced by small cargo vessels who bring supplies in from Vladivostok and return with the fish products.

John and Gavin draw up a weather forecast based on the position of the mother ship twice daily. Because the Russians are sensitive about disclosing the number of vessels in the region or their locations, the trawlers are not authorized to communicate directly with another entity.

The meteorologist sighs. "I'd better put a warning together

for them. They were about two hundred miles southwest of South Georgia last night."

He drafts an e-mail.

> To: Captain Vladimir Khlanostikov, *Akademik Knipovich II*
> From: Falkland Islands Met Office, Stanley
> Priority Level: Urgent
>
> Severe storm warning. 70° south 37° west, cyclonic depression 874 mb and falling. Moving northeast at 4.7 knots, expected to turn northwest over South Sandwich to reach your last position at 0700 within 24 hours. Tempest extends 3,041 km current. Whiteout conditions imminent with sustained winds at 91 knots from the east to southeast, increasing to 192 knots over the next 86 hours. Mean temperature dropping to minus 17° centigrade, wind chill minus 42.7° centigrade. Advise you seek immediate shelter at Grytviken.

Gavin looks across at him just as he clicks Send. "Are you going to mention anything about the storm in the next local forecast?"

"Yes." He ponders for a moment. "I think this constitutes an emergency. I'd better call the governor and brief him before we release it." John reaches for the handset. He has a king-size crush on the administrator's sophisticated thirty-five-year-old private secretary and begins to have inappropriate visions of the woman about to answer the phone. But it can never be more than a wild fantasy. She's well out of his league.

"Government House; this is Linda Russet."

"Hello, Miss Russet," the meteorologist says politely. "This is John Starker at the met office. May I speak to Sir Glenwick, please?"

"Would you like to leave a message? I'll make sure he gets it as soon as possible."

"Uh ... no. It is urgent."

Linda doesn't object and responds pleasantly. "Okay, please hold, Mr. Starker."

He waits for a full minute before the robust baritone voice of the royally appointed sixty-year-old civil commissioner booms over the line. "How can I help you, John?"

"A dangerous storm with the potential to do a lot of damage is developing in the south, and its predicted path will bring it over the islands during the next twenty-four to thirty-six hours."

"Can you define 'dangerous' with more clarity?"

"It's a subzero depression that's expected to produce whiteout conditions and sustained winds of more than two hundred miles an hour."

There's a long pause before the governor responds, speaking in a slow, reflective tone. "I see. How long do you think it will last? A few hours? A day?"

"That's difficult to project, sir, but it is a slow-moving storm, very unstable, and could be with us for a few days at least. I will know more in another six or seven hours, but there *will* be structural damage, and power lines will be brought down. A warning will be released in tonight's broadcast."

Sir Glenwick's response is sharp. "No. If this is going to be as bad as you seem to think, we need to start taking precautions right away. The residents need to know so they can stock up with food and other essentials. I'm going to declare a state of emergency and authorize the immediate closure of schools, nonessential services, and all other government offices. I want you to draft a provisional warning for broadcast within the hour. Be sure to advise everyone to remain indoors once the storm breaks."

"Yes, sir."

"Keep me updated. I must be kept in the loop."

Before John can respond, the civil administrator hangs up. The meteorologist looks at his underling, who is staring at a new chart.

"C'mon, lad. There's work to be done. I'm going to issue a severe weather warning, and as soon as it's broadcast, the telephone is going to ring off the wall." A wicked grin spreads across his face. "You can deal with the punters."

"Oh, *thank* you," Gavin replies indignantly. "I get the *shit* end of the stick. What am I supposed to tell them?"

"The truth. It's as easy and as simple as that."

Gavin's demeanor changes, and John sees an evil glint flash into his eyes. "Can I have some fun and exaggerate to anyone I don't like?"

The meteorologist gazes at the apprentice with an astonished expression on his face, which gives way to another big grin. "Go ahead, lad. I'd *love* to hear how you're going to embellish on the parameters of *this* storm."

"Doom, gloom, death, and destruction," Gavin mutters.

John stands up and splays his fingers out on top of the desk to support his weight as he leans toward the young man. He speaks in a low voice but there's a sinister tone to it. "Be careful what you say, munchkin. Truth is spoken in jest, and you've already made one wish today."

14

Infinity Meteorological Database Systems, Inc.
Hamilton Ave, Palo Alto, California
Coordinates: 37° 26' 40.3" N, 122° 09' 36.2" W
Monday, June 22, 2020, 1417h

The entrance doors to the Infinity tower slide open, and Steve walks into the lobby at a brisk pace. He greets the security guard with an unassuming nod as he makes a beeline for the elevators. The CEO is returning from a business luncheon with the executives of Massey Electronics, who want a license to tap into their satellite system. Brad was supposed to attend the meeting too, but when Steve called the lab at eleven-thirty to remind him about the appointment, the CTO said he couldn't go. In a voice thick with frustration, he told Steve that his immediate primacy was to get the defective satellite operational again. As the talks were preliminary, his partner advised him to steer the topic toward the business end and avoid technical aspects until another session could be arranged.

Steve reaches the elevator and hesitates with his finger poised over the call button before changing his mind. The CEO turns right and walks along a tiled corridor that leads to the laboratories and assembly center, which are housed in a large, spacious single-floor building at the rear of the main structure. This was once the Palo Alto Police Department, which was gutted and split 25–75 to accommodate two different operations. The smaller section, accessible through the corporate tower, is known as the soft lab. This is where the software is developed and maintenance of onboard satellite equipment is performed. Thousands of databank storage units and control servers are lined along the back of the laboratory, secured into neatly rowed racks. Tiny red, orange, green, and blue LED lamps tirelessly flash on and off as they download, process, store, or search through trillions of gigabytes of data every second. This is Brad's domain.

The work carried out is sensitive and shrouded in corporate secrecy. There are no windows, entry is restricted, and a solid wall divider separates the soft and hard labs. Access to the second laboratory is attained through an entrance on Forest Avenue. Brad employed an undermanager to supervise a team of technicians and design engineers who adapt the hardware to be installed and wired into various satellite designs from blueprints provided by the client. Most of the frames and bracketing that secure the equipment are built by 3D printers, and a small team travels to the site to mount it.

Steve reaches the double security doors of the soft lab. He pulls an identification card from his wallet and swipes it through a wall-mounted reader before entering a PIN into the keypad. The electromagnetic locks deactivate with a solid clunk, and the doors slide open.

The three technicians glance up as he enters, but Brad appears to be engrossed in a thick stack of data sheets with a deep frown across his forehead.

"Any luck, BB?" Steve asks, approaching from behind.

The CTO leans back in his chair with a heavy sigh and swivels around to face his friend. "You're in time. I downloaded the data streams before deleting the RAM and ROM files from the onboard equipment. Danny will be finished reprogramming the satellite from the master discs in a few minutes."

Steve is anxious. "Do you think that'll work?"

Brad's reply is blunt. "It *has* to; otherwise, I don't know what to do next." He hesitates. "However, another situation came up twenty minutes ago."

"Oh?" Steve recognizes the dark expression on his partner's face and braces himself for bad news.

"A Russian subscriber called at two o'clock. The Siberian satellite shut down with an error message: 'Invalid input command; data out of range.'"

It takes several seconds for Brad's words to sink in. "You mean a second unit's gone down with the *exact* same problem?"

"Yes."

The odds of two malfunctions on the same day is inconceivable, but both with the same symptom? The CEO pulls a chair up close to Brad's desk and slumps into it.

"Sweet Jesus. We have a board meeting tomorrow afternoon, and this isn't going to help our argument for another ten satellites."

"I hope they'll be back online before then," Brad exclaims indignantly. "We're going to be in deep shit if they're not." Steve is troubled by the second failure, and his consternation grows as the CTO tells him where they're at with the investigation. "I had Jim run a diagnostics test. It shows normal functionality too, but when he reboots it, the whole caboodle shuts down again."

"When did these units go into operation?"

"The Australian one was launched in April 2014, and the Russians put theirs up in June 2016."

Steve is deep in thought for several seconds. "Could it be a component failure?"

Brad shakes his head. "That would've shown up in diagnostics, but analytics show nothing is wrong and all operations are normal. No failures. No malfunctions. It even passed a fucking simulation test with flying colors, for God's sake, but as soon as we put it back online, the onboard computer shuts down. It doesn't make *sense*."

"Is there a chance we might lose more satellites?" Steve asks, and the angst in his voice is clear.

"We shouldn't be losing *any*."

"Could the problem be in the communicators?" Steve asks. These are the earthbound units that commune with the onboard computer and print up the weather charts, maps, and forecasts at the request of the meteorologists.

"No," Brad replies confidently. "The user's communicator was eliminated the moment ours returned the same error message. Whatever the problem is, it's up in the sky."

Danny Walker, the supervising technician when Brad is absent, calls across to his boss. "Program reinstallation of the Australian satellite is complete, BB."

"Rebooted?"

"Restart successful, and ... *oh* ..." The young technician's voice trails off.

Steve leaps to his feet. "'Oh,' what?" he asks sharply.

"'Invalid input command; data out of range,'" Danny reads direct from the screen. "It's shut down again."

Brad slams the ball of his clenched fist on top of the desk. "*Christ!*"

Steve sinks back into the chair.

"Do you want me to reinstall the software into the Russian unit?" Jim asks.

BB shakes his head. "No. Danny's wasted several hours doing that, and it hasn't worked. We've overlooked something and need to figure out what it is pretty fast."

The quiet hum of electronic equipment pervades an uncomfortable atmosphere that's fallen across the lab. Steve reaches out and lays a hand on Brad's shoulder.

"BB, you've been working on this for twelve hours straight. You're tired, irritated, and your mind isn't functioning properly. You need to go home and get some rest, and with any luck, you'll wake up with a different perspective."

Brad protests, but the fatigue in his voice is hard to miss. "We can't leave this in limbo until tomorrow."

"We're not going to. We'll work on this thing around the clock until we get it resolved, but I don't want a team who are too tired to concentrate. That's how stuff gets overlooked, how mistakes are made, and how accidents happen. I need you at the board meeting tomorrow with a clear mind. Danny, Jim, and Bill can go on three overlapping shifts so someone is working on the problem until we know what's going on."

It's clear that Brad is against the suggestion, but acuity prevails. He gets to his feet and addresses the three technicians in a reluctant voice. "Okay, guys, this is how we'll do it. I'm going home to rest up, and I'll be back at midnight—"

Steve interrupts in a sharp voice. "*No* you *won't*. If you come back in tonight, you're not going to be worth shit by the time the meeting rolls around."

Brad throws an angry glare at his friend and hesitates before turning back to the technicians again. "Danny, you'll continue working on the Australian unit and go home at eight. I need you back here with a fresh mind at eight o'clock in the morning. Jim, I want you to stay on until midnight and come back at midday tomorrow. Bill, you can go home now, but you must be back by ten tonight. That will give Jim two hours to update you on where he's at so you can continue when he leaves."

"You're putting them on twelve-hour shifts?" Steve asks.

"Yes," BB replies. "It worked last December when we went on an emergency shift to clean up the mess left by all those big earthquakes."

The CEO concedes with a nod, and Brad turns to finish giving instructions to his crew. "I'll be back at six in the morning. Our priority is to get the Australian unit back online, so I want all heads to focus on the same thing. Once we discover what the problem is with that one, we'll probably find that the Russian satellite has the same ailment. If *anything* happens, or you discover the cause of the malfunction, you *will* call me on my iPhone regardless of the time. Is that clear?"

They acknowledge with a nod of heads. They're a good team, and Steve knows his partner has faith in them. He takes a deep breath and adds his gratitude. "Thank you, lads. We'll make it up to you after this is over."

Brad looks at Bill. "Okay, off you go."

The technician walks toward the door and waves to his colleagues with a big grin on his face.

Steve turns to Danny. "I have to go back up to the office. I'll be back down around four o'clock. You and Jim think about what you'd like to eat, and I'll buy it for you." He looks at Brad. "What are *you* still doing here?"

BB grunts. "Okay, *okay* … I'm leaving."

The chief technician heads for the door. Steve knows his friend is going to worry far too much to get the rest he needs, but he won't be alone.

15

M/V Akademik Knipovich II
South Atlantic Ocean
Coordinates: 55° 36' 34.1" S, 41° 12' 14.2" W
Monday, June 22, 2020, 2104h

Captain Vladimir Khlanostikov paces back and forth across the bridge of the *Akademik Knipovich II*, keeping in perfect synchronization with the vessel's roll. At 167 centimeters tall, the sixty-four-year-old bachelor is the typical image of a salt, complete with a white beard and bald dome. The odds he'll ever get married are next to none, and retirement is not an option in his eyes. He's spent 78 percent of his life on the ocean, and it's where his final resting place is going to be.

His career began as a cabin boy at fifteen. Intelligent, ambitious, and dedicated, he studied hard, moving up through the ranks to earn his master's certificate by the time he was twenty-two. A year later, he took command of his first vessel. The *Kiel* was only a small supply ship, but it filled him with pride. Now, after fifty years at sea, he's a veteran captain of the Russian Fisheries & Research Institute. Not only is he the first master of the largest factory ship in the world, but his command encompasses a flotilla of fifteen trawlers. Vladimir's knowledge of the southern ocean is vast, and he knows where to place the fishing boats at any given time of year to attain maximum haul. He sees himself as an equivalent to a fleet admiral in the Russian Navy, although no such rank exists in merchant shipping.

Captain Khlanostikov was appointed to the *Akademik Knipovich II* when she was commissioned as a replacement for her smaller predecessor in 1991. Not only is he the first skipper to be given command of this ship, but he's also the only one she's ever known. This puts him at twenty-nine years of service on the same craft—a triumph that deserves a note in the record books. While he's accountable for the safety of the vessel and every soul on board, he doesn't have jurisdiction over the factory workers. A production manager is in charge of the gutting, processing, and canning of the catch, and for the employees.

Vladimir turns the collar of his thick duffel coat up against the harsh cold, opens the door to the port bridge wing, and steps outside. He's concerned about the increasing swell. The sky directly overhead is crystal clear, illuminated by the stars and gaseous nebula of the Milky Way, but the view to the south is disturbing. The moon is obscured by heavy cumulonimbus clouds that stretch along the east–west horizon, but its ambient reflection draws a defined silvery-white outline along the puffy top of the cloud bank. He received a storm warning from the Falklands earlier in the day, which advised they seek shelter in Grytviken. However, protocol dictates that he must get permission from the authorities in Vladivostok before entering a foreign port, albeit a tiny museum settlement with a population of twenty and a defunct whaling station. They were fast to respond to the petition, and he chews the words over in his head as he gazes at the skyline.

> Satellite image of 0900 hours your local indicates no cyclonic activity in, near, or approaching your location. Request to enter Grytviken harbor is denied.

The direct contradiction between the two communications is bothersome. He's obtained daily weather forecasts tailored to their locale from the Falklands for years, and they have *always* been reliable. As captain he can override the orders, but it will open an inquisition into disobedience. If he sends the trawlers into Grytviken and no storm materializes, it'll be impossible to vindicate the decision. Punishment is harsh and often ends up with the revocation of the skipper's credentials. The company can't take away his certificate, but the government can, and if his license to plow the seven seas is rescinded, his life will be finished.

He curses beneath his breath. He should have followed his prior gut instinct and taken measures to neutralize the risk by positioning the flotilla close to the island but outside of territorial waters; it would have given them a short distance to run. But if the clouds along the southern horizon *is* a storm barreling toward them, it's already too late. South Georgia is 165 nautical miles northeast, and they're too far away to reach the haven in time.

Icicles are forming on the guardrails, and Vladimir rests his gloved hands on the top bar as he leans over to look down at the trawler moored alongside. The M/T *Mikhail* is illuminated by bright floodlights beaming down from the mother ship, and Captain Khlanostikov notes how hard the small boat is getting buffeted against the rubber pontoon that protects the hulls of both vessels. The seas are heavier than they were twenty minutes earlier. He reaches into a large pocket in the duffel coat where he keeps a two-way radio used to communicate with the trawlers when they're tied up alongside. He calls down to the skipper of the smaller ship.

"Are you almost done, Stefan?"

A long silence follows. Vladimir is about to call a second time when a rapid series of beeps are emitted followed by a brief crackle of static, and Captain Abarnikov responds.

"Aye, we've finished offloading the catch. The crew are preparing to load our supplies. We should be casting off in thirty minutes … forty max."

"Good. I don't like the way the seas are building."

There's a loud, hollow thud as the wash slams the trawler against the pontoon, and a spray of water shoots upward between the two vessels.

The radio beeps again. "It looks like we're in for a rough time, sir?"

"I have conflicting weather forecasts. When you cast off, set a direct course for Grytviken, and hove to outside the territorial limit. It will give you an opportunity to seek shelter in the harbor if a serious storm does break out."

"Aye, Captain. Understood."

Captain Khlanostikov steps back into the shelter of the bridge. The temperature isn't much higher than it is outside, but he's protected from the cold bite of the wind. He glances at Fyodor Boyarov as he heads across to the chart desk. The lanky twenty-three-year-old helmsman has a quiet, unassuming disposition and obeys orders without question or complaint. He's been doing a decent job at keeping the huge vessel steady despite the increasing swell.

A door at the rear leads to the ship's communication center. It opens, and Mika Nardin walks on to the bridge. The 158-centimeter twenty-nine-year-old is the chief communication officer who has been with them for the last two years. She's a pretty woman with a desirable figure, but it's always hidden beneath layers of bulky clothing. She holds a communiqué out toward him.

"Captain, I have an urgent message from the *Walvisbaai*."

"Read it to me," Vladimir requests, looking down at the chart to note the last recorded position of the trawler.

"They're experiencing heavy seas, and the skipper says the vessel is taking on more water than the bilge pumps can handle. He fears the safety of his ship and crew is in jeopardy."

Captain Khlanostikov stands upright and turns to face the young woman. "What are their coordinates?"

Mika tears the top page from a small notepad and hands it to him. The *Walvisbaai* is less than three kilometers east of her last location, and about a hundred forty kilometers to the southwest of the mother ship.

"It'll take four or five hours to reach her *if* the seas are in our favor," he mumbles.

Mika seems to be uncertain whether he's talking to himself or addressing her. She speaks with a little hesitancy. "I'm sorry, sir; I didn't catch what you said."

Vladimir chooses not to respond and studies the chart to find the nearest trawler to the *Walvisbaai* before speaking again. "Send a message to Captain Boris Poltorak. The *Nemanskii* is eighty kilometers east of the *Walvisbaai's* current location." He hands the notepaper back to her. "Order him to these coordinates, but remain on standby until we get there. Under no circumstances must he attempt to transfer the crew from the *Walvisbaai*. If they need to abandon ship, they must do so via life raft, which will allow the

Nemanskii to carry out a safer and more effective rescue operation. The last thing I want is for the two vessels to slam together, leaving me with a double disaster on my hands."

Mika is about to exit the bridge to execute her instructions when Vladimir calls out to her. "Miss Nardin?"

She swings around to look back at him.

"When you're done, send a communication to every vessel in the fleet; order them to head for Grytviken but stay outside of territorial waters. If conditions continue to deteriorate and threaten to compromise the safety of the vessel and the crew, they are to contact us for directions."

Mika scribbles the instructions into a small pad. "Is that it, sir?"

The captain pauses. "No. If we fail to respond in three minutes, the skipper *must* seek shelter in Grytviken harbor." He wavers for a second before dismissing the officer. "Thank you, Miss Nardin."

As Mika leaves for the communications center, Captain Khlanostikov strides across the deck, pulls the door open, and steps onto the port bridge wing again. He leans over the guardrail with the radio in his hand and looks down at the *Mikhail*. The stiff breeze has developed into a gusty wind that's whipping across his cheeks in icy blasts. Vladimir depresses the transmit button and speaks into the microphone.

"Stefan, are you done yet?"

"I need another fifteen minutes."

The captain's response is firm. "You can't have them. Cast the moorings now."

A brief pause ensues before the skipper of the *Mikhail* replies in the same dispassionate tone. "Aye, Captain."

A dark figure appears on the starboard wing of the boat below. Vladimir listens to the wind-lashed voice shouting orders to the crew. Moments later the ropes are cast and the vessel starts to drift away from the side of the mother ship. The water churns at the stern of the *Mikhail* as the propellers bite into the murky black seas of the South Atlantic, and the throb of diesel engines floats up on a gust of wind. Like a dark specter melding into the shadows, the trawler slips out of the halo of the floodlights and into the darkness beyond. The boat's navigation lights and a couple of dimly lit portholes are the only visible sign that the trawler is there.

Vladimir steps back into the wheelhouse, walks across to the control panel, and makes an announcement to the crew through the ship's speaker system. "This is Captain Khlanostikov. Batten down the hatches and secure the booms. Deck foreman, report to me after inspection."

Mika stumbles back on the bridge, trying to keep her balance as the vessel rolls in the heavy swell.

"Captain!" He turns to acknowledge her with a glance. "The *Nemanskii* is on course for the *Walvisbaai*, but the skipper is concerned. Gale-force winds and increasing seas are restricting headway."

"I understand the captain's dilemma, Miss Nardin, but he's the only vessel in the vicinity until we get there."

Mika holds a sealed envelope toward him. "I have another communiqué from Vladivostok."

Vladimir takes the missive from her. "Thank you, Miss Nardin." He dismisses her from the bridge with a final instruction. "I will come to you if I need to send a response."

She disappears back into the communications center as he breaks the seal and pulls the slip of paper from the envelope.

> Urgent! Severe storm warning issued as of 2100 hours your local. Increased cyclonic activity with surface wind speed in excess of 100 knots bearing toward you from

the south. Cease all operations. Permission is granted to take haven in Grytviken harbor. All vessels are to comply.

The captain's mouth tightens, and a dark shadow of bitterness moves across his eyes. *So much for protocol*, he thinks with resentment as he crumples the message into a tight ball and drops it into the right pocket of his duffle coat. He's weathered his way through some fearsome storms during his life on the ocean, but the negligence of an administrator in Vladivostok is forcing him sail into the jaws of the largest one Antarctica has ever generated.

He picks up the telephone and dials the extension to the factory manager's office. "Khalani, stop production now and strap down anything that can move."

"Closing the factory is not an option, Captain," the manager retorts.

"My responsibility is for the safety of the men and women on board my ship, and with respect, my orders override yours. If you refuse, I will hold you in contempt, and I won't hesitate to report you to Vladivostok and request your immediate suspension."

Without waiting for Khalani to respond, the captain replaces the handset. Not a lot of benevolence exists between the two men, but they are able to tolerate each other because it's unusual for a conflict of professions to pit them at odds. Vladimir will allow the manager fifteen minutes to halt production, and then he'll order the chief electrician to cut the power to the factory, with the exception of emergency lighting.

The door on the starboard wing opens, and the deck supervisor walks in. "All hatches and ports are sealed, Captain."

"You are dismissed," Vladimir snaps, and he picks up the microphone again. "All personnel and deckhands are ordered below decks. Topsides are out of bounds until further notice. A compulsory order for all crew and factory workers to wear life vests is in full effect."

He walks over to where several life vests are hanging on the rear wall and pulls two of the garments free.

"Mr. Boyarov."

The helmsman turns his head, and the captain throws a vest in his direction. "Put this on; then strap yourself to the helm."

Both men pull on the bulky jackets and tighten the cords. A giant wave slams into the port bow and washes over the forecastle, causing the ship to lurch violently. A hollow boom echoes through the hull of the ship, and Captain Khlanostikov snatches at a handrail to prevent himself from being thrown off his feet.

"Man at the helm," he calls out. "*Full speed ahead.*"

The muted bell of the telegraph in response to the command is received from the engine room, and the helmsman confirms the successful execution of the order by repeating the captain's words in a loud voice. Vladimir can feel a strong vibration beneath his feet as the engines power up and the propeller shafts engage.

"Steer two hundred twenty-seven degrees."

The bow of the *Akademik Knipovich II* pitches up and rolls to starboard as the helmsman brings the huge vessel around to an approximate 45-degree angle into the wind and swell sweeping up from the southeast. The bow yaws and plunges down into a dark, murky wave. Moments later, a giant plume of white spray is illuminated by the running lights as it breaks over the ship. Vladimir's exterior is calm, and he appears to be in full control, but for the first time in his long career, he feels afraid.

The captain takes up a stance behind the helmsman, with his feet planted apart. Bracing his body and synchronizing himself to the motion, he glances at the compass. He speaks to the young man at the helm in a calm, controlled voice.

"Keep her steady at two hundred twenty-seven degrees."

For the next thirty minutes, the wind and seas continue to increase in strength. Powerful waves smash into the port bow quarter and ram the vessel to starboard by more than twelve degrees. Vladimir studies the helmsman as he struggles to bring the craft back on course, but thirty seconds later, another sturdy breaker pushes them around again.

"Bring her to bear, two hundred fifteen degrees," Vladimir commands in a loud voice so the helmsman can hear the orders over the successive booming of waves crashing against the hull.

A few wind-driven snowflakes swirl against the transom, and within minutes they are in the grip of a howling blizzard. Visibility drops to absolute zero, and the wipers struggle to keep the snow from sticking to the windows.

The door from the communications center slams open, and Vladimir turns in time to see Mika skating through on her feet, caught out by a violent yaw. The deck slopes in the opposite direction, almost throwing her back through the door again, but she has a tight grip on the handrail. Seconds later, a much larger wave breaks over the bow and a heavy spray of water slams into the bridge. Mixed with the snow, it begins to freeze on the windshield. The noise of the water smashing into the hull and superstructure is making it difficult to converse without shouting.

"Captain Khlanostikov."

Vladimir saves his own breath by acknowledging her with a simple nod.

"The *Walvisbaai* ... the crew are abandoning ..."

This is news he didn't want to hear, and he is bitter, frustrated, and angry for following protocol instead of trusting his own instincts.

"The *Nemanskii*?"

"They're unable to effect a rescue." The communications officer pauses as the ship pitches wildly. "The skipper of the *Nemanskii* is preparing to abandon ship too. They've sustained significant damage to the hull and are listing fifty degrees to starboard. He fears they may not have more than a few minutes before the boat capsizes."

Captain Khlanostikov weighs the situation. With two trawlers on their way to the bottom of the ocean, he could continue to the last coordinates of either vessel, but it's unlikely he'll be able to recover the crews from the lifeboats while the tempest is in full fury. It would be safer to remain in the tiny crafts until conditions improve.

"Do you have radio contact with the lifeboats?"

Mika nods. "Yes, sir. Two from the *Walvisbaai*, and one from the *Nemanskii*."

"Why one?"

"The second boat is waiting for the skipper to make a final transmission and take a headcount to make sure he's the last to leave the vessel."

There are no protocols to follow when fifteen trawlers and the mother ship are under threat. Although he's responsible for the fleet, his immediate priority must be for the *Akademik Knipovich II* and the lives of the 350 crew members and factory workers on board.

"Have any of the other trawlers issued a distress call?"

"No, sir. They've been instructed to head for Grytviken as per your orders."

Vladimir knows they won't make it to the old whaling station. There are a couple who might be foolish enough to run before the wind, but most should be hove to.

"Keep the radio channels open. Tell the crews in the lifeboats to conserve their battery power until the storm blows over. Without the radios, we'll never be able to find them. They are not to use their flare pistols. They will be wasted, and the flares will help us to locate them after the storm has passed. I also want a roll call on the trawlers every thirty minutes."

Mika turns toward the communications center. Captain Khlanostikov shouts out to her. "Miss Nardin, would you like to be written up for breach of regulations?"

Mika stops and, keeping a firm hold on the guardrail, turns to look at him with an astonished expression on her face.

"Disobedience and failing to comply with orders," he yells, and he points toward the orange life jackets hanging on the wall. "You are not exempt."

She acknowledges him with a nod before disappearing through the door. Captain Khlanostikov tries to peer through the iced-up windows, but he can't see anything. The wipers have been rendered ineffective, and the rubbers simply slide over the frozen film of moisture.

"Mr. Boyarov, new heading: one hundred thirty-seven degrees ahead half, and hold steady."

Fyodor repeats the command and brings the ship around into the wind. Vladimir intends to ride out the tempest by holding this position, unaware that the *Akademik Knipovich II* is only on the outer fringes of the massive storm and in the direct path of the hub that's still five days out. The winds are rotating around the eye at 204 knots and still increasing in speed, whipping 3.1 million square miles of Southern Ocean into a boiling white froth in unrelenting fury.

Three hours later, Captain Khlanostikov is more afraid than he's ever been. The factory ship is getting tossed around with no effort, and they are completely at the mercy of Mother Nature. The stern rises out of the water, and the bow plunges into the huge waves, immersing the vessel in a wind-driven spray that sweeps right over them.

"The controls are getting sluggish, sir," Fyodor calls out.

Vladimir steps over to the wheel and takes over for a moment to make his own assessment. The vessel is far heavier than it should be. He hands the helm back to the young man. With seas like this, they'll be taking on water, but no more than the powerful bilge pumps can handle. He calls down to the engine room.

"The helm is getting heavy," the captain tells the chief engineer. "Can you check the hydraulic lines and make sure they haven't sprung a leak."

"Aye, sir, I will get them inspected right away."

"If you don't find anything, I want the cargo and storage holds checked to make sure a hatch hasn't been left open and we're taking on water."

Vladimir hangs up. He hears a loud creak over the booming crash of the waves. It's not a sound he's familiar with, and it bothers him. The rolling is becoming more pronounced and sloth-like, and the vessel seems to be taking longer to recover than he's comfortable with.

Twenty-five minutes later, the chief engineer appears on the bridge via the communications center, and Vladimir immediately picks up on his worried expression. By this time, Fyodor is struggling with the helm.

"Captain, the hydraulic lines are fine, and all the hatches are secure. I went back to make sure the gates on the stern ramp hadn't been left open." He pauses and swallows hard. "They're shut, but I found the problem." He points at the iced-up transom. "It's the ice."

A frown forms across Vladimir's face as he tries to figure out what the engineer is talking about. "What do you mean, 'it's the ice?'"

"When I tried to reach the stern ramp, the door was frozen closed. It took me ten minutes to get it open a few centimeters by using a blowtorch. The snow and spray from the ocean is freezing, and the decks and superstructure are encased in a layer of thickening ice. The storm is turning us into a fucking iceberg, and it's weighing us down. If we don't find a way to stop it, we'll get top-heavy and capsize."

Vladimir's heart jumps. "How thick is it?"

"Perhaps a hundred to a hundred thirty millimeters, but it's hard to be sure. I tried to open several doors that lead on to the decks, but they're all frozen closed. We're trapped in here."

Captain Khlanostikov stares at the engineer in disbelief. He heads for the starboard wing door and almost loses his balance as the deck shifts beneath his feet. The latch is frozen, and brute force fails to release it. The ice has turned the windows into opaque white sheets, but in close proximity to the glass he can feel a searing cold radiation as it exchanges the outside temperature with the warmer air on the bridge. Anxiety is burning in his chest as he turns back to the engineer.

"Are the crew able to reach the lifeboat stations if necessary?"

"No. The boats and davits are encased in a … a … I guess it can be called an ice cube. We'll have to chip it away to free the davits first, but it's likely that the cables are frozen to the drums too. The temperature outside is less than minus fifty."

The captain echoes the engineer's words in a weak voice. "Less than minus fifty? Exactly *how* cold is it?"

"I don't know. The deck thermometer doesn't go any lower, sir."

The captain is overwhelmed by a sense of hopelessness. They're trapped in what is essentially a floating coffin if they can't find a way out. "I want you to get a team together to work on freeing the doors to the boat decks, and find a way to get the davits deiced."

It's hard for Vladimir to read what's on the chief engineer's mind as he leaves. He makes his way into the communications center. Mika, now with a bright orange life vest strapped to her body, is making entries into a log book. She looks up at him, and the captain can tell by her eyes that she's frightened.

"I need to send a message to Vladivostok."

She shakes her head. "I'm unable to transmit, sir."

"Why?"

"I'm trying to figure it out, but I think there's a problem with the mast. I'm getting RF feedback, and if I make any attempt to transmit before repairs are made, I'm going to burn out the final stage. I need to go outside to fix it."

"Miss Nardin, I have reason to believe that the masts are encased in ice."

She hesitates. "What are you saying, sir?"

Vladimir isn't obligated to explain anything to her, but under the circumstances, it's not going to make any difference. "This ship is encased in a block of ice. We're going to capsize, and nothing short of a miracle will prevent it from happening."

The confession startles Mika. "There must be *something* we can do."

"Prayers—and hope they get answered," the captain states. He stumbles out of the communications center without saying another word.

The bow of the mother ship lifts up and rolls at an even steeper angle. It hangs suspended at almost 60 degrees for several long, heartwrenching seconds. The vessel is seriously contemplating whether to continue with the roll, but slowly, the ship rights itself again. This is not the way Vladimir ever thought he would go.

Eighty minutes later, the *Akademik Knipovich II* succumbs to the sheer weight of the ice and capsizes with all hands entombed within. No one has a chance of escaping the ice-enclosed sepulcher, but it spares the occupants the unpleasant sensation of drowning. The same element sealing them in is keeping the water out. Stuck inside a frigid air bubble, the terrifying ordeal of impending death extends itself. The temperature plummets, and with no power, lighting, or heating, the disorientated men and women snuggle up to each other in the darkened hull in an attempt to keep warm. Frightened sobs echo throughout the vessel between the deafening crash of the sea slamming against the steel plates of the overturned hull, and together they pray in the darkness. The chance of getting rescued this far south is remote.

They shiver in the cold, clinging on to life for more than five hours, but slowly hypothermia picks them off one by one until there are no lives left for the waters of the South Atlantic to claim—if it ever finds a way in.

16

Met Office
Stanley, Falkland Islands
Coordinates: 51° 41' 54.9" S, 57° 50' 58.8" W
Tuesday, June 23, 2020, 0916h

John stares at the nine o'clock image in astonishment and is shaken by what he sees. The eye is keeping to the path predicted by the spaghetti chart, but its diameter has expanded to an incredible 2,500 miles. The outer band of clouds is only 50 miles to the southeast of the Falklands, and the wind speed recorded by the satellite show that the leading edge is going to pack a hard punch.

"I'll be taking you home soon, lad."

Gavin glances out of the window. "Why? The sky is still clear."

John taps the face of the latest satellite picture. "Not for much longer. In another hour we're going to be hit by a ferocious blizzard, and I intend to be in the comfort of my home when it gets here."

"Strange," the young trainee mutters, his eyes locked on the computer monitor.

"Everything about this weather system is strange."

"No, I mean our Russian friends. They haven't sent any OBS this morning."

"Hmm, that's not like them," the meteorologist replies. "They're always punctual with the report. I hope they made it into Grytviken safely." He gazes at the image again. South Georgia is obscured by a blizzard with 185-mile-per-hour sustained winds, and the chart shows they are expected to increase to 239 miles per hour as the hub creeps closer to the British outpost. Gusts in excess of 300 miles per hour are prevalent, and he can only shake his head in awe at the dynamics generated by the storm.

He stands up, walks across to the exit, and takes his jacket from the coat peg. John pulls the garment on and is still zipping the front as he steps out into the crisp air. The thermometer on the exterior wall beside the entrance shows the temperature is minus three degrees centigrade. He shivers as he strides down to the end of the annex and turns the corner to get a view of the South Atlantic Ocean across the headland.

A huge bank of angry cumulonimbus clouds stretches along the southern horizon. The dark purple-gray base is at sea level, and John stares in awe at the intimidating wall of cloud billowing upward on strong updrafts until boiling outward at the tropopause. The sun reflects off the top of the moisture, which resembles puffy white cotton wool.

After several minutes, he heads back to the office. "The leading edge is visible in the south."

As the young apprentice runs outside to take a look, the telephone starts ringing. The meteorologist answers it to the rumbling voice of Sir Barry Glenwick.

"What's the latest on the storm, Mr. Starker? The schools and government offices are closed, but some people are asking questions because it's such a beautiful morning out there."

John laughs nervously. "I assure you, sir, in less than an hour this beautiful morning is going to turn ugly, and it will not be one of Mother Nature's friendliest visits."

"You're still expecting the worst, then?"

"Yes. The eye will pass less than fifty miles to the north of us, but for all intents and purposes, it's not going to make any difference."

"How long will it last?"

"Well, it's two and a half thousand miles in diameter, and it doesn't seem to be in a rush to go anywhere fast. The eye is halfway between the Weddell Sea and the Sandwich Islands, and for the past fourteen hours, it's been traveling at a leisurely three and a half miles an hour. We could be in for ten days of hell, give or take twenty-four hours."

"Do you think it will speed up?"

"Not according to the Infinity forecast."

Twenty seconds of silence follows, and John suspects that the civil administrator is not impressed. "Emergency services will be withdrawn thirty minutes prior to the storm's arrival to give personnel time to get home. Most of the doctors and nurses have volunteered to live-in at the hospital for the duration, and the radio station will remain on air. Two announcers have offered to play music and whatnot to entertain the residents, so send in a detailed forecast before you go home."

John is aghast. "I don't think that's a wise thing for them to do, sir. There will be structural damage, and they won't be able to broadcast once the power goes down."

"All things they are aware of, Mr. Starker. They've stocked up on food and a couple of camp beds, and they argue that they're just as safe hunkering down there as they are at home. It's irrelevant where they are, providing they understand what lies ahead and they've made adequate preparations."

"Well, I'll be closing the station by ten o'clock. I'm going to make sure my apprentice gets home, and then I'll be doing the same thing. I'm sorry, but I'm no hero."

"I'm not looking for heroes," Barry replies, and he brings the conversation to a close. "I'll talk to you on the other side."

Deep in contemplation, John hangs up. His thoughts are interrupted by a beep from the satellite communicator, and he walks over to the console. A message on the screen reads, "Invalid input command; data out of range," and the meteorologist scratches the side of his head as he tries to recall the correct procedure to reset the device. After going through the sequence, he waits for the recommended thirty seconds before transmitting a new request. The alarm beeps again, and the same error message flits onto the screen.

John groans and walks back to the desk. It won't make a difference what chart is used for the final forecast anyway, but first he sends an e-mail to the British Antarctic Survey office in the United Kingdom to advise them of the malfunction.

Gavin returns from outside. *"Wow! Those clouds are stupendous!"*

The meteorologist mumbles an acknowledgment as he begins to sift through some paperwork. "Give me about ten minutes to finish this, and then we'll leave."

Gavin slumps into his chair and sits in silence for almost fifteen minutes. John stands and holds a sheet of paper out toward him.

"Here, lad. Fax this over to the radio station, and then shut your terminal down."

The trainee follows the instructions of his supervisor. A few minutes later, the pair are pulling on their jackets when the room darkens even though the fluorescent lights are still on.

Gavin looks at John in alarm. "*Yikes!* What just happened?"

"The clouds have moved across the sun. It makes a big difference, eh?"

John's eyes sweep around the office to make sure everything is off, and with the apprentice leading the way, the two men step outside. He locks the door and walks toward the Land Rover with his eyes turned upward. Long fingers of dark cloud stretch across the heavens ahead of the main formation.

"Déjà vu," he mutters, and a cold chill runs down his spine. The nightmare he had on Sunday springs to the forefront of his mind, and with a shiver, he pulls the jacket hood over his head.

The ten-minute drive is made in silence. The clouds are racing across the sky, yet it's still flat calm on the surface. As he pulls up in front of Gavin's home, the first snowflakes start to float down from the sky. They are more than two inches in diameter and are the largest flakes John has ever seen. He looks at the apprentice as the young man opens the door to get out.

"Make sure you stay warm."

"Don't worry; I will," the trainee replies. "Thanks for the ride."

"You're welcome, lad."

The meteorologist watches the trainee unlatch the gate and retreat up the garden path. With a heavy sigh, he slides the gear shift lever from neutral into first and slowly drives off down the road. Five minutes later, he parks the Land Rover on the street outside of his house. By now the snow is falling heavier, transforming the world before his eyes. After getting out, he contemplates whether to drain the radiator but changes his mind. He wants to prevent damage to the cooling system, but vehicle maintenance changed the fluids the previous morning and never advised him of any action he should take. He dismisses the thought and turns his attention to his immediate vicinity.

In less than ten minutes, the snow is an inch deep. It crunches in an uncanny way beneath his feet. The huge flakes are sticking to his clothes, and with visibility at less than a hundred feet, sounds beyond the range of perception are muffled. Little natural light is able to penetrate the thick clouds, leaving him in an ominous gray-white twilight, and the meteorologist suddenly feels alone in the eerie, unnatural world. He's almost afraid to make a sound for fear of disturbing some evil entity lurking outside of his visual range. John clears his throat in a deliberate act to introduce some corporeal noise into this chillingly quiet world, but there's no resonance.

"Hello?" It's flat calm, and with no physical object in visual range to reflect his voice, the vocalization is absorbed into the snow-filled air.

John opens the front door and steps into the warmth of the house. The islanders have a natural propensity for their environment, and they inherit a special aptitude to support each other beneath a dome of sensitivity far removed from the cold, remorseless world he was born into. He turns the radio on. The scheduled programs are cancelled, and the announcers are improvising by inviting the listeners to call in and suggest song titles that reflect the current weather conditions. The elderly are encouraged to share lighthearted stories and yarns of years long gone, or tales about their ancestors, most with a warm thread of humor. He's amazed at how the townsfolk can still reach out to comfort each other over the airwaves, and John has a sudden yearning to be part of this world, but he feels like too much of an outsider. *How can I slot into this unique way of life?*

He opens the pantry door to see how much food he has on the shelves. There are enough fresh victuals to get him through the week, and sufficient canned provisions to last a month. He ponders for a moment. The electricity will fail for sure, so he places a flashlight on the table where he can find it in the dark. There are plenty of spare batteries in the kitchen, and more in a drawer beside his bed.

Satisfied there isn't anything else he needs to do, he makes a grilled cheese-and-onion sandwich and a cup of coffee. He glances at the clock. The time is ten forty-five. This is what the islanders call *smoko*, a midmorning snack between breakfast and the midday meal. As he munches on the sandwich, Steppenwolf's "Snowblind Friend" is playing on the radio. He gets caught up in the spirit and tries to come up with an appropriate song to call in, but only Christmas carols come to mind.

The current track ends, and the announcer speaks. "I have Gavin Fletcher on the line. Most of you will know he's our local weatherman-in-training. Good morning, Gav."

John tilts his head to one side and listens with attentiveness.

"Hello, Josie. Nice of you to keep us company. Can you play 'Snow (Hey Oh)' for me?"

"Isn't that by the Red Hot Chili Peppers?"

"You got it."

The announcer laughs. "Hey, did you conjure up this weather just to get a few days off?"

Gavin chortles. "Y'know, John is a great tutor and always takes the time to explain details to me, but he hasn't taught me how to invoke it yet."

"I hope your boss will join the party and call in later. We'd all love to hear from him. The morning started off nice and sunny, and now it's snowing hard out there. What can you tell us about this storm, Gavin?"

"Are you sure you want to know?"

"We all do, chay. I bet there are a lot of people greasing the runners on their sleighs as we talk."

The meteorologist chews slowly on the sandwich as he listens to the trainee with amusement. Whatever the young man was going to say next, John will never know. A violent shudder rips through the house frame, and a picture falls off the wall as the storm hits the small town with a vengeance. It heralds its arrival with a gigantic gust of wind that roars across the town at eighty miles an hour. It slams into the side of his home with a bang so sudden, loud, and intense that John drops the remains of the sandwich in fright. He leaps to his feet with his heart thumping like a jackhammer and gasps desperately for oxygen as the air is sucked out of the room. The temporary vacuum, combined with an incredible change in air pressure, results in a searing pain in his ears and across his forehead.

The shriek of the wind howling around the exterior of the house drowns the radio, and a moment later the lights flicker and go out. He had an idea things would change fast, but he never expected it to arrive as a literal wall of force. An icy draft races back into the house through cracks around the doors, and the carpet balloons upward several inches as blasts of freezing air are forced up between the floorboards.

John sits alone in the near darkness with the chilling scream of the wind for company as it shrieks around the house like a crazed banshee. It's the most ungodly natural sound he's ever heard, and there's no doubt that Satan himself has unleashed some unholy demonic wraith to run amok across the earth. Waves of fear surge through his body as his home shudders on its foundations under the enormous gusts.

The temperature is falling fast, and the need to keep himself warm has suddenly become top priority. The storm is going to be far worse than he even feared.

17

Infinity Meteorological Database Systems, Inc.
Hamilton Ave, Palo Alto, California
Coordinates: 37° 26' 40.3" N, 122° 09' 36.2" W
Tuesday, June 23, 2020, 1022h

Steve sits behind his desk, twiddling a pen between his fingers, and stares at the opposite wall with a perturbed expression on his face. When he came in, the laboratory was his first stop; there he learned that no advances had been made to resolve the issue.

"Could it be a structural problem in the software rather than a technical one?" Steve asks.

"I can't see how," Brad replies. "The software was designed around your knowledge of meteorology, and it's worked without a glitch for the last eleven years. If you left out any details or I misinterpreted your instructions, the issues would have exposed themselves *long* before now."

"Could it have outgrown itself?"

"What do you mean?"

"Well … you devised a form of artificial intelligence so the system could teach itself about preclimatic conditions and the development of weather patterns over time," Steve says. "It's been working well, but isn't there a limit as to how far it can go? I mean, a lot of data are stored on a daily basis, but the memory isn't boundless. It must get full at some time?"

"You *know* that can't happen. Unused files are dumped into the database banks twice daily to free up space for new information."

"That's what I *mean*. What if the processor needs to refer to something that was discarded into the recycle bin seven years ago? It could be stuck in an eternal loop, searching for information that's no longer there." Steve is smart and knows his stuff where meteorology is concerned. He's an excellent businessman and of course understands how to *use* technology, but when it comes to how it works, his knowledge is quite superficial.

"That *can't* happen," Brad replies, and he sweeps an arm toward the racks holding the data storage units. "*Not*hing gets recycled, and every byte since the first satellite went online is stored in these boxes. They are the satellite's subconscious, and in the unlikely event it requires information not in the onboard databank, it searches through here on the next scheduled update. If it can't find data relating to the subject, a whole new facet is set up automatically."

"I don't suppose you were able to retrieve the last forecast from either satellite?"

Brad nods. "Yes, it's all in the database. Jim discovered that the satellites are still going about their business as though nothing is wrong."

"What do you mean?"

"Well, the sensors are still gathering, processing, and storing the data, and we can access the individual streams from storage after the download. That leads me to believe the error is being invoked at the interface, where the information is compiled into a forecast, and that's where our current focus is."

"BB, do me a favor. Send a copy of the last imaging and graphic charts saved by both satellites to the printer in my office. I'll take a look and see if I can find an anomaly in the general meteorological physics that might be contributing to the error."

Brad taps several command functions into his keyboard before turning back to his partner. "I hope you come up with something because we're at an impasse down here."

Steve returns to his office and for the next two hours, pores over the charts spread out across his desk. His frustration is growing. He can't find anything that suggests the meteorologies are a direct cause. A knock on the door breaks his concentration, and Brad walks in. The grim expression on his partner's face tells him that they are no closer to a solution.

"Don't forget about the board meeting at three," Steve says as BB slumps into a chair on the opposite side of the desk. "We'll have to do some clever talking. The investors won't even *consider* funding the new program while this is going on."

"Don't tell them."

"You know that's not an option. If we persuade them to invest in the other ten units without disclosing our current problem, it amounts to fraud. The Russians are upset over the failure. It's the only one that covers Siberia, and now they're threatening a lawsuit. Peter Noble in PR is doing a diplomacy number, but he won't be able to stave them off for too long if the outage continues. They subscribe to four satellites, and we can't afford to lose their business, so we need to appease them before they wake up their old ones."

"They can't switch back."

"Why not?"

"The 2017 International Space Act has been in full implementation since the end of 2018. The garbage disposer has cleaned out almost every defunct satellite and piece of detectable junk, including the old weather satellites that went dark after we put our network up."

The act Brad is referring to was a mandate proposed to reduce the buildup of space junk orbiting the planet. There was a real danger of a fatal collision, and every nation with a current or past space itinerary, except for North Korea, signed a treaty to remove nonfunctioning equipment from orbit. The cost to design, construct, and launch the special unmanned craft was shared between the space agencies. The intentional destruction of a satellite was prohibited, and a statutory fee is charged to the owner for each piece of junk removed. The garbage disposer is kept docked at the International Space Station and drags anything no longer in service by remote operation to a lower orbit before sending it on a trajectory to burn up in the earth's atmosphere on reentry.

North Korea showed contempt for the directive with the deliberate detonation of two rockets after the implementation of the act. This led to missile bases in South Korea, Japan, Guam, and Hawaii to successfully intercept and destroy all rockets after they were launched by the DPRK, but before they reached the upper atmosphere, much to the chagrin of Kim Jong Un.

"*Crap!* I'm not sure if that's a good or a bad thing," says Steve.

Brad clears his throat. "I never came up here to talk about this afternoon's meeting or the garbage disposer. A call came in from the British Antarctic Survey. Their satellite that covers the Falkland Islands, dependencies, and territories on the Antarctic Peninsula went down about forty-five minutes ago."

"Another one!"

"With exactly the same symptoms," Brad confirms.

"But how can that *be?*" He stares at his partner in silence for almost a minute, trying to come up with something that makes sense. "Is it possible that someone has hacked into our network?"

"I think that probability is remote," Brad replies. "Our security software is some of the best in the world."

"I agree, but hackers are smart, and catching them isn't easy. Because *we* have the notion our system is impenetrable doesn't mean it isn't."

The CTO hesitates, and Steve can tell he's cast a sliver of doubt in his partner's mind. Brad unclips the iPhone from his belt and turns the speaker on before dialing down to the lab.

Danny answers. "Yes, BB?"

"Run a security report. See if you can find an attempt to hack into the network."

"I've already done that. No breaches have been recorded."

Steve leans over the desk, and speaks in a loud voice so Brad's phone can pick it up. "Most cyberpunks are smart enough to cover their tracks before they exit a network, though, aren't they?"

"No," the technician replies. "A hacker can't erase the trail completely. I can run another report though."

"Thank you," Brad says. He turns the iPhone off, and continues to talk to Steve. "Even if someone *did* succeed to get in as far as the interface, you *know* there's no way he or she will ever get past Mad Max."

The Infinity system operates on a unique code developed by the CTO, and it can't be read or decoded by software outside of the company. "Mad Max" is a nickname given to a firewall designed by Brad that is installed on the satellite at the input and output interface. All communications to and from the onboard computers go through this device. But while it can identify the Infinity and standard machine codes, it can't translate from one language to the other and obeys only a limited number of preset commands. To install malware onto the onboard computer, it needs to be converted to Infinity code first, and Krazy Kath is the only machine in existence that can translate the two languages and create the master discs used to program the satellites.

Brad speaks again after a brief silence. "Give me one good reason why anyone would *want* to compromise our systems?"

"Because they can?"

His partner dismisses the idea with a snort. "That's a lot of effort to go through for someone without a serious agenda. They'll need to crack our code first, and *that* will take decades, if they can ever do it. The only device capable of reading it is Krazy Kath, and we are the only two people in the world who knows it exists."

Steve glances at an artist's impression of an Infinity weather satellite suspended in orbit above the earth. Krazy Kath is a one-of-a-kind machine that resembles a slim-line DVD recorder, and a sliding panel behind the picture conceals the safe where it is kept, along with the blueprints for their entire system.

"Corporate theft?"

A look of astonishment appears on Brad's face. "Who would want to *steal* it? We don't even have any competitors."

"I'm only saying we shouldn't eliminate any possibility until we're one hundred percent certain. Three satellites have failed with an identical problem, and that is more than a mere coincidence when you consider how impeccable our record for technical failures has been until now."

Steve stands and paces back and forth across the office in

frustration. "We're flogging a dead horse. We need to expand our search from the improbable to the impossible. It will be foolish to put total faith in our security wall when the one thing we *haven't* dismissed is a viral infection."

Brad opens his mouth to say something but closes it again without speaking. Steve sits back down and continues to rant as he leans back in the chair. "Don't forget about the Chameleon. No one knows for sure what its capabilities are."

The Chameleon is a clever but deadly virus discovered by the FBI several months earlier. They suspect it's been around for some time, doing untold damage to computer systems across the globe. It mimics background codes to slip through some of the most complex security software on the market without detection, evolving as it shifts from one file to the next to remain transparent. The discovery was made by accident, but cyber forensics had difficulty when they tried to isolate the alien intruder. So far, they haven't been able to figure out how it works, and until they do, there's no protection against it.

"It will never get past Mad Max," Brad says.

"I disagree. If it's been planted in the development computer, it could insert itself on the transfer disc and get translated by Krazy Kath to the master."

His partner groans. "Don't even *go* there."

The conversation is interrupted by the buzz of the intercom, and Steve glances at the wall clock, noting that he and Brad have been in discussion for nearly an hour. He leans across the desk and depresses the button to connect to his secretary.

"Yes, Nancy?"

"Can you take a call from a Mr. Samuel Peters of the Canadian Meteorological and Oceanographic Center?" Steve casts a suspicious glance at his partner, who is preparing to leave, and motions with a hand for him to sit back down.

"Put him through." There's an almost inaudible click as the connection is made. "Mr. Peters?"

An irate voice confirms the identity of the person on the other end of the line. "Is this Mr. Jaeger?"

"Yes, it is. How can I help you?"

"One of your weather satellites has broken down. It would be nice to get it back into operation again."

Steve rolls his eyes, and a horrible sensation simmers in the pit of his stomach. The Canadians also subscribe to multiple units.

"Which one?"

"The satellite covering Nunavut Territory and the Northwest Passage."

"Can you tell me the what the symptoms are?"

Samuel's response is pompous. *"Symptoms?* There *aren't* any symptoms, Mr. Jaeger. The fucking thing shut down on us and won't come back online."

Steve speaks in a slow, calm voice in an attempt to soothe the enraged man on the other end of the line. "Are there any error messages on the screen, Mr. Peters?"

The Canadian pauses before replying, and the sharpness in his tone softens. "Yes, I'm looking at it now. 'Invalid input command: data out of range.'"

"Thank you, Mr. Peters. Our techs are already working on the problem. In the meantime, I'm going to transfer you back to my secretary. She'll take your telephone number, and someone will call you back when it's in service again."

"Thank you."

Steve places him on hold while he calls Nancy. "I'm sending Mr. Peters back to you. Can you take his contact details for me?"

"Okay, Mr. Jaeger."

He hits the transfer button, and as the intercom disconnects, the telephone starts ringing. The caller ID shows it's Peter Noble from the PR department.

"Yes, Pete?"

"I've received a complaint of another malfunction."

Steve scowls. "Yes, I know. I spoke to Mr. Peters a few moments ago."

"Who?"

"Samuel Peters … from Canada."

The public relations officer hesitates before speaking in an uncertain tone. "I never talked to a Samuel Peters. The call came from David Bower of the Alaskan Weather Center. Their satellite has failed with an 'Invalid input command: data out of range' error message."

Steve can feel the blood draining from his face. "We still have no idea what the cause of the problem is yet. The technicians are doing their best to resolve it. I need you to keep on top of diplomacy until we know what's going on, Peter."

"I will," the public relations officer confirms, "and by the way, the Russians are warning that an affidavit is being prepared by their lawyers, which they intend to file with the US Department of Justice if their satellite isn't back in operation by midnight."

"*Fuck!*" Steve shouts. "Thank you, Peter." He holds the handset several inches above the cradle and drops it into place with a clunk before looking across at BB with weary eyes. "The Alaskan unit is now kaput, too."

"Same error message?" Brad asks.

Steve nods his head, and replies in a tone bordering on cynicism. "Of *course*. Now the ante's been upped to two at a time. What the hell is *happening?*"

BB is silent for a few moments. "Interesting."

"What is?"

"I need to go down to the lab and check something out. I don't know if it will have any bearing, but if I'm correct, the Nunavut and Alaskan satellites are in orbit on the same parallel."

Steve gets up and walks a few paces to the bookcase. He turns his head to the side to read the spine labels and, after a few seconds, pulls a softcover publication from the shelf.

"I have a copy of the satellite directory here," he says as he sits back down, and opening the first page, he slides a finger down the index. He leafs through to a page about a third of the way through the book. "You're right, BB. They're both on the sixty-fifth parallel."

"I don't see how or why that would be relevant, but it's worth investigating."

Steve clasps his hands in front of his stomach. "I'm convinced more than ever that a virus is the problem and somewhere along the line Mad Max has failed to recognize it. I think this is the direction you should pursue."

"I'm still dubious," Brad says. "If it *is* a virus, it hasn't displayed any of the characteristic signatures associated with a malicious code. The operation of each satellite is initiated from different countries, and no one has access to a unit they're not subscribed to."

"No one may be able to get in by conventional means, but they are linked together in an unobtrusive manner. Infect one satellite and the virus could be passed from one to the other through data networking."

Brad's body stiffens at the insinuation. "You're scaring the *shit* out of me, Steve." He stands up. "I'm going to sever the link between the defective units and the functioning satellites. *If* a virus exists, it should prevent more shutdowns." He walks toward the door singing "A-hunting we will go, A-hunting we will go," but with cynicism in his tone.

"BB?"

Brad stops his out-of-tune aria with one hand on the doorknob and turns his head to look back at his partner.

"Don't forget the meeting at three o'clock. You need to be there."

The chief technical officer nods his head in silent affirmation before leaving the room without saying another word.

Steve rests his elbows on the edge of the desktop and props his head up on his hands with a heavy sigh. He has no alternative but to revise the scheduled agenda of the investors' conference and disclose the problem to the board members. It's better they hear about it from his own lips than from the television or radio. Things aren't going to move in their favor even if the technicians stumble across the cause between now and three o'clock.

18

Infinity Meteorological Database Systems, Inc.
Hamilton Ave, Palo Alto, California
Coordinates: 37° 26' 40.3" N, 122° 09' 36.2" W
Tuesday, June 23, 2020, 1347h

After BB leaves the office, Steve simmers in his own excogitations, and the longer he stews, the more convinced he becomes that the malfunctions are being caused by a virus. He calls the FBI at eleven-thirty, and they promise to send a cyber forensics team out to investigate. By one fifteen, he has calmed down again. But then Brad reports another failure—this one a satellite shared by Finland, Sweden, and Norway—bringing the total number out of commission to six.

Steve calls his partner on the arrival of two federal agents, and while he waits for Brad to come up to the office, he gives them an overview. Clarke Richards listens intently. As Richards is six feet tall, the CEO doesn't miss the self-assured swagger in his gait. His physique is that of a man who works out regularly; he is clean-shaven with a crew cut, and exudes the confidence of one who is competent and knowledgeable in his field. By comparison, his partner is shorter and on the pudgy side. Ben Thomas is three years junior to his associate, but his demeanor is less affable. He makes notes on a legal pad but keeps staring at the CEO with piercing eyes. Steve feels as though he is being psychoanalyzed.

"Do you have tangible evidence that your network has been hacked?" Clarke asks Brad.

"That's the problem. I don't have anything conclusive."

"Then what leads you to believe that the satellites are infected by a malicious code instead of something technical like faulty wiring or component failure?"

"Diagnostics show the units are functioning properly, but when we reboot them, the onboard systems shut down again. They all display the same error message, and a virus is an option I need to keep on the table until it can be eliminated."

"And you're unable to trace the source of the code?"

Brad grunts before answering. "Analysis indicates it shouldn't even exist."

The FBI agent purses his lips for a few moments. "It's possible that the error message *is* the virus."

"Hmm, I never considered that angle," Brad mutters.

"There's another reason why we suspect a virus," Steve adds. "We've never had a technical failure in eleven years until yesterday morning."

Clarke appears surprised. "You do anticipate that failures will occur, don't you?"

"Yes, of course we do, but we don't expect six malfunctions to happen with the same symptom in less than thirty-six hours."

"I will concur to that argument, but if it's the work of a virus, how do you think it was introduced into your network?"

Steve throws a glance at Brad, who responds. "That's something I can't explain. The scanners never tracked a breach in security, and neither could we find a single instant where an attempt was made to hack the system."

For the next ten minutes, Steve listens as BB explains to the agent about the tight security measures they employ. After Brad has finished expounding, the agent rubs his chin with a thoughtful expression on his face.

Ben speaks for the first time. "It's beginning to sound like an inside job."

"Even *that's* a high improbability," Brad responds sharply.

Clarke raises his eyebrows. "Why do you say that?"

"Well, *no* one has access to the codes except for Steve and myself."

The agent appears astonished at the declaration. "I imagine your techs need to use them, don't they?"

Steve jumps in to answer the agent. "There isn't a need for them to know the codes exist. Updates are made on a computer that runs a simulation of our systems in binary. BB analyzes the compatibility to ensure the adjustments are glitch-free before they are translated into Infinity code by Krazy Kath. The master disc used for reprogramming can't even be read by a regular PC or laptop."

Clarke inclines his head in an inquiring manner. "Who is BB?"

"Oh, uh … yes, that's Brad Bentley," Steve replies, indicating his partner with a casual sweep of his hand. "It's a soubriquet that's stuck to him since childhood."

Clarke smiles. "Then who is Krazy Kath? I presume that's an alias as well?"

Steve grins. "Krazy Kath is a special computer that translates standard binary to the Infinity encryptions. She's the *only* piece of equipment in the world that can do this. We keep her locked away in a secure location, and no one knows of her existence. That includes the techs."

"Have you considered industrial sabotage?" Clarke asks.

Steve shrugs. "As far as I know there aren't any competitors in our field."

The agent sits forward in the chair. "It doesn't have to be a rival business—only a greed-driven corporate ambition to claw at a viable and successful company."

The CEO is startled by the agent's allusion. "You mean the Luther Corporation?"

"Yes."

"I've heard rumors about the underhanded tactics they employ to acquire assets and the way they conduct business in general, but aren't those only suspicions and hearsay?"

"What you've heard is probably true. They are under investigation, but it's an ongoing case that I'm not able to discuss." He turns his head and looks at Brad. "Is there a pattern to the failures that indicates the presence of a virus?"

Brad shakes his head. "That's what makes the whole thing so *bizarre*."

"It is possible that a latent virus was planted in your network years ago."

"A dormant code is usually awakened by a date–time combination, and perhaps activated by a specific action, but if this *is* a virus, I'm pretty certain that the activation key is far more complex than a time or date process."

"What makes you so sure?"

"We have sixty satellites in orbit. If the prompt is a date–time element, they would've all gone down within twenty-four hours."

Clarke frowns at Brad's rationalization. "How do you figure?"

"Regardless of what time the virus was woken up, it would take an hour for the satellite to perform every possible function that could be used as an activation key. This gives a maximum window of twenty-four hours for them to fail. A lapse of thirty-six hours occurred between the first and last failures, and they didn't drop out with the progression of the timeline; they jumped indiscriminately between time zones. I think that eliminates the basic date–time theory."

"*Ahh*, I see what you're saying." Clarke pauses. "I'm not prepared to rule out a disgruntled employee just yet either."

"I can't imagine why," Steve says. "We don't have a revolving door when it comes to staffing. They get good pay, benefits, and bonuses. In fact, we've only had one resignation since we began employing technicians, and that was only because he moved out of the area to get married." He glances at BB for support.

Brad nods his head in confirmation. "Yes, a bright lad by the name of Harvey Worrell. I was sorry to see him go. He and Danny are good friends, and I think they still keep in touch with each other."

"The department with the highest turnover in staff is janitorial," Steve adds.

"Don't you subcontract the cleaning to an outside company?"

"No."

"Interesting," Clarke remarks, and he hesitates before speaking again. "I'll need access to your employee files. I'm going to start with a security screen and see if any names are flagged."

"Which departments are you most interested in?"

"Janitorial through to management, which includes Mr. Bentley, you, and the board of directors. *Everyone*, past and present, must be regarded as a potential suspect until he or she is cleared."

"I don't have a problem with that," Steve says, looking up at the clock. It's almost three o'clock, and he needs to bring the interview to a close. "Listen, gentlemen, Brad and I have an investors' conference to attend. I will call down to Human Resources and tell the manager that you have unrestricted access to the employee records."

"Will you be discussing this at your meeting?"

Steve throws a wistful glance in Brad's direction before answering the agent. "There's a transparency clause in the investorship agreement, and I'll be in violation if I fail to disclose it. This isn't something small that can be buried and forgotten in two minutes. We are a multibillion-dollar business, and it's going to be impossible to keep this out of the media for much longer." A frown forms across his forehead. "I'm worried about the shockwaves it will send through Wall Street once the news does get out."

"I understand. It won't compromise the investigation, and who knows, it might flush the rat out if there is one."

The two agents leave, and Steve looks at his partner as he grasps the handle of his briefcase. "We'd better get over there."

The investors are sitting around the conference table chatting among themselves when Steve walks into the boardroom with Brad on his heels. They fall silent and begin to stand, but the CEO motions with one hand as he walks at a brisk pace across to his chair at the head of the table. "Please, remain seated."

He pulls a file from his briefcase before glancing around at the two women and nine men on the panel, and he takes a deep breath. "Good afternoon, ladies and gentlemen." His voice doesn't have its usual effervescence, and the grim expression on his face alerts them that something is wrong. "Due to a crisis, I am forced to invoke paragraph ten of the investors' agreement. The intended agenda for today is postponed and will be rescheduled for a later date. This is an informative session only."

He pauses, and an uncomfortable hush settles over the room. It's the first time he's summoned a citation in eleven years, and no one is sure what to expect.

"*That* doesn't sound good."

The owner of the voice doesn't make himself apparent to Steve, but it's not hard to guess who made the remark, and he ignores it. "A string of failures since early yesterday morning has taken six satellites offline, leaving eight subscribers without access to weather-related services. I'm going to hand you over to Mr. Bentley, who will provide you with an update on what we know from a technical standpoint."

The CTO delivers a précis of the problem and the diagnostic procedures they've applied in their attempt to trace the source. Five minutes later, he finishes talking. "We are mystified because analysis shows there is no fault with the equipment."

Jack Mason springs to his feet, and Steve rolls his eyes. This is a man who is always in opposition to any development the company proposes, and he never fails to complain about something. "How can you say it's *not* a fault when it's so damn clear that a fault exists? If it's a *malfunction*, it's a fucking *fault*—end of debate."

Steve has little tolerance for the cantankerous seventy-one-year-old, but Brad's patience is far less genial. "Let me elucidate, Mr. Mason. Our satellites have given us eleven years of service without a problem, so what are the odds of six suddenly malfunctioning in less than two days? Give it some thought for a moment."

"Why don't you employ proficient technicians who *know* what they're doing?"

Brad's face turns red, and fearing things are about to get out of hand, Steve intercedes by placing a hand on his friend's shoulder. "I'll handle this," he mumbles into his ear. BB gives him a sharp glare and hesitates before sinking into his chair.

The CEO locks eyes with the sanctimonious old man and reproves him in a calm voice. "Mr. Mason, we are trying to deliver a report, and there are people in this room who are interested in what we have to say even if you're not. With respect, please refrain from interrupting until we have finished." He turns his attention to the rest of the board. "The techs are working around the clock to isolate the problem, but because of the nature and number of failures, we can't rule out that this has been deliberately orchestrated by one or more individuals."

"Are you suggesting the computers may be compromised by a virus?"

Steve looks at the concerned expression on the face of fifty-six-year-old John York. "That's something we can't rule out, Mr. York."

Jack raises his voice again. "Incompetence and negligence by you and your staff are the real villains here. You convinced everyone on the board except for me to invest in a costly security system with the promise that it would make the satellites impenetrable, and you said the network could *never* be hacked."

The old man irritates Steve, and while his demeanor remains placid, he's unable to disguise the sharpness in his voice. "Please stand corrected, Mr. Mason. I said the firewall would *lessen* our chances of getting hacked, not eliminate them. I think everyone around this table will agree that we do our best to prevent intrusions into the network, but it's *never* a guarantee. The technology we employ is revolutionary and remains unpublished. There are corporations out there who are desperate to get their hands on the blueprints, and that in turn spawns individuals who will try to dip their fingers into the pit for the rewards they'll reap. We are probably a top target for hackers, and I don't need to stress how the profits and high dividends we all enjoy will take a dramatic dip if *anyone* duplicates our technology."

Rita McLeod, one of the two female investors, raises a hand, and Steve acknowledges her with a nod. "Mr. Jaeger, are you not made aware if a hacker tries to get through the firewall?"

"Yes, Mrs. McLeod, and that deepens the mystery because the security logs show no attempt has been made to hack into the network."

Jack cuts in again and makes sure that everyone can hear him by speaking far louder than necessary. "If the failures are as abnormal as you'd like us to believe, and no one has hacked into the network, which you're *also* telling us, I'd be thinking by now that this has the traditional hallmarks of an inside job, wouldn't you?"

"I wouldn't say there's a traditional sign of *anything*, Mr. Mason, but that avenue is under investigation by the FBI. I called them in this morning, and they're downstairs right now, exploring every possibility from an individual with a personal grudge through to corporate sabotage. All persons associated with Infinity, past *and* present, are being scrutinized, and that means *everyone*."

Jack sneers. "I hope that includes you."

"Yes, it does. Mr. Mason. Mr. Bentley, myself, and everyone sitting at this table are not exempt."

The investor's face turns red, and he bellows back at Steve in outrage. "You do *not* have the authority to subject any of us to this kind of harassment."

Steve is taken aback at Jack's outburst. "No one is being harassed, Mr. Mason, and no one will even be questioned unless something suspicious is uncovered." He looks around, making brief eye contact with each person. "Does anyone else want to object to an FBI investigation?"

Jack gives a loud, contemptuous snort. "Of *course* they do. They're all too pussy to admit it."

The vulgar insult brings an angry reaction from the rest of the investors, but John York speaks first. He adjusts the glasses on the bridge of his nose and addresses the old man directly.

"Mr. Mason, I, for one, don't have *any* objections because I *know* they won't find me involved in anything nefarious. I am also a director on the board of a renowned Internet security company and am well acquainted with the problems consumers and businesses face from hackers on a daily basis. Dozens of new threats appear by the hour, and I'm sad to say online security is not a onetime event. Security software needs to be updated regularly; otherwise, it has no value. Mr. Jaeger is making an effort to get to the bottom of this tragic situation, and I applaud him for taking the initiative." He turns his head to look at Steve. "Mr. Jaeger, I apologize for jumping in without addressing you first."

"No offense taken," Steve replies.

"You suggested corporate sabotage," John continues. "Do we have competitors in this field now?"

"We are not aware of any, Mr. York, but the FBI hinted that we shouldn't dismiss the Luther Corporation as the instigators behind the satellite failures."

"Those bastards." John's retort is venomous, and Steve is surprised at the angry passion in the usually calm investor's voice. "Their activities are reprehensible. They force viably profitable companies, both private *and* corporate, into bankruptcy and then launch a takeover bid to bail them out of trouble. Those who don't accept their terms are forced into insolvency."

"They dispose of their competitors in the same manner," Rita McLeod adds in a bitter voice. "They stomped on my husband's business and completely ruined him, but he can't prove anything against them."

"I think we all know how dangerous the Luther Corporation is," Steve replies.

Fifty-nine-year-old Leon Chesney speaks out. "I've heard of them, but I'm not familiar with their operation."

"The pattern is always the same," Steve says. "A reputable company starts to spiral downward for no apparent reason. The Luther Corporation steps in and offers to buy them out at a fraction of their value. A business that's a threat to any of their assets is closed down thirty days after they acquire control, but others have a sudden reversal in fortune. They go about their despicable operation all over the world, but so far the FBI have been unable to come up with sufficient evidence to indict them."

A dark scowl appears on John's face. "It's said that in some countries, businessmen who refused their proposals have died or vanished under mysterious circumstances. However"—he hesitates before finishing the dialogue—"*if* the Luther Corporation has infiltrated this company, it can only mean that one of us in this room is a traitor."

A stunned silence falls over the table at John's revelation, and everyone gazes at him in astonishment. This is something that Steve has contemplated since Clarke Richards planted the seed a little earlier.

"One of *us* is a corporate spy?" Leon exclaims. He's a quiet, amiable person but a shrewd businessman.

"I'm inclined to concur with Mr. York's suspicion" the CEO says. "The chance that one of us *could* be a spy for the Luther Corporation is real."

Jack reacts angrily and insults Steve by addressing him by his surname. "What a *preposterous* accusation, Jaeger."

"I never *made* an allegation, Mr. Mason. I am merely pointing out the possibility, but you are the only one who seems to be taking it personally."

"What are you implying?"

"You figure it out," Steve fires back.

"I already have," Jack yells. "When word of this fiasco gets to Wall Street, the value of our stocks are going to sink faster than a sack of shit in a goldfish pond. We will lose hundreds of millions of dollars all because of your ineptitude at running a business the way it *should* be run."

"Mr. Bentley *and* I have more to lose than money," Steve responds. "Our reputation and integrity are at risk, and I do *not* intend to lose either."

"What fucking integrity, Jaeger? You *have* none. I want to call for a motion of no confidence in your role as company CEO"—he glances around the table at the other investors—"but no one else has the guts to tell you to your face."

Enraged, Brad jumps out of his chair and lays into the obnoxious investor before Steve can respond. "Mason, you are a complete and utter *prick*. Mr. Jaeger is more qualified than anyone to be CEO of Infinity. He knows this business from top to bottom, he's respected by his peers, and he puts the interests of this company, its employees, *and* its investors before his own."

"Bullshit!" Jack spits, his voice full of scorn.

Brad clenches his fists, and Steve gets ready to intervene. "*Bullshit?* Mr. Jaeger has more integrity in the tip of his little finger than you've *ever* accumulated in that tiny pin-brain of yours. You fight against every proposal we make to improve services and launch into outbursts of offensive slurs against the investorship when a vote doesn't go your way. I've often wondered why you were the *only* person who was against the security upgrades, and perhaps the answer is right before our eyes. Improved security would inhibit plans to infect the network with a virus."

"You need to show more respect," Jack rages. "I *am* your highest investor, and without *my* cash, you'd still be in the gutter. If you think I'd throw money away by compromising the company, then you're more of a dimwit than I imagined."

"I'm no idiot, Mr. Mason. Anyone affiliated with the Luther Corporation wouldn't lose a dime. The acquisition of Infinity will triple their investment at *least*." He hesitates. "But if you're *that* unhappy, I suggest it's time for you to cash in your stake and move on. We can operate as effectively without your money as with it."

Brad's anger has moved into eggshell territory, and Steve doesn't want the exchange to escalate any further. He reaches out and gives the sleeve of Brad's jacket a gentle tug.

Leon obviously feels the same way and intercedes in a calm voice. "I propose we wait and see what the FBI turn up. If the problem is something that could've been avoided, then we'll decide on what our next course of action should be. It does no good to point fingers or cast the blame on an individual when we don't know what the problem is yet. I recommend an adjournment, and we'll reconvene once the FBI have submitted their report."

The rest of the board mutter their approval at Leon's suggestion. Jack Mason snatches his briefcase up from the floor, gets to his feet, and glances around the table with an angry glare before his eyes settle on Steve. "Jaeger, you have until tomorrow morning to get a grip on this ignominious debacle. If business isn't back to normal by then, you can expect my support to be withdrawn." He spins on his heels, storms across the room, and exits the boardroom. The tension in the room dissipates as the door slams closed behind him.

Steve turns to Leon. "Thank you, Mr. Chesney, and I apologize to everyone for suspending the scheduled agenda. Please, feel free to call in at anytime for an update."

He gets to his feet and leaves with Brad close behind.

19

National Weather Center
Buenos Aires, Argentina
Coordinates: 34° 37' 47.2" S, 58° 22' 05.5" W
Wednesday, June 24, 2020, 0811h

A cold, blustery wind sweeps across the cemetery, and Carlos Castelli glances up at the dark clouds blowing across the sky from the southeast. Heavy rain showers are in the forecast, but he's hoping the precipitation will hold off for a couple of hours.

The forty-eight-year-old brown-skinned man is a devout Catholic. He is 175 centimeters tall with an average body build, his cheeks are slightly sunken, and he has a full head of black hair that's graying at the sides. His forty-four-year-old consort, Isabella, is eight centimeters shorter and still looks like a million dollars in his eyes. She has a slender body, an elfin face, and thick shoulder-length black hair. Like Carlos, her skin is light brown, but lines of age are showing on her face. Over the years she's become codependent

241

on him, and though he doesn't expect it, she always abides by his decisions like a dutiful wife. Isabella trusts him implicitly, and he genuinely has her best interests at heart.

When they were married twenty-two years earlier, the young couple carefully planned out the way their life would go. Carlos had a promising future at the National Weather Center, where he's now head of the meteorology department, and unlike many newlyweds, they were financially stable. He bought a five-bedroom house in Santa Rosa in anticipation of the large family they intended to have, but that's where things went awry. Isabella's failure to conceive led to a visit at a fertility clinic. They were devastated when tests revealed that her chances of pregnancy were less than one percent. The consultant told them that *in vitro* fertilization would likely be unsuccessful. Over the next year, her yearning for motherhood became intolerable, and it almost tore their marriage apart. Then a true miracle happened. Against all odds, Isabella fell pregnant.

The meteorologist opens two folding chairs beside the grave and places a knee pad on the damp grass in front of each one for kneeling during prayer. Because it's midwinter, the weather is usually bleak, and while Carlos sets up a huge beach umbrella to ward off the wind and rain, Isabella props a large wreath against the headstone. She steps back, loops her hand through her husband's arm, and lays her head against his shoulder with tears in her eyes. Her voice is distant, but the heartbreak in her tone is discernible.

"Today is his eighteenth birthday."

The meteorologist needs no reminding but doesn't rebuke her. He lays a gloved hand on top of hers. At the beginning of the eighth month, the baby developed an erratic heartbeat, and the doctors made a decision to deliver the boy by cesarean seven weeks premature. An ultrasound scan revealed the heart had failed to develop properly, and the consultant prepared them for the sad news. He would survive for only a few hours.

Carlos called their priest from Santa Bartholomew, who rushed to the hospital and gave Pablo a special bedside baptism. It was a harrowing experience. Isabella was inconsolable because one minute after the hastily arranged christening, the monsignor administered the last rites. The infant passed away two hours later.

"I know it hurts," he replies, "but he was suffering. We need to be grateful that God was merciful and took him to a better place."

She tightens her grip on his arm. She doesn't say anything, and they stand in silence for several minutes. His iPhone begins to ring, and Isabella turns her eyes up to her husband.

"Why didn't you turn that thing off?"

"I wasn't expecting anyone to call," he replies, taking the device from his pocket. The display shows "National Weather Center," and he gets irritated. His colleagues are aware of the reason he isn't in today, so he lets it go to voice mail.

"Who is it?"

"Someone from work," he replies. "They *know* not to call me until after midday."

"Let's say a prayer."

The two kneel on their respective pads, and holding hands, they recite the Apostles' Creed together. "Amen" has barely rolled off Carlos's tongue when the iPhone rings again. The office is still trying to get him to answer. He'll check the messages after they get back home, and deal with the guilty party tomorrow morning.

They continue to pray for another fifteen minutes. Isabella removes a tissue from her handbag and uses it to dab the tears from her eyes. Time has reduced Carlos's own emotions, but his wife's grief is as prevalent today as it was eighteen years ago.

The phone rings.

"Why don't you turn it off?"

He ignores her question and pulls the device from his pocket. The caller ID shows his office is still calling, and he gets annoyed. "Let me see what they want."

Isabella remains silent.

"Hello?"

"Mr. Castelli, this is Jose ... from the weather center."

Jose Panteras is a nineteen-year-old intern. Carlos was horrified when the teenager disclosed how he was orphaned at fourteen. He had gone to a friend's house to work on a school science project, and while he was there, his parents were savagely murdered in a brutal home invasion robbery. Jose returned to find their battered and bloodied bodies in the living room. Carlos couldn't even begin to comprehend how traumatic the experience must have been. Because he's an empathetic person, he took the young man under his wing.

"Jose, have you forgotten what today is?"

"I'm sorry, sir, but some strange weather data are coming in that I think you should know about."

"There are supervisors there who can assist you. That's what I've employed them for. I don't want to be bothered anymore today."

Jose hesitates. "They're the ones who told me to call you, sir."

"No balls, huh?" he snaps, and his tone softens. "What's the problem, son?"

"*Uh*, well, you need to see for yourself. The chart shows a storm is moving in over Terra del Fuego, but the forecast makes no mention of it."

"If there's *that* much of a conflict, then draw up a manual forecast. You don't *always* need to rely on technology."

"I can't, and it seems that no one else can either."

Carlos is confused. He had checked the satellite charts before going home on the previous evening, and there wasn't anything to indicate that a drastic change was on the way. The meteorologist glances at his wife, who is looking at him with an anxious expression in her eyes.

"I'm going to come in and see what's going on," he replies, making no attempt to hide his annoyance. "It might be time for some heads to roll." He closes the connection and speaks to Isabella as he slides the phone into a pocket. "I'm sorry, sweetheart, but I have to go into the office for a little while."

The disappointment on her face fills him with guilt. "*Why*, Carlos? This is *always* our day with Pablo."

He takes both of her hands in his. "I'll try not to be too long, honey, but in case I get delayed, I'll take a taxi and leave the car for you."

"If you can't get back by midday, stay at the office. I'll drive over to meet you."

He hands the car keys over and gives her a kiss before setting off at a brisk pace toward the main exit. A taxi pulls up to drop off a fare just as he reaches the cemetery gates, so he jumps into it.

Twenty minutes later, Carlos enters the main office at the National Weather Center and stops. Fearful of his wrath, everyone in the room stares at him in silence. The tension is heavy. Carlos makes no effort to hide the displeasure on his face, but he chooses to ignore the others for now. His eyes rove around and settle on Jose, who is on the other side of the room. He beckons the young intern to follow, and with long, purposeful strides, he heads for his office. The meteorologist is already sitting behind the desk when Jose catches up, holding a manila folder in one hand. He places the file on the desk, and Carlos opens the cover.

"What are we looking at?"

"The seven-day forecast for southern Argentina is cold but clear and sunny," Jose replies nervously. "There's no mention of the storm that's poked its nose in at the bottom of the image. It's just moved across the boundary into the area covered by the satellite, but there's no mention of it in the forecast."

The ambit of the satellite's sensors ranges from Puerto Lobos in the north, to south of Cape Horn, fifty kilometers east of the Falkland Islands, to the Southern Pacific Ocean, west of Chile. The unit leased by the British Antarctic Survey transfers information on the events moving out of its own territory into its neighbor's domain, which is integrated with its own data, but the failure of the BAS satellite has left a blind spot in the network. It's not receiving the necessary intelligence to update the data bank, so the outlook is being calculated using the only source available—a constant loop of the last transmission.

Carlos studies the image. Heavy clouds in the bottom right quadrant obscure the Falklands and sweep in a gentle arc to the southwest across the tip of Tierra del Fuego. A sustained wind speed of 210 kilometers per hour is stamped around the outer limits of the system, but the chart is void of all other data. He presumes that the storm needs to move further into range before the sensors are able to detect the barometric pressure, moisture content, temperatures, and so on, but he's puzzled. That should have been passed on by the British satellite.

The meteorologist pulls a small box from the top drawer of his desk and removes a compass, protractor, ruler, and a pair of dividers. "I can barely recall the last time I used these."

"What are you doing?" Jose asks.

"Simple mathematics," Carlos replies. "The cloud formation suggests they are rotating around a central core. There's enough of an arc to calculate the circumference and diameter, which will give me an idea of where the center of the low-pressure system is. I don't know why the satellite isn't giving us any vitals, though."

Jose points to the figures imprinted on the image. "It shows a scary wind speed."

"I doubt whether that information is reliable, son," Carlos replies. "I can tell by the arc that it's a pretty big storm, but I don't think the winds are 210 kilometers per hour in the outer extremities." He draws a straight line in a southeasterly direction from the edge of the curve to a point in the vicinity of the South Sandwich Islands, and he whistles.

"When did this image come in?"

"About an hour ago, sir."

"Run another one for me."

While the intern is gone, Carlos rechecks the calculations. He estimates that the tempest's radius is at least two thousand kilometers, which means it has the potential to do serious damage if it moves across mainland Argentina. The new chart should indicate the speed and direction of movement.

Jose returns and lays the new printout on his boss's desk. The wind speed is still 210 around the edge of the outer band, but overall there's no significant change between the two images. The apparent direction seems to be northwest, which will bring the system across the southern tip of Argentina and Chile, but what he fears most is the speed. It's moving at less than four kilometers an hour, and if his calculations are correct, a storm of these dimensions could inundate the South for days. With much of the data missing, he wants to dismiss the accuracy of the wind velocity, but one simple fact nags at his consciousness. During the six years they've been looped into the Infinity system, not once has he had to question its reliability.

He picks up the forecast for the cape and reads through it slowly. Cold but clear weather is predicted for the next week, but there's no hint of a storm. It leaves no doubt in his mind that something serious is amiss, and that puts him into a quandary. *Do I believe the forecast, or do I trust the map?*

"I want an image on my desk every fifteen minutes," he demands gruffly. He's forgotten about Isabella, and where he should be. Carlos ponders for a moment. "Tell me, son, would you trust the map or go with the seven-day projection?"

"The map, sir."

The meteorologist is surprised by the intern's fast response. "Why?"

"Well, the portion of the storm that's visible in the chart has moved a little, so I would think it has more substance than the report."

Carlos contemplates the logic in Jose's answer, which the intern is quick to clear up. "The seven-day forecast is false, sir."

The meteorologist looks up at him in astonishment. *"False?* How did you figure *that* out?"

"Read it. Each day is exactly the same. When have you seen seven consecutive days and nights with precisely the same metrics? The forecasts are duplicated every twenty-four hours."

His jaw drops open as he realizes that Jose is right, and he feels a little foolish for not spotting the discrepancy. That means he needs to process the worst-case scenario, but if the sustained winds *are* that high on the storm's outer limits and his calculations on its size are correct, how bad *will* the worst be? After several minutes of silent debate, he picks up the telephone and dials the switchboard.

"I need to speak to President Hernandez, or an official at the *Quinta de Olivos* who has direct contact with him. Call me back once you've established a line."

Carlos has nothing but contempt for Argentina's head of state. He's an obnoxious leader who puts his own personal interests before the needs of the nation, and his narcissism is taking the country down a dangerous path. Corruption is rife within the administration, and he predicts a power struggle will transpire before too long. A military coup to oust is inevitable.

Twenty minutes pass before the telephone rings. "President Juan Hernandez is on the line," the operator tells him, and he hears a click as she makes the connection.

Despite his abhorrence for the man, the meteorologist greets him in a civil manner. "Good morning, sir. This is Carlos Castelli at the National Weather Center."

"I know who I'm talking to," the president snaps.

The weatherman is taken aback by the president's arrogance but tries to brush it aside. "I'm about to issue a severe winter storm warning for southern Argentina, sir."

An awkward pause follows before Juan's sardonic response comes down the line. "Correct me if I'm *wrong*, Mr. Castelli, but I believe that *is* your job, isn't it?"

His air of superiority irks the meteorologist. "Yes, you are right, and the other part of my job is to inform the president of Argentina when unusual weather conditions arise that might pose a threat to the nation."

"Then *inform* me," Juan says impatiently.

Anger wells up in Carlos's chest, and fears that his forecast could be inaccurate dissipate in an instant. "It's an extraordinary storm—unstable, erratic, but predictably dangerous. It's over the Malvinas and Terra del Fuego and is moving into Ushuaia as we speak."

"Define 'extraordinary' for me."

Carlos takes a deep breath. "It's more than four thousand kilometers in diameter and moving northwest at less than four kilometers an hour. It could engulf southern Argentina for up to a week. I predict heavy snow, blizzards, subzero temperatures, and sustained winds in excess of three hundred kilometers per hour. Loss of communications and power is inevitable, and there will be structural damage. It's likely that people are going to be killed."

"How poetic. I couldn't have said it with more flair myself," the president fires back in a tone that borders on mockery. "Tell me, Mr. Castelli, do you think I'm a fairy godmother with a magic wand I can wave to make it all disappear … *poof?*"

Carlos is repulsed by the president's nauseating attitude. "No."

"What *are* you expecting me to do, then?"

The meteorologist feels debased, but his reply is firm. "I'm doing my duty, which is to counsel you on a serious and potentially dangerous weather system. What *you* do with the information is your decision. I thought you might want to proclaim a state of emergency and make plans for disaster relief."

President Hernandez gives a loud, raucous laugh. "It's hardly likely I'll announce a state of emergency or declare southern Argentina a disaster zone *before* any kind of catastrophe occurs. Likewise, how the hell do you expect me to put a search and rescue mission together when there's nothing to search for or rescue?"

Carlos is embarrassed by the president's reproachful stance and decides to bring the worthless conversation to an end. He has better things do. "Thank you, Mr. President." Without anything further to say, he terminates the call abruptly by replacing the handset.

"We have an imbecile for a president," he mutters angrily.

Jose returns with a new image and chart. The outer band has inched its way across Terra del Fuego and over Ushuaia, but the satellite prediction shows the current weather conditions over the windswept town are calm and clear. He connects to the online telephone directory to find the number for the town's weather office. Twenty seconds later, an animated voice gives him a clue that a disaster is in the offing.

"We are unable to connect your call at this time. Please try again later."

20

Infinity Meteorological Database Systems, Inc.
Hamilton Ave, Palo Alto, California
Coordinates: 37° 26' 40.3" N, 122° 09' 36.2" W
Wednesday, June 24, 2020, 0927h

Seventy-five minutes after the conclusion of the board meeting, two more Russian satellites failed, which left the nation with one functional unit. After a second night of discomfort, Steve headed into work early and went straight to the soft lab, where he learned that Russia's last satellite went offline at 0245. The country is weather-blind, and he has uneasy premonitions of the repercussions.

"The two that went down at the same time are also in orbit on the same parallel," Brad told him. "Bill ran an experiment overnight. He downloaded the software from the defective Siberian unit and used it to reprogram one of our own that covers the southwest quadrant of the United States."

"What was that supposed to achieve?"

"That's what I asked him, and I was surprised when he told me that our satellite worked perfectly. It encouraged him to download and transfer the operational data from a working satellite into the Russian one, but it failed the moment it went online."

"So we're back at square one?"

Brad nodded his head somberly. "I can't understand why it works in one and not the other."

Exasperated, he goes up to his office, and he has barely sat down at his desk when there's a knock on the door. The company's public relations officer enters and doesn't waste time getting to the point of his unscheduled visit.

"The Russians held a press conference last night and released a scathing report to the media."

"*Christ!* What did they say?"

"Well, they carried out their threat and filed a lawsuit with the International Court of Justice."

"I thought they were going to go through the State Department?"

Peter strokes his chin, a habit he has in uncomfortable situations. "It seems they've changed their minds because they've decided to file a litigation against the federal government too."

Steve is astounded. "Can they do that?"

"I'm not sure. I guess it depends what their claims are against the administration. The international courts will assess the allegations, and if they validate the plaintiff's affidavit, we can expect to be served within thirty days."

The CEO's voice is bitter. "Oh, I have no doubt it will get approved."

"I'm not a lawyer, but if I were the litigant, I would want restitution for every hour the satellites are down," Peter warns.

"Advice?"

"Right now, none. We'll have to wait until our lawyers receive the deposition and see what claims are being filed."

Steve stares at the PR officer in silence for several seconds. "You said their press release is scathing. How far did they go?"

"Well, the cold relationship between Russia and the United States since Putin is still prevalent. They've accused the administration of willful intent by allowing us to deliberately compromise their meteorological services. Bazhenov is going to call Sinclair and demand that the White House desist if they wish to prevent an escalation of hostilities."

"That's *all* we need is for this to trigger an international incident." Steve falls silent as he toys with an absurd thought. "Do you think the CIA or the NSA could hack in and take control of our satellites?"

Peter shakes his head. "I don't know if they have that capability, but if they did, why would they knock out the Australian and Canadian units … even our own one in Alaska?"

The public relations officer has a point. "Your guess is as good as mine. I doubt if the White House will get involved. I think the president will chalk this up to Russian paranoia and give it a wide berth." Steve sighs. There's nothing he can do except run with it for now.

"After the Russians made the announcement, the Canadian, Finnish, Norwegian, and Swedish governments followed with their own press releases and told their citizens they are no longer able to provide forecasts either."

The CEO stares at the PR officer. "Do you have *anything* good to tell me?"

Peter gives a nervous cough. "I know this isn't what you want to hear either, but our stocks opened up with a one percent dip on Wall Street this morning."

This has been one of Steve's biggest fears since Monday, and he curses under his breath. "What about Australia and the British Antarctic Survey?"

"They've been quiet so far, but I guarantee they'll jump on the wagon now that it's on the roll." Peter folds his arms across his chest. "How do you want to respond?"

"Don't volunteer anything," the CEO tells him after a moment of contemplation. "If you get calls from the media, be diplomatic with your answers but keep them as opaque as you can without giving them the impression your evasion is deliberate."

"That'll be an impossible task."

"Then be as discreet as you can."

After Peter leaves, the CEO sits forward, rests his elbows on the desk, and, close to despair, holds his head in both hands. He needs to get himself together.

The intercom buzzes, and he opens the connection. "Yes, Nancy?"

"Mr. Mason is here to see you, sir."

Steve rolls his eyes in dismay. "He's the *last* person I want to see. Tell him I'm occupied, and make an appointment for next week."

He didn't realize that Nancy was using the speaker, and before she has a chance to reply, Mason's angry voice booms through the intercom. "Like *hell* I will!"

The secretary hesitates. "I'm sorry, Mr. Jaeger. He's heading toward your office. Shall I alert security?"

"No, this isn't anything I won't be able to handle"

The door bursts open, and a furious Jack Mason storms in. Striding into the center of the room, he goes straight into a diatribe. "How *dare* you treat me as an inferior. I'm *not* one of your fucking peons."

The urge to respond with an insult is irresistible, but Steve remains calm. "My serfs are more classy and less vulgar, and they know how to knock on a door before they come in ... but I forgot, respect and politeness are not your forte."

Jack's eyes blaze in fury. "Fuck you, Jaeger. How do you intend to prevent this debacle from getting into the media?"

Steve's reply is bland. "I don't think that's any concern of yours."

"It's *every* concern of mine," the old man fires back. "This is *my* money you're farting around with."

"Mr. Mason, you're not the only person with an invested interest in this company. We are doing everything possible to protect everybody's money until we can diagnose and resolve the problem."

"And *that's* a goal that you and your bunch of vaqueros seem to be incapable of achieving," Jack fires back.

Steve's desire to rip this bad-tempered individual apart like a wild animal is overwhelming, but he retains some measure of professionalism and extends an invitation. "Why don't you assist us if you're so concerned?"

Jack removes a sealed envelope from the inside pocket of his jacket with a loud, contemptuous snort. "Go fuck a pig, Jaeger."

The seventy-one-year-old throws the missive toward the desk, where it lands on the top with a slap and slides along the polished surface. The CEO keeps his hands clasped in front of him, making no attempt to arrest the letter as the momentum carries it across the desk. Steve watches it slip over the edge, and drop to the floor with a nonchalant expression on his face.

"That's my resignation. I am withdrawing my support as of this moment."

Steve's lips curl into a tiny smile. "You do realize that if you sell your shares today, it will be perfectly illegal."

"What?"

"Trading with insider knowledge is against the law, Mr. Mason. Have you forgotten that under the investors' proviso, resignations from the board are not effective until ninety days after submission? It looks like you'll have to take the fall along with the rest of us after all."

Steve gloats over Jack's discomfort, and the investor yells back at him so loud the CEO is certain everyone in the adjacent offices can hear him.

"You *can't do this!*"

"I'm not. The law is." Steve hesitates and moves to the front of his chair. "I have some more news for you … I believe journalists call it a tidbit. The media knows of our problem, and Wall Street is far from happy."

Jack splutters and starts salivating like a rabid creature, his eyes transfixed on Steve. The CEO knows that the best way to antagonize his adversary is to stay calm. A carefree attitude is far more effective than an affront.

"Now, if you *don't* mind, Mr. Mason, I have more pressing matters to attend to. Please feel free to slam the door when you leave."

Jack is incensed, and for several seconds he continues to glare in silence at the CEO with so much loathing in his eyes that someone more timorous might have felt intimidated. The investor hunches his shoulders, clenches both hands into fists, and—with a loud, angry snort—punches them down toward the ground.

"My lawyers will be in touch, Jaeger. You haven't heard the last from me by a long stretch." Red-faced and fuming, he turns for the door and yanks it open with as much force as he can muster. It swings on its hinges and slams into the doorstop on the baseboard.

Steve smiles with satisfaction as the old man storms out of the office.

The encounter with Jack Mason has lifted his spirits, but it's short-lived. After closing the door, the CEO sits back at his desk and combs his fingers through his hair in frustration. A couple of minutes later, he decides to go down to the lab and bug his partner for a while, but as he gets to his feet, Clarke Richards arrives. Steve invites him to sit down before sinking back into his own chair again.

The agent places a folder across his knee and opens it. "I'd like to ask you about one of your investors—a Mr. Jack Mason."

Steve throws his head back and laughs.

"What's so funny, Mr. Jaeger?"

"You missed the crabby old bastard by minutes. He was here to hand in his resignation. I took pleasure in reminding him of the ninety-day clause that prevents him from selling his stock beforehand. It pissed him off for sure, but I don't care. He's been nothing but a thorn in our sides."

"Is he your top investor?"

"He was." Steve becomes curious, and sits forward. "Why are you asking about Jack Mason in particular?"

"I shouldn't say anything, but the FBI has been interested in him for quite some time. Because of the nature of your situation, I think I should furnish you with some details, as he *may* be the root of your problem."

"*Oh?*"

"Are you aware that he's on the boards of several companies besides Infinity?"

"No," Steve admits, "but our financiers aren't required to declare other investment interests under the terms of their agreement."

"Each is undergoing a financial crisis with a risk of bankruptcy on the horizon."

The CEO raises his eyebrows in consternation. "Are you *serious?*"

"At the moment, we have insufficient evidence to indict him, but we're certain he's with the Luther Corporation." Steve stares at Clarke in astonishment as he listens to the agent. "Mason has a remarkable track history. He's been the top financier of twenty-three companies who have collapsed under unusual circumstances. He withdrew investments at a time when they were vulnerable, which sent them into a tailspin; and until this week, Infinity was the *only* business he's linked to that didn't have a problem." The agent leans forward, rests his right forearm across the folder on his knees, and lowers his voice. "Your ninety-day clause is an inconvenience, but it may not be enough to save your company."

"What are you talking about?" Steve is numbed by the bombshell.

"Guess who comes to the rescue when Mason quits?"

"I think you're going to tell me it's the Luther Corporation?"

"Uh huh, and he made two more acquisitions this week alone."

A puzzled expression falls across Steve's face. "How the hell is he doing it?"

"That's what we're trying to figure out. Every case points to industrial sabotage, but we can't nail anything specific to him. Of course, the Luther Corporation executives claim they are helping the companies to get back on their feet, which in itself isn't illegal, but there's more behind the veil than we can see. Their operation is a high-tech, mafia-style takeover scam that stretches right across the globe."

Steve sits back, clasps his hands together across his stomach, and twiddles his thumbs nervously. "I did some Internet research on the Luther Corporation last night, but I couldn't find too much about them. They are nothing more than a panel of twelve advisory investment directors with no other employees. All executives were named, but Mason wasn't among them ... unless they're all aliases."

"Oh, the names are real enough, and you're right, they don't employ workers per se. The titles of the directors are publicized for legal reasons. Because they're under public scrutiny, they are squeaky clean ... too clean. What they *don't* mention are the fifty-one ad hoc investors they're not required to proclaim because they are freelancers. We have circumstantial evidence of Mason's acquisitive involvement with the corporation, but we lack anything of substance to ensure a successful prosecution. He's also under investigation by the IRS because his lifestyle far exceeds his annual income declarations, so we'll get him on something."

Steve is gobsmacked. "How do these twelve ... or fifty-one men get control over so many businesses?"

"There's an ingenious operation going on, and we will bust them eventually," Clarke assures him. "The money that Mason invested in your company as a private shareholder is *not* his own."

The CEO is startled by the agent's declaration. "You're not going to tell me it belongs to the Luther Corporation, are you?"

"Every bronze cent."

Steve squirms in the chair. "So when he resigns, he sells his shares to them?"

Clarke nods with a grim expression on his face. "They already own them. They'll make an offer to get you out of trouble, but only on their terms. For a business like this, they will want control, so you'll be required to sell them enough stock to give them a fifty-five percent stake in your company. Businesses they consider to be competitors in a market they already have their paws into are closed down. Freelancers like Jack Mason reap a high reward for each acquisition—something like fifty percent of the profits they generate. He makes more money in one month than you and I earn combined in our lifetimes, but at no time is his own wealth *ever* at risk."

"*Jesus!*" Steve exclaims. "He must be raking in *millions.*"

"Try billions, Mr. Jaeger," Clarke replies, and he smiles. "He's sitting on more than one and a half trillion."

The CEO is getting more flabbergasted with each statement rolling off the agent's tongue. "We all like money, but he'll *never* spend that much in his lifetime. I guess his family will be well off when he dies."

"The freelancers have a satisfactory arrangement with the Luther Corporation in exchange for a life of luxury, but they must bequeath seventy-five percent of their net worth to a specified charity in their will. The other twenty-five percent is left to their beneficiaries, but as you can imagine, their families will still be well off for the rest of their lives. If there are no heirs, then one hundred percent must be left to a designated charitable organization. The will is drawn up and signed before the investors are allowed to climb on board."

"Let me guess. The specified trusts are set up by the Luther Corporation, and the money filters back into their pockets."

A big grin spreads across Clarke's face. "Now you're catching on, Mr. Jaeger. And because the charity is registered, taxes are nondeductible."

"Tax evasion *too*? Isn't there a way you can get one of the freelancers to come clean?"

"No. You see, Mason and the rest of the cohorts aren't employees of the Luther Corporation, but neither are they as free as a lancer should be. They're *all* part of the organization, and that's where it starts to get complicated. Trust me, we haven't even chipped the tip of the iceberg yet."

Steve becomes anxious again. "So what about *our* immediate problem?"

"Without evidence, we can't do anything against Jack. Who we *are* looking for is another employee who may be a contracted operative."

Steve's brow wrinkles. "What do you mean?"

"Mason is not in a position to place a virus in your system. The best way for the Luther Corporation to learn your weakness and exploit flaws in your operation is by placing a freelancer on the board of directors. Once they find a loophole, they will entice a current employee, preferably someone long-term who has the complete trust of his or her administrator, and utilize that person as an operative. Quite often it is someone as lowly as the humble janitor."

"I'd like to think that all my employees, especially the ones who have been here for years, are loyal to me."

"Money talks, Mr. Jaeger, and they can offer a payday that will set them up for life. They are careful, though, and they need to be confident that their target will turn. The alternative is to get a gopher employed or contracted by Infinity. It's done through a third party, and whoever the perpetrator is, they won't know they're getting paid by the Luther Corporation; but neither do they care. The fee is large enough to stop them from asking questions, and if they are caught, their knowledge is too limited for them to give up any useful information under interrogation."

"*Fuck* them. I'd rather lose *everything* than give them a chance to triumph in something BB and I started with our bare hands." He pauses for a moment. "Do you think they're behind the Chameleon?"

Clarke sighs. "We have our reservations but, again, no evidence. I called forensics this morning to get the most recent update, but our knowledge of the bug is next to nothing. They seem to think they've only got part of the code, which makes it impossible to figure out how it works."

Steve is puzzled. "How can they only get *part* of a virus?"

"They added a marker so they could track its progress through an isolated system, but nothing happened. Now they think it might be incomplete. They don't have the other pieces of the puzzle to be able to determine its intended purpose."

"I still don't understand how it can be *part* of a virus, though."

"Forensics suspect it's formed by several codes and each one carries a portion of the virus's instructions. When a system is infected, the routines scatter and hide in various files. They are not only harmless when they're on their own, but they're undetectable to the antiviral and firewall software on the market. They can sit dormant for years while waiting to be activated. When they're awakened, they congregate at a predesignated location and plug into each other to complete the equation. The attack is swift and often deadly."

Steve's face pales. "Good *God*. How can we ever protect ourselves against such a powerful foe?"

The telephone rings. Brad's name is on the caller ID, and he apologizes to the agent for the interruption as he lifts up the handset.

"BB, please tell me you've got some news."

Brad's tone is grim. "I do, but none you're going to like. We've lost another two satellites."

The CEO groans. "Who are they subscribed to?"

"Canada."

"Both of them?"

"Yes. They went offline at the same time."

Canada subscribes to three units, and that means they're all out of commission. "Are they on the same latitude?"

"Fifty-six degrees north," Brad confirms.

"We're up shit creek, and the paddle is floating farther away. Do you think we're going to lose them all?"

BB grunts. "I've no desire to answer *that* question, but a pattern *is* emerging, and I think I can predict the next failure in advance. If my calculations are correct, the next subscriber to lose service will be the United Kingdom, somewhere between thirteen-thirty and fourteen hundred hours."

"Does that help us to isolate the virus?"

A note of irritation creeps into Brad's voice. "Steve, I still don't know how the code is being activated, and until we do, well …"

Exasperated, Steve boils over. "BB, if it isn't going to help resolve the problem, why are you wasting time predicting which units are going to crap out next? You should be using the time to get them operational again because, to be quite honest, it's running out on us. The news is now in the media, and our stocks took a hit on the opening bell this morning. Find that fucking virus, and get our network back online."

"Don't speak to me like that," Brad fires back. "I'm as frustrated as you are, and we're out of options. The lads are trying to trace malware that I don't think exists, and if I can forecast which satellite will fail next, it's a step that might help unravel the mystery."

"How?"

"It's a pattern, and—"

Steve cuts him off. "*You're* the technician. Do what needs to be done."

"I'll call you back later."

"Gator," Steve replies.

He replaces the handset and wipes his forehead with the back of a hand. "We've lost two more satellites."

"What repercussions will it have on the ones that are still working?" Clarke asks.

"It's causing too many black spots, which will result in a catastrophic failure of the entire network."

An awkward pause follows. "Out of personal curiosity, Mr. Jaeger, what's unique about your weather satellite program that's made your company so successful?"

"Our technology has been described as futuristic by many scientific publications. Each satellite is fitted with hundreds of sensors that monitor the atmospheric pressure; air, surface, and ocean temperatures; humidity levels; moisture density; wind speed and direction; oceanic currents; and a whole plethora of scientific data that get shared with the immediate neighboring satellites. Each unit amalgamates the networked information with its own, analyzes the dope, and teaches itself to make more accurate predictions over time as weather systems move from one quadrant into another."

"Are you trying to tell me that down the road they'll be able to tell us what the weather will be at any location on a given date, weeks or months in advance?"

Steve laughs at the agent's speculation. "I would like to say this is where we are going, but I don't want to be too presumptuous. Our system is powerful, and its learning abilities have far exceeded expectations, but it will be a novel concept to plan a vacation around the kind of weather you want and be sure you're going to get it."

A smile breaks across the sober face of the FBI investigator. "I do like that idea." He hesitates. "Why do countries like Russia and Canada subscribe to more than one satellite?"

"The reliability of a prediction is only accurate over a small area," Steve explains. "The sensors in most of the satellites are set at an optimum obliquity of one point two eight eight degrees, which covers an area of one million square miles. A wider angle corrupts the data, owing to atmospheric refraction. This would make the information that gets networked too indistinct for the neighboring satellite to process."

Clarke closes the folder on his knee and prepares to leave. "It's fascinating stuff, Mr. Jaeger, and it's piqued my interest, but I'd better get back downstairs. Ben will think I've scarpered and left him to do all the work."

The agent crosses the floor and pauses with a hand on the doorknob. "Is it possible that only one satellite has malfunctioned and, because its data never got transferred, it's triggered a shutdown of the network?"

"That was ruled out right at the start. The first failure happened over Antarctica, and the second one happened over Siberia. They couldn't be any farther apart, and there is absolutely no communication link between them."

Clarke waves the folder in his hand. "I haven't found any meteorologists in your employee files yet."

"If you do, then I'd like to know who they are. We don't employ people with meteorological skills."

The agent gives the CEO a quirky gaze but doesn't ask any more questions on the subject. "If Mason happens to stick his face in the door again, call me right away. I'd like to speak to him."

"Somehow I think I'll be dealing with his lawyers from here on out."

"That's even better!" Clarke exclaims. "His councilors will be employed by the Luther Corporation, and I'd like to know who they are as well. I'll catch you later." With those departing words, he disappears through the door.

Steve sits back in the chair and puffs his cheeks out before expelling the air through puckered lips. *How much does Mason know about the satellite failures? If he is the problem, it means his accomplice is still with Infinity, and that's a very troubling thought.* He decides to call the company lawyers to prepare them for a major lawsuit, but he is secretly hoping they will give some advice that will make him feel better. The attorney only repeats what Peter said earlier. They need to see the official statement first before making a comment. After thirty minutes, he hangs up feeling no more reassured. Steve glances at the paperwork piling up on the side of the desk, but with no motivation to tackle it, he decides to go downstairs.

The quietness feels unnatural as he enters the lab and walks over to Brad's terminal. The CTO must be aware of his presence, but his eyes remain glued to a data chart on the monitor. Not wanting to break his partner's concentration, the CEO pulls a chair up to one side and watches in silence.

After several minutes, Brad leans back, removes his reading glasses, and rubs his eyes. "I suppose you're here to pressurize me some more?"

"No. I'm only getting bad news upstairs, so I've slipped out for a while."

Brad sighs. "Well, I'm afraid I don't have anything good for you either."

"I didn't think you would. Do you want to take an hour for lunch?"

"No. I'm tracking a new thread, and I don't want to break away from it. You can take Danny, though. He's been working damn hard, and I want to move him off the task he's on anyway."

"What's caught your attention?" Steve asks.

"Well, I'm convinced the problem isn't technical. I'm not even sure it's a virus, either. A pattern *has* emerged in the way they're going offline, and all I need to do is figure out why." Brad turns to the console and minimizes the current screen before opening another window to reveal a 3-D image of the globe. Their satellites are positioned around it, and several are flashing red.

"These are the units that have shut down," the CTO explains, and he points to the one farthest south. "The Australian Antarctic Division was the first to fail." Steve's eyes follow Brad's finger as he points to and identifies each one in sequence. "The Siberian satellite followed, and the third was the British Antarctic Survey. Back north, we saw the concurrent collapse of the Canadian and Alaskan units."

"Now, were they simultaneous failures, or was there a time lapse?"

"They went down within a millionth of a second of each other."

Steve remains silent while his friend brings up another chart on a second screen.

"Whether the satellites are in the Northern or Southern Hemispheres is irrelevant," Brad tells him. "The failure pattern is in their orbital latitudes. Australia's Antarctic Division is the southernmost at seventy-two degrees. Russia's Siberian unit is the northernmost at seventy-one degrees. The second malfunction in the Southern Hemisphere is the British Antarctic Survey, placed at sixty-seven degrees. The Canadian *and* Alaskan units are on the sixty-fifth parallel, the next one is at sixty-four degrees, and the two Russian satellites that went down at four thirty yesterday afternoon are on the sixtieth. Can you see the sequence?"

"Seventy-two, seventy-one, sixty-seven, sixty-five, sixty-four, sixty," Steve murmurs. "They're going offline in some kind of sequential countdown."

"Exactly!" Brad exclaims. "And on a constant timeline. To be more precise, the failures are moving toward the equator from the north *and* south at a constant rate of twenty-six point six six arcseconds per second, or one degree every two hours and fifteen minutes. This enables me to calculate the date and time a specified satellite will go offline in both hemispheres."

Steve is curious but remains skeptical. "Which one will go out of service next?"

"I told you earlier, the United Kingdom. It sits at fifty-four degrees north and will go down at thirteen forty-five."

The CEO still isn't convinced, despite the conviction in his partner's voice. "Why are there only two satellites offline in the South while a whole bunch have gone down in the north?"

"We don't have as many units in the south. More than eighty percent of the Southern Hemisphere is ocean, which is where the blind spots are that need to be filled by the ten new units. The next failure to occur south of the equator will happen at twenty-three hundred tonight. Another one will go down about two hours later."

"Who owns those?"

"Argentina and Chile. The last satellite will go dark around three o'clock on Monday morning if we don't get things resolved by then."

"If you're so sure it's not a technical issue or a virus, what else *can* it be?"

Brad shrugs. "I have a gut feeling it's something indirect."

"Indirect?" Steve blurts with a blank expression on his face. "Now I *am* lost."

"Indirect, as in a natural phenomenon that's interfering with the electronics. It could be anything from an X-ray emission to a magnetic disturbance or unusual RF signals from deep space playing havoc with one or more of the sensors."

The CEO's cynicism increases, but he doesn't mock his friend. "Is that possible?"

"I don't see why not. We don't know everything that's out there in the universe. I think one of the sensors is picking up data that's not aligned to information in the database and the computer has locked itself into an infinite loop trying to locate a set of values that doesn't exist. The error code is being invoked to bring it to our attention."

"What about sunspots or solar flares?" Steve asks. "I know we were on edge a couple of years ago when the activity peaked at an exceptional level."

Brad shakes his head. "It caused serious damage, outages, and inconvenience to different global services, but it never interfered with our equipment. I've checked the current sunspot activity, but they're at a minimum, so that's factored out of the equation. I'm leaning toward something that happens periodically—perhaps a supernova or some other rare event for which we don't have enough data to know what its effects are."

"This is perplexing," Steve mutters. "The subscribers can communicate with the satellites, and the systems are still recording and storing the data. That would mean the malfunction must happen when the computer crunches the statistics."

"Correct," Brad confirms, "but do you realize how much data passes through the interface every millisecond? I need to narrow down the vicinity; otherwise, I'm searching for a pin in a field of haystacks."

The two friends fall silent for several minutes. Steve goes through every detail of the known facts in his head. He's unconvinced that a natural phenomenon is the culprit, and he can't shake the possible connection between the Luther Corporation and Jack Mason from his mind. The CEO looks across the room to the lab's senior supervisor.

"Danny?"

The twenty-eight-year-old looks up. "Yes, Mr. Jaeger?"

"C'mon, we're going to lunch."

The young man casts an inquiring glance at Brad, who motions with his head toward the door. "Get out of here. I have a different assignment for you when you get back."

21

Dover Heights
Sydney, Australia
Coordinates: 33° 52' 36.5" S, 151° 16' 56.1" E
Wednesday, June 24, 2020, 1347h

The affluent community of Dover Heights, an eastern suburb of Sydney, sits on top of a cliff overlooking the Tasman Sea. A grassy verge runs in front of the houses, and a safety fence has been erected along the edge to prevent walkers from accidentally falling over. Fifty-nine-year-old Graham Lane stands in the doorway of his home and briskly rubs his hands together. Dressed in a thick, fur-lined jacket, the 174-centimeter-tall retiree squints his eyes against a cold onshore breeze as he stares out over the ocean. The focus of his attention is a huge bank of dark, foreboding clouds that have been building up several kilometers out to sea since early this morning. The storm has remained stationary, but it's grown heavier, darker, and more threatening by the hour.

His wife is a small, thin woman with straggly shoulder-length hair, easily excitable and often flustered. Martha wears clothes that look a size too big, and they hang rather than fit over her frail body. Yet after more than forty years together, Graham can't imagine life without her. Whether they are good for each other or not, no doubt exists that they rely on one another to survive.

This is the harshest winter Graham can recall. The low temperatures are topping the headlines on every news broadcast and making the front page in the papers. The meteorological center confirmed that a new record of minus two degrees centigrade was recorded at Observatory Hill for one hour and eleven minutes overnight, which beats the previous record set way back in the day—so far back he can't remember it.

He continues to watch the storm clouds for a while longer. The clouds boil furiously from the surface and surge to a high altitude on strong updrafts, where they spill outward to form a huge anvil. The cell is organizing itself into a fearsome entity that'll deliver a powerful punch if it decides to move ashore.

With a shiver, he steps back into the warmth of the house and removes his jacket. After hanging it on a coatrack, he ambles toward the living room. Martha hurries into the hallway from the kitchen and heads for the same door, reaching the portal one step ahead of her husband.

"That's one mean-looking mother out there," he says.

She brushes past him through the doorway as if he isn't there. "Aw, don't worry about it, Gramps," she answers in a thin, whiney voice. She bustles across the room and picks something up from the sideboard. "We gots more concerns to fret over on this earth than a drop of rain."

She breezes back out of the room, and he shakes his head in stupefaction. Martha has a strange conception of life that he's never been able to interpret, but he's gotten used to it over the years. He sinks into his favorite chair and picks up the remote to increase the volume of the television. The newscaster is summarizing the headlines.

Graham calls out to his wife. "Martha, bring me a Foster's from the cooler."

He can hear some unintelligible mutterings from the kitchen. A few moments later, she blusters into the living room and hurries over to her husband. Without saying a word, she stretches an arm out at shoulder level and lets the canned beverage fall from her hand. He grimaces and, with a deft movement of his right hand, snatches it from midair just before it lands on his genitalia. Martha is already heading back toward the door as if she's late for something important. She's been in a feisty mood ever since she woke up this morning, and though he has no idea what's eating her, she's acting as if he should.

"God *damn* it, Martha. You didn't even crack it for me," he complains. He never expects her to wait on him, but because of her strange temperament, he wants to rankle her a little more.

"Why don't you ask me to drink it for you too?" she retorts as she disappears into the hallway once again.

Graham shrugs, pops the top with a hiss, and settles into the armchair. He turns his attention to Quinton Andrews, who is talking about the cold snap.

"This chilly weather is being brought to us by a bizarre wind condition," the meteorologist tells his TV audience. "A massive stream of bitter air is being swept up from Antarctica and pulled across the Australian continent, but the real problem ..."

Graham is startled by a scream from the kitchen and almost drops the beer can. He leaps to his feet and mutters under his breath as he bounds across the living room. "Martha, Martha, what the hell have you done this time?" The retiree charges down the hallway and bursts through the kitchen door. Expecting to see the frying pan on fire, or blood spurting out of her hand after slicing herself with a sharp knife, he comes to an abrupt stop and his jaw drops open in bewilderment. His wife is staring out of the window into the back garden, jumping up and down in childish excitement.

"Look, *look, looookae*," she yells, pointing through the glass pane.

Graham's initial response is anger. "Goddamn, woman. You almost gave me a friggin' heart attack."

Martha ignores the rebuke. She's worked herself up into an excited frenzy, and her voice gets squeaky. "Look … quick."

"Okay, okay," he mumbles, irritated by the dramatics as he walks across the room toward her. "Don't get your knickers twisted, woman … I'm coming."

"Look … it's snowing!"

Graham peeks out into the yard to see snowflakes floating past the window. Suddenly energized with as much excitement as his wife, he hurries out of the kitchen and down the hallway, pausing only long enough to snatch his jacket from the coatrack. He pulls the front door open and steps out into the calm but cold air while still inserting his arms into the sleeves. White flakes are falling, and there's been a significant temperature drop in the last ten minutes, but it's something he's not going to dwell on. This is the first time he's ever seen it snow in Sydney, and he looks out over the cliff top at the storm that's been brewing in the Tasman Sea. It's still several kilometers offshore, but the huge black clouds are now moving toward them at a pretty fast lick.

Martha appears in the doorway behind him and walks into the

front garden. Her eyes open wide in wonderment as a white flurry swirls on a light wind eddy. Graham cups a hand to catch one of the flakes and studies the fine particles of ice.

"This isn't snow!" he exclaims disappointedly. "It's graupel."

"Quit complaining, Gramps," Martha scolds. "It's the same thing to me, and it's still so beeeauutiful."

She walks over and stops beside him. Her eyes gaze past him, and he turns in time to see a small sailboat about a kilometer off the coast get engulfed by the black veil. It disappears from sight in an instant.

Unexpectedly, an object flies past his left ear with a short but noisy hiss, and he ducks reflexively.

"Strewth!"

Graham glimpses a white flash from the corner of his eye, but it's gone before he can focus on it. A split second later, there's a loud, metallic clang behind him, and he swings around. His mouth drops open in astonishment as an empty fifty-five gallon drum on the corner of the house teeters and falls over. He had placed it there to serve as a temporary water catch until he could get the drain runoff for the roof gutter repaired, but whatever slammed into the barrel with enough force to bowl it over like a skittle put a huge dent in the side too.

"What the fuck was that?" he says, bewildered. He doesn't see anything in the vicinity, but it was moving so fast it probably ricocheted and could be anywhere. A shiver runs down his spine. He'd just cheated death by less than a couple of centimeters. If it could do that much damage to the drum, a direct hit would have smashed his head open like a watermelon.

The horrific vision is short-lived. A loud crash to his right makes him flinch, and he turns his head in time to see his precious 1947

Riley RMB rocking from side to side. It takes several seconds for his eyes to settle on a twenty-five-centimeter hole in the soft roof panel, and as he gazes at the damage, alarm bells start to go off in his head. A strong gust of wind sweeps across the top of the sea cliff, and he's suddenly consumed with a sense of imminent danger.

Panicked, he turns to his wife. "Get into the house."

Martha is rooted to the spot with a horrified expression on her face. A blast of air catches the front door. It swings on its hinges and slams against the wall with a loud bang. Graham takes a tight grip on his wife's arm and drags her toward the house. *"Get the fuck inside!"* he yells in desperation as he vies to compete with the increasing noise of the wind. He pushes her unceremoniously into the house and grapples with the handle as he fights to pull the door closed. Graham secures the locks and leans with his back against it, panting hard from exertion.

Martha is close to hysteria and starts shouting at her husband in a shrill voice. *"What's happ—argh!"* she screams, and she cowers away, raising her arms protectively over her head as a solid object slams into the front door with a deafening thud. A hard jar transferred through the wood thumps across Graham's shoulder blades, and his reflexive impulse is electric. He leaps away from the door with a pounding heart and cusses unintelligibly beneath his breath. The sound of a loud crash on the roof is almost obliterated by an ungodly shriek as the wind whistles around the corners and through the eaves of the house. The structure trembles on its foundations, and a terrified Graham races down the hallway to a door beneath the stairs.

"Get down into the cellar!" he yells as he yanks it open, but Martha is petrified in sheer terror and doesn't move. A spasm of panic rises into Graham's chest, and he bellows out to her again. "Get your arse downstairs, you stupid fuckin' bitch."

A round white projectile smashes through the decorative oval window in the center of the door panel and misses the woman by a couple of centimeters before embedding itself into the opposite wall.

"Jesus Christ!" Graham exclaims in horror. A gigantic hailstone close to 250 millimeters in diameter is glaring back at him like an evil white eye. Without a second thought, he charges back along the hallway to his wife, and taking a firm grip on her arm for a second time, he pulls her forcefully to the cellar door. Fearful she might fall down the stairs, he picks the quivering woman up in his arms and, taking care not to lose his own footing, carries her down to the basement. He stands her back on her feet and races up to close the door.

Martha is whimpering and shaking in fear. The sound of the wind is subdued from the basement, and taking her hand, Graham leads her across to the far corner beneath the strongest part of the house.

"Sit down." She is trembling so hard that he is scared she'll end up falling over, and he forces her to the floor. The noise above their heads is muffled but getting louder, and she begins to moan. He makes her as comfortable as he can before lowering himself onto the cold concrete beside her. Seconds later the electricity goes out, plunging the windowless room into pitch blackness. He wraps his arms around her shoulders and pulls the terrified woman close to him, unsure if he can comfort her when he's feeling so afraid too.

The best Hollywood script could never generate the amount of dread and horror the couple endures over the next twenty minutes. Huddled together in the darkness, Graham is certain they are reliving the last minutes of their lives. A loud explosion above their heads sends a sharp jolt reverberating through the concrete floor and the walls of the cellar. The aging couple wrap their arms tightly around each other as their dark world shakes and trembles as if it is in the throes of a miniature earthquake. A noise scarier than anything Graham has heard before echoes down through the ceiling. The demonic howl of the wind and the deafening pounding of giant hail could easily be a legion of hellish ghouls trying to smash their way through to them. The racket is so loud he can't even hear himself shout.

The cellar trembles harder, and the crescendo from above sounds like a dozen freight trains have taken a detour through their home at the same time. Graham doesn't relinquish his protective hold around Martha for a single moment, and though he can't hear her, he can sense his wife's fearful moans through their body contact. The combined effect of the darkness, noise, and shaking is so terrifying that her body has become rigid, and he's worried that she'll go into cardiac arrest.

Fifteen minutes pass with no abatement, but to the Lanes, cringing in terror, it's a lifetime. Then, as quickly as it started, the storm passes. The silence that descends over them is so sudden it's as frightening as the noise of the tornado was, and for several minutes the terrified couple remain in their refuge. Martha sobs uncontrollably with her head buried in her husband's shoulder, and as he holds her in silence, he realizes that the grim reaper paid them a visit and left empty-handed.

After five minutes, he plucks up the courage to go upstairs. He's worried about what he might see, and afraid to speak in a loud voice, he whispers to his wife. "Martha, wait here while I go upstairs and check things out."

She doesn't respond but continues to weep as he gets to his feet. The retiree makes his way slowly to the foot of the wooden staircase. Feeling for the risers in the darkness with his toes, he begins a cautious ascent. Graham reaches the door and pauses with a hand on the doorknob while he presses an ear against the wooden panel. He listens for any unusual sounds on the other side, but all seems to be quiet. He turns the knob and pushes the door. It doesn't budge. He shoves harder. It gives a little, but something behind is preventing it from opening. He leans his shoulder against it, and applies a steady force. The door opens wide enough to allow him to squeeze through.

His jaw drops open in utter disbelief. The sun streams down from a cloudless blue sky, and Graham finds himself in a doorway beneath a partial staircase, which is the only upright structure left standing in the ravaged community. Dover Heights has been reduced to fifteen square kilometers of flattened wasteland. Every home was picked up by an enormous vortex, and the debris lies scattered over incredible distances far beyond the district.

"Bloody Norah," Graham whispers in breathless awe. He's unable to grasp the scale of the disaster, and he's not sure if he should laugh or cry at the paradox. His prized Riley RMB sits amid a bed of wheel-deep hail, crushed beyond recognition. The roof has been pummeled into the seats, the boot is dented beyond repair, and the bonnet has been hammered down so hard it now has the shape of the valve cover. He's unable to gauge his emotional status and rips his eyes away from the automobile.

People who were fortunate to have a retreat where they could escape from the freak storm are emerging from their shelters. Not far away, something pokes up through the giant balls of ice, and as his eyes focus on the object, he recoils in revulsion. An open hand with its fingers partially curled reaches up through the hail, and the white surface in the immediate vicinity is stained with red where the warm blood has seeped through from underneath before congealing. In other places, the icy chunks have started to thaw, slowly revealing the pummeled bodies of dozens of victims who were stoned to death in their homes. Many have been battered with such severity that they're beyond visual recognition, and the gory scenes make Graham feel nauseated. There's little doubt in his mind that Mother Nature's vicious blitz was of incomprehensible proportions.

Martha's trembling voice floats up from the cellar. "Gramps? Is everything okay?"

"You'd better stay down there for a bit," he calls back, but how can he break something like this to her gently?

"Why? I don't want to stay down here."

A scuffle from below warns him that she's making her way up the stairs. The best way is probably to let her see for herself. "We don't have a house anymore, Martha. Our home is gone … it's *all gone* …"

Her voice rises to a shrill pitch. "*Whaaat?*"

She pushes her way through the cellar doorway and stands beside him. Graham puts a comforting arm around her shoulder, and the couple simply look around in silence. Even the sound of emergency vehicle sirens and the distinct chopping of helicopter rotors somewhere in the blue sky above don't offer any comfort.

22

Infinity Meteorological Database Systems, Inc.
Hamilton Ave, Palo Alto, California
Coordinates: 37° 26' 40.3" N, 122° 09' 36.2" W
Wednesday, June 24, 2020, 1506h

Brad scratches the side of his head and stares at the monitor with a perplexed expression on his face. Nothing has panned out. He sits back and rubs his eyes. Danny had checked in when he returned from lunch with Steve.

"Do you still want me to search for the virus, BB?"

The CTO answered without taking his eyes away from the screen. "No. You can punt for a bit until I'm ready to assign you. Jim called in and said he'd be late because of a family emergency, but he should be in by four or five."

Since then, two hours of silence have passed. Brad sits back and rubs his eyes. They are getting sore from staring constantly at the monitor. "What are you up to, Danny?"

While waiting for instructions from his boss, the young

technician had embarked on a series of capricious mini-tasks to keep his mind active. "I'm testing the sensors on the Australian unit, and I've found something a little unusual."

The latter part of Danny's sentence captures Brad's interest. "What is it?"

"I'm getting a brief spike in the current at the database interface when information is submitted by one of the astral sensors, but it's so small I can't see how it would have a negative impact. It's about one thousandth of a microamp."

Brad mulls it over for several moments. "It's probably nothing more than the transference of data. It's too small to be anything else."

"That was my first assessment, too, but when I tried to find out what the peak parameters are, I couldn't find any references about it in the technical manual."

"It's probably under a different section."

Danny shrugs. "It doesn't matter. I made comparisons with a few of the other satellites instead."

"Did it reveal anything worth exploring?"

"Yes—at least I think so. A similar spike is produced when the same sensor exchanges data with the database on the units that have gone offline, but when I ran a similar check on a couple of the operational satellites, it isn't there."

Brad gets to his feet, walks over to Danny's terminal, and looks over his shoulder at the monitor. "What sensor are you activating?"

"The one that maps the sun."

An idea slips into the CTO's head. "Access the stored files and compare the technical data of its last successful transmission and the first communication where the error message comes up."

"I've already done that, and there is no spike prior. The first peak is concurrent with the first error message."

This ignites a new flame of hope. Brad suppresses the expectation that they may be on to something at last because he can't perceive any logical reason why such a minuscule power surge would result in a shutdown of the onboard systems. The function of the astral sensor is basic; it is the least complex of them all. They've run multiple diagnostics, which would've picked up on anything unusual; but they didn't, and that casts more doubt over the significance of the spikes. The fact that they are there at all intrigues him and because it's the only thing to come up in sixty hours, he decides that it should at least be eliminated as the cause.

"Come over to my desk," Brad says, walking back to his terminal. "You can explain to me how you discovered it."

"I wish I could impress you by offering a technical justification, but I can't," Danny replies. "I found it by pure accident."

Brad looks at him and smiles. "I'm still impressed."

The two men are huddled at Brad's console, conversing in epigrammatic phrases, when the electric locks on the entrance door activate with a clunk. Steve storms into the lab, and he's barely inside when he launches into a furious tirade.

"Are you two going to get a handle on this, or do I need to bring in someone who knows what the fuck they're doing?"

Danny's jaw drops open, but Brad remains unreceptive to Steve's rant. Without taking his eyes away from the monitor he ignores the CEO and speaks to Danny in the same low tone they'd been conferring in. "I'm going to override the code dominion, which will allow us to progress through the sequence by manual input." His fingers flit over the keyboard as he punches some commands into the computer.

Danny looks flustered but continues the dialogue with his boss. "Can we slow it down enough to make a reasonable prognosis, though?"

Steve stands behind the two men, shrugs, and gesticulates with his hands to convey a sense of incredulity. "Am I a nobody now?"

"Yes," Brad replies in an unruffled voice, but his answer is in response to Danny's question although he's sure the CEO will think he's replying to him. The technician's furtive glances between himself and their visitor don't go unnoticed.

"Oh, disregard him," he adds evenly.

Steve is seething. "*What* the *fuck?*"

BB swivels around in the chair to face his partner. "I will talk to you when you've calmed down and stopped threatening my staff. But if you think you can bring someone else in to resolve this, please, be my guest. Danny and I will go home and leave you to work things out among yourselves."

Steve pulls a seat toward the console, sinks into it, and buries his face into his hands for a few seconds. He makes no apology for his outburst but lowers his voice to a more acquiescent level. "The UK satellite went down, just as you said it would."

Brad remains silent but glares sturdily at his friend.

"I've just come from a tense meeting with our financial advisors," Steve continues after a several moments. "Wall Street has hit us so hard I'm not sure we'll be able to recover once we're back in business again."

"Don't be pessimistic," Brad says, but the news disturbs him. "How much have we lost?"

"Thirty minutes before the close of business, our stocks dropped three point five percent," Steve says. "The last half hour saw an unprecedented sell-off, and I think we now hold the biggest loss recorded for a private company in a single day of trading. We are down by fifty-three percent at the final bell, and the futures are *not* looking good."

Brad feels the blood draining from his face and turns back to the computer without responding. He can't afford to dwell on the subject, because it'll distract him from the immediate issues at hand, and he switches the subject away from their pecuniary woes. "We're following a fragile thread, though I'm not sure if it'll lead to anything significant yet."

The CEO leans forward to get a clear view of the monitor between the shoulders of the two technicians. "What is it?"

"Danny discovered a minor surge in the current at the database interface when an astral mapping sensor activates. I'm not sure what relevance it might have, but it's only happening on the nonoperational satellites."

"How long before you know?"

"Oh, only a few minutes, I hope," Brad replies.

New columns of figures appear on the screen, and a minute later, Danny points to one of the rows on the screen. "Isn't this the intel collected by the astral sensor?"

"Yes," Brad confirms, and he turns to look at Steve. "I'm doing an inspection of the sun-mapping data by advancing each step manually through the sequence." He returns his attention to the monitor but continues to explain the progress of each event for the benefit of the CEO. "Okay, the collected data are in the RAM ... and now it requests confirmation of the sunrise and sunset times from the database." He pauses to type in a recovery string. "It's searching for the relevant file ... and here is where it recovers the appropriate information."

"What information is included in the database report?" Danny asks.

"A preset chart pertinent to the present date and time at specified coordinates, and nothing more," Brad replies, tapping another string into the keyboard. "Reoccurring info is stored in the database, which keeps space freed up in the random access memory for new data. Comparisons are made with the ROM and are discarded when a match is confirmed. It prevents the RAM from getting cluttered with redundant files."

"Will it overwrite the files in the database with new information if there's a discrepancy between the readings?" Steve asks.

"No, the database *can't* be overwritten. The only way to do that is to erase and reprogram via the master disc. Whenever anything is conflicted"—he glances toward the thousands of servers that take up more than half the space in the soft lab—"it's flagged for further research. We upgrade the onboard equipment with anything that needs to be updated or modified, but that almost never happens anymore."

Brad enters another command string. "Okay, it's found the information, and it's being inspected by the RAM." He progresses to the next event with a series of taps on the keyboard. "Now the new data are compared to that being read." He taps the Enter key. "And this is where validation occurs ... *oh*."

"Hey, *that's* the spike," Danny says excitedly. His finger is pointing to a set of readings halfway down the data column on the monitor.

"What's going on?" Steve asks, sounding anxious.

Brad suddenly feels energized. "The error code has been invoked. The spike is initiating the system shutdown. Now we know the source of the problem, but we need to figure out the reason behind it."

Puzzled wrinkles form across Danny's brow. "A data mismatch between the database and the solar map sensor?"

The question perplexes BB, too, and he takes a moment to

ponder. "I can't see how. We've used the same solar records since the launch of the first satellite. All the sensors do is revalidate it with every reading."

"Perhaps that's where the virus is?" Steve suggests. "Are you able to reconfigure the forecast structure to bypass the sunset and sunrise information, and isolate the sensor? That should contain the virus and prevent it from escaping to another location."

Brad's response is distant. "That *might* work. The astral data aren't an integral part of the forecast, and they're on the Internet for anyone who needs them. Television and radio broadcasters use …" His voice trails off.

"What?"

"I'm not sure," BB mutters, and he turns to Danny. "I want you to scrutinize the data coding and algorithms two seconds prior to, and follow through to three seconds beyond, the peak of the spike. If a virus is lodged in the interface, that's where you'll find it. Let's eliminate that probability once and for all."

Steve inclines his head to one side. "Clarke Richards told me that the Chameleon is made up of more than one code that can separate and take refuge in any file in the system. It's undetectable because it duplicates the codes of the file it's hiding in."

"Ahh, now I understand," Danny says. "Because we know exactly when and where the code is coming together, you think we should be able to trap it by isolating the sensor at the precise time of activation?"

"That's what I have in mind," The CEO says, smiling for the first time today. "The FBI forensics team will be more than appreciative to get their hands on a complete virus."

Brad is growing more annoyed. His partner is so obsessed with the idea that a malicious code is responsible for their misgivings that it's given him tunnel vision. "*Christ*, Steve, you're making it sound like a jog in the park. Anyone smart enough to write a devious code like the Chameleon will have made sure it has the ability to clone itself once inside the targeted network."

Steve looks startled by the remark. "What do you mean?"

"The pieces that connect will be clones sent out on a suicide mission. Once they do the deed, they self-destruct before they can be purged by the system's security software while the master hangs out in a safe place to reproduce again when it's ready. Short of scrubbing the operating system clean and reinstalling everything from scratch, we'll never get rid of it."

Steve has a dubious look in his eyes. "I thought you tried reprogramming?"

"I did, and that validates my point. The code is either in Krazy Kath, which is practically impossible, or our services are *not* being compromised by a virus, period."

"I think you're wrong."

Brad hesitates. "Everyone is entitled to an opinion, but you've forgotten one small detail."

"What would that be?"

"The virus is lodged in a computer that's in orbit. It's not something the FBI can pick up and carry off to their laboratory for examination."

"Can't you download it to disc?"

Brad snorts. "I would never recommend such a dangerous undertaking. If it gets loose down here, it'll definitely be over for us. For now I need to figure out how to reroute the forecast routines around the astral sensor without interrupting the millions of other calculations that are going on."

"What should I tell our customers ... and the media?"

The question horrifies him. *"Don't* make a public statement yet."

A dark scowl forms on Steve's face. "Why not? We need to release some positive news to try to reverse the sell-off trend on Wall Street."

Brad sighs. "I know you're keen to instigate damage control, but a presumptuous announcement at this juncture could be more damaging and detrimental to our integrity than staying quiet. Once you issue a press release, the media will want a detailed explanation, and the subscribers will expect their satellites to be back in service within hours. If that doesn't happen, then you've paved the way for a total disaster."

Steve doesn't put up an argument, but Brad can see he's far from happy. The CEO decides to go back up to his office, and as the security doors close behind him, BB turns to Danny. "You look like you have a question?"

"What gives you the idea that this *isn't* a malicious code?"

Brad leans back in the chair, and fold his arms. "A couple of things preclude a virus. What we know so far would indicate that something pretty darn complex would need to be tailor-written to each satellite and introduced one at a time."

"I concur, that's risky," Danny says. "The chance of detection would be far too high for anyone to hack into each individual unit."

"That's right, but now the second question is, how many people in the world could author a malicious code?"

Danny frowns. *"Huh?* I'd say hundreds of thousands ... perhaps even millions."

The CTO shakes his head. "You've missed the point. Let me rephrase. How many people are capable of writing one that's customized with a specific intent to strike at *our* satellites?"

"Oh ..." The technician falters on the first syllable.

Brad can tell by Danny's facial expression that the implication has dawned on him. "A total of five—excluding Steve—because I know he doesn't have the knowledge to even write a basic program. A customized virus could only be written by someone with an intimate understanding of our network, and that narrows the field of candidates down somewhat."

Danny appears dumbfounded by his revelation and speaks in a hushed voice. "You, Bill, Jim, and myself. That's four."

"What about your friend who used to work here?"

The technician's eyes open wide in surprise. "Harvey? You *can't* be think—"

Brad cuts him off midsentence. "Not for a single moment. That's why I'm adamant that something else other than the Chameleon is at the root of this mess."

"Steve will go loopy if he knows we've stopped looking for a virus."

Brad smiles. "Don't worry about Steve. I'll handle him. I'm your immediate supervisor, and we have to work out how to isolate the sensor without allowing a gaggle of conflicted statements to run wild in the system, but first …" He turns back to the console, leaving the sentence unfinished.

23

The Oval Office
The White House, Washington, DC
Coordinates: 38° 53' 50.6" N, 77° 02' 14.5" W
Wednesday, June 24, 2020, 1559h

Tiny globules of sweat bead the forehead of the forty-fifth president of the United States. This is the hottest June on record, and meteorologists have warned that no relief is projected for the foreseeable future. Every nation across the Northern Hemisphere is reporting temperatures that are broken almost daily, and concerns that it's a step up in global warming have alarmed ecologists.

President Lloyd Sinclair is a robust, high-energy, fifty-six-year-old. He stands five feet ten inches tall with broad shoulders and a sculpted body that suggests a regular fitness regimen and a health-conscious diet. His facial features are chiseled and clean shaven. He has amber eyes and sports a full head of curly brown hair treated with Grecian Formula to hide the gray.

He's an avid gardener with a special passion for roses. When he moved into the White House, he allowed his fifty-three-year-old wife and first lady, Diane, to assume full authority of the internal furnishings and decor while he made a controversial transformation to the rose garden. By the end of the first summer, it resembled an English country garden. The only structure missing is a rustic thatched cottage at the end of the winding gravel pathway that cuts through the center of the lawn. The trail is lined with a wide variety of rosebushes both common and rare. Set behind them are rose trees carpeted in colorful blooms.

Lloyd pauses and looks around with pride. This is his haven—his world away from politics. It's where he prefers to hang out in his spare time instead of playing golf like many of his predecessors. Here he can relax, gather his wits, and make peace with the world. His favorite time is early evening, when the sun is sinking and the heat of the day is on the wane. That's when the soothing aroma of roses drifts and swirls around on an imperceptible movement of air, hugging the pathway and clinging to everything around.

The war cry that won the election in 2016 was his hard-line, no-nonsense policies against Islamic State fundamentalists and jihadist groups. He made good on many of the promises, but the last twelve months saw a decline in popularity. Although he still clings to the lead in the polls, they are in the final months of an election year, and it's necessary to discuss new tactics with his campaign manager in an attempt to reverse the trend. He's a decisive leader, but tenacity is his one outstanding fault. Most of his decisions are calculated, but once made, they stick. This doesn't mean that every call he makes is met with approval, and there have been times when he's backed himself into a corner by making a rush to judgment.

Damage control is not his forte, but the admission of a mistake grinds against the egotistical side of his nature.

Every president inherits the country's domestic and foreign turmoil from the previous administration and passes on a different set of issues to the next when he leaves office. Relations with the Chinese over the construction of artificial islands in the South China Sea deteriorated into a military standoff in November of 2017, but the North Korean dictator, Kim Jong Un, stunned the world on New Year's Eve by launching a horrendous triple attack in support of their alliance with China. A barrage of missiles intended to hit US military and naval targets on Guam were intercepted long before they got close to the Micronesian island in the Western Pacific. The Japanese made a valiant effort to destroy the rockets meant for them, but one got through. Amid the peal of bells, firework displays, and celebrations, it exploded in a densely populated suburb of Tokyo, killing more than seven hundred civilians. Another two thousand suffered life-altering injuries. However, his savage attack on the South Korean city of Seoul was brutal, successfully hitting 75 percent of the civilian targets marked for attack. His grand finale was a nuclear warhead, and it was fortunate for sixty million citizens that it failed to detonate. The despot was so incensed his signature event was a dud that he ordered more than a million ground troops across the border in a bloody orgy of murder, pillage, and rape.

President Sinclair was reluctant to commit the nation to another war, but he had no alternative but to act in accordance with the military alliance treaty. With full congressional approval, he authorized the deployment of the largest military defensive in US history but fell short of sanctioning the direct engagement of ground troops across the North Korean border.

The world's top psychologists have never been able to unravel the complexities of Kim's mindset, which gave him the impression he could manipulate the South China Sea dispute to his advantage. It's not known whether China instigated the North Korean offensive or whether it was a singular decision by Kim, but suspicions of Chinese involvement were aroused when the leadership delayed their condemnation for more than a week. Field intelligence hinted that China gave false promises to support North Korea militarily in exchange for the initiation of limited hostilities on the south. It's thought to have been a diversionary tactic, but Kim went too far, and the Asian superpower was forced to back off. Instead of honoring the pledge, they distanced themselves from the North Korean leader.

One month later, Israel discovered an underground facility in northeastern Iran where Persian scientists were engaged in the full enrichment of uranium in defiance of the Joint Comprehensive Plan drawn up in 2015. An enraged President Reuven Beinisch didn't hesitate to take action, but because of its depth, the construction was impervious to bunker bombs and penetration missiles. Bound to yet another treaty he couldn't back down from, he committed two hundred thousand ground troops to the defense of the Jewish state.

Lloyd sighs and ascends the steps to the oval office. The vice president should be arriving at any moment for a briefing on the Middle East crisis, and as he closes the doors, his eyes fall on a copy of the *New York Times* lying on top of his desk. The bold headlines across the front page glare up at him. "Is Syria a Russian State?" The strangely complex war against ISIS in Syria and Iraq took a new twist earlier in the week. Unconfirmed reports that the Russians had detained Bashar al-Assad and assumed authoritative control over the nation triggered a wave of fear throughout the western coalition. An extraordinary emergency session of the United Nations Security Council was called, and the secretary of state had called with an update thirty minutes earlier.

The northwest door opens, and Terry Schofield saunters into the Oval Office with one hand thrust deep into a pocket. The first words out of his mouth are a complaint.

"*Jesus!* It's *hot* out there."

President Sinclair nods in agreement and waits for him to sit. Lloyd and the five-foot-eleven-inch, 220-pound vice president have known each other for years, although Terry's physique hasn't held up as well. His face is lined, and a receding hairline gives him the appearance of being the older of the two men.

"I suppose you've read the headlines in the *New York Times*?"

"Yes, and I'm trying to find out how legitimate the claim is, but they won't reveal their source—privacy agreement and all that bullshit."

"No need to worry about it, Terry. I spoke to Brian a short time ago," Lloyd says, referring to the secretary of state.

"How long is he going to be in Geneva?"

"He's on his way back."

"Already?"

The president stares at Terry with a grim expression on his face. "I told him to walk out. We need to find a way to revoke Russia's position on the security council."

The vice president gazes back at him with astonishment in his eyes. "That's never going to happen."

"The Russians have announced that Syrian airspace will be under their control as of midnight, and unauthorized aircraft will be intercepted and shot down by their fighters or surface-to-air missiles."

"Under whose authority?"

"Direct from President Bazhenov."

"An announcement like that can only be authorized by al-Assad."

"Brian asked them if they have annexed, or intend to annex, Syria as a Russian state; they refused to confirm or deny. He delivered a message to the security council from me and then left."

Terry inclines his head inquiringly. "Which is?"

"Our airstrikes on ISIS in Syria will continue, and if any coalition fighters are shot down, it will be deemed a deliberate act of war. The motion was backed by France, Great Britain, and the ten nonmembers who walked out with Brian."

"China?"

Lloyd snorts. "What do *you* suppose? Tien's second home is inside Bazhenov's pants."

"What actions have you authorized so far?"

"None yet. Until they shoot down any of our aircraft or make a declaration that Syria is Russian territory, we are not at war. NATO has called an emergency meeting for later today, and here at home, I want SWAT teams placed on standby, but out of sight, close to every Russian embassy in the country."

"*SWAT* teams?"

"Yes. When they fire that first missile, we will execute an immediate hostile takeover of all five consulates."

"What about plans for action abroad?"

"I will wait until I see what resolutions are made at the NATO meeting first."

Terry nods and switches the subject. "What about this other business with the weather satellites?"

The president sits back in his chair and ruminates over the

question before responding. "It's not our practice to interfere with a private business unless it poses a threat to national security. While they're not precipitating such a risk, it has provoked tensions among our allies and other crucial relationships. Foreign companies and governments poured billions of dollars into a system developed by an American company of their own free will, and now they expect us to accept partial liability? There's no chance of that happening. It's up to Infinity to acknowledge accountability, which I believe they have, and they're the ones who need to resolve it."

"We shouldn't ignore it and pretend it doesn't exist, either," Terry warns. "There will be some nasty negatives if we do."

"Elaborate."

"It's going to strain some of the more tenuous relationships we've spent decades building up, and in addition, the encouragement of international trade growth in US manufactured technology could suffer an interminable shock."

"You're suggesting that we should make this an exception?"

"It's my humble opinion that we can't brush it off to the side without suffering serious repercussions somewhere along the line."

The president muses over Terry's concern for more than a minute before he speaks again. "I think we need to show empathy and give them reassurances that we will take appropriate, but limited, action in their best interests *without* accepting liability."

"I concur, but it's escalating fast, and we need to act before the end of the day."

"I want you to arrange for the feds to step in, but our involvement must be restricted. Make sure the company's business accounts and assets, including the personal chattels of Jaeger and Bentley, are partially frozen at midnight. We will not be liable for any contractual infringements, because that's a negotiated subject between Infinity and the subscriber. Our objective is to secure the maximum amount that can be recovered for restitution."

"What do you mean by 'partially frozen'?"

"Financial control will be held by the feds. The company's access to funds will be restricted to sustain essential expenses, such as employee salaries, utility bills, and expenditures required to maintain enough functionality to resolve the problem. Pecuniary support for projects, production, and research will be suspended."

"That's not going to make them happy."

"Too bad," Lloyd replies. "Their accounts and assets will be unfrozen when the satellites are back online and applicable restitution proportionate to the inconvenience is bestowed to the clientele, or an appropriate compensation is agreed to by negotiation."

"I'll make sure that a federal auditor is appointed to take up residence in their HQ by the start of business tomorrow morning," Terry says.

"I understand their CEO called in an FBI forensics team to investigate. They suspect that the satellites have been compromised by industrial sabotage, so be a little fair and instruct the agent to drop the bad news to company executives before the auditors arrive."

"I don't think *they'll* take it as being fair," Terry replies. "Will the feds be laying off employees?"

"No, that will be a corporate decision, but the auditors are authorized to furlough nonessential staff indefinitely," Lloyd says.

"What about the price tag for our intervention? We can't expect the taxpayer to bear the cost."

"Infinity operates a specialized, one-of-a-kind service, and it's important to ensure its not closed down. I know it doesn't qualify under the Fed's 'too big to fail' policy, but our options are limited. They're still obligated to maintain a service to the satellites that are working."

"We can navigate that ruling because we're not offering the company a bailout loan. Do we have an estimated value of Infinity's assets?"

"We'll know what can be pumped out once the auditors go through their books. That might take up to a week. I'm sure there won't be enough to reimburse the full amount to every litigant if the entire network shuts down, though."

"We'll need to put together a contingency plan in case we have to cross that bridge." A short period of silence follows before Terry speaks again. "I wonder if they have an insurance policy that covers this sort of thing?"

"The auditors will figure that out." The president sighs. "Getting back to the Middle East crisis, I have a briefing with General Morgan in my study at eighteen hundred. I want you there."

"I'll see you then," Terry replies, and he gets to his feet.

After the vice president has left, Lloyd swivels around in his chair and stares through the window into the rose garden. *If only the rest of the world could be as peaceful.*

24

Infinity Meteorological Database Systems, Inc.
Hamilton Ave, Palo Alto, California
Coordinates: 37° 26' 40.3" N, 122° 09' 36.2" W
Wednesday, June 24, 2020, 1637h

Brad is talking on his iPhone when Steve walks into the lab. He called fifteen minutes earlier and asked the CEO to come down, although he didn't elaborate. Steve is optimistic because the techs have taken a step forward, albeit a small one, so he anticipates more good news.

"I *know* what the charts say, Mr. Seville, but I'm trying to get your satellite back into operation again," Steve hears him say as he approaches Brad's console. "It's *crucial* that you get a real-time eyeball tonight *and* in the morning. I'll be waiting for a callback regardless of what the time is." He pauses before he thanks the person on the other end and disconnects.

"Who's Mr. Seville?"

"Alex Seville, head meteorologist at the Alaskan weather center.

I've asked him to carry out a physical check on the time the sun sets tonight and rises in the morning."

Steve gazes at his partner in astonishment. "*That* information is in the database!"

An irritated resonation in Brad's voice warns him to be careful of what he says. "I'm aware of that. I'm not a *complete* moron. I need someone to carry out a physical check, okay?"

The CEO wheels a chair to his partner's workspace. "So you haven't found the problem?"

Brad points to the computer screen. "Look at this."

Steve leans forward to get a good view of the monitor. "I think you need to tell me what I'm looking at."

"These first two columns show the time that the sun is supposed to rise and set. The third and fourth are the actual times registered by the astral sensors. As you can see, they don't match with the database."

He compares the data for almost a minute. "That's impossible! Didn't we set the margins of tolerance well beyond the expected maximum parameters to prevent this exact thing from happening?"

"Happen it did. Why? That's what I'm trying to determine. If you remember, we decided a variable is possible but calculated that it would be less than one thousandth of a second. Precise accuracy isn't critical for the required applications, which is why the data gets rounded up. We allowed a forty-five-second margin of error because it would be impossible to exceed." Brad leans forward and, with the click of a key, opens another window. "These samples are from the failed satellites. The database shows the sun should set over South Georgia at sixteen oh nine and eighteen seconds, but the solar map sensor registers an actual time of sixteen oh seven and twenty-eight seconds. That's a full one minute fifty seconds early—*well* outside the margin of tolerance by two hundred forty-four point four four percent. When it searches the database, the readings conflict with the preset information, and *that's* why the error code is being invoked."

Steve scratches the side of his head, uncertain what to make of this new development. "Did you check the files for inconsistencies? Perhaps it was programmed with the incorrect info for this date?"

"That was the first thing I verified. The database is correct, so the mystery lies in the data being collected by the sensor." He pauses for a moment before reading from a list he compiled in advance. "Stanley, Falkland Islands: The sunset for yesterday was recorded one minute three seconds early. Today the time has increased by forty-seven point six two percent to one minute thirty-three seconds. Yesterday's sunrise in Anchorage, Alaska, was fifty seconds too soon, but this morning it was one minute thirty-four seconds early. The sun rose prematurely in Helsinki, Finland, by one minute seven seconds, and this morning it's one minute fifty-one seconds. Ushuaia, Argentina: Yesterday's sunset was one minute ten seconds in advance, while today it went down one minute forty-four seconds early." Brad turns his eyes toward his partner. "Would you like me to continue?"

Steve has heard enough and responds with a shake of his head. "Did you collect sun-mapping data from the satellites that are still in operation?"

"Yes, and they *all* show a shift in sunrise and sunset times, except they haven't reached the forty-five-second margin yet. That's why they are still online. I recalibrated the sensors, but it hasn't made any difference."

"Does that mean the virus is hiding inside the sensors?"

Brad sits back in his chair and strokes his chin thoughtfully.

"There's a pattern in the way the times are being recorded that's rather discerning. The daylight period in the Southern Hemisphere is still getting shorter instead of longer, while in the north, the reverse is happening—the daylight hours are increasing. This conforms to Newton's third law of motion, which begs the question, why would anyone go to the trouble of writing a code with such complexity when he or she could jeopardize the entire system with something more basic?"

"Who knows what goes through a hacker's mind?" Steve replies bitterly.

"What I'm trying to tell you is that this is well beyond the scope of a virus no matter how multifaceted it might be. If Alex Seville carries out my request like I asked, I will be able to prove it."

Danny interrupts the conversation by calling out in a loud voice, "I've found it."

Steve glances across to the technician. "The virus?"

Brad responds to the question. "No. I had him pull data from the storage banks so we can pinpoint when these anomalies began. We checked the first day of each month, going back six months." He takes a moment to read through some notes scribbled on a piece of paper. "This is the result from one of the Chilean satellites. On the first of January, the sun rose thirty-seven seconds late and set thirty-four seconds late, but on the first of March, it came up thirty-two seconds *early* and sank thirty-one seconds early. That's a swing of one minute nine seconds from late to early over a thirty-one-day period. The sunsets are of an almost equal swing in the opposite direction. The first of May shows that it rose late again by twenty-six seconds and sank twenty-four seconds early."

"That's within the time margin of forty-five seconds, so why is that a problem?"

Steve is surprised by the level of earnestness in Brad's voice. "Those kind of swings shouldn't be *happening*. How did something important like this get missed by scientists?"

"Perhaps they didn't miss it. Maybe they know what the anomaly is and consider it to be inconsequential."

"I can guarantee you they're not unimportant anymore," Brad fires back. "In some way, it has the answer to our satellite problem. The first incidence happened between the first of December, 2019, and the first of January this year."

"How did you figure *that* out?"

"Danny went back another six months to June of last year, and the variations through to December are within the expected parameters. They are negligible: less than five ten thousandths of one percent of one millionth of a second in either direction."

"What's causing the huge swings since January, then?" Steve asks.

"Danny is checking each day through December to find the answer, and in fact ..." he leaves the sentence unfinished as he turns to face the technician who stops between the two men with a piece of paper in his hand.

"December 26, 2019," the young man says. "The sun rose within the normal parameters but set thirty-nine seconds late."

Brad's forehead wrinkles. He connects to the Internet and types the date into the Google search engine. At the top of the first page he reads, "The Andaman Event, December 26, 2019, *Wikipedia*, The Free Encyclopedia."

"Yes, the Andaman Event," the CTO mumbles.

Steve stares at his partner in bewilderment. "Are you trying to tell me that something that happened six months ago is shutting our satellites down *now?*"

"The Andaman Event caused the entire planet to oscillate, swinging back and forth in space like a pendulum," Brad replies. "That explains the strange swings between sunrise and sunset times. The oscillations subsided over subsequent weeks and months, but I was never aware that our equipment could detect anything like this, especially so well defined."

Steve's frustration is growing at his failure to understand the relevance, and he is getting heated up again. "Okay, I *get* that, but what *I* want to know is why it's affecting us *today?*"

The discovery has energized Brad. "It's not the oscillation that's causing the problem. I need to run some more tests, but I won't have a solid answer until Alex Seville calls me back. What I think is happening is too ridiculous for words, so I don't want to be presumptuous."

"If you're not going to tell me, I would suggest you find a way to take the solar map sensors out of the loop so we can get the satellites back online," Steve says with some petulance. "Once they're back in operation, *then* we'll focus on this and get it figured out."

"I'm going to be here all night."

The CEO raises his eyebrows in surprise before he admonishes his partner. "Don't be so stupid. You need to get some sleep, too."

"I'll be okay," Brad replies in a reassuring voice. "Bill will be here with me, and I can snatch a catnap while I'm waiting for the data to upload to the satellites, but I must be here when Alex calls."

Steve studies his friend with a wary glaze in his eyes before heading toward the exit. "I'll bring something back for you to eat between seven and eight," he promises as he leaves the laboratory.

25

*CPC Central Headquarters
Zhongnanhai, Jing-Jin-Ji, China
Coordinates: 39° 54' 55.4" N, 116° 23' 04.3" E
Wednesday, June 24, 2020, 1800h*

With his usual punctuality, Yuan Tien enters the conference chamber where the other six members of the standing committee are waiting. He walks at a brisk pace to the empty chair at the head of the table, opens a briefcase, and pulls out several documents. Yuan is the general secretary of the central committee, the country's leader, and a perfectionist who expects nothing less from everyone else. They wait for the chairman to sit before following suit, and as the rustling dies down, the bespectacled premier adjusts the glasses on the bridge of his nose.

"The North Korean issue is on today's agenda," he says with brusqueness, which is a characteristic warning that his mood is temperamental. In general, he is soft-spoken, but everyone on the committee has fallen foul to his wrath more than once. "The implementation of the air defense identification zone was calculated to antagonize the Japanese, American, and South Korean administrations. Each operation we've carried out since has been conspired to irritate them while reinforcing autonomy over our own territory. It's advantageous to understand the enemy, but as witnessed, unforeseen and dangerous elements can blight the perfect equation. Kim Jong Un's missile strikes on Guam, Tokyo, and Seoul were unjustified despite his claim that they were made as a sympathetic gesture for China."

"Someone at this table inspired him to believe it's what we wanted him to do," Sun declares. His suspicions that Kim was set up as a pawn in a greater plan is confirmed by Yuan's demeanor. He's too calm not to be in the loop of a preexisting arrangement with the dictator.

Mao clears his throat. "Negotiations *were* taking place with regard to a specific operation. The details are classified, but the maneuver was postponed at the outbreak of hostilities."

Sun appears offended and sweeps an arm around the table. "I protest strongly. We are here to govern, and one individual doesn't have the authority to carry out a surreptitious act without the approval of this committee."

"The proposal would have been laid out before this committee once the minutiae had been established, but Kim added his own twisted touch without our knowledge. Ninety-five percent of what occurred was of his own volition. I give surety that our consultations did not include military action against the Americans and Japanese."

Yuan interrupts, afraid that Mao is about to pin himself into a corner. "Kim's desire for an armed conflict with the West has consumed him for some time, but let's not forget that despite the bravado, he is fearful of defeat. He's an opportunist who tried to use the South China Sea dispute to engage us militarily with the enemies of the DPRK as his ally, but he made a gross miscalculation. It was a foolish move unsanctioned by this committee, and our refusal to cross that boundary irks him."

Chiang Yat-sen, the committee's vice chairman, speaks. "The Western world still believes we encouraged him with promises of military support we failed to keep."

Yuan takes a deep breath. "Earlier today, I had an audience with an emissary for the North Korean diplomatic agency on behalf of Kim Jong Un. They are making a formal appeal for assistance that extends beyond the aid we've rendered to date. The mess he's gotten himself into is of his own conception, and he is undeserving of our benevolence, but his foolishness has put us in an unsatisfactory position. We cannot allow the regime to collapse to a Western power or an alliance state of the same. We need to take some course of action to prevent them from occupying a country whose border butts up against ours."

"We are providing munitions and limited hardware," Mao Xiaoping says. "That shouldn't be construed as a gesture of goodwill. The purpose is to extend the conflict to give us time to implement a plan that leads to a more favorable solution."

Chiang looks at him. "The American, South Korean, and Japanese coalition will not stop while Kim is in power. They want his head. We are lucky the Americans took up a defensive stance in the South, but we don't know how long the status quo will last. South Korea's strike-and-retreat tactics are working for us at the moment, but the rate of success is questionable, and they're not going to keep that strategy indefinitely."

"I don't think the intention is occupation," Mao argues. "Their primary directive is to undermine and destroy North Korea's nuclear capabilities for decades into the future. There are no doubts they will eventually succeed in this goal. The US secretary of state called me last night. He believes we can influence Kim and has asked us to intervene diplomatically to bring the conflict under control. We need to take advantage of the opportunity so we can manipulate the outcome to our benefit."

"Interesting," Zhu Duxiu mutters. "I expect they're making specific demands?"

"Yes," Yuan confirms. "They want Kim's unconditional surrender, and for him to place himself into the custody of the United Nations."

"We all know *that* won't happen," Chiang retorts, "and neither can we agree to such conditions. The best they can hope for is a truce, which, as we are all aware, will be celebrated as a victory by the North Koreans. What we *don't* want is his capture or assassination. It will throw the country into greater turmoil with repercussions that will place *us* at a grave disadvantage."

"No, we can give them Jong Un," Zhu says, enthusiastically. "What we need to do first is force a change in leadership."

Yuan holds a hand up in a signal for silence. "I have not responded to the American request yet. The Japanese want him because the missile strike on Tokyo was an unwarranted, vicious attack on a civilian target. The South Koreans want him for the unprovoked bombardment of Seoul and for sending a nuclear warhead that failed to detonate only because someone forgot to arm it before launching." He pauses for a moment. "We will arrange for a dialogue with Kim to broker a truce agreement between the United States, South Korea, and Japan. A cease-fire must be implemented first, but because of our own interests, I'm *not* prepared to go further than that."

"We need a secondary plan," Chiang responds. "I'm convinced this idea is doomed to fail."

"We can't allow anything less than a Communist power to govern the north, and if Kim won't comply, we will fund a coup to force a regime change. He *can't* be replaced by someone from his own administration, though." Yuan looks from one committee member to the next while he speaks. "We will groom someone who is politically motivated and believes in the values of communism to assume control, but he must be a man we can influence once he's in power."

"Do we know where Kim is or how we can contact him?" Mao asks.

Yuan stares back at him with an icy glaze in his eyes. The committee man bites his lip, realizing the mistake he's just made.

"Not yet, but I'll give you that opportunity," the general secretary says softly. Whenever a hurdle is placed in the way, Yuan never fails to assign the task of clearing it to the person who put it there. Mao has a habit of falling into the trap.

The chairman leans forward, rests his forearms on the conference table, and clasps his hands together. "I'm sure it will take a little time, so I hope you'll have the necessary information by this time next week." Yuan gives him a cold smile before glancing around at the rest of the committee. "Meanwhile, I have sent more ground troops to our border with the North. They've been ordered to establish a thirty-kilometer dead zone to prevent unauthorized crossings. We will not accept refugees, and anyone found within the boundaries of the prohibited region will be killed regardless of status or nationality. Our own people who live within that region will have twenty-four hours to evacuate."

The chairman glances around the table. "Do we have any other business that needs to be addressed?"

Chiang stands up. "Yes. There are sporadic pockets of civil disobedience in the Da Hinggan Ling prefecture, Heilongjiang Province. The weather in the North is unusually hot this summer, and they are demanding a temporary change in work ethic so they're not exposed to the heat at the peak of the day."

"What calefaction are we talking about?" Zhu asks.

"Thirty-five degrees centigrade."

"*That's* not *hot!* Perhaps they should work in the South, and experience *real* incalescence."

"The average summer temperature in the Heilongjiang region is twenty-three degrees," Chiang replies. "They've had more than a month of temperatures well above normal, and too many incidents of heat fatigue are occurring. I'm going to dispatch additional police into the area to quell further disturbances."

"Do it," Yuan barks. "A hot summer is *no* excuse for insubordination. Be sure they are aware the penalties will be harsh for anyone who fails to comply."

The chairman turns his eyes toward Mao. "Are the security plans completed for next Wednesday's celebrations?"

July 1 is the CPC Founding Day, but this year it will be special. The integration of Beijing, Tianjin, and seven other cities in Hebei Province into a massive megacity will be certified. It will be seventeen times larger than Sydney and have a population in excess of 132 million, which is six times greater than New York. The inauguration will be carried out at midnight in Tiananmen Square, where the renaming of the supercity to Jing-Jin-Ji will become official. The main event will be the largest firework display ever conceived, with the simultaneous launch of shell bursts from more than 200,000 locations. The shells will be fired every second to keep the entire 134,140-square-kilometer region under a red—and, in some places, yellow—umbrella for three minutes. The yellow shells will be strategically placed to display the Chinese flag when observed from the International Space Station, and it will be the first firework display to ever be observed from space. To ensure it will be seen with clarity, all electric power to the supercity will be cut for the three-minute show.

"Yes," Mao replies. "I will be addressing the event organizers on Sunday to ensure the coordination of the celebrations is synchronized."

"Good. You can give us an update on Monday." The chairman closes his briefcase with a snap and gets to his feet. "We will meet at the same time tomorrow."

Yuan dismisses the conference with his usual abruptness and strides toward the door.

26

Infinity Meteorological Database Systems, Inc.
Hamilton Ave, Palo Alto, California
Coordinates: 37° 26' 40.3" N, 122° 09' 36.2" W
Thursday, June 25, 2020, 0758h

A frown forms on Steve's face as he turns right from University Avenue onto Ramona Street. One block ahead is the Infinity tower, and several television and radio news vans are pulled over to one side in the vicinity of the building. A large satellite dish is installed on top of one vehicle, and a tall periscope mast extends into the air from a second van. He slows down on the approach to Hamilton Avenue, where he turns left. A sizeable group of reporters mill around in the courtyard, and a couple of TV cameras have been set up for action. He'd expected an influx of media attention but assumed most of it would go through the company's public relations officer by telephone.

He drives past and turns into the underground car park unobserved. After pulling into the space reserved for him, he remains in the driver's seat and runs through the options open to him. He's reluctant to face the crowd on the forecourt, so he could make his way through to the back and use the service bay entrance. On the other hand, if he ran the gambit, he might be able to use the media to Infinity's advantage. The third alternative would be to sneak back out and go home, but that isn't going to solve anything.

Steve pulls the iPhone from a pocket in his trousers, and dials Brad's number. The ringtone buzzes several time before his partner answers. "BB, are you in the lab?"

"I've been here all night," the CTO reminds him.

"I'm in the car park. Do you know why there are so many news reporters and TV camera crews outside?"

"I didn't know anyone was out there until Danny came in and told me," he confesses. "It seems that our satellite outage is a major focus for the media, you know … front-page news."

Steve groans. That's the kind of publicity he doesn't want. "Did you get the satellites back online?"

"No."

"I thought you were going to bypass the solar sensors?"

Brad hesitates. "It's become a bit more complicated. The lunar map sensor is in disagreement with the database too. It didn't show up, because it's further down in the sequence, and the error code was already invoked prior to running the application."

"You *are* kidding, *right?*"

"I wish I were." He pauses briefly. "I'm pretty confident I know what's going on now, although I must warn you that you'll find it hard to swallow."

"I'm coming straight to the lab," Steve replies, removing the keys from the ignition and climbing out of the car.

"I think you'd better go up to your office first. Nancy's called down a couple of times looking for you. Clarke Richards is waiting in her office, and she says it's urgent."

The CEO opens the rear door to retrieve his briefcase, and a few choice words pass through his head. "Thanks."

He gives the door a sharp push to close it and locks it with the remote pad attached to the key ring. Deciding not to face the press, Steve walks through to the loading bay entrance. He fights a strong desire to head for the lab but stops at the elevators. Clarke needs to be handled first. Once in the office, he removes his jacket and hangs it over the back of the chair. Still on his feet, he leans forward toward the intercom and presses the Speak button.

"Good morning, Mr. Jaeger," Nancy greets in a soft, cheerful voice. "Mr. Richards is waiting to see you."

"Good morning, Nancy. You can send him in."

He sits down, and a couple of seconds later there's a light tap on the door. It opens, and the FBI agent greets the CEO in a somber tone. "Good morning, Mr. Jaeger. I see you have a welcoming committee outside."

Steve gives Clarke a silent invitation to sit with a hand motion as he replies in an enervated voice. "It looks like they've settled in for the duration. It's going to be another hot day, so if I'm lucky, the heat will drive them away."

"I think you know *that* will never happen."

"I hope they get sunstroke, then."

"You *are* in a spiteful mood this morning, aren't you?"

"What do you expect?" Steve replies bitterly.

Clarke averts his eyes from the CEO's gaze to a folder placed across his knees. "I hate to be the bearer of more bad news."

Steve's body stiffens, and he waits for the agent to continue.

"I've been instructed to inform you that Infinity's bank

accounts, investments, and assets were partially frozen at midnight last night. All financial business is now under the supervision of the federal government."

"*What?*" Steve leaps to his feet and places both clenched fists on the desktop to support his body as he leans forward. The FBI agent doesn't appear intimidated by the threatening stance and blazing eyes, but he still gestures defensively. He speaks in an even, almost soothing tone, which has a calming effect on the CEO. "*Please* hear me out, Mr. Jaeger." Clarke waits for Steve to sink back into his chair before he continues. "The order came from the White House, direct from President Sinclair."

"What the hell has *this* got to do with the fucking president?" Steve snaps. "He has no right to stick his nose into my business. How am I supposed to get the satellites back into operation if our financial ability to do so is choked off?"

"It is unprecedented for the White House to interfere with a private business, and I assure you the president is reluctant to do so now. However, he is under pressure from your subscribers who have lost their services. The Russians are calling on the government to take responsible steps to secure their investments and minimize their losses. You know that other nations are going to epitomize their lead, and it gives Mr. Sinclair no choice but to intervene. The crisis has the potential to influence annulments or dissolutions of international agreements currently under negotiation, and other friendships that have taken years to restore since the 2013 NSA scandal. The implementation of federal control is to ensure that maximum funds are available to reimburse your clients."

Steve's tone is bitter. "In other words, he wants to make sure I don't disappear or whisk billions of dollars out of the country."

The agent's admission is blunt. "In a proverbial nutshell, yes. I don't know the finer particulars of the sequestration, but I can tell you that funds required to resolve the crisis will *not* be cut off. It's their intention to transfer financial control back once the satellites are functioning again and the threat of litigation is over."

Steve's tone is morose. "How do they intend to manage it … or us?"

"I'm told that federal auditors will move into your finance department in the next hour or so. Providing your controller and accountants don't complicate, inhibit, or try to undermine their authority with hostile behavior, they will be allowed to stay. It'll be in your best interests to make sure they cooperate."

Steve's head slumps forward, and he gazes with miserable petulance at the floor for several seconds before raising his eyes to look at Clarke again. "My wrists are bound."

"I'm afraid so, but a word of advice, Mr. Jaeger: comply with the auditors' demands. They will do whatever they want regardless of any remonstrations you make. While they're here, they are God."

Steve grunts. "I won't impede them deliberately, but I don't intend to worship them either. I won't get on my knees for anyone except …" He finishes the sentence by turning his eyes upward.

Clarke's nod is almost imperceptible. "As the prime investigator, I did submit a report to the White House early this morning and notified the president that there are strong indications suggesting Infinity is the victim of industrial espionage. It won't alter his current stance, but it will be on record that you took positive steps to counteract the problem prior to the filings." He pauses for a moment. "It's a good thing you called me in when you did."

"At least I should thank you for taking the time to do that. You are still going to continue with your investigation, though, aren't you?"

"Yes, of *course* I am!" the agent exclaims, and he pauses. "Is there anything else you'd like to bring up?"

"Only the foul-tasting bile rising into the back of my throat."

"I understand, Mr. Jaeger, and I wish there were something I could say or do to make you feel more positive." Clarke stands up. "I'll be in Human Resources if you need me."

Steve gazes at the agent's back as he walks across the floor and exits without looking around. He continues to stare at the closed door in a daze for several minutes before reaching for the telephone. He calls the business controller to advise him of the federal takeover, and to tell him to cooperate with the auditors in every respect when they arrive. After a two minute conversation, he hangs up and places a second call to Brad.

"Hey, Steve, are you finished with the FBI guy?"

"Yes."

"I think you'd better get down here then."

There's an urgency in his friend's voice that cuts through the misery, and his mind is alert in an instant. "Have you found something?"

"Let's say there's a significant development."

Enthused once again, Steve leaps to his feet as he hangs up the handset and grabs his jacket. He's halfway across the floor when there's a knock on the door.

27

National Weather Center
Buenos Aires, Argentina
Coordinates: 34° 37' 47.2" S, 58° 22' 05.5" W
Thursday, June 25, 2020, 0823h

Carlos walks across the lobby to the receptionist's desk. She is on the telephone but catches his eye and acknowledges him with a smile as he pulls the log book toward him. After signing in, he replaces the pen to the breast pocket of his shirt and turns for the elevator to see the director, Gabriel Santos, making a beeline toward him.

"Good morning, Carlos," the executive greets somberly.

The head meteorologist doesn't feel so amiable either but responds to his superior in a pleasant manner. "Good morning, sir."

"I've received a complaint from President Hernandez."

Carlos stares at the director in astonishment. "About what?"

Gabriel's voice is calm. "The incompetence of your division and, in particular, your attitude toward him. What's going on?"

Carlos' brow wrinkles in puzzlement. "If you can be more specific, perhaps I can give you a satisfactory explanation."

"He said you called him yesterday and warned of a winter storm that was imminent in the south of the country."

A dark scowl rolls across Carlos's face. "Yes, I was following protocol. I don't see how *that's* being incompetent. He'll need to strategize for an emergency response once it passes."

"That bad?"

"I had every reason to believe it could be a dangerous storm that will do a lot of damage at best."

"He alleges that you were vague about the details and, dare I say, evasive about the storm's severity."

Carlos doesn't hesitate to jump to his own defense. "I was not. I informed him of everything I knew at the time. He reacted to my warning with unwarranted arrogance."

Gabriel speaks in a stern voice. "I'm not pointing fingers until I make further investigations, but he told me that he received grievances from the mayor of Comodoro Rivadavia and the governors of Chubut and Santa Cruz Provinces regarding the insufficient amount of time you gave them to prepare. It's my understanding that a blizzard moved in yesterday evening and terminated communications to the South."

The contempt in Carlos's voice is unmistakable. "Hernandez is not accepting accountability for his own decisions, and he's trying to shift the blame onto an underling as usual. I'm *not* going to be his fall guy, if that's his intention."

"I don't want your political opinion," the director says sharply. "I want to know why you took so long to issue a warning."

"I heard on the news this morning that several weather satellites have malfunctioned, including the one owned by the British

Antarctic Survey. My guess is that it failed before an information exchange could take place with our southern unit. The outer edge of the storm didn't move into its range until yesterday. There was no hard data to make a definitive forecast, so I made a manual calculation based on the limited intelligence available. If I hadn't, there would have been no forewarning whatsoever."

"I want you to submit a written statement to my office along with charts, satellite reports, and any other information to corroborate your argument *before* the end of the day. I will decide whether you need to face disciplinary measures for ineptitude."

"That *won't* be a problem, sir," Carlos replies huffily. He's not annoyed at the director's neutrality because it's the way he handles disputes, and his investigations are always thorough and fair, but he is angry at the president for deviating from the truth. Without another word, he storms across to the elevator, and a couple of minutes later he steps into the control room. He strides across the floor toward his office, and once behind his desk, he calls Jose's extension.

"I want to see you in my office *now*."

Less than thirty seconds later, a nervous-looking intern appears in the doorway.

"I want the latest charts and satellite images of the South."

"W-we don't have any," the young man stammers.

"Why not?"

"Er … the southern satellite's been offline since ten forty-five last night. I tried to reboot the computers, but they keep shutting down with a default message."

"'Data out of range'?"

"Yes."

The meteorologist mutters something inaudible and, clenching one hand into a fist, slams the ball down on the surface of his desk.

Jose flinches. "What about the last reports that came in?"

"Bring them to me."

The young man leaves the office and returns a couple of minutes later with a folder. Carlos takes it and opens the cover. The top document is a satellite image, and the meteorologist stares at it in amazement. Two hours after he left for home, enough of the storm had moved in for the satellite to collect adequate data to revise its files.

"Holy *hell!* Why didn't someone call me last night?"

The intern shrugs. "I don't know."

"Bring me the logbook so I can see who was on duty." He hesitates before changing his mind. "No, scrub that. I'll schedule a staff meeting later and remind everyone that I expect the departmental rules to be obeyed."

Jose is silent for about ten seconds. "The southern satellite managed to network enough information to our northern one to create a model for the next seven days before it failed."

"Show me."

Once again the intern leaves the office, and he reappears two minutes later with another folder. He hands it over to his boss.

"Excellent. The data transfer will be a tremendous help," Carlos says, opening the cover. He searches through the documents for the one-day computer-generated outlook, and he gasps in disbelief. Clouds are visible in the southern range of the satellite that stretch northwest from Puerto Madryn on the east coast across the country to the Chilean border. The metrics are in excess of anything he's ever thought possible, and it scares him. He reaches for a weather center directory on the side of his desk and flips through the pages. Moments later he lifts the telephone receiver and dials the number to the Chilean Weather Center in Santiago. The ringing goes on for a long time, and he's about to hang up when the operator finally answers.

"May I speak to the head of the meteorology department." He spends another couple of minutes on hold before someone picks up. "This is Carlos Castelli, head meteorologist at the National Weather Center in Buenos Aires."

"How can I help you, senor?"

"Our Infinity satellite in the South has malfunctioned, and a dangerous winter storm with the potential to wreak havoc is forecast by our northern unit," Carlos explains. "Can I bother you to fax me the latest reports, images, and charts from yours?"

"Our southern satellite malfunctioned at one o'clock this morning, and it's not back in service yet."

Carlos curses to himself. "What about the futures it transmitted before failing?" He's clinging to the hope that their defunct unit managed to network with the Chilean satellite before going offline.

"Nothing exceptional is showing. The chart is in front of me, and the seven-day forecast is fair with no expected change."

"No changes are showing because the satellite didn't network," Carlos warns. "The computers are recycling the last information received prior to the failure, and I assure you it's far from reliable. A treacherous blizzard is going to hit the southern half of Chile sometime today." He pauses for a moment as he studies the map. "Puerto Montt ... even Osorno ... and everywhere south to Cape Horn is in its path."

A long silence on the other end ensues. "I'm sorry, but there's nothing like that on any of our charts," the Chilean meteorologist reiterates.

"The chart you have is *wrong*," Carlos says in earnest, trying to convince his counterpart of the incongruities. "Give me your e-mail address. I'll send you all the info I have. It's limited because of the satellite problem, but there's enough for you to see how bad it's going to get."

"Thank you, Senor Castelli."

After scribbling the contact information on a note pad, the meteorologist replaces the handset and turns to the intern. "Jose, I need you to draw a lineament on the chart from Puerto Madryn on a northwest trajectory to San Carlos de Bariloche in the foothills of the Andes. Issue an imminent winter storm warning to the entire country on the south side." He pauses before adding to the instructions. "Increase the moisture content, temperature, and wind parameters by twenty percent. I know it's an exaggeration, but we don't have the ability to monitor its progress anymore. I'd rather err on the side of caution."

"By scaring the shit out of everybody?" Jose asks.

"If that's what it takes to get everyone to hunker down," Carlos replies. "Now, draw another line north of the first one from Punta Alta across to Chos Malal. Send out an advisory for all places between the two parallels."

"How long do you want the warning to be effective for? Twenty-four hours?"

"Is that what the seven-day outlook says?"

"I ... er, I didn't look, sir," the intern confesses.

"By my calculations, the storm is about four thousand kilometers in diameter and moving at four kilometers an hour. It could last for as long as a week, or more."

"That long?" Jose exclaims.

"I'm praying hard that I'm wrong," Carlos mumbles. He continues to study the data from the northern satellite. "The only thing I can't factor in with any degree of confidence is whether the speed will increase. It's moving too slowly, and my biggest fear is that it'll become stationary before the hub moves across the coast."

"Won't it pick up speed and break up when it comes ashore?" the intern asks.

"A superstorm like this?" He shrugs. "With its current alacrity and size, that's at *least* three or four days out at best." He shuffles the documents together on the desktop and places them back into their folders. "Issue a four-day warning because if it goes beyond that, coupled with the harsh temperatures and high winds, I don't think it will make much difference."

"Difference to what, sir?" Jose asks, clearly alarmed by the statement.

"I wish I knew," Carlos sighs, and he refrains from repeating the thoughts going through his head. He doesn't want to speculate the amount of damage a storm of this caliber could do in just fifteen minutes, let alone a prolonged blitz lasting several days. This thought reminds him that he needs to submit copies of the charts, satellite information, and a written statement to the director. He pushes the files from both satellites across the desk toward the intern.

"I need a photocopy of every document in these folders, pronto, *and* every byte of data collected by the northern and southern units over the last three days. Oh …" He'd almost forgotten the promise he made minutes earlier. Carlos continues to talk as he rips the top page out of his note pad. "This is the e-mail address to the Chilean Weather Center. I want you to send the last satellite reports we received to them first. They need to get their hands on them as soon as possible, though it won't save them from a catastrophe."

"Yes, sir."

He leans forward with a thoughtful expression on his face as the intern leaves, and picks up the telephone receiver. He punches in an internal extension number and waits for the director to answer the phone.

"Mr. Santos, I think you'd better come down to my office. We have a crisis, and it's far from pretty."

28

Infinity Meteorological Database Systems, Inc.
Hamilton Ave, Palo Alto, California
Coordinates: 37° 26' 40.3" N, 122° 09' 36.2" W
Thursday, June 25, 2020, 0902h

Steve is about to go down to the lab when there is a knock on the office door, and Peter Noble walks in. After a forty-five minute discussion, he leaves, and anxious to find out what Brad has discovered, the CEO stops by at Nancy's office to tell her where she can contact him. Two men are in the office with her.

"Mr. Jaeger, these gentlemen have just arrived. They say you should be expecting them."

A man turns to Steve and holds a business card out between his fingers. "I'm Kevin Porter. This is my associate, Jeremy Hill. We've been appointed to oversee Infinity's financial infrastructure and need to run through some details with you."

The CEO feels a subjacent numbness in his stomach despite his preparedness. They are brisk, with an air of self-importance that rubs him the wrong way; but his hands are manacled, and he senses it wouldn't be wise to stir the pot.

"Come to my office," he says, and moments later he's back behind his desk.

Kevin takes up the role of spokesperson. "Mr. Richards said he forewarned you."

"He told me that the company accounts and assets are frozen, gave me a brief outline, and said you were coming this morning. Beyond that, I'm still ignorant."

The auditor makes a correction. "*Partially* frozen. Expenditures not associated with the resolution of the satellite failures will not be embraced. That includes accounts payable to vendors, with the exception of utility bills, and payrolls for designated employees."

"You will allow the payment of invoices due prior to today's date?"

"No."

Steve protests. "That's unwarranted."

"We have stipulated guidelines to follow," Kevin tells him.

The CEO keeps his anger in check. All he can do is hear the agent out for now, but he will call the his lawyers for advice after the interview is over.

"Staff not involved with solving the crisis will be furloughed," Kevin continues. "Whether you send them home with the promise of back pay once they're allowed to return is your decision, but they will not be paid until the company's accounts are handed back."

Steve remains stoic. He knows they won't deviate from their directive no matter how much he begs. Despite a deep resentment, he has no intention to give them an opportunity to gloat.

"The departments affected by the furlough will be Research and Development, Production, and Sales. Outside contractors will also be affected, and there will be a reduction in accounting staff. Furloughs will occur in other sectors as necessary within the federal guidelines. The technicians involved in fixing the satellites will not be furloughed. If you need to purchase materials to repair the satellites, a requisition with specific details must be filed through Mr. Hill or myself, and we will authorize the release of the funds."

Steve slumps back in his chair and twiddles a pen between his fingers. This isn't what he expected to hear. "That's a bit harsh," he remarks. "Production schedules and contracts still need to be met."

"The White House thinks it's pointless for you to continue with manufacturing until you know what's interrupting your services. It's more perceptive to identify the problem so you can incorporate the modifications into your schedule. We think it's unlikely that your clientele will be interested in your product until fixes are implemented and you can guarantee the same thing won't happen again."

The CEO takes a deep breath. In this respect, Kevin speaks the truth. He decides to make a plea to the auditor. "Please tell me the federal intervention isn't going to be publicized until the satellites are back online?"

"I do sympathize with you, Mr. Jaeger, but a press release will be made by President Sinclair later today. This isn't to discredit your company; it is to reassure the end users that the White House is doing everything to minimize the defalcation."

"If you want to maximize the amount for restitution, doesn't it makes more sense to keep this between us?" Steve persists. "Our stocks are taking a massive hit, and when Wall Street knows you're here, we're going to lose billions more."

Kevin hesitates. "That's good sagacity, and I will put that in a memo, but I think the idea will be rejected. He needs to show the world that he has their interests in mind."

Steve throws his arms up in despair. "I see this is *all* about politics. The president doesn't care whether the problem is resolved or not. I hope you guys make the same effort to bring the perpetrator to justice and get remuneration for our losses once the source is identified."

"You can be assured that judicatory proceedings before a federal judge will be brought against any individual indicted for criminal behavior, but restitution will need to be pursued through a civil court, and that will be your responsibility."

An awkward silence falls between them. Steve's gaze is stalwart as he stares for several seconds at the auditor with blazing eyes before responding in a bitter voice. "Are you finished?"

"Unfortunately, no," the actuary replies. "A federal judge decreed that all personal bank accounts owned by you and Mr. Bentley are to be frozen, credit cards suspended, and liens placed on your properties, including house, land, and vehicles. You will be required to declare other properties not mentioned in the diktat, and any chattels on or within these domains must not be removed. If more funds are required to settle with the litigants, they will be sold by auction. Investments made by your board of directors are frozen too. They cannot withdraw any of their investments until the crisis is over."

"How can you freeze the investor money? Those are private funds."

"Risk by association. They chose to invest, which means they suffer the consequences of the fall."

Steve groans before blurting out, "So, in other words, I'm *fucked.*"

The auditor's reply is blunt. "If that's how you perceive it, Mr. Jaeger, then yes, you are."

The rage festering in his chest is about to burst, and Steve feels that he's on the verge of flying off into a frenzy. He has an urge to rant and rave around the office in unmitigated fury, but this won't achieve anything. His speaks in a weak voice. "What else, Mr. Porter?"

"That's it for now," Kevin replies. "We are taking up residence in your accounts department, and I expect close cooperation from your staff. We'll go through the employee files, and I'll give you a list of names that *must* be served with a furlough notification by the end of their shift today."

Steve stands and paces back and forth across the office floor in silence for several moments before speaking again. "How am I supposed to live if my bank account and credit cards are suspended? I don't carry cash on my person, and I still need to pay the utility bills and purchase groceries."

"Does your wife work?"

"No, she's a volunteer at a special hospice for children with chronic disabilities."

"Perhaps she should consider a paying job as a temporary means to get by. You will get a salary to cover basic living expenses, but don't expect to afford luxuries. I will authorize a petty cash payment for you and Mr. Bentley on the last day of each month." He pauses for a moment. "Do you have enough food to last the next five days?"

"I think so, but I'll need gas for my car so I can travel between home and work. I can't speak for Mr. Bentley, though. I don't know his current predicament."

"I'll ask him later," Kevin says. He hesitates, and for a moment he appears sympathetic to the CEO's plight. "I can arrange for a petty cash payment for fuel before you go home today. I'll need a receipt for each gas purchase you make, though." He opens a briefcase and removes a couple of thick documents consisting of about forty pages clipped together. "There are two copies of the executive order here. I need you to endorse the last page on one copy to confirm you understand the terms and conditions and agree to abide by them. The other one is your copy."

Steve's voice is sour. "What if I disagree and refuse to sign?"

"That would be your appanage, but regardless of whether you consent or not, the order will still be enforced," Kevin replies, but there's a sharpness in his tone that warns the CEO not to test his limits. "I believe you are an intelligent person, Mr. Jaeger. If you work with us, and don't put obstacles in our path, we'll be more sympathetic in respect of your position and treat you with equal esteem. On the other hand, if you choose *not* to"—he shrugs—"you'll find we can be as disobliging. I'll leave the documents on your desk to give you a chance to read them, but they must be signed and returned to me by the end of the day. If you want a lawyer to review and negotiate one or more clauses on your behalf, print 'legal representation pending' beneath your signature, but he only has seven days to file a complaint."

Steve's iPhone buzzes, and he reaches into his pocket. Noting that the call is from Brad, he apologizes to the two visitors. "Excuse me one minute; I need to take this."

"*Steve!* What's happened? I thought you'd be down here by now?"

"I got waylaid, BB," he replies flatly, and he looks at Kevin. "Are we finished?"

"For now."

"I'm on my way down," the CEO tells his partner as the assessors get to their feet and leave without saying another word. He disconnects and throws a scornful glance at the documents on his desk. He'll fax them to the lawyer after he comes back up from the lab.

Danny is sitting beside Brad at his terminal, and the pair are in a deep discussion as Steve walks into the laboratory. The CTO looks up and grunts.

"*Humph!* It's about *time*. Pull a chair up."

"The morning isn't going well," Steve replies as he sits down. He's not going to tell his partner that the federal auditors have taken over in the presence of staff, so he refrains from saying anything about it.

"Prepare yourself, then. I think I'm about to blow it apart," Brad warns.

"Have you found the cause of the malfunctions?"

"I believe so, but I don't think you're going to like it."

Steve's eyes open wide, and in an instant he feels uplifted. "Whether I like it or not is irrelevant. Get it fixed so we can get this show back on the road."

Brad stares at him with unwavering eyes. "There's nothing to fix."

"What do you mean there's nothing to fix?"

"If something isn't broken, there isn't anything to fix. Our system is fine. There *is* nothing to be repaired."

Steve frowns. "If there's no malfunction, the satellites should be *working*, and they *aren't*."

"The satellites *are* working," Brad fires back before raising a hand to his forehead, and he lowers his voice. "We're not on the same page." He swivels around on the chair to face the computer monitor and selects an icon to bring a chart up on the screen. "We lost four more satellites overnight," he says, making selections with the cursor. "Argentina south, Chile south, Poland, and Kazakhstan."

"Isn't the Polish satellite a multiple subscription?"

"Yes, they share it with Belarus, Romania, and Ukraine. Danny checked the solar sensors on the new failures. The spike appears on all four satellites, but only *after* the failures. They weren't there beforehand."

"So there *is* a virus?"

Brad shakes his head. "No." He falls silent for several seconds, and his eyes don't waver as he concentrates on the data scrolling up on the screen. "Ah … here we are." He sits back in the chair so Steve can get a clearer view of the monitor over his shoulder. "These four columns refer to the rising and setting of the sun. Columns one and three are when it's supposed to rise and set as per the database. The second and fourth are the *actual* time as recorded by the solar mapping sensor." He pauses to give Steve time to synchronize. "We're going to analyze line five. This is the information taken from the Alaskan unit that failed on June 23. You can easily see the discrepancy. The sun rose one minute and twenty-five seconds early, which is forty seconds in excess of the preset margin and is the reason why the data are out of range."

Steve begins to speak. "As strange as—"

Brad holds a hand up and cuts him off. "The inconsistency appears to shut the satellite down, but in reality, it's not doing that. The only thing it's doing is blocking the charts at the print interface. The insertion of the solar and lunar information is required to format a forecast, but because it's outside the preset boundaries, the function fails. The daylight period should now be shortening as we move toward winter, but instead, the days are still growing longer."

Steve's skepticism grows as Brad points to the third line in the chart. "This is a download from the British Antarctic Survey unit. The latitudinal times vary, so these samples are established for

Stanley. On January 23, the sun was supposed to set at 3:49 p.m. local. Instead it was recorded at 3:47:22, which is two minutes and six seconds early. Yesterday it set prematurely by three minutes eight seconds, and so far today, the solar mapping sensor has recorded an additional lag. It's predicted to sink at 3:46. That's another thirty-five seconds earlier than the previous day—an overall time of four minutes sixteen seconds. This is where the days *should* be growing longer, but they're still getting shorter."

"So is the malware making changes at the sensors or in the database?"

The expression on Brad's face changes to one of frustration. "*No*, Steve. You have tunnel vision. You need to get the idea of a virus out of your head and look at the bigger picture. Samples taken from several working satellites in the Northern and Southern Hemispheres paint a mural that's so consistent I can now tell you what units are going to fail, and when. The reality is that the sun is rising earlier in the north and setting prematurely in the south."

Steve pulls his eyes away from the monitor and gazes at his partner. "Can you prove that the false times *aren't* being generated by a virus, though?"

Brad clasps his hands together behind the back of his head, leans back, and takes a deep breath. "Alex Seville called me back early this morning. He carried out a visual observation of the sunrise and recorded a time of 0419 hours. That is a precise match to the solar mapping sensor—and five minutes earlier than the database says."

Steve understands where his partner is trying to go, but he has serious issues with his conception. "What does it all mean?"

"I'm not an astrophysicist, but I'd say the summer solstice hasn't peaked yet."

"The summer solstice was on June 21."

"Not this year. If the recorded data are accurate, and Alex Seville has confirmed they are, the Northern Hemisphere is still tilting toward the sun."

Steve emits a short, uncertain laugh and stares at his friend in astonishment. "That's not possible, BB. The earth's axis doesn't change. It sits at a fixed angle that changes in relation to its orbital path around the sun. We *all* know that."

Brad swings a hand in the direction of the chart on the computer screen. "Then *you* explain this. I'm willing to consider *any* rationale that makes more sense than mine. You've got to believe me; I'd give my right hand to be proved wrong. What I see here scares the crap out of me."

"Why?"

"This is going to have a profound effect on the earth's ecosystems."

"*How?* I mean, it's only a couple of days and a few minutes off—if you're right."

"A couple of days and a few minutes off?" Brad echoes. "It shouldn't be off at *all*. Can you tell me the last time when something like this happened?"

Steve hesitates, and his eyebrows snap together. "I can't."

The head technician sits forward in his chair and speaks with more passion. "A couple of days and a few minutes longer exposes the Arctic to higher temperatures for a longer period of time, which contributes to additional melting of the polar ice cap, warmer oceans, and more intense storms."

The CEO is hesitant to accept Brad's assertion, but he's unable to come up with a rational argument in dispute. "I'm sorry, BB, but changes to the ecological structure of the planet are the least of our concerns right now. What we *need* is a fix to get our satellites operational again."

"We *do* need to be concerned," Brad fires back. "I will work on a bypass for the astral sensors, but we *can't* ignore the connotation shown by the data."

Steve doesn't understand why his friend is pinning more importance to the cause than to a counteraction on how it's affecting their network. "What do you suggest we do, then?"

"We've got to report it to the proper authorities. I'm surprised they haven't picked up on it yet"

"Perhaps they have," Danny remarks.

"You might be right, but it's still our place to say something."

"Who would we report something like this to?" Steve asks.

Brad shrugs. "I'm not sure, but I think we should drop this into President Sinclair's lap and let him handle it."

"Why don't we just tell the media in the next press release," Danny suggests.

Brad gives the technician a fiery glare. "No."

The young man appears taken aback by the unexpected sharpness in BB's reply. "Why not? It'll get them off our backs."

Brad drops his voice. "That would be irresponsible. We're not qualified to make these kinds of affirmations, and I don't want to be liable for recreating the Orson Welles syndrome."

Danny gazes at his boss with a puzzled expression on his face. "What's *that?*"

"In 1938, the CBS network broadcast a radio adaptation of *The War of the Worlds*. The first twenty minutes was presented as a series of simulated news bulletins, and terrified listeners believed an actual Martian invasion was in progress."

The technician begins to laugh. "You're joking?"

"No, I'm not," Brad replies. "Look it up on the Internet if you don't believe me. Back then, radio broadcasts only had a short reach, so the audience was much smaller than it is today. If we release this kind of information to the press, it'll be sensationalized, and social media will carry the news around the world in a matter of seconds. The panic it would create would be on a far grander scale."

Steve is more concerned about getting the feds off their backs than about something that happened eighty-two years ago. "As the White House has poked their noses into our business, proof that the problem is natural and not technical will exonerate us."

Brad casts a horrified glance at his partner. "How is the government involved?"

"I'll explain later," Steve replies with a smile. "The natural disaster clause in the contracts stipulate that we're not legally responsible for damage to, or failure of, our equipment resulting from a natural event emanating from within the cosmos. They can only claim for indemnity, and that's an argument between them and their underwriters."

"They're covered by more than one insurance?" Danny asks.

"Yes. Only the onboard weather equipment is warranted by us for twenty-five years." The CEO turns his eyes to Brad. "Who's going to tell President Sinclair that the earth is ... is doing whatever it's doing?"

"You're the chief executive officer."

Steve becomes obdurate. "Oh *no* I'm not. He'll *nev*er believe me. *You're* the one who's more knowledgeable about what's going on."

"I need to work on a fix and get the satellites back into operation," Brad replies. "I'll gather all the evidence into a package and include my own report with it. The president already knows we have a problem, so even if he *is* skeptical, he should follow through with qualified sources at *least.*"

Steve is apprehensive but reluctantly accepts that the

responsibility falls on his shoulders. "What if you're wrong, BB? I'll be ridiculed and end up being the butt of every fucking joke on late-night television."

Danny grins. "Look at it this way. If Brad *is* right, you'll be an international hero overnight."

"Well, I guess the only way is up," Steve mutters discontentedly. "I'm an international villain at the moment." He takes the iPhone from his trouser pocket and dials Nancy's extension. "I want you to track down Clarke Richards and ask him to meet me in my office in fifteen minutes."

"Do you have his number?" she asks.

"No, but you should find him in Human Resources."

"Okay."

The CEO slips the communications device back into his pocket. "I'm going upstairs. Call me when you've got everything together that'll convince the president I'm not a nutcase. I need Richards to pull some strings to get me a face-to-face."

"Don't tell anyone, *including* the FBI," Brad warns. "We need to keep this under our hats and let President Sinclair decide whether the information should be made public or not."

"I don't intend to," Steve replies. He doesn't want to make himself look like an ass more than necessary. "Let me know once you've found a way to bypass the sensors."

The CEO leaves the lab, heads down the passage toward the lobby, and waits for an elevator. A bell dings, signaling the arrival of a car, and the door slides open. He stands at one side to allow the passengers to exit, and Clarke Richards walks out. The agent doesn't see him and walks toward the main doors.

"Mr. Richards."

The FBI agent pauses in midstep and turns his head. "Oh, hello

Mr. Jaeger. I'm sorry; I wasn't expecting to bump into you down here."

Steve takes a few paces toward him and lowers his voice. "Brad thinks he's discovered the cause of the failures."

"That *is* good news," he replies. "Is it a virus?"

"Not exactly, but I can't discuss the nature of the problem because it might be … well, a bit sensitive."

Clarke appears offended. "Oh? Why are you bothering to tell me, then?"

"I need an audience with President Sinclair, and I want you to make it happen."

The agent hesitates. "I don't have that kind of authority, Mr. Jaeger. Perhaps if you share some details with me, I can ask my chief to pull a few strings if he validates the request."

Steve shakes his head. "No offense intended, Mr. Richards, but I can't disclose the information to anyone except the president. I assure you it needs his personal attention, and he can decide where and how it is handled."

"I think it will be impossible to induce the chief of staff to arrange an appointment without a solid outline. Is it to do with the decision to place your company under federal control?"

"No, and I've no intention of broaching the subject." His mind races. He needs to be more deceitful and wonders if Brad's discovery could be categorized as a threat to national security. Steve takes a deep breath and chooses his words with care. "The cause of our satellite failures isn't restricted to Infinity. *Every* satellite in orbit is under the same threat. Ours just happened to be first."

"You have my assurance that whatever you say *will* be in confidence, Mr. Jaeger."

"You're not the one I distrust, Mr. Richards. I don't have faith in bureaucracy or the people who will handle the information beyond yourself."

"Well, I'm sorry you feel like that," Clarke replies slowly. "I'll see what I can do, but I can't promise anything. Perhaps if you're lucky, he might agree to slip you into his schedule in the next week or two."

There's a new intensity in the CEO's voice. "This is *urgent*, and I assure you ... I'm *not* playing games. It could be too late if I wait that long. I *must* see him today."

The agent regards Steve with suspicion in his eyes. He's aware that the agent is trying to figure out whether a threat to the nation is real or whether it's an attempt to influence him psychologically.

Steve throws his hands up in a submissive gesture. "I guess have no choice. I'm going upstairs to draft a press release for the media. I think he'll be unhappy that I didn't brief him first, but at least I tried."

"Why would you do that?"

"If it's left to some bureaucratic imp to validate my request, it won't get approved," the CEO says. "The truth is, they're not going to believe me, and neither will you." He gesticulates toward the main entrance. "There are dozens of reporters out on the forecourt, and you know what they're like once they get their hands on the scoop of the year. At least they'll dig deeper for more facts, and once that happens, the shit is going to hit the fan. If a press conference is the only option, then I will use it."

The agent inclines his head. "And that should bother me because?"

"No particular reason," Steve replies. "I will answer every question I am asked, and I think President Sinclair will be pissed when he learns that the FBI blocked me from briefing him prior to a press release." He pauses to let his words sink in and then adds, "And I *won't* be afraid to tell them I asked for your assistance."

"Why do I feel you're being overdramatic?"

Steve smiles wryly. "That's your prerogative, Mr. Richards."

Clarke is starting to look uneasy. "How do you intend to get to Washington if I *can* arrange a meeting for you?"

"We have a company jet."

"Have you forgotten that the federal government has seized your assets?"

Steve curses beneath his breath. With his credit cards suspended, he won't even be able to purchase an airline ticket. "You'd better find a way to get me to the White House before the end of the day," he says firmly. There's a ding as another elevator car arrives in the lobby. "I have a statement to prepare for our clientele and the press, so I'll talk to you later, Mr. Richards."

Without waiting for the agent to respond, he spins on his heels, and storms toward the elevator. Sometimes a flair for the thespian is crucial to get the necessary attention, but he doesn't have time to continue the argument. His only interest is to avoid any furloughs taking place, and if Clarke doesn't pull some strings before he leaves for home at the end of the day, he will hold a conference.

He steps into the car and turns to see the FBI agent still standing in the same spot, gazing back at him as the doors close.

29

The Oval Office
The White House, Washington, DC
Coordinates: 38° 53' 50.6" N, 77° 02' 14.5" W
Thursday, June 25, 2020, 2104h

It is midday when Kevin Porter comes to Steve's office. "Mr. Richards tells me you want a personal meeting with the president?"

"Yes."

"I've spoken to the chief of staff, and he said they might be able to set up a five-minute telephone conference for later today."

Steve lays a hand on top of a thick folder. It contains the documentation that Brad prepared and brought up thirty minutes earlier. "I have physical evidence I need to give him."

Kevin nods. "Mr. Richards told me you wouldn't reveal the motive for the request. It's highly irregular for the chief of staff to approve a meeting without adequate information. The decision to grant a one-on-one is based on how important he considers your adjuration is, so can you give me some particulars to pass on?"

"The cause of our satellite failures is external. In essence, there isn't anything wrong with our equipment. I will go as far to say that an abnormal natural phenomenon is being recorded by our sensors, and the consequences could be devastating for everyone, but I'm not prepared to disclose anything else except to the president."

"Do you perceive it as a national security risk?"

Steve laughs. "What do *you* think, Mr. Porter?"

"My opinion is irrelevant, Mr. Jaeger," the auditor replies coldly. "You won't tell me what the phenomenon is, so I'm not in a position to make that assessment. What I need is a yes or no answer to my question."

"In that case it's an unequivocal yes."

Kevin takes a few seconds to weigh Steve's affirmation. "Do you think your satellites can be put back into service again?"

The CEO is cautious with his reply. "Brad is working on a fix, but as it stands right now, the chances of getting them back online is fifty-fifty. He won't know whether he'll be successful until later today or sometime tomorrow. Our clientele and the media will demand answers to some pretty tough questions if we do manage to get back online, which is why it's essential to apprise the president ahead of time."

"Why is it important to brief him first?"

"Mr. Bentley's personal interest in the subject matter gives him a better concept of the corollary than I have, but he did scare the shit out of me. He has evidence to back him, and I assure you it's not something the president will want to learn from the front page of the *Washington Post*."

"Are you making an unambiguous statement that the president of the United States is in danger?"

Steve is getting exasperated by the inquisition. "Yes, but he's not the only one. The entire world is in peril. I thought I'd made that quite clear by now."

Ten seconds of silence ensues before the auditor makes a decision. "I will speak to the chief of staff again and get back to you."

When the auditor leaves, Steve reads through the contractual clauses that relate to acts of nature. Despite his agnosticism to Brad's asseverations, it's the only thing that might save Infinity from a complete financial disaster.

Thirty minutes later, Kevin returns. "Okay, the chief of staff has granted you acquiescence for an audience with the president, but he's done so with reluctance. You will have five minutes to impress him."

"Will you allow me to use the company jet?"

"It's been impounded. You're going to Washington on my watch, and if this is a clever ploy to get on your plane and abscond, I will be held responsible."

Steve feels like a little boy under castigation by his parents for some innocent mistake he's made.

The auditor continues to give instructions. "Mr. Richards will drive you to San Carlos Airport, where you'll board a federal jet that leaves for Washington at three o'clock." He glances at his wristwatch. "That gives you forty-five minutes to get your stuff together. I suggest you travel light and take only what's necessary to prove your case. A car from the White House will meet you when the plane lands."

"Thank you, Mr. Porter. I appreciate your help."

"As you are meeting with the president today, I will suspend the proposed furloughs for twenty-four hours." Steve is surprised but grateful to find some humanity buried deep within his persona after all.

The flight from Palo Alto to Ronald Reagan International Airport takes five hours. Three federal agents are on the plane but show no desire to engage in conversation despite several failed attempts. In the end, he opens the folder that Brad prepared and reads through the documents a couple of times.

Toward the end of the flight, he is subjected to a security search. Ten minutes later, the small aircraft touches down on the tarmac with a screech of tires. The jet taxies to an isolated hangar at the far end of the airport, where a black Lincoln is waiting. There are no civil greetings between the car's occupants and his fellow passengers, and chatter between them is brief and direct.

"Has he been screened?"

"Yes."

An agent holds the rear door open and invites the CEO to get in with a silent gesture of his hand. Twenty minutes later, Steve walks into the White House lobby flanked by two Secret Service agents. They escort him down a corridor past the vice president's office and turn left. An agent steps forward, opens a door, and seconds later he's in the Oval Office.

President Sinclair is standing to the right of the desk with his legs apart and his hands clasped behind his back. He dismisses the agents and waits for them to leave before greeting Steve in an agitated voice. "Good evening, Mr. Jaeger. If your visit is related to the federal order imposed over your company, this interview is terminated."

Weary from the long flight, President Sinclair's disharmonious disposition riles the CEO. "I'll be equally blunt, Mr. President. Infinity is *not* responsible for the failures. We are attempting to fix the situation as a matter of courtesy to our clients, but there are no guarantees."

Lloyd raises his right eyebrow. "If I may clarify my interpretation of your position, you're disclaiming liability for the failure of *your* equipment?"

"With due respect, sir, that's *not* what I said. Our onboard computers are not defective. The network is compromised by a developing situation dissociated from Infinity."

President Sinclair saunters a few paces toward Steve with his hands still clasped behind his back. "What kind of a situation are you talking about, Mr. Jaeger?"

The CEO pauses and takes a deep breath. This is the moment of truth, the thin line between crazy and mad. "The data we've analyzed shows there may be a change in the planet's axial inclination—a shift large enough that some of the information recorded by the sensors is no longer within computing range."

The president gazes into Steve's eyes, and it's not difficult to detect the skepticism in his voice. "I thought the earth's axis was always shifting, but perhaps I'm wrong. Shouldn't you be seeking the opinion of a scientist?"

"I'm not looking for opinions, Mr. Sinclair." Steve squats down and fumbles with the locks on his briefcase for a moment before they pop open. He removes the documentation Brad put together and stands upright again. "Our satellites began to record a continual shift in the planet's axial inclination since last Saturday, but the change wasn't great enough to start taking them offline until the early hours of Monday morning. Twenty units are now out of service, and one of our own went down as I left my office in Palo Alto. This file contains documented evidence and data from the satellites. I think you should get it checked out by someone who is more qualified than Mr. Bradley or myself."

"I fail to see why it's *my* responsibility to get confirmation. You need to report it to the appropriate authorities."

"I *am* reporting it to the proper authority," Steve replies firmly. "My partner, Mr. Bentley, describes the earth as 'tumbling.' He's staunch in his belief that it poses a significant danger to the ecosystems and geological structure of the planet, and, dare I say it, life."

President Sinclair unclasps his hands from behind his back and folds his arms across his chest. "That's a rash statement. I hope you don't intend to include that in your clientele report?"

"I'm certainly not going to tell them that they're the proud owners of billions of dollars in space junk without providing an explanation."

Lloyd takes a couple of steps back toward his desk with a thoughtful expression on his face. "Mr. Jaeger, I need you to reconsider the content of that report before you make it. You've made an unsubstantiated declaration of an Armageddon-style event we only see in science fiction movies. I don't think it will be wise to claim that mankind is under threat of extinction ... which is what you're implying, isn't it?"

"I suppose I am," Steve replies, "but I did use the word 'possible.'"

"Three tiny syllables that will be overlooked by the media if they so desire. We're in an era where news flashes around the world in seconds, and an overstatement of facts could result in a global panic if others come up with the same assumptions." He hesitates. "To be honest, I'm not buying into your story without hard evidence. If you *must* provide your clientele with an explanation, I suggest you stick with the virus. That's far more credible than something wild like this."

Steve stares at the president in surprise. "I can't do that, sir."

"Why not?"

"I've already *told* you—our equipment isn't to blame. It will be a fabrication if I blame a virus that doesn't exist, and it'll indicate a failure in our security systems that never occurred. A false confession will make us legally responsible, and we'll be wide open to litigation when a natural disaster clause in our contracts exonerates us from liability."

The president regards him warily for a few seconds before he speaks again, gesticulating with his right hand at the same time. "Tell me, Mr. Jaeger, are you on any medications or controlled substances for an undisclosed medical condition?"

The CEO stares at Lloyd in disbelief, and makes no attempt to hide the scorn in his voice. "I don't have *time* for that crap, Mr. Sinclair. I came to you with legitimate concerns, but I see I'm wasting my time." He makes a move to leave.

"Are you going to bring the satellites back into service?"

Steve pauses and turns back to face the president. "Mr. Bentley voiced some doubt because the problem is still fluid. The data initiating the shutdown is used to calculate thousands of equations for other applications, and removing it could result in a catastrophic failure of the entire network."

"What I don't understand is why you're the first person to bring this to my attention," Lloyds replies softly. "I'm sure if something serious were happening, I would have been informed before now. I can't imagine there's been an oversight by every scientist on the planet."

"Mr. Sinclair, I came to you because I made a logical supposition that other units could start to shut down too—your military and spy satellites, for example. I perceive *that* as a major threat to our nation." Steve can tell by the president's expression that he's succeeded in casting some doubt in his mind.

Lloyd is silent for several seconds before he speaks again, but his tone is less authoritative. "I have reservations that other satellites and networks will be affected, but I'll make some inquiries. In the meantime, I want you to stall any reports or statements to your clientele and the media until Monday afternoon."

Steve considers the request before he answers. "That won't be easy, sir. Mr. Bentley predicts that our last satellite will go offline in the early hours of Monday morning. What you're asking will destroy Infinity. This is my company, my business, and I'm *not* prepared to let that happen."

"I understand, Mr. Jaeger, but I'd like to follow through with someone who is qualified to confirm the substance of your story. That could take a day or two."

Steve twists his lips as he ponders again. Monday is too far away, but undisputed scientific support will be essential to enforce the act-of-nature clause. "I concede, but I do so under protest."

"You do understand that if your hypothesis turns out to be valid, it won't result in the automatic release of the federal imposition?"

Steve gazes at the president in astonishment. "*Why*?"

"There's a probability that the natural disaster element in your contracts may be contested. It affects too many entities worldwide, and I still need to be cautious. Even if the clause *is* valid, we may still take special steps to have it annulled."

The CEO is stunned and takes a few seconds to recompose himself. "You can't do that. Contracts are legal and binding. That's why there are indentures, and not even the federal government, the White House, *or* congress can override a signed agreement between two parties to suit their own self-indulged interests."

"Perhaps, Mr. Jaeger, but let's cross that bridge *if* we get to it." Lloyd walks toward Steve with an outstretched hand for the documents Brad prepared. "I appreciate the effort you made to convince me, but I'm not sold on the notion that the planet is doing what you seem to think it is."

Steve is on the verge of an outburst of fury, and the only way he can control it is to remain silent. He hands the folder over to the president.

"I need to find out where these have to be sent for clarification," Lloyd says. "An official response will be on your desk by midday Monday."

Steve's voice is icy. "I should be getting back to Silicon Valley."

"Thank you, Mr. Jaeger."

The CEO turns sharply, walks over to the door, and exits the Oval Office. Two secret service agents are waiting outside to escort him back off the premises.

As the door closes behind Steve, President Sinclair turns and heads for another door in the west wall that leads to his private study. He drops the Infinity folder on top of the desk, walks around the side, and sinks into the chair. He remains in a thoughtful repose for almost a minute before pulling a cell phone from his pocket and pressing a direct dial button. It rings twice before the vice president answers without formality.

"Hello, there!"

"Terry, Mr. Jaeger has just left, and he's come up with an incredible pretext for the failure of their weather network. If anything, he has an incredible imagination."

The vice president laughs. "What kind of tale is he trying to fob off?"

"He claims that the earth's axial inclination began to shift five days ago and it's impacting their satellites in a negative manner."

"Hmm, that's a strange proclamation."

"I agree, but we need to find someone qualified to confirm that a skittle is missing at the end of his lane. He claims that an Armageddon-style event is in motion, and I want facts to discredit his integrity if he decides to go public."

"Did he submit evidence in support, or does he expect to be taken at face value?"

"He gave me a thick file, but I can't tell whether it's fact, fiction, or a mixture of both." Lloyd hesitates. "Who do we go to with this? Hell, how do I know? I'm only the fucking president."

"I would think it falls somewhere in the spectrum of physics, but shouldn't this be their responsibility?"

"That was my initial response until he made the assertion that every satellite is under the same umbrella. It might only be a matter of time before they fail too."

Terry scoffs. "I'm inclined to refute that assessment."

"I want to dismiss it as BS too, but Jaeger's threatened to go public. Whether this 'tumble' thing is true or not, it could resonate negatively around the globe. I tried to persuade him not to release a report until Monday, but he's pretty disgruntled, so I don't know if he will."

"I *think* what we need is an astrophysicist," Terry says reflectively.

"Can you root one out for me?"

"I'll call NASA. They'll have the answer."

"No, see if you can single out a qualified individual rather than an entity. If there's a sliver of truth, NASA will go public too. Jaeger's file is on my desk if you need it, but I want a preliminary assessment as soon as possible. This needs to be squared away. We have a campaign going on, and fact-chasing to satisfy some feral world of science fantasy is a distraction I don't need."

"Okay. Will there be anything else?"

"No, that's all for now."

Lloyd bids a good-night and places the iPhone back into his pocket. He gazes distantly at the cover of the folder for several moments.

He opens it and begins to read the first page of the top document.

30

Infinity Meteorological Database Systems, Inc.
Hamilton Ave, Palo Alto, California
Coordinates: 37° 26' 40.3" N, 122° 09' 36.2" W
Friday, June 26, 2020, 0814h

Steve leans back in the chair, clasps his hands behind the back of his head, and gazes across the desk at Brad. A comfortable sleep evaded him on the overnight flight back from Washington, and all he could do was doze off into light, fitful slumbers. The aircraft landed at San Carlos Airport at 0435, and he had to call his wife to pick him up.

"Well, did the old man believe you?"

"It wasn't easy to gauge what he was thinking," Steve replies. "He was pretty cynical but gave me an allusion he would follow through."

"It makes no difference to us whether he acts on the information or not. That's his prerogative. We fulfilled our obligations by bringing it to his attention."

"We still need to get the satellites back into operation, though," Steve says. "How many units are down now?"

"We lost twelve since ten o'clock yesterday morning."

The CEO wasn't prepared for this answer. "You've got to be kidding."

Brad's face is grim. "The French satellite, which is a joint subscription with Germany, Spain, Italy, and Austria; Mongolia; New Zealand; four of the six covering the good old US of A; Turkey; the second Chilean unit; Japan; and two of the three Chinese satellites."

Steve screws his face into a pained expression. "We must have lost half the fleet by now."

"We're past halfway. There are twenty-five left in service."

"Do you think the axis will keep on shifting?"

"I hope not. It's got to stop at some point otherwise the world is going to be turned upside down."

The CEO takes a moment to reflect. "I suppose we'll need to upgrade the databanks to conform to the differentiations when it does?"

Brad takes a few seconds before replying. "We can't even begin to evaluate what the new normal will be until the earth stops tumbling, but we will have to do an extensive overhaul of our systems programming before we can get them back online again."

"Yesterday you told me you thought the tumble would affect the planet. Do you believe half the stuff you told me, or were you just trying to scare me?"

"What I said is real enough, and the longer the globe takes to correct its fall, the worse it will be. How bad? The answer is beyond the boundaries of my wisdom."

Steve smiles. "Perhaps that's a good thing, BB."

The CTO sighs heavily. "Anyway, back to the current situation. We have three guys downstairs who made a valiant attempt to rescue this company last night."

Steve inclines his head and gazes at his partner with curiosity. "Oh?"

"They didn't disclose their plan to me, but they worked together throughout the night to try to figure a fix. Danny pulled off a twenty-four-hour shift. I tried to send him home this morning, but he refuses to leave until he knows if it's going to work."

Suddenly overwhelmed with emotion at the loyalty of their staff, Steve sits forward in his chair. "Do you think they were successful?"

"They wrote a new routing program, fixed the rogue codes generated through kill-zone eviction, and presented the package to me when I came in this morning. I ran a preliminary scan, service run, and activation, and so far it's passed every test."

Steve raises his eyebrows in surprise. "Good *Lord*, that's no easy feat. Do you remember it took us months to flush the rogues out when we developed the software or made modifications and expansions?"

Brad gives a short laugh. "That was twenty years ago. We were venturing into unknown territory in those days. Things have improved since then."

"Did we ever write new software that passed the first time around?"

"Actually, never." A tiny smile of pride curls at the corner of Brad's mouth. "Our guys are the best, and their teamwork is impeccable. That's the only reason why they pulled it off so fast. The definitions look good, and the program is going through a final simulation. We'll know in a few more hours whether it's ready for Krazy Kath."

"The big question, though—are you *sure* this will work if the axis continues to change?"

"No. We can only preprogram the system with a new profile in preparation, but we can't update the database with the parameters until we know a reversal is taking place. Kick-in will be automatic, and the computers will calculate the necessary adjustments for the new positions before they reboot to bring the satellites back in service, but the earth has to get its act together first."

"I hope that happens soon. I promised the president not to release any reports until midday on Monday."

"Do you think Sinclair will pull through on his end of the bargain?"

Steve shrugs. "I'm not sure, but if I don't hear from him by the agreed time, I *will* issue a public statement regardless."

"I take it he wouldn't agree to release the company from federal control until our data are verified, then?"

"Not a chance. The disaster clause is the only thing we have to protect us. On top of that, he wants to find a way to invalidate the related paragraphs in the contracts."

Brad's jaw drops open, and he stares at his partner in speechless stupefaction for a few seconds. "He can't do that. A contract is legally binding to all parties."

"One would think so, but he's more interested in saving his own face." A tiny smile appears on Steve's lips. "We don't have anything to fear. He doesn't have that kind of power."

"What makes you so sure?" Brad asks dubiously.

"If such a ruling *is* made, agreements, treaties, and contracts across the board will no longer be legally binding," the CEO explains. "It'll be exploited hell west and crooked, and it's sure to do irreversible damage to foreign commerce. Businesses will disengage from international trading when contracts can be invalidated with so much ease every time an overseas client is dissatisfied. It's simply not going to happen."

The conversation is interrupted by the buzz of the intercom, and Steve leans forward to turn the speaker on. "Yes, Nancy?"

"Mr. Porter is here to see you."

The CEO looks at Brad and rolls his eyes. "Send him in."

"Who's Mr. Porter?"

"One of those damn auditors. He's probably here to discuss the furlough list."

Brad stands up and stretches his arms. "I need to be getting back to the lab. I'll stop by a little later." He starts to walk toward the door.

"BB?"

The CTO turns and looks back at him.

"Tell your guys not to talk about this outside of the lab. I promised to keep it quiet until Monday."

"They already know. I had a chat with them yesterday afternoon."

"Thanks."

Kevin has a hand raised to knock on the door when Brad opens it. Steve notes how the two men eyeball each other with some hostility as they pass without acknowledging each other.

"How did your meeting go with the president?" the auditor asks, crossing the floor toward his desk.

"It was satisfactory," Steve replies pleasantly. He can tell that Kevin seems surprised at his amiable attitude—and perhaps a bit curious. "I expect you're here to give me the furlough list?"

"Uh … yes I am. Are you ready to go through it?"

"Let's get it done."

31

The President's Private Study
The White House, Washington, DC
Coordinates: 38° 53' 50.6" N, 77° 02' 15.1" W
Friday, June 26, 2020, 1123h

President Sinclair flips to the second page of a three-sheet fax and continues to read it with a heavy frown on his face. It's the third time he's gone through the document since it came in thirty minutes earlier. A knock on the study door interrupts him.

"Come in."

The secretary of state, Brian Harding, and Robert Klaus, the secretary of homeland security, enters the room. At sixty-two, Brian is six years senior to the president, but a professional relationship between them goes back thirty years. Sinclair is less familiar with Robert, but he was a suitable candidate for secretary of homeland security based on his record, a no-nonsense policy, and years of experience within the department. At first the president was concerned by the overambitious inclinations of the forty-nine-year-old, but he grew more satisfied with the man's performance as time progressed.

The president is in a mediocre mood and makes a gesture toward a reading table in the center of the room. "Gentlemen, make yourselves comfortable. Terry will be here in a minute."

As the two men sit down, the president goes back to reading the fax in silence. No one speaks a word until the door opens and the vice president joins them.

"Good morning," Terry greets, walking across to the table. Brian and Robert return the greeting as he sits down.

Lloyd gets to his feet and walks around to the front of the desk with the fax still in his hand. "Infinity has blamed the failure of their weather satellites on a natural phenomenon that, to me, sounds too far-fetched to be credible."

Robert inclines his head to one side. "Excuses?"

President Sinclair casts a sharp glance at the Homeland Security secretary before addressing Brian and Terry. "Their CEO came here last night to submit circumstantial evidence indicating that an incongruity existed, but it remains inconclusive. The documentation is full of scientific expressions, charts, and abstract mathematical calculations that make no sense to me." He pauses to perch himself on the front edge of the desk with one foot on the floor and closes his eyes for a brief moment to recompose his thoughts. "The report infers that the angle of the earth's axis is changing and the planet is slowly tumbling head over heels. Jaeger fears that it's a potential catalyst for a global disaster of incomprehensible proportions."

Robert throws his head back and begins to laugh, but the mirth is short-lived. The expressions on the faces of the president and

Terry remain solemn, while Brian appears to be suppressing some amusement.

The Homeland Security secretary shrugs in bewilderment and gestures with his hands. "Am I the *only* one with a sense of humor this morning?"

Lloyd ignores the remark and picks up where he left off. "As I've already said, I was skeptical of his assertion, but because he provided documentation, I followed through with the intent to discredit him. Terry faxed the Infinity report to Dr. Jack Bailey, PhD, a respected astrophysicist and professor at Harvard." He raises the papers in his hand. "He faxed a preliminary report back to me, and despite my cynicism, there may be more substance to Jaeger's fairy tale than I'm willing to accept." A hush falls over the study and Lloyd throws a glance at Terry before looking back down to read from the fax. "The earth's obliquity to the ecliptic is typically twenty-three point four four degrees. The current angle at ten forty this morning is twenty-four point nine one four two. I can confirm that the planet's axial inclination has advanced by one point five degrees from the position considered normal."

"What does he mean by oblique to … uh, whatever?" Brian asks.

"Obliquity to the ecliptic is a scientific term used to express the angle of the axis. I had to do some research to understand what it meant, but the obliquity is the angle between the rotational axis and orbital axis of the planet, while the ecliptic is the celestial sphere of the apparent path the sun takes through the stars, as observed from earth."

Terry raises his eyebrows in amazement. "*Jesus* Lloyd! Where did *that* come from?"

Brian shakes his head. "I didn't understand a word of that."

"I'm confused too," Robert admits.

President Sinclair continues to relay the contents of the fax. "Dr. Bailey writes that evidence to suggest the obliquity to the ecliptic is still shifting is inconclusive; another twenty-four hours is required before advancement of the planetary alignment can be substantiated."

"Did the doctor respond to Jaeger's perception that a potential natural disaster is imminent?" Brian asks

The rustle of paper resounds in the electric silence as the president flips the first page of the fax and lets it dangle down from the top corner, where it's stapled together. "His assessment supports the Infinity evaluation, and Dr. Bailey writes that while a shift of one point five degrees may seem insignificant, in reality, major environmental changes can be expected across the planet. He doesn't elaborate other than to say that irreparable damage to the earth's fragile ecosystems is likely to occur."

"That's a pretty vague statement," Robert remarks.

"The professor goes on to say that he doesn't want to draw premature conjectures and that any statements issued will be based on facts. He adds that he will get a better idea of the consequences once he's confirmed whether the earth's axial inclination is still shifting or not." President Sinclair gets up from his perch on the front of the desk and begins to walk around to his seat again. "To be honest, Dr. Bailey's brief evaluation doesn't comfort me. We need to keep this out of the media. The *last* things we want are scaremongering and an unnecessary panic on our hands." He sits down. "I'm assigning the code name Tumble to this file, and until we understand what's going on, it stays classified. This will remain between the four of us, and if I need to bring anyone else in, I will do so at my privilege."

"Don't you think this is best handled by the CIA?" Robert asks.

Lloyd glares back at him with scornful eyes. "There are more leaks at Langley than you'll find in a rusty bucket."

Brian sits forward with a concerned expression in his eyes. "Sir, we aren't the only ones who are privy to this information. We must assume the employees at Infinity know, and Dr. Bailey probably has assistants too. It'll be pretty hard to contain."

"With regard to Infinity, it appears that the only people who know are Jaeger, Bentley, three technicians, and possibly Jaeger's private secretary. That's where it must be contained. There are four federal agents in the building, and none have reported anything in their daily updates, so it's not general gossip at the moment. The trouble is, I don't know how long it will stay that way."

"And there's the rub," Robert mutters. "Ninety-seven percent of the human population find it difficult to retain a secret for longer than twenty-four hours on average."

"Why don't we give them temporary accommodation at the Nevada facility for a few days?" Terry suggests.

Robert doesn't hesitate to oppose the vice president's proposal. "The existence and location of the Nora Hartley Center are classified. It's not a hotel to hide people; that's what safe houses are for."

"A safe house is to conceal people for their own protection, but it's not going to keep their mouths shut," Lloyd replies thoughtfully. "The people who need to be stymied are the ones we have to rely on for more information."

"There's an empty level at Nora Hartley," Brian says. "It *is* a research facility, and I think that's exactly where they should be."

Lloyd turns his eyes to Robert. "I want Dr. Bailey quarantined until he's able to give us a definitive prognosis."

"What will you do if his research supports Infinity's conjecture?" Terry asks.

"Then I may have no alternative but transfer him to the Nora Hartley Center," Lloyd replies firmly, "but let's not get ahead of ourselves. I expect this will be behind us once the doctor has made a full assessment, and in another twenty-four hours we'll be talking about other things."

"What about Infinity?" Robert asks.

"Now, they're a little more problematic. I've been told that their satellites are still going out of service, but the data they are collecting may be of immediate value. This Brad Bentley seems to be a pretty sharp tool." President Sinclair takes a moment to contemplate. "I want him taken to the Nora Hartley Center with any specialized equipment he needs to maintain communications with his equipment in orbit, but it *must* be done today, and it *must* be done with discretion."

Robert scribbles a few notes into a small pad. "Is he married?"

"I don't know," Lloyd replies, "but if he is, his wife and any children under twenty-one can go with him."

"What of Jaeger and the rest of the geeks at Infinity?"

"Robert, *you're* in charge of homeland security. Do whatever is necessary to keep things under wraps until Monday afternoon, but he must *not* be allowed to go public under any circumstances until I give him consent."

"I understand."

"You're excused. I want this handled right away."

As Robert tucks the notebook into a pocket and leaves the study, Terry clears his throat. "Aren't you overreacting? I don't think it's necessary to place everyone under sequestration."

"I'm merely being cautious. *Tumble* will remain a red-light priority until we have it in perspective." He pauses for a moment. "Tell the campaign manager to reschedule tomorrow's rally in Kansas for another date."

"You have two back-to-back appearances on Sunday," Terry remarks. "Do you want to have them postponed too?"

"Sunday? *Sunday?*" Lloyd mutters, recalling where he should be. "Oh, that's a definite no. Those are in Ohio, and I can't afford to blow them out."

The vice president stands up. "I'll be in my office for the rest of the day if you need me. I have a lot of shit to catch up on."

"Tell me about it," Lloyd groans. He pulls a folder across the desk and opens it. "I have some congressional paperwork that requires my attention, so I'm going to be stuck here for a while too."

Terry smiles before heading for the exit with Brian close behind.

32

Infinity Meteorological Database Systems, Inc.
Hamilton Ave, Palo Alto, California
Coordinates: 37° 26' 40.3" N, 122° 09' 36.2" W
Friday, June 26, 2020, 1242h

Steve walks across the floor and slumps into the chair behind his desk. In compliance with the federal auditor's instructions, he's just returned from the unpleasant task of announcing to the employees that most would be furloughed by the end of their shift. He's never had to perform such a tasteless mission before, and he had no problem pointing the finger at the two agents who followed him around. Despite a guarantee that the employees would not lose their jobs, there was still a lot of umbrage and anger among the staff.

He opens a spreadsheet and throws himself into a chore that requires a lot of concentration. The plan is to keep his mind engaged, but after ten minutes he realizes that it's not going to be so easy to push his emotions aside. The telephone rings, and he answers it in a despondent voice.

"Mr. Jaeger, this is Robert Klaus, secretary of homeland security. I'm calling on behalf of the president of the United States." The tone in the secretary's voice is formal and somewhat prickly.

Steve stiffens. "Hello, Mr. Secretary."

"By the time this conversation is over, two of my agents will be in your office. You *are* required to comply with their instructions. Do I make myself clear?"

An angry scowl appears on Steve's face. "What are they—"

The voice on the other end of the line cuts him off sharply. "Have I made myself clear?"

"Yes, *loud* and clear, and I—" But there's a click, followed by a buzz, as the caller hangs up while Steve is in midsentence. Infuriated by the secretary's rudeness, Steve slams the handset back on its cradle. He swings an arm over to the intercom and presses the Talk button. Nancy doesn't answer right away, but when she does, there's a definite note of hostility in her voice. Her name was included in the furlough, and despite pleas to the auditors to keep her on, they deemed her expendable. The reduced company trade and production no longer justified her continued employment, and they considered the workload would be small enough for Steve to handle on his own.

Nancy is a valuable asset, and he doesn't want to lose her. Afraid she might seek alternative employment, he pulled her off to one side, and asked her to treat the time off as a vacation. He gave her assurances that she'd receive full back pay as soon as the feds released the accounts from appropriation, but she was too upset to respond.

"Yes, Mr. Jaeger?"

"The Department of Homeland Security called to tell me that a couple of goons are coming to see me. Let me know when they get here."

She lowers her voice. "They're here, Mr. Jaeger, and they're heading for your office even though I asked them to wait. They are *rude*."

Steve rolls his eyes. "Thank you, Nancy."

He hears a scratchy sound at the door and is startled by a head peering around the corner. The stranger tries to open it with stealth, but now that he's been spotted, he steps into the office with an egotistical swagger and an air of arrogance. He's a burly man in his midtwenties who stands a little over six feet tall and is dressed in a smart, dark suit.

"The polite thing to do is knock and wait until you're invited to enter," the CEO snaps, making no attempt to hide his indignation at the man's sneakiness. "You don't have the right to come marching in here like you own the place."

The agent doesn't respond to the complaint, and a second man—a little shorter, but just as muscular—follows him into the office. They walk into the center of the room and stop. Steve is repulsed by their behavior, but despite their anarchic attitude, he makes an effort to be cordial.

"Please sit down, gentlemen."

They ignore the invite and continue to display an aberrant deportment that's intended to intimidate. While their stance is unsettling, the CEO is not a person who is easily coerced.

"You don't scare me if *that's* what you're trying to do," he says in a contemptuous tone, and he looks from one to the other with a denigrating leer in his eyes. "Quit playing silly games and tell me why you're here?"

The first man has a gruff, grainy voice. "We're here to escort Mr. Brad Bentley to the White House."

"You need to tell *him*, not me."

"We have orders to assist Mr. Bentley with his equipment."

"*What* equipment?"

"Whatever is necessary to communicate with the satellites."

"I want to see identification," Steve replies dourly. The first man reacts to the demand with a fiery glare, as if Steve doesn't have the right to question their authority.

"Didn't you get a telephone call from our boss?"

"You are *rude*. You haven't told me who *you* are, let alone who the fuck your boss is."

"Robert Klaus, the sec—"

The CEO cuts him off with a scornful snort. "I had a brief exchange with someone who *claimed* to be the secretary of homeland security, but I didn't get an attestation as to whether he's the person he says he is. For all I know, you could all be imposters."

"Didn't he tell you to cooperate with us?"

"Yes, he did, and like you, he had no manners either. Our equipment is unique and is protected by corporate *and* private rights. I need to see some credentials before I allow *anything* to be removed from the premises. You have thirty seconds before I call the police."

It's clear that they loathe Steve's demands, but they reluctantly comply. The two men produce a gold five-pointed star and a picture identification, but they make no effort to walk over to the desk. The CEO beckons with a finger. "Don't be shy! My eyesight isn't *that* good."

The pair hesitate but finally walk over to the desk, where Steve deliberately antagonizes them further by taking his time in scrutinizing the cards. He has no idea whether the badges are authentic or not, but they identify the men as Roland Jennings and Paul Robbins.

"Thank you," he says with controlled politeness.

Steve is puzzled as the two agents step backward into the center of the room again, but he makes no comment. He's still averse to letting any equipment leave the tower, but the fact that Brad will be in charge of the apparatus consoles him. The CEO is beginning to realize that there must be more substance to Brad's theory than he was willing to believe, and his eyes glint with curiosity. "Why is Mr. Bentley required in Washington? We can communicate quite effectively with the satellites from here."

"We don't question our orders, Mr. Jaeger. We obey them," Roland replies in a hostile tone.

Steve reaches for his iPhone. "Hey, BB, I need you to come up to my office."

"I'll be there in a couple of minutes."

He disconnects. "He's on his way."

The agent acknowledges with a single nod. Both men are standing in macho style with their arms folded, staring at him in silence. The thick atmosphere makes the CEO uncomfortable, so he tries to break the status quo.

"Would either of you like a cup of coffee or anything to drink?"

"Not for me," Roland replies, and he paces across the floor to a window in the west wall that overlooks Hamilton Avenue. It's behind Steve, and he swivels the chair around to a position where he can keep the agents in the corner of each eye.

Undaunted, he tries to engage them in small talk. "I hear the weather is as hot in Washington as it is in California."

Roland places a finger and thumb between the slats of the venetian blinds and stretches them apart to peer into the street below. "Hotter."

"You still have July and August to get through yet."

Steve's attempt to strike up a conversation falters. The agent is still on the prowl and ambles in silence to a bookcase on the south wall, behind the CEO. Now he's unable to keep an eye on both, but because Roland is the one on the mooch, he swings the chair around to keep an eye on him. The library is full of technical manuals but nothing of a sensitive nature. The agent angles his head to one side to read the titles on the spines. He selects a tome that seems to catch his interest and flicks casually through the pages.

To Steve's relief, the door opens and Brad enters. The CTO glances from one agent to the other, and then at his friend, with inquiring eyes. Roland closes the volume and, to the CEO's surprise, replaces it in the correct location.

"BB, these two ... uh, gentlemen ... are from Homeland Security."

Roland saunters back toward his partner, but he keeps his eyes locked on Brad. Steve is astonished by the unexpected softening in the agent's attitude as he greets the CTO in a pleasant tone. "Mr. Bentley?"

Brad is hesitant. "Yes."

"We've been asked to escort you, and all essential equipment necessary to communicate with your satellites, to the White House. President Sinclair needs you to analyze data that may be of use to him."

The chief technician frowns. "Analyze *what* data? Why does he want me to go to Washington? I'm communicating with them from here twenty-four seven."

"I'm only following orders, Mr. Bentley. The president likes his advisors close at hand during a crisis."

"Advisor? Crisis?" Brad echoes in astonishment.

"You *are* the expert when it comes to your satellite systems, yes?"

BB appears perplexed. "Well, yes, but there's a lot of sensitive, heavy, and bulky equipment."

"That won't be a problem," Roland replies. "A truck is waiting in the service bay at the rear of the building. We've been ordered to render assistance to get your apparatuses loaded and transported safely."

A wary expression creeps into Brad's eyes. "You seem to have anticipated that I'll agree to go."

"Are you refusing?"

"I haven't made up my mind yet. I'll let you know on Monday."

Roland's response is blunt. "You're coming back with us today, like now."

Brad reacts with a horrified expression in his eyes. "*Today?* I can't. My wife will kill me if I bail without warning."

"That's *not* an issue, Mr. Bentley. A limousine is on its way to your house to pick her up, and you'll join her at the airport. The first lady is affable, and I'm sure your spouse would love the opportunity to spend a weekend at the White House."

"You know where I live?"

"Of course."

Brad's face is in a state of confusion. "I don't know … we still need to arrange a sitter for the kids."

"That's not necessary," Roland continues persuasively. "You'll be in a family-friendly environment, and it'll be an adventure for the children too. They'll be the envy of their friends when they start the new semester with tales of their summer vacation. Call your wife and tell her you're taking the family on a surprise trip, but be sure you *don't* tell her where you're going; otherwise, it wouldn't be a surprise, *would* it?"

Steve can see that his friend is unhappy over the way he's being shanghaied. "I still need to go home and pick up some clean clothes."

The agent gives a short, gruff laugh. "I'm sure your wife is capable of packing something for you. I know this is unexpected, but it's urgent, and we must get your equipment operational as soon as possible."

The CTO looks at Steve for support with a silent gesture of his hands. Steve shrugs with a big grin on his face, and resignation slides across Brad's face. "It looks like my best friend has sold me out, too." He heaves a heavy sigh. "I'll need high-speed cable connections to communicate with the satellites."

"That won't be a problem," Roland replies. "The White House has the fastest in the world."

"Well, that I *can* believe," Brad mutters.

The agent smiles. "Call your wife. A chauffeur-driven car will arrive at your house to pick her up in about twenty minutes."

Brad gives a sardonic laugh. "It's clear you don't have much experience with women."

"I've had my fair share, Mr. Bentley, trust me," Roland replies. "Let's go to your lab, and get your stuff together."

Brad glances at his partner with exasperation on his face before he turns and walks toward the door. As he begins to exit the office, Steve calls out to him.

"Have a good weekend, BB."

The company's technical executive doesn't respond; he disappears into the corridor with the two agents close on his heels.

33

Bir Lehlou
Western Sahara
Coordinates: 26° 21' 00.2" N, 09° 34' 33.1" W
Friday, June 26, 2020, 1317h

Bir Lehlou is a tiny oasis town located in the northeastern sector of Western Sahara. The dusty desert village is inhabited mainly by Sahrawis and comprises a few shanty homes, a small shop, a mosque, a dispensary, a school, and a crude gas station. A Land Rover is parked outside of the general supply store, which sells basic necessities for the townsfolk and serves as a post office. Several Arabic children stand around and watch with curiosity. Visitors to the village are rare, and word spreads fast when a stranger drives in.

Randy Middleton appears in the doorway of the tiny mart. The heat is brutal, and his forehead is beaded with perspiration as he grips the ears of a large sack of rice over his shoulders. He stumbles down the three wooden steps under the weight, and trudges across to a Land Rover parked close by. The tailgate is down, and with a loud grunt he lets the load slide from his back onto the platform. Before pushing it into the rear of the vehicle, he pulls a handkerchief from a pocket and mops the sweat from his face.

The fifty-one-year-old is the leader of a small British archaeological expedition who are here at the invitation of the Polisario government. The team were asked to investigate large fossils discovered in an old phosphate mine, and as they brushed the sand away from the aged bones with painstaking patience, excitement began to mount. They'd stumbled across the mass grave of an undiscovered species of dinosaur, and preliminary tests dated them back 220 million years. This placed the creatures close to the beginning of the Triassic Period, and Dr. Middleton is waiting for confirmation to come back from the laboratory. If true, the reptile is three times larger than those known to exist during that era.

The importance, value, and immense size of the ancient graveyard required additional workers. Randy sought permission to employ local Sahrawis to perform manual labor duties. They are one of the major Bedouin ethnic tribal groups in the region, but the language barrier was an obstruction until he came across nineteen-year-old Sekkouri al-Taheel. The young man spoke English and Hassaniya, an Arabic dialect common in this part of the country, and because of his language skills, Randy gave him a supervisory position.

Although Bir Lehlou is a 250-mile drive across a hot, sandy, and unforgiving wilderness, it's the nearest town to the archeological site. He had to coordinate the import of provisions and equipment through the supply depot. The old man who owned the store seized the opportunity, and extorted a fee to allow the shipments to pass through the town. This infuriated the archaeologist, but his options were few. He needed someone to hold the supplies until someone drove in to pick them up. The task usually fell on Sekkouri, but this week Randy wanted a diversion from his daily routine.

He casts a casual glance at an older model jeep as it pulls up close to his with a beefy roar, and shoves the handkerchief back into his pocket. A tall, slim Arabic man in his midforties jumps out of the vehicle and approaches with a big grin on his face.

"*As'haab*, Randy! This is a surprise. How are you, my friend?"

A smile of recognition breaks across the archeologist's face, and he greets the man with a hug. "Firkin al-Mouhand! By all that's holy! What brings you to this dusty, sandy world?"

"Allah, and my jeep," the newcomer replies, and laughs. "I'm doing a dig in an abandoned phosphate mine to the west of here."

"You and me both." Randy stands back and looks his old friend up and down. "I see you're just as skinny as ever."

"It's the bloody diet," Firkin replies. "I'll never be able to get a belly like yours if I can't get some decent food inside of me."

"I know what you mean. Even the occasional stewed camel would be a welcome change."

The Arab begins to probe the archaeologist's presence. "I can't imagine you're here on a pleasure trip, so I think you must be on to something big, yes?"

"I'm leading a British team at a dig about 250 miles northeast of here," Randy explains. "I'm here at the invite of the Polisario government to investigate some fossils in an old mine."

Firkin turns his head and spits on the ground. His voice is full of scorn, and his eyes are dark with hatred. "Fuckin' Polisarios. They're as worthless as the piss that dribbles down a camel's hind legs." He looks back at Randy. "Nothing personal against *you*, my friend, but they never give us the opportunity to explore anything of importance. They are always given to foreigners."

The British archaeologist is sympathetic. "I'm sorry the politics haven't changed."

The dark expression on Firkin's face dissipates as fast as it appeared. "I suppose this is a big find, is it not?"

"It's bigger than I expected. We've uncovered fossils of a brand-new species of dinosaur."

Firkin's mouth drops open in astonishment. "You don't say, you lucky dog. You Britishers smell like roses while my foot stands in camel shit."

"Why don't you come back with me? You can stay for as long as you like."

The Arab's expression changes to one of excitement. "As'haab, Randy, you will allow this for me? It will make me happy."

Firkin can change facial expressions faster than a light switch can be flicked on and off—a habit he's had for all the years that Randy has known him—and a moment later he looks forlorn. "I can't come today. I, too, have come for supplies, and my men can't wait for too many days. Mayhap we can arrange something for next week?"

"What about next Friday? I'll drive in on the next supply run."

Firkin is unable to contain his excitement. "I will be here early, as'haab."

An older man of Sahrawi descent appears in the shop doorway holding a large cardboard box. He speaks to the British archaeologist brusquely in Hassaniya. Firkin glances at the supply store owner before translating for his friend.

"He says this is the last carton."

Randy walks up the steps and takes it from the man. "*Shu-kraan.*"

The old man nods his head once. "*Ma-sa-laam,*" he says, and he disappears back into the building without saying another word.

The archaeologist carries the box to the Land Rover and sits it in the rear. He closes the tailgate before dusting the palms of his hands together. "All done for another week." He glances at his wristwatch before placing a hand on Firkin's shoulder. "Listen, I would love to stay and chat for a while longer, but I must leave. I have a long drive, and I want to be back at the site before darkness falls."

"I understand. I am in similar circumstances."

"I'll meet you here next week, then?"

Firkin takes his British counterpart's right hand in a firm grip and gives it a solid shake. "But of course, as'haab! I want to see this monster you dig up, and sup a few glasses of quality scotch while we reminisce. Drive with care, my friend, and beware of the dust devils."

Randy climbs into the Land Rover and starts the engine. It's hot inside. He wipes the sweat from his brow and takes a swig of tepid water from a bottle lying on the passenger seat while he waits for the climate control to fill the interior with cooler air. Two minutes later, he pulls out onto a dusty trail and heads out of the village. Three miles out, he turns off the track and drives northeast into the open desert. There are no landmarks, and the GPS is the only device that can guide him back to the dig site.

For the next thirty minutes he drives through territory where the sand dunes rise up into imposing sentinels. For thousands of years, the ancient barriers have challenged the strength and courage of travelers and explorers as they've shifted, changed, and marched before the wind across this foreboding, unforgiving desert. A thick ecru cloud kicked up by the tires stretches out behind the vehicle like the vapor trail from a jet for more than half a mile before it dissipates in the still air.

Out in the wilderness, it's easy to drift off course, and Randy keeps a regular check on the GPS. Lost in his own introspection, he peers out of the windshield at the golden-brown dunes rolling across the landscape. A discoloration on the horizon draws his attention. Puzzled, but not concerned, he slows to a stop and climbs out. The heat outside the bubble of cool air in the cab is fierce. He removes his sunglasses and shades his eyes from the glare of the sun with the open palm of his right hand. It's usual for the outline of the distant dunes to stand out with sharp clarity against the clear blue sky, but a thin brownish hue from east to west blends the land and firmament together.

"Ahh, it's an illusion caused by the hot air currents rising from the surface," he concludes, and satisfied that there's nothing to worry about, the archaeologist climbs back into the cab. Fifteen minutes later, he comes to a standstill for a second time. The hue along the horizon is growing and has changed to a darker reddish-brown in color.

"Well, bugger me," he mutters. "If it isn't a bloody sandstorm."

Conventional cell phones are useless out in the desert, and Randy grabs the satphone from the passenger seat. He climbs back out of the vehicle and dials the number to one of his associates at the dig site. While he waits for the call to go through, he keeps a wary eye on the advancing wall. Dozens of dark vertical streaks undulate from side to side in a slow, wavy dance like snakes under the mesmerizing movement of a charmer's flute.

A red light on the telephone unit begins to flash, indicating a failure to connect with the satellite. This has never happened before, and he makes a second attempt, but the result is the same.

"Damn!" He assumes that the storm has disrupted communications and tosses the phone back into the Land Rover in disgust. The cloud moves across the sun, turning it from a dirty gold to an angry gray-black. It's not the first time he's been caught in a sandstorm, and he knows how formidable they can look, but this one is frightening.

A gentle, hot breeze swirls, and it ruffles his hair. Randy is alarmed. The wall of sand is bearing down fast; it is a menacing, living, breathing entity. Familiar with the intense energy it takes to generate a creature like this, he leaps back into the vehicle in panic. Fully exposed to the storm with nowhere to seek shelter, the archeologist slams the transmission into gear with a crunch and turns the Land Rover so the rear is toward the approaching storm to mitigate the chances of getting rolled. The problem with hot air storms is that while they move in one direction, the wind can sweep in from another.

Randy pulls the parking brake on, cuts the ignition, and waits with his eyes glued to the rearview mirror. The air is heavy, sultry, and the silence is ominous. He begins to wish that he's still at Bir Lehlou, but the archaeologist is unaware that the tiny town is about to be obliterated by the greatest sandstorm to ever rise up from the desert. Born in southern Egypt and northern Sudan, it's the leading edge of a huge frontal system that's marching across the North African continent with relentless fortitude. The five-hundred-mile-wide freak has swept through more than two thousand miles, destroying hundreds of desert towns in its path and exterminating an unknown number of tribal communities across parts of Libya, Chad, Niger, Algeria, and Mali, and now as it crosses Mauritania, Western Sahara, and southern Morocco.

A small sand devil swirls upward close to him and dies a few seconds later. Farther away, a second one spins up from the ground, and that, too, disintegrates; but a third one is closer, larger, and more sustained.

Time ticks by too slowly. A faint rumble grows in intensity, and in less than a minute, it develops into a cross between a roar and a godless howl. A constant ripple of shockwaves causes the vehicle to vibrate as the approaching wind pounds the surface. The raw, naked helplessness is enough to strip the heroism from the bravest warrior, and a shiver runs down his spine. Randy is afraid, and he supplicates for compassion as the sand kicks up around him.

The roar builds up to a howling crescendo, and moments later the storm slams into the rear of the Land Rover with unparalleled fury. It lurches forward for several feet on locked wheels. The noise is indescribable as the rattle of millions of sand grains smash into the vehicle like tiny pellets of hail. In the space of thirty seconds, daylight is vanquished by the huge volume of solid material in the atmosphere, and the surrounding dunes are obscured from view. The Land Rover rocks violently as enormous gusts buffet it with incredible ferocity. Gripped by sheer terror, he clenches the steering wheel so tightly that his knuckles turn white, and with every muscle in his body taut with fear, he prays fervently beneath his breath.

Several minutes of gut-wrenching dread pass. The rear window, weakened by the pitting of millions of sand grains smashing into it at excessive speeds, suddenly implodes. An instantaneous change of air pressure within the vehicle ruptures both of Randy's eardrums, and he screams in pain, covering the organs reflexively with the palms of his hands. The howl of the wind becomes a distant muffled roar, overridden by a high-pitched whine in his head.

But he doesn't get time to dwell on the injury. The windshield, door, and side windows shatter simultaneously into thousands of tiny fragments under the intense air pressure that took only a matter of seconds to build up inside the vehicle. Glass particles hang suspended before his eyes for a brief moment before they're whipped away by the ferocious wind into the dark world outside.

Randy screams in excruciating pain. Millions of sand grains stream in through the back window and exit the vehicle by means of the windshield opening. The tiny granules blast the back of his neck and head, tearing into his skin, stripping the flesh off in layers. His instinctive reaction is to protect the back of his skull from getting peppered by what feels like searing hot needles, and he clasps his hands together around the back of his head to shield it. Moments later, his fingers and arms begin to burn as though he's plunged them into a fire. He quickly pulls them back to the front and stares in horror at the bloody mess. Shredded tentacles of flesh hang from white skeletal bone, and blood trickles down the torn strips before dripping into his lap. Much of the tissue has been ripped away the top lower forearms, exposing parts of the radius and ulna.

The vehicle lurches and pivots 180 degrees into the face of the storm. The sand blasts at his face and chest, dissolving the flesh into a bloody red pulp. White skull and breast bone appear as the fine grains continue to rip into his body.

In a final gesture of dominance, the high winds flip the sturdy vehicle and roll it across the ground with the ease of a cardboard box.

34

Infinity Meteorological Database Systems, Inc.
Hamilton Ave, Palo Alto, California
Coordinates: 37° 26' 40.3" N, 122° 09' 36.2" W
Friday, June 26, 2020, 1446h

Danny looks at his boss as he absently wrings his hands and casts a critical eye over the electronic equipment, cables, and connectors stacked on the laboratory floor.

"I *think* this is all I need," Brad mutters, and he glances around one last time.

The young technician is satisfied that everything is there too. "What about the fixes we worked on last night? The simulation finished thirty minutes ago."

"Any glitches?"

"None. It was a one-hundred percent pass."

Brad beams at him before looking at Jim and Bill. "You guys have made me proud. I couldn't expect better teamwork from anyone. When I get back from this little jaunt, I'll make sure you all get the reward you deserve." He pauses for a moment and turns to Bill with a pessimistic tone in his voice. "Are we still losing satellites?"

"Yes. Portugal/Morocco and South Korea went down earlier. The Uruguayan satellite went offline about fifteen minutes ago."

"There's no rush to upload the fix until the situation goes into reverse," Brad says. "I suggest you all enjoy a well-deserved weekend off. I think next week will be busier than hell."

Danny's eyes light up. "Oh, *great!* It's my kid brother's twenty-first birthday today, and he's having a big party tonight."

Brad smiles. "Have fun. You'll have two days to nurse your hangover. I'll call you if I need anything." He pauses. "Don't forget to take the new fix up to Steve before you go home today. The data needs to be recoded, and he'll do that for you."

Danny wonders why Steve and Brad are the only two in the company who are able to validate new software, but it's a question that can wait. He turns to the two agents from Homeland Security who are standing near the exit and sweeps his arm over the equipment. "This is ready to load."

Roland is the one who responds. "Will there be anything else, or is this it?"

"That's everything."

The agent turns to Brad. "I'll walk you out to the car. It's waiting in the car park. Your wife is already at the airport, and from what I hear, she's a little feisty."

"You've poked a sleeping dog with a sharp stick, there," Brad replies. "The trouble is, I'm the one she's going to bite."

Roland doesn't even smile at the quip; he looks at the three technicians. "Okay, lads, take this stuff and load it into the van. My partner will help, and *you*"—he points to Danny—"can stow it in the box. You know what equipment can be stacked and what needs to go as top-load."

Brad sighs. "Well, I'll see you on Monday." He pauses before giving the senior technician a final reminder. "*Don't* forget to take the fix to Steve before you go home. Now, enjoy the weekend." The CTO turns and exits the lab with Roland.

"I'll be back to help once Mr. Bentley is on his way," the agent calls out as the doors start to close.

Paul speaks for the first time. "Anyone got a dolly?"

"There are a couple in the loading dock," Jim replies. "I'll be back in a minute."

Twenty-five minutes later, Danny lashes the last piece of equipment into the box truck. After it's tied in place, he makes a final inspection. Satisfied that everything is secure, he walks to the rear, reaches up, and, taking a firm hold on the canvas grip cord, leaps to the ground. The door rolls down behind him, and he looks at Paul.

"Hey, you got the key for the padlock?"

The agent steps forward, but rather than hand the key to the technician, he locks the box door himself. Danny shrugs it off.

"So much for your buddy coming back to give us a hand."

Paul doesn't respond, but Danny isn't surprised. He's spoken to them only when necessary, and with as few words as possible. At that moment, Roland appears at the front of the van with a vexed expression on his face.

"Perfect timing, man," the technician says. "We're all finished."

The agent ignores the remark and inclines his head. "Does he always fuss and dither?"

"Who? BB? He's far from being a ditherer."

"Twice he came back to the lab because he'd forgotten something," Roland complains. "He even wanted to come back a *third* time to change some instructions, but I had to stand firm and told him I'd relay the message. If I hadn't, he would have ended up missing the flight."

An awkward silence ensues. Danny is puzzled because it doesn't make sense. Brad is flying to Washington on a private flight, and it begs the question as to why they are desperate to rush him to the airport. The plane can't leave without the equipment. But Roland and Paul are an odd couple, and since he doesn't read anything into their strange behavior other than eccentricity, he lets it slide.

"What did BB want to tell me?"

"He's cancelled your weekend leave."

Danny's heart sinks at the unexpected change. "Did he say why?"

"He said something about data downloads, but it was all above my head."

"He's got all the equipment to do that himself," Danny quips. "It doesn't make sense for me to download here when he can do that at the White House."

Roland shrugs. "I'm not familiar with your procedures, so I can't tell you why. I'm only the messenger."

Bill turns to Danny. "Listen, don't miss out on your brother's party. I'll come in tomorrow. It shouldn't make any difference who's here as long as someone is."

Roland interrupts. "Uh, excuse me, but he requested for the *three* of you to come in. He made that quite clear to me."

"*All* of us?" Danny exclaims in astonishment. His shoulders slump, and feeling disheartened, he reluctantly agrees to abide by the new instructions. "Did he say what time he wants to start?"

"He said he'd call you at six o'clock."

Danny rolls his eyes and groans. "Oh, my good *gawd!* Why so fucking early?"

"Washington is in a different time zone," Roland says. "He *was* going to start at seven until I reminded him of the three-hour difference."

Disappointed, the technician stares down at his feet for a few seconds. "We'll be here." He turns his eyes to Bill and Jim while he speaks. "Won't we?"

It's clear they're as unenthused about the sudden switch as he is, but both men give affirmation with a simple yes. The three technicians head across the service bay for the elevator without saying another word to the agents. Danny gazes back at the truck while he waits for the car. Something doesn't feel right. He considers sharing his anxieties but decides to keep them to himself as the van pulls out of the loading bay.

"I don't see the need for three of us to come in tomorrow," Danny says. "You two take the weekend off, and I'll take full responsibility if BB goes into a shit fit."

Bill shakes his head. "I'd rather not take the chance. His instructions are specific, and he wouldn't do that without good reason."

"I agree," Jim adds. "United we stand, and all *that* bullshit. I'll be here too."

A bell dings to signal the arrival of the car. The elevator door opens, and as the three young men step inside, Danny pulls his iPhone from a pocket.

"Who're you calling?" Bill asks.

"BB. I want to confirm his instructions and ask him why he needs all of us." The call is redirected to Brad's voice mail. "*Damn!* He's turned his phone off." He waits for the beep and leaves a message asking him to call back regardless of time.

At four twenty, Danny heads up to the top floor with the USB memory sticks that need to be recoded. He stops by at Nancy's office to make sure the CEO is alone before charging in, and he is quick to observe her brooding mood.

"Hey, what's wrong?"

"I've been furloughed," she replies.

Danny is dumbfounded. He can see she's fighting back tears, and a wave of empathy sweeps through his body. She isn't married and doesn't have children, but she has a mortgage and car payment. If the temporary discharge lasts for too long, both her house and car could be repossessed.

His voice is firm and sincere. "Nancy, you have my number. Don't hesitate to call me if you need *any* financial assistance. I'm still working, and I have a decent amount saved up. You can pay me back after you return to work."

She reaches out and takes one of his hands. "Thanks for the offer, and your kindness is commendable, but I can't use a friend in that way."

"Goddamn it, Nancy, that's what friends are for. Now you've got to make a pledge."

She pulls a tissue from a box on her desk. "Okay, I promise."

"Is Steve alone in his office?"

"Yes."

"Then I'll be back after I give him these memory sticks," he says. "I'm taking you out for dinner."

"I appreciate the offer, but I'm not in the mood."

"It's not an offer. I'm going to my brother's birthday party later, so I won't keep you out late." He grins. "Scout's honor."

Her lips curl into a weak smile. "Okay, I accept."

Steve shuffles some papers into a neat stack and places them on the side of the desk, where they will be ready to deal with on Monday.

He takes his jacket from the back of the chair, and as he slips his arms into the sleeves, he hears a knock on the door. It opens, and Danny steps in.

"BB asked me to bring these USBs up before I go home."

"Are they the fix for the satellites?"

"Yes."

"Put them on my desk. I'll come in over the weekend to recode them."

Danny walks across the office with the package. "Do you think BB will be back on Monday?"

"That's what he hopes, but I have my doubts," Steve replies. He leans against the side of the desk and folds his arms. "I want you to report to me at nine o'clock on Monday morning. I have a proposal to make."

He can see that Danny's curiosity is aroused, but it's too late in the day to divulge a plan to promote the technician. It will be a pleasant start to the week.

"Not even a hint?" the young man asks.

Steve laughs. "No clues. If I say anything now, neither of us will get to go home tonight."

"I still have to come in tomorrow," Danny tells the CEO.

"Why? BB told me he was giving you guys the weekend off?"

"For some reason he's changed his mind."

"How many units are out of commission now?"

"Eleven went offline today, so that makes a total of thirty-four. Another two are predicted to go down before midnight."

"BB will let me know when the trend starts reversing," Steve says as he snaps his briefcase closed. "I'll need you to upload the new software into the satellites once I get them done."

"Not a problem."

"Well, I'm going home now, and I suggest you do the same thing."

"I will just as soon as I've set the security alarms," Danny replies. "Have a nice weekend, Mr. Jaeger."

As the technician leaves, Steve picks up his iPhone and sends a text to his wife. Five minutes later, he steps out of the elevator and walks across the lobby toward the exit. The automatic doors slide open, and he exits the building into the hot afternoon air without slowing his pace. He'd forgotten about the media, and the sight of the huge crowd packed into the forecourt brings him to a stop at the top of the steps. The yard erupts into an unintelligible wall of sound as reporters bawl out in an attempt to be heard over the next person, and the CEO places the briefcase on the ground before motioning for silence. The noise subsides, and an expectant hush falls over the courtyard.

"Ladies and gentlemen." His voice echoes around the alcove, which amplifies it to a level where it's heard with perspicuity by the captive audience below. "This week has tested our integrity, strength, and resolve to work through some serious issues with our satellite services. The technicians have identified the cause, and corrective measures are now in progress. However, satellites will continue to go offline over the next day or two while the modifications are integrated into the software. I want to apologize to our subscribers, who will receive a detailed report, and extend my gratitude to the staff at Infinity for their efforts to identify the origins so we can bring this unpleasant chapter in our history to a conclusion."

Intuition tells Steve to walk away, but he hesitates. A scurry, followed by a low murmur, ripples across the forecourt like a wave and explodes into a barrage of questions. He makes the mistake of responding and motions for silence once again. The noise dies down.

"I can't understand anything when you all yell at once. *Please.*" His eyes sweep over the crowd below, and he points to a reporter close to the bottom of the steps. "You, sir, in the plain blue T-shirt."

The journalist wastes no time. "How many satellites have failed to date?"

"Thirty-four."

Another voice yells out. "Mr. Jaeger, if you know the cause of the problem and have a fix for it, why are you going to cause further inconvenience by allowing more satellites to shut down?"

"The technicians are still writing the bypass codes, but I assure you corrective measures are being implemented with haste." He turns his eyes to another reporter. "Yes, sir—you in the sunglasses and green cap."

"Mr. Jaeger, what is the exact cause of the problem that brought down so many satellites? Is the fault in your own computer systems, or was it something else?"

He should have been prepared for the obvious question, and he knows it won't bode well if he declines to answer or if he becomes evasive. Steve opens his mouth to explain how inappropriate it would be to enunciate the details publicly before he submits a clientele report, but in a moment of uncertainty, he wonders if it will be enough to satisfy their curiosity, and he hesitates.

Perhaps it is the vacillation, or it might be his demeanor or his body language that are misinterpreted, but someone is afraid he's about to reveal the truth. The CEO doesn't hear the distant crack of a high-powered rifle; nor does he feel the high-velocity bullet penetrate the center of his forehead between the eyes. The parietal bone explodes with a sickening but distinct pop that echoes around the alcove as the projectile exits the back of his skull. The air is so still and quiet that the splat of blood and clumps of brain matter hitting the glass door behind him is heard by the people below. A loud gasp resounds around the courtyard as the tissue slides down the smooth surface, leaving a bloody trail in its wake.

He is dead before he begins to collapse. Dozens of reporters stare in silent horror as his legs bend at the knees. His body crumples into a lifeless mound with a muffled thud in front of the business he started from nothing with his lifelong friend.

The people in the forecourt gaze at the motionless form in stunned silence.

Somewhere, a woman screams.

35

*Los Robles Avenue
Barron Park, Palo Alto, California, USA
Coordinates: 37° 24' 44.4" N, 122° 07' 50.6" W
Saturday, June 27, 2020, 0601h*

Danny is lying faceup on a king-size bed with both arms stretched out to the sides. He's dressed in a pair of faded blue jeans, a once-white T-shirt with an ugly brown stain down the front, and a black sneaker laced on his left foot. A sock hangs off the other one.

He groans, rolls his head on the pillow, and opens his eyes. It takes a few seconds to focus on the bedside clock. The time is two minutes past six, and he sits up in panic. *"Holy crap!* I'm late." His head is throbbing, and he raises both hands to hold it with another loud groan. He has no idea how much alcohol he consumed or how he got home. Steve's assassination had dispelled all desire in him to socialize, but not wanting to snub his brother on his twenty-first birthday, he made an appearance. It wasn't long before he wished he'd stayed home.

When he got home at five on the previous evening, he called Nancy to see if she'd heard the news about Steve. He couldn't imagine that she'd want to go to a restaurant after what happened, but he wanted to let her make that decision. Her voice mail picked up after four rings, so he tried again at the prearranged time of six o'clock. When she failed to answer again, he left a second message. An hour later, Danny made a last attempt to contact her, but by now he was getting annoyed with her for ignoring his calls.

The technician swings his legs out of bed and gets to his feet. He staggers to the bathroom, strips the dirty clothes from his body, and leaves them in an untidy heap on the floor. His coordination is not good, and after splashing cold water on his face, he ambles unsteadily back to the bedroom to get dressed. Ten minutes later, he's speeding northbound on route 82.

Steve's death is foremost in his mind, and as he gets close to the freeway exit, his iPhone begins to ring. Without taking his eyes off the highway, he reaches out with his right arm and fumbles around to retrieve it from where he'd thrown it on the passenger seat. He's left the Bluetooth earpiece at home, and though it's illegal use a phone without the device while driving, he takes the chance.

"Hello?"

Jim is on the other end. "Danny, where the hell *are* you, man? Bill and I are getting worried."

"I'm on my way in. Has BB called?"

"No, not yet."

Danny breathes a sigh of relief and steers the car toward the off-ramp. "I'm getting off the freeway now, so I'll be there in six or seven minutes. If he calls, tell him I'm on the shitter or something."

Jim laughs, but it sounds forced and humorless. "Okay."

"Are the feds still there?"

"Nope, they're all gone. They were just leaving when I got here."

"Man, I still can't believe what happened to Steve."

"Me too. Were you here when he was shot?"

"Yes, but we'll talk about it when I get in," Danny replies. "I forgot my Bluetooth, and the last thing I need is to get pulled over by the cops."

"Okay. See you in a few."

The technician disconnects the phone and tosses it on the passenger seat again. He drives the blue Toyota Corolla along University Avenue a little faster than the posted speed restrictions, which forces him to brake sharply to take the corner at Ramona Street.

He's one block from the Infinity headquarters when a bright white flash suddenly encompasses the entire ground floor. Danny slams his foot down on the brake pedal, and the vehicle skids to an abrupt stop with a screech of tires. The technician stares in horror as a massive horizontal sheet of flame blasts outwards before curling up and flickering into huge orange tongues that lick around the first and second floors. The shockwave shatters every window on each floor in succession as it travels up through the frame and exits the top of the structure in a massive shower of dust and debris. Millions of glass shards fly in all directions before raining back to earth in a wide circle around the tower.

At the same time, shockwaves traveling through the ground hit the Toyota from underneath with a hard, resounding thump that rocks the vehicle wildly. A few seconds later, several huge explosions erupt from behind the main edifice where the laboratories are located, and giant fireballs roll up into sky.

Danny grips the steering wheel tightly with both hands, and his mouth sags open in disbelief. Huge plumes of thick black smoke billow out from the first two floors and cling to the side of the building for about half its height before drifting away at a gentle angle into the clear morning sky. The only noise that permeates the air is the roar of the fire as gigantic flames flicker through the smoke and lick up from the ground floor with so much ferocity that he feels the heat through the windshield.

Danny is numbed, and for the next few minutes his breath comes in short accelerated pants as he tries to process what has just happened. Something doesn't measure up. There are no chemicals stored on the premises that could cause such a powerful blast. The distant sound of emergency vehicle sirens reaches his ears, and an intuitive sense tells him it wouldn't be wise to be seen in the vicinity. Still dazed, he restarts the engine, makes a U-turn, and drives back toward University Avenue.

The traffic signals are green, but he stops to let several fire engines and a police cruiser turn onto Ramona. After they've passed through the junction, he drives straight ahead. The blue Corolla makes a left at Lytton Avenue and a right onto Alma Street, and it continues for another mile before pulling into the parking lot of a McDonald's restaurant opposite the Menlo Park train station. He parks in an empty space in the far corner.

The technician cuts the ignition and leans across the passenger seat to retrieve the iPhone from the floor, where it had been thrown when he braked hard. His hands are shaking as he redials Jim's number. Deep in his gut, he knows the probable fate of his colleagues, and as he expected, the call goes straight to voice mail.

In a state of blind confusion, he calls Nancy. It's almost seven o'clock, and he assumes she's probably still asleep, but he needs to talk to someone. The phone rings three times before a sleepy, toneless male voice answers.

"Hello?"

Danny didn't think she was in a relationship, and caught off-guard, he stammers in surprise. "Uh ... hi. I-I'm sorry for calling this early. Is Nancy there?"

A long pause ensues. "Who is this?"

The technician feels awkward. "Danny ... Danny Walker. I'm a colleague."

"Oh, yes, you're the one who left messages on her voice mail. I intended to call you later today. I'm Brian Pritchell, her younger brother."

Danny is relieved that it's not someone who might get jealous at his trying to contact her, and he continues to explain himself. "She was furloughed because of the satellite crisis, and I promised to take her out for dinner. She asked me to call her at six o'clock, but she never answered or returned my messages."

Another long, uncomfortable silence follows, and he decides to clarify why he's calling so early in the morning. "I don't want to speak to her about that, though. I ... uh, *Christ*, I don't know how to say this ..." His lips quiver, and for the first time, tears well up in his eyes. "The Infinity tower and laboratories ... there's been an explosion ..." An emotional lump forms in his throat and begins to restrict his speech. "I think Jim and Bill are dead ... and anyone else who was inside. I saw it. A *huge* explosion ..." He falters. His emotions collide, and he sobs. "Steve ... her boss ... the CEO was assassinated last night, and I wanted to tell Nancy, but can you tell her for me?"

Brian remains silent for such a long time that a noise in the background is the only indication that they're still connected. "Nancy was killed in a car accident on her way home from work yesterday."

This is the last thing he expected to hear, and he feels as though he is getting slammed in the gut with a sledgehammer. His head spins as Brian continues to talk in a strangled voice. "The police said the brakes failed when she was coming down Mason's Hill."

"I-I'm so sorry," Danny stammers in a hoarse whisper. "I don't know what to say …" Mason's Hill is a dangerously steep incline with a sharp bend at the bottom, and he always avoids it unless there's no alternative route.

Brian becomes choked up. "They need to do forensic tests on the brake hoses first, but the detective thinks they were deliberately cut."

Tears run down the technician's cheeks. "Who would *do* such a thing? She's such a beautiful person and wouldn't harm *anyone*."

"A witness said he saw flames inside the car before it hit the wall. It'll take several days for the autopsy and forensic reports to come back, but the coroner is expected to rule her death as a homicide." His voice gets angry. "If her death *is* deliberate, I *will* track the bastard down and kill him with my own hands."

"Have you been to the morgue?"

"They won't let me. Her car exploded into a fireball when it hit the stone wall at the foot of the hill. They said she was burned beyond recognition and had to confirm her identity from dental records."

Danny shudders. It's a brutal way to die, and he can barely speak. "I'm so sorry. Can I call you later?"

"Yes."

"Thank you."

He slides the iPhone into a pocket, closes his eyes, and lays his head against the headrest. Danny goes over the horrific moment after he secured the lab on the previous afternoon. He set the intruder alarm and was on his way to the lobby when a distant scream penetrated the corridor. Quickening his pace, he strode past the elevators into the foyer, and as he turned the corner, he saw an ugly red splatter that looked like blood with tiny rivulets running down the glass doors. Two security guards were kneeling over a motionless form lying on the ground outside. Driven by curiosity, the technician took a few more hesitant paces forward, but he couldn't discern what was happening or who had collapsed. Henry Jackson, a crippled black guard who usually remained behind the security desk logging staff and visitors into the tower, was standing close to the main door, brandishing a walking cane to turn people away. Another guard ushered them through the building toward the rear entrance.

"What's going on, Henry?"

The guard stared back at him through wide, tear-filled eyes. "Someone just shot Mr. Jaeger."

Danny's heart beat hard, and his head spun wildly at the guard's unexpected announcement. "H-how bad?"

"Worse than awful, son. He's dead."

His stomach sank into a deep pit, and a wave of nausea swept through his body. Several seconds passed before he was able to speak in a raspy voice. "Nancy? Did you see *Nancy?*"

"Miss Pritchell left a few minutes ahead of Mr. Jaeger."

As he sits in the Toyota, Danny tries to put everything into perspective. What are the odds that four Infinity employees would die in three separate but extremely violent incidents less than fifteen hours apart? *Steve. Nancy. Bill. Jim. BB is at the White House… or is he?* And if he hadn't overslept, he would have been a victim too. Even for the diehard skeptic, that's far too many to be coincidental, but keeping it realistic, who would go to this much trouble to make sure they were dead, and why?

Something tells him it's linked to the phenomenon recorded by the satellites, but the question is, how? *If it was an upset customer who came gunning for Steve, where's the logic in going after Bill, Jim, and Nancy? And Brad? He hasn't answered his phone or returned any of the messages left on his voice mail. Is he dead too?*

When BB explained to him on Thursday what could happen to the planet, the technician thought it sounded abstract and too apocalyptic. Now he's beginning to wonder if the implications are more serious than his skepticism allowed him to believe. Even if there *is* some substance to the speculations, it's not a good reason to kill people. No one except for President Sinclair knew about Brad's suspicions. *Unless ...*

He wants to dismiss the notion of a government conspiracy as ridiculous. It's something he'd expect to read in a John le Carré novel, but it would *never* happen in reality—or could it? Had they accidentally stumbled on a secret operation that the government was trying to hide? There must be a rational explanation, and all he needs to do is figure out what it is. He's too confused to think straight. He decides a black coffee and an egg burger will help to clear his head.

He gets out of the car. To the west, a distant plume of black smoke mars a blue sky, and he hurries across the parking lot. There are only a few people in the fast-food restaurant, and after making a purchase, he sits at a table where he can watch the early morning news on the television. All eyes are on the fire raging out of control around the Infinity tower. The first eight floors are engulfed, and the newscaster reports that at least two technicians, and possibly a third, were inside at the time of the explosion.

Danny frowns. The statement was specific and sounded unambiguous. How did they know *who* was in the building so soon after the explosion? The fire is so fierce that the firemen are still in defensive mode and haven't been able to get close to the tower. His iPhone rings, and he pulls it from his pocket to see Brad's number on the display. Overwhelmed with relief, he answers.

"BB?"

"Is this Danny Walker?"

The baritone voice doesn't belong to his boss, and he becomes cautious. "Yes."

"I'm calling on behalf of Mr. Bentley. He's been trying to call you at the office, but he's not getting a reply. Where are you?"

An alarm goes off in Danny's head, and he hesitates. "May I speak to Brad?"

"He can't come to the phone right now. Where are you?"

The hairs on the back of his neck prickle. "I'm in the lab."

"Now we both know that's not true," the person replies in a near condescending manner.

A wave of panic sweeps through the technician. He keeps his voice as normal as his agitated state will allow. "Tell Mr. Bentley I'll call him back."

"Where are you?" the speaker repeats, but this time his tone is demanding.

Danny closes the connection. How did *they* know he hadn't been killed in the explosion? His suspicions that the deaths of his colleagues were intentional are becoming a conviction, and now they want him, but the evasive question is, why? Nervous, confused, and scared, he pushes the tray with the half-eaten burger away from him. His iPhone rings again. He turns it off and removes the sim card. If they *are* desperate to find him, they can track his location by ping triangulation. He leaves the restaurant and drops the card into the trash as he walks out. Before getting into the car, he throws the phone into some bushes at the far end of the parking lot.

The blue Corolla pulls out of the car park and turns right. His priority is to drive as far away from here as possible, as fast as he can. Danny has no idea where to go, but he can't go back home. If he is being chased by the government, it's probably under surveillance by now.

36

The President's Private Study
The White House, Washington, DC
Coordinates: 38° 53' 50.6" N, 77° 02' 15.1" W
Saturday, June 27, 2020, 1017h

The expression on President Sinclair's face is one of indifference as he absorbs the contents of a fax that came in from Dr. Jack Bailey less than five minutes earlier. The telephone rings, and without taking his eyes away from the document, he reaches out to pick up the handset.

"Yes?"

Brian Harding is on the other end, and he speaks with some exigency in his tone. "Mr. President, a new satellite situation is emerging."

Lloyd waits for the secretary to continue, but after several moments of silence, he scowls in irritation. "Well? Go on, I'm listening."

"DirecTV began to receive complaints of lost reception from their consumers about two hours ago, but now the affliction has spread to global corporations like Sky, Art, ABS-CBN, and a bunch of other major broadcasters."

A contemplative expression moves across the president's face. "Did they clarify what they mean by 'lost reception'? I understand that pictures aren't being received, but are they able to communicate with their satellites from a technical standpoint like Infinity can?"

"Yes, but the signal is erratic, and they're scared of losing it altogether. I've just gotten off the phone with DirecTV's CEO, who admits that the outage has stumped their technicians. They're anxious to contact someone at Infinity to find out how they resolved their satellite issues."

The president's forehead wrinkles. "Do you think it has something to do with the change in the earth's axis?"

Brian's reply is hesitant. "I'm not sure. Maybe. The TV satellites are in a geostationary orbit, so I guess it *could* be possible, but I'm not a NASA scientist. I mean, Jaeger contends that the shift is responsible for taking down their network, so why wouldn't others be affected?"

"I don't have full verification from Dr. Bailey in support of Infinity's allegations yet, and until we do, their excuse remains an open debate." Lloyd places the fingertips of his right hand against his temple and closes his eyes to mull it over before speaking again. "If a satellite is in geostationary orbit, doesn't it stay in the same position without moving? I'm sure that's what it means."

"Geostationary satellites move, but their orbital speed is synchronized to the earth's rotation. That's what makes them *appear* to be stationary from our perspective on the surface." Brian pauses. "If the earth has moved out of alignment with the satellites, wouldn't their positions change relative to a fixed point on the ground? At least, that's how *I* perceive it."

"Damn!" An angry grimace appears on the president's face. "Does this mean every satellite will be affected?"

"To be honest, that's a question I can't answer."

"I think you should find out," President Sinclair demands in a gruff voice. He sighs and glowers down at the fax in his hand. The pitch of his voice shifts to a softer tone. "Brian, I think Dr. Bailey is qualified to give us a detailed overview on what to expect. I'm going to have him flown in, and we'll see where it goes from there. Can you be here by 1500 hours?"

"Yes."

"Bring Barbara with you. I'm sure Diane will be overjoyed to have guests to entertain. God knows I've not been the best company for her of late." Lloyd replaces the handset, and after a few moments of thought, he picks it up again.

"Terry, are you in your office?"

"Yes."

"Can you come over to my study for a moment?"

Two minutes later, the vice president walks into the room. Lloyd flaps the fax in the air. "This came in from Dr. Bailey about fifteen minutes ago. It states that the planet's obliquity to the ecliptic has increased by point two one oh six degrees in the past twenty-four hours. As of ten o'clock this morning, it sits at an angle of twenty-five point one two four eight."

Terry is silent for several seconds before he makes a comment. "So he confirms that the earth is still, uh, tumbling, as it's been so eloquently described?"

Lloyd affirms with a nod of his head.

"Is that *all* he says?"

The president shakes his head. "No. He's added a footnote that disturbs me. The shift will trigger natural forces of titanic proportions that will result in unprecedented environmental changes across the planet. The consequence will be the mass extinction of millions of species across the board. Mother Nature won't discriminate, and mankind is not immune."

A startled expression appears on the vice president's face. "Does he expound on that statement?"

Lloyd places the fax on top of the desk and clasps his hands in front of him. "No, which is why I need the good doctor brought to the White House. I want a detailed assessment as soon as possible."

"Is he still in Cambridge?"

"Yes. Bring his wife and two children, too. After I've had a one-on-one with him, the family is to be transferred to the Nora Hartley Center."

"Does he have any assistants?"

"No, he's been working on his own since yesterday."

"That makes it easier. I think it would catch someone's attention if half of Harvard were suddenly whisked off into the fog."

Lloyd sighs. "His disappearance will cause more of a stir than a few assistants would. He's not your average Joe."

Terry gets to his feet. "How soon do you want him here?"

"Today. At fifteen hundred." President Sinclair raises an index finger in the air. "Oh, there's been an extensive loss of communications with satellite television across the globe. It began more than two hours ago, and broadcasters are unable to offer an explanation for the blackout. I want to know if it's related to the shift in the axis or if it's something else."

"I'll see what I can find out," Terry promises, and he leaves the study.

The president reads Dr. Bailey's fax once again.

37

Petro Santa Nella Service Station & Diner
Gustine, California, USA
Coordinates: 37° 03' 17.1" N, 121° 00' 57.6" W
Saturday, June 27, 2020, 1114h

Danny's focus is to get away from Palo Alto. Scared, he heads south on the 101 freeway. He needs some noise to blast the fog out of his head, so he slips a Tony Blair Witch Projekt disc into the CD player and cranks the volume. Although the traffic is light, he keeps the speed at a steady seventy miles per hour down to Gilroy. Worried that a government posse might be somewhere on his tail, he takes the transition to 152 eastbound. At one point he debates whether to remain on the highway, but he's not familiar with the surface streets in this area.

Half an hour passes, and he glances at the fuel gauge. *Damn!* It's getting low, and he needs to make a service stop for gas. The next exit is Gustine, where a combination filling station and diner comes into view, and he drives off the highway. A few minutes later, the blue Corolla pulls onto the forecourt and stops beside a pump. He feels this is a good time to pause and get organized. He can't drive forever with nowhere to go, so he needs to come up with a sensible game plan if he wants to outsmart whoever is trying to track him down. People are dead, but now is not the time to dwell on misfortunes. The important thing is to stay alive. He can mourn later.

Danny turns the ignition off and opens the door. A blast of heat floods into the cooler interior of the vehicle. The canopy over the pumps, intended to shade customers from the unrelenting sun, does nothing to protect them against the brutal heat. The temperature is similar to that in Silicon Valley, but the air is raw and dry, and there's no effective humidity in the strong breeze blowing in from the desert.

The technician swipes his credit card through the reader. While he waits for authorization, he removes the fuel cap and inserts the nozzle into the filler tube. Seconds later he hears a beep as the transaction is approved, and the machine begins to pump gas into the tank.

Harvey Worrell. He's an old friend and ex-colleague from way back when Infinity was in its youth. Why didn't he think of his African American friend before now?

The two met when they turned up at an open interview, competing for the only position offered by the company. Brad was their interviewer, and because no other applicants turned up, he decided to take them both on. The pair became inseparable until the day Harvey met Anita. She lived east of Los Angeles in San Gabriel, and he began a long-distance courtship. The young couple married two years later, and Danny was honored to be best man.

Harvey chose to move south rather than bring Anita up to Silicon Valley. Infinity had just installed a communicator at LAX that enabled them to loop into the satellite network, and his friend submitted a successful application for a meteorologist position. His experience and knowledge of the system gave him an unfair advantage over more than two thousand candidates.

Danny has seen little of Harvey since his marriage. Even telephone and e-mail conversations have been pretty rare. He knows they intended to buy a house in South San Gabriel, but he can't recall the name of the street. In fact, he's not even sure if he has his pal's telephone number, and he wonders if his address book is still in the glove compartment. If there's anyone he can trust, it will be Harvey.

The lever on the nozzle clicks off, and he replaces the hose on the cradle. He glances across the forecourt at the diner while he waits for the receipt to print. It probably has a public telephone inside. He walks around to the passenger side and rummages through the glove box. Of course, telephone numbers are kept on his iPhone these days, but he discarded the device back at McDonalds. His spirits rise when he finds the small black book at the bottom of the pocket. He snaps the compartment closed and then moves the car to a parking space close to the diner.

A pleasant aroma of freshly baked cinnamon buns tickles his nose as he steps into the almost empty restaurant, and he makes a promise to leave with one inside of his stomach. Danny looks around but doesn't see a pay phone. He questions a pretty waitress with an accent who is perhaps a year or two younger than him.

"Over that-a-ways by the entrance to the loo ... I mean, restrooms," she replies in a sweet voice, pointing to the far corner. "Will you be eatin'?"

He flashes a smile. "Yes. A couple of cinnamon buns and a latte."

"They sniffin' good, don' they?" she says. "Sits anywheres you wan' to. I'll 'ave 'em ready for you when you finished natterin'."

"Thank you," he calls back as he walks toward the telephone.

He opens the address book, and punches the ten digits beside Harvey's name into the pad. A chime sounds, and his ears are greeted with a prerecorded message from the telecommunications company. "The number you are trying to call is no longer in service."

Danny curses beneath his breath and rechecks the number. The area code is for Palo Alto. He never updated the book because the new number is on his iPhone, but at least his friend's San Gabriel address is there. He studies the writing a little closer and smiles. It's not written in his hand. Harvey must have added it when he went to his wedding.

The technician walks back into the dining area. The young waitress is standing at a window table, trying to catch his eye, and he heads across the diner toward her.

"Here you goes. Make yourself nice n' comfy. I'll bring your latte an' buns over in a mo."

There's something rather cute about her, and he can perceive she has an interest in him. "You have a fascinating accent. Are you Australian?"

She giggles flirtatiously. "Nah, mate, I'm from Essex, in England."

For the next twenty minutes she hangs around his table when she's not serving. "So, are you only passin' through or what?"

Danny grins and whispers, "I'm on the run."

He's pretty sure she won't believe him. Her eyes open wide, but it's more of an excited expression rather than one of fear. "Are you a real-life fugitive?"

Danny nods his head and takes a bite of the soft, hot dough of the bun. He savors the delicate flavor of cinnamon.

"How *erotic!*" she exclaims in a loud whisper. "I can come wiv you if you needin' extra protection?"

The technician is stunned. He didn't expect the pretty waitress to believe him, and he squirms in his seat. "I was only teasing. I wouldn't be sitting here eating these delicious buns if I were being chased now, would I?"

She smiles. "Good, ain't they?"

Some customers enter the diner, and she scoots off to serve them. While she's busy, he finishes the food and coffee; and after leaving a good tip on the table, he prepares to leave. She comes over to him and slips a piece of paper into his hand.

"My number," she whispers. "I finish at four if you wants to give us a ride 'ome."

"Only if you promise not to break my heart," he replies. She takes his hand and gives it a brief squeeze before walking off to wait on more customers. He can't deny that he's attracted to her, but he's also a probable fugitive. It would be wrong to drag an innocent person into a dangerous situation even though he's not guilty of committing a crime—but neither were Steve, Nancy, or any of his colleagues at Infinity who are already dead. He decides to keep her phone number in case of an emergency.

He walks back to the Toyota. Interstate 5 is a few miles farther on. He doesn't have Harvey's telephone number, but he's got an address. His friend is going to be surprised when he turns up on the doorstep, but it will give him an opportunity to determine how well-founded his fears are.

38

LAX International Airport
Los Angeles, California, USA
Coordinates: 33° 56' 41.1" N, 118° 24' 13.3" W
Saturday, June 27, 2020, 1326h

Flight Captain James Faraday carries out a routine check of the instrument panel as the 787 comes out of a banking turn and lines up with the runway five miles ahead. The engine thrust is decreased, and the large aircraft begins its final descent.

His career began with a seven-year stint in the Royal Air Force, where he flew military transporters over Iraq. After coming out, he spent the next sixteen years flying 747s for British Airways. In 2016, he switched to Eton Airlines, a new company based in Dublin, Ireland. The move was for the benefit of his Irish wife, who wanted to be close to her elderly parents. The veteran pilot was required to take a training course on the 787 Dreamliner, but the hi-tech cockpit took the fun out of flying. Prior to 2018, the choice to land manually was at the behest of the airliner's captain, but a string of accidents attributed to pilot error brought about a mandatory change in the rules, extenuating circumstances excepted. The new regulations necessitating aircraft to use automated GPS systems to land was first implemented by the FAA, but it didn't take long before the CAA and ICAO adopted the same policy.

James glances at the copilot, First Officer Patrick O'Ryan. This is his first flight with the burly Irishman, and his jovial demeanor, sociability, and laid-back attitude strike an accord with the captain. "I hope it won't be long before we fly together again."

Patrick flashes a smile. "Aren't you going on vacation when we land at LAX?"

"Yes. I'm off to Hawaii for two weeks. My wife is on a flight that's scheduled to arrive in another hour, and then we're off for a fortnight of pleasure in paradise."

"What about her parents?"

James sighs. "As far as the elderly go, it's not their physical condition so much as the ability to care for themselves. They both suffer from dementia and forget the simple things, like how to wipe their arses, but we've hired a nurse to babysit while we're away."

He glances at the LCD screen that displays the horizontal situation indicator. The attitude of the aircraft is steady, and below that, the GPS shows they are locked on a perfect glide path.

In the control tower, Air Traffic Controller Eddie Masters tracks the approach of the Eton Airlines flight on radar. Something disturbs him, yet he's not sure what it is.

"Sir, something isn't right with this one."

The on-duty supervisor, Larry McDermott, walks over to the

console and leans over his shoulder. He takes a few seconds to assess the information on the screen. "What's not right about it?"

The coordinator pauses and studies the radar for a little longer before replying hesitantly. "I can't lay my finger on it, but I don't feel comfortable with the landing path."

"It looks good to me."

Eddie continues to gaze at the radar with a grave expression on his face. A Qantas 747 is in descent toward runway three under the supervision of Bobby Flowers, an associate who sits at the next terminal. Both aircraft are due to touch down at about the same time, but they are a safe distance apart, so why does he feel apprehensive? He shrugs and speaks into the headset. "Echo Tango 364, you are cleared for runway one."

Captain Faraday has a faint smile on his lips as he listens to air traffic control. Why tell *him*? It's the goddamn computer that's flying the aircraft. The approach *and* landing are out of his hands. He gives the first officer a sidelong glance as he responds.

"Roger, Control. We are on final approach."

He sits back and looks ahead at the approaching runway. The smile on his face fades and is replaced by a frown. His eyes flit across the instrumentation and take in the information on the dials before he speaks to the first officer.

"Verify our approach, Pat."

The copilot leans forward to check the readings on the navigational panel. "It's all good, Captain. This baby's going to put down right on the center line."

The officer's reassurance doesn't quell the captain's anxiety, and he speaks to the tower again. "Control, this is Echo Tango 364. Something isn't right with our glide path and descent."

Eddie stares attentively at the sweeping radial arm of the radar. "Echo Tango 364, can you elaborate?" He turns his head to look up at the chief. "The flight captain isn't happy with the approach either."

"Let me sit there," Larry orders.

The controller slips out of the seat and hands the headset to the supervisor, who tosses it to the side of the console. He pulls a desk microphone in front of him and redirects the communications through a speaker. "Echo Tango 364, state the nature of your problem."

Eddie notes how calm Captain Faraday sounds.

"Control, I've flown into LAX thousands of times during the past twenty-one years, and from my perspective, we are not on a good landing path."

He listens to the chief's response. "Captain, I have you on radar. You are locked in, and your approach is good."

"Confirmed. The GPS and navigational instruments indicate that everything is fine, but my visual concerns me. I want permission to take manual control."

Eddie's concern continues to grow as he stands behind his boss, looking at the radar screen over his shoulder. He anticipates the chief's decision will be to deny the flight captain's request, and he interpolates. "Chief, there are two of us who feel that something isn't right, and one of them is up in the sky. I think you should authorize manual control."

He can see by the expression on Larry's face that the comment irritates him, and the supervisor responds sharply to Captain Faraday. "That will *not* be necessary. Our instruments show you are coming in for a good landing. Your request is denied."

The chief mutes the microphone and swivels around in the chair. He glares up at Eddie. "How *dare* you question my authority."

The controller starts to protest. "Sir, I was *not* questioning your authority, and I don't—" But his grievance is cut short by Captain Faraday's voice.

"This is Echo Tango 364 to control. I knew I wasn't wrong. If I manage to get out of this one, your arse will be on the roaster, boy, and if I don't, I'll be waiting for you at the gates of hell."

The starboard wheels of the 787 touch down on the tarmac, but the port side wheels miss the runway by six feet. The aircraft bumps violently as they roll across the hard, uneven surface. The unequal traction drags the Dreamliner to the left and pulls the nose down too fast. The front landing gear slams to the ground with tremendous force, and the wheels miss the runway by two feet. A vicious judder races through the airframe as the tires blow out, and seconds later the rims strike a giant pothole. Already weakened by the first jar, the front gear collapses. The undernose crashes to the ground. A portion of the fuselage skin peels back amid the deafening screech of tortured metal, and a shower of sparks and debris. The huge aircraft careens out of control across the median that separates the taxi lanes from the main runway, missing another airliner by a matter of feet.

Sepulveda Boulevard is a busy highway that runs through a tunnel beneath the airport runways. The doomed plane smashes through a low concrete parapet and plunges down toward the road. The nose slams into the south wall of the underpass, and the speed of the impact causes the fuselage to crumple like an accordion. The Dreamliner explodes into a gigantic fireball, blowing dozens of cars into the air, and a deadly ball of fire rolls through the 1.3-mile tunnel.

In the control tower, Eddie hears a double explosion. The shockwaves have the effect of a small earthquake, and everything around him rattles. He stares in horror at the thick clouds of oily black smoke that billow up from behind a terminal building.

Bobby is still at his console, and he looks up at Eddie and Larry. His face is white. "*Chief* ... oh, my *God* ... *chief!* The Qantas flight from Sydney has crashed," he yells, close to panic. "*Shit* ... it's *exploded.*"

The two men continue to gaze in disbelief at the heavy plume of smoke climbing higher into the sky. Larry responds in a choked voice. "No, that was an Eton Airways flight from Dublin. It's just crashed on runway one."

"*No*, chief," Bobby shouts back. "It's definitely Qantas. It's missed the runway ... out on number three."

Eddie turns around. Through the windows on the opposite side of the tower he can see heavy plumes of black smoke boiling into the atmosphere. Huge, hungry, fuel-fed flames flicker and roll up in angry balls of fire from the broken fuselage of a 747.

39

The Oval Office
The White House, Washington, DC
Coordinates: 38° 53' 50.6" N, 77° 02' 14.5" W
Saturday, June 27, 2020, 1434h

President Sinclair walks over to General Barry Morgan with a facsimile in his hand. He disagreed when Terry made a recommendation to bring the fifty-year-old five-star military commander into the small circle of confidants, but changed his mind after he gave it more thought.

He hands the document to the general. "This is the fax I received from Dr. Bailey." Despite concerns stirred up by the professor's facsimiles, he's still cynical about the brief evaluation.

The general's eyes shows some reservation as he reads the short statement. "It's pretty indistinct."

"He'll be here in another thirty minutes. There are more important things that need our attention, so the sooner I can shovel it under the rug, the happier I'll be."

The vice president walks up to the two men. His facial muscles are taut, and he glances at Barry. "I'm sorry to interrupt." He turns his eyes to Lloyd. "There's been a spate of fatal airline accidents. A few minutes ago, the FAA ordered an indefinite mandatory grounding of all aircraft in US airspace with immediate effect. The CAA and ICAO, supported by the ANC and CANSO, issued the same mandate a few moments later."

"What the hell does *that* translate into?" Lloyd asks, bewildered.

"Private, commercial, and military aircraft around the globe are grounded," the vice president replies, and he glances at some hastily scribbled notes in his hand. "At least forty-seven planes on automated landings missed the runway by a few yards. Every single one crashed at 1339 hours, give or take a couple of seconds."

President Sinclair inhales sharply. "Does that number include private aircraft?"

"No—commercial airliners with more than sixty passengers only. Two in Los Angeles and one in Miami exploded on impact. There are hundreds of injured and dead in Atlanta and New York." Terry looks back down at the notebook. "Heathrow and Gatwick in the United Kingdom have been closed. Other countries reporting similar incidents are Germany, Russia, South Africa, Australia, and Brazil, to name a few, which indicates how widespread this is."

For the first time in his presidency, Lloyd doesn't have an immediate response. A cold dread flows through him. "Do the aviation authorities know the cause?"

"The FAA are being cautious with their analysis, pending further tests, but they think that the in-flight positioning data received by the onboard navigational systems is corrupt. It places the aircraft in one location when it's actually in another, albeit a matter of only a few yards."

Lloyd is perplexed. "Could it be an attack by cyberterrorists?"

"We don't know, yet," Terry replies. "GPS-controlled landings are mandatory at most major airports now. Crews have been instructed to bring their aircraft down under manual control, but assistance by air traffic controllers is restricted because their systems are affected too. All they can do is keep them separated to prevent a midair collision, but the risks are still high."

"I assume they've tried to recalibrate the navigational equipment?" General Morgan asks.

"I've been told they have, but it hasn't made any difference," Terry replies. "The dilemma extends beyond landing, though. The aircraft are being taken off course during flight, too."

The general voices the president's fears. "I think the GPS satellites have been affected by the same phenomenon that's bringing the weather and TV networks down. The FAA and ICAO are justified in taking these extraordinary measures under the circumstances. The coordination and execution of a nearly impossible task of this size in such a short period of time is remarkable."

Lloyd's shoulders slump. "We can't hide *this* from the public."

"The media are all over it like flies around a bucket of shit," Terry confirms. "The pressroom is filled to capacity with journalists waiting for an official statement."

"What can I tell them when I don't know what's going on yet?"

"You need to tell them something," the vice president replies. "If you don't address this soon, they might make their own presumtions or dig into corners we want them to stay away from."

"I concur with Mr. Schofield," the general says. "You need to stall them and quench their thirst with anything acceptable until we know exactly what's going on."

"I've got to speak with Dr. Sinclair first," Lloyd replies.

"You can't wait that long, sir," Terry says. "Every minute you procrastinate is an extra sixty seconds in favor of the undesired. The presence of an astrophysicist at the White House will only elevate their curiosity—especially one with Dr. Bailey's credentials."

President Sinclair thrusts his hands into his trouser pockets. Frustrated, and deep in thought, he walks away from the general and vice president. He stops in front of the window and looks out into the rose garden, but his mind isn't focused on the colorful blooms that line the winding gravel pathway.

On the opposite side of the Oval Office, Robert is in a conversation with Brian when the iPhone in his pocket starts to vibrate. He apologizes to the state secretary and steps away to receive the incoming call from Kent Marlowe, the head of the special operations division for Homeland Security.

"Yes?"

"One of Infinity's technicians, identified as Danny Walker, survived the blast this morning."

The Homeland Security secretary casts a furtive glance around to make sure no one is in earshot. Brian is walking toward General Morgan and Terry, but he still keeps his voice lowered. "Are you sure?"

"Three cars were in the company's parking lot. We've checked the VIN with DMV records. They're registered to James Beattie and William Chester, who are two of the techs, and a Henry Jackson, who is a security guard employed by Infinity."

Robert bites his lip nervously. "That's not good. How did that happen?"

"I don't know. They were told to be there at six, so I can only surmise that he was either late or slipped out to get breakfast. When I realized his car was missing, I called him. He terminated the conversation and turned the iPhone off. We can't trace him until it's back on."

"If he suspects anything, I can guarantee he won't use it again."

"The call was triangulated to a McDonald's restaurant, but he was gone by the time we arrived."

"Of *course* he was," Robert retorts. "He probably dumped the phone into the trash on his way out."

"We got two hits on his credit card a short while ago. He used it at a gas station and a diner in Gustine, so we know he's on route 152 east. An agent is on the way to interview the diner staff."

"Send someone back to McDonald's, and search the trash cans for his phone," Robert demands. "We need to find out what acquaintances he has outside of Palo Alto because he's heading for one of them."

"Yes, sir."

"I want to isolate him from the public," the Homeland Security secretary continues. "Issue an APB and release a terrorist alert including a picture, driver's license, car details, last known location, and any other shit you can dredge up ... and keep me in the fucking loop."

"Yes, sir," Kent replies. "Do you want to offer a reward?"

"How much is in the remuneration fund?"

"Uh ... something like half a million."

"Then use a quarter of a mil."

"*Jeez*, you want him *that* bad?"

"Do your job, Mr. Marlowe. You know better than to ask questions." Robert pauses. "What about Jaeger's secretary?"

"Case closed."

Robert terminates the call and strolls across the room to join Terry, Brian, and General Morgan.

President Sinclair stares across the rose garden, formulating a story for the media in his head. It'll be ad-libbed because there's no time to write up a script, but that doesn't bother him. He's an accomplished speaker, but he needs a temporary yet realistic scapegoat. He turns away from the window and makes his way back to the vice president and General Morgan. They've been joined by Brian and Robert, and as he walks up, the Homeland Security secretary is talking.

"I've just issued a terror alert for one of the Infinity techs."

"Why tag him as a terrorist if he isn't one?" the general asks.

"He knows why the satellite failures are occurring and probably has an idea of the effect it may have. Public awareness should deter him from going to the media for fear he'll be turned in."

"He can still use social networking to get the message into the public domain," Barry warns, "and it will be far more effective."

Lloyd's eyes light up. "What's the name of this tech?"

"Danny Walker," Robert replies.

The president pulls a pen from the inside pocket of his jacket and scribbles the name on the palm of a hand. "Okay, let's get this press conference out of the way."

"Do you know what you're going to say?" Terry asks.

"Yes." He doesn't elaborate, and the vice president eyes him with curiosity. Before he can inquire further, Gordon Reece walks into the Oval Office, and the forty-one-year-old chief of staff makes a beeline for the president.

"Dr. Jack Bailey and his family are here, sir."

"Good. I have a brief press statement to make. Take his wife and kids over to the residence. Diane is expecting them. The doctor can wait for me in here."

Gordon walks off, and Brian turns the television on. The podium where the commander in chief will soon be standing appears on the screen. Lloyd subconsciously adjusts his tie and straightens his jacket before heading for the exit. Alan Price, the bespectacled thirty-four-year-old press secretary, is waiting in the corridor.

"Ah, *there* you are," the president mutters. "I see your skill at avoiding me until the last minute has been honed to a fine art."

"Sometimes it's prudent to keep a low profile, sir," Alan responds candidly.

Lloyd walks along the passage at a brisk pace. "Are there any updates I need to know before I go on?"

The press secretary keeps in step. "I haven't heard from the FAA yet. The ICAO have revised the number of commercial airline crashes to sixty-three."

"Do they know why the satellites failed?"

"Be careful how you phrase it, sir. They're sensitive about the use of 'failure' because the satellites are still working. It's the data that's corrupt."

Lloyd gives a short, cynical laugh. "So much for political correctness."

Alan ignores the remark. "The cause still hasn't been established, but multiple countries are involved in the investigation."

The two men reach the entrance to the press room. "Is that it?"

"It's all I have."

"*Christ*, why can't you tell me something I *don't* already know," the president complains. Without another word, he enters the media room. The incessant drone of voices fades, and his footsteps echo on the wooden floorboards as he walks across to the podium. After stepping onto the dais, President Sinclair looks around at the dozens of upturned faces and clears his throat.

"This is an informative brief only. I will not be answering

questions." He's an excellent orator, and his speeches tend to be more fluent when he doesn't have a script or use an Autocue. "America is facing the biggest threat ever posed by organized terrorism. A fatal cyber attack against our technical infrastructure began last Monday when weather satellites began to fail after being infected by a malicious virus known as the Chameleon. It has now spread to other networks. An attack on GPS systems a couple of hours ago resulted in a large number of airline crashes, forcing aviation authorities worldwide to ground all aircraft to prevent further casualties. This is the first time in more than a hundred years that there are no man-made machines in the skies anywhere in the world."

He takes a moment to catch his breath and glances down at the palm of his left hand. "Danny Walker, a trusted technician employed by Infinity, is suspected of introducing the Chameleon into the network. Investigations into Walker's background reveal an association with a terror organization that has a much larger agenda. He's also responsible for the assassination of the company CEO and the huge explosion at the Infinity headquarters this morning. Danny Walker is armed, dangerous, and desperate, and Homeland Security has offered a substantial reward for information leading to his capture. The White House press secretary will provide you with more details on the fugitive after I've finished this update."

The sound of clicking as reporters type into their notepads sounds strangely loud in the hushed media room. President Sinclair picks up a glass of water and takes a sip to hydrate his mouth before he resumes in a more vehement tone. "The financial damage is only a by-product and is not the real motive behind these atrocious attacks. Our intelligence agencies have exposed a horrendous plot to detonate at least one thermonuclear device and employ other weapons of mass destruction on mainland USA, but we don't know what, or where, the intended targets are yet. The severing of satellite networks is an attempt to prevent us from tracking radioactive signatures emitted by the weapons while they are moved around the country. I give you my unequivocal assurance that these monsters will *not* succeed."

A buzz of excitement sweeps through the audience but quickly dies down.

"Over the coming days, people may observe a military presence where none would normally be seen. This is not a cause for panic. Exercises and emergency drills between armed forces and first responders will be ubiquitous. I will *not* hesitate to recall troops from war zones abroad to protect Americans at home, and I appeal to *all* citizens to be extra vigilant. Report anything suspicious regardless of how trivial it seems. America is dependent on your alertness in the same way you rely on our servicemen and women to protect your liberty." President Sinclair brings the briefing to a swift close. "God bless America!"

He steps down from the podium and walks briskly toward the exit. Alan has left, but the vice president is standing in the corridor, and his displeasure is apparent. "Don't you have any conscience at all?"

"Would you prefer I tell them that we don't know what's going on?"

Terry makes no attempt to hide his anger. "I'm not in concordance of absolute denial under the circumstances, but you've got no evidence to purport Walker's association to terrorism, whether or not he's responsible for Jaeger's assassination or the explosion at Infinity this morning. You're persecuting an innocent man."

Lloyd remains calm. "I've given the media something to keep

them busy until we talk to Dr. Bailey. I needed a temporary fall guy, and Walker just happened to be in the wrong place at the right time. It can be explained away as a case of mistaken identity afterward."

The vice president responds in a calmer voice as they make their way back to the Oval Office. "It's unwise to sow false speculations."

Lloyd doesn't share the same view and shrugs it off, but Terry isn't finished.

"What about the other crap you prattled on about? Where did all that come from about nuclear devices, weapons of mass destruction, increased military presence, and a troop recall? *Christ*, Lloyd, this will backfire and go awry in an instant."

"It might be unorthodox, but it's bought us a little time. So what?"

They've reached the open door of the Oval Office, and the president walks in before Terry can counter. A portly man about five feet ten inches in height is standing close to the Resolute Desk with hands thrust deep into his pockets. Except for a line of gray hair over his ears, he's bald; but a thick, well-groomed beard makes up for the locks missing from his head. A briefcase sits on the floor between his feet, and the fifty-three-year-old appears to be quite agitated. Lloyd walks over to the newcomer with a pleasant smile on his face and greets him with cordiality.

"Dr. Jack Bailey?" The president extends a hand toward the visitor, but the professor makes no attempt to respond. He keeps his hands in his pockets and stares back with a cold, hard glare that makes the commander in chief uncomfortable.

Several seconds pass before the academic speaks. "I've *never* heard so much bullshit in my life."

The president recoils in surprise. This is not the response

he expected, and the smile quickly dissipates from his face. He withdraws his hand. "What do you mean?"

"Oh, come *on* Mr. Sinclair," Jack replies in a denigrating tone. "All that crap you pumped into the heads of good American citizens? You *know* a virus doesn't exist. You know an organized terror plot or WMD threat doesn't subsist. How can your conscience allow so many blatant falsehoods to slip through your lips?"

The astrophysicist's hostility triggers a rapid change in the president's mood, but he keeps his anger in check. "Dr. Bailey, there's a time and place for criticism, but it isn't here or now. I didn't bring you in to air your discontentment, views, and opinions of me or how I do my job. You're here to help me understand so I *can* do my job." Lloyd doesn't miss the resentment in the doctor's eyes, and for some reason, it amuses him. "You don't like me too much, do you, professor?"

"*Too* much?" Jack retorts. "I don't like you at *all*, Mr. Sinclair. I never have, and I doubt I ever will."

"Do I need to be concerned about your cooperation?"

The professor appears to be offended by the question. "I take pride in my profession, and I conduct business without the interference of personal prejudice. You will get my assistance despite the fact that I've had no sleep for the last twenty-four hours and I've been kept under constant surveillance. I've been denied my egalitarian rights, and now you're forcing my family and me to go to an undisclosed location against our will. That's an unconstitutional breach of our civil liberties as American citizens. I believe the correct term would be 'kidnapping,' which is a federal crime."

"You don't mince words, do you?" Lloyd asserts. "But I'm relieved you won't let personal issues obstruct the debrief."

"Mr. Sinclair, a surgeon might hate his patient, but when a

surgical procedure is required to save his or her life, he makes every effort to keep the person alive and *still* continues to despise them afterward. Professional satisfaction is the path *most* of us prefer, which pretty much sums up the direction our relationship will take."

President Sinclair looks down at his feet and shakes his head with a tiny smile on his lips. They could be in for a weird, if not awkward, discussion. He raises his eyes and makes a gesture in the direction of two white-leather couches positioned on each side of a long, low glass-topped table. "Let's waste no more time, doctor. Please, take a seat."

Dr. Bailey walks across the room and sinks into the center of a couch. He removes an overstuffed manila folder from his briefcase, and lays it on the table. President Sinclair sits on the couch opposite with Terry and General Morgan on each side. Robert and Brian sit down beside the academic.

"I'm sorry; I should introduce you to everyone before we start," Lloyd says.

Jack glances at him over the rim of his reading glasses. "There's no need, Mr. Sinclair. They introduced themselves when I arrived—except for Mr. Schofield ... and I'm not so dumb as to not know who he is."

Lloyd is still tense from their initial meeting and decides not to respond. The professor opens the folder to reveal a thick bundle of documents and a bunch of loose-leaf papers with notes and calculations scribbled haphazardly all over them.

Dr. Bailey looks around at the five men. "What I have to tell you won't be easy to absorb, but I will make it as comprehensible as possible. Don't be afraid to stop me if you need clarification on something you don't understand. Just because *I* know what I'm talking about doesn't mean everyone else does." His lips curl into a gentle smile, and he chuckles. "You can ask my students about that."

Robert and Terry laugh at the professor's quip, and Lloyd feels his tension easing. Jack seems to have a natural ability to relax his audience. Dr. Bailey picks a paper up from the top of the stack and glances at it before speaking.

"I want to start by reconfirming that the planet's obliquity to the ecliptic is still shifting. Someone described it as a tumble, which is pretty much what the earth is doing. Imagine a freighter caught up in heavy seas when the cargo breaks free and is thrown to one side of the hold. The imbalance causes the vessel to list, and the greater the weight, the more pronounced the list will be. Now use this analogy to visualize our planet as the ship, the mantle as the freight, and magnetic, gravitational, kinetic, and other influential forces as the ocean. An internal shift in the earth's mass has created a disparity on the same principle."

"Is it something that occurred naturally?" Robert asks.

"No. Only a major destructive force could generate an insurmountable scenario like this, and the only catastrophic event in the planet's recent history is the Andaman Event."

General Morgan appears perplexed. "That was six months ago. Why did it wait until now to start tumbling?"

Dr. Bailey smiles. "Physics. The displacement placed the earth on a precarious balance, but the counteraction of the sun's gravitational pull kept it in equilibrium until now. Where and how it was dislodged is an open debate, but it's reasonable to assume it ended up beneath the Bay of Bengal."

"Wouldn't something need to replace the area vacated by the mass?" Barry asks.

"It probably filled with less-dense material, but that's speculation. It'll be months, or even years, before we have a conclusive answer … which means we'll never know."

Terry looks startled. "What does *that* mean?"

"All in good time, Mr. Schofield," the professor replies. "I don't want to miss something by getting ahead of myself."

Robert reiterates the question asked by General Morgan. "What's different *now* that's making the earth tumble?"

"The planet's orbital position in relation to the sun changed when it passed through the northern summer solstice. The same gravitational influences that kept the planet stable are now conspiring to pull from the opposite direction, and with no counteractive dynamic in play, the earth is complying."

Lloyd clears his throat with a nervous cough. "How long will it be before it stops?"

"Once the earth reaches a natural equilibrium with the external environment. My preliminary estimation is based on the assumption that the displacement occurred as a result of the Andaman Event; therefore, the tumble will stop when the obliquity to the ecliptic reaches ninety point two degrees. That will happen in another three hundred eleven days, sometime on May 3, 2021. I must stress that my results *are* fundamental, which means they're susceptible to updates *if* we get the time to learn more."

Lloyd doesn't miss the pessimism in Jack's words, but Terry is the one who questions him. "That's the second time you've used a negative implication, Mr. Bailey. Is that intentional?"

The professor compliments the vice president. "You're a good listener, Mr. Schofield. I assure you that if I speak in negative axioms, I do so deliberately." Jack rifles through some loose sheets of paper in the folder, pulls one free, and studies it for a few seconds before speaking again. "Three main elements have been in play since the earth began turning four billion years ago: rotation, precession, and nutation. In the last twenty-four hours, I've discovered the manifestation of a new directional constituent, which is the key influence that initiated the tumble." He pauses for a moment. "The first movement is one you're all familiar with—axial rotation. The earth spins like a top on an imaginary pivotal line known as the axis. I conducted a brief examination on the revolution velocity and did not detect any changes. It's still the dominating force that's keeping the biosphere together."

"That's a relief," Robert remarks.

"The second movement is axial precession. This is a slow gravity-induced shift in orientation concentrated around the rotational axis. It's best described as a wobble. While rotation takes twenty-four hours to complete one revolution, the precession takes twenty-six thousand years to move through a full cycle. It may have sped up, slowed down, or become less or more pronounced, but that will take time to ascertain."

"Wouldn't it produce colder winters and hotter summers if the wobble became more prominent?" Terry asks.

"Over a long time period, yes, but it would be negligible in the life span of an individual," Dr. Bailey replies with a smile. "I know what you're thinking, but that's not the reason for the record-breaking weather we're getting this year. If the precession had increased to a degree where we could perceive it on a daily basis, or even over several generations, the tremendous forces generated would have torn the planet asunder by now."

President Sinclair's impatience is growing at what he deems to be an earth science class, but he doesn't interrupt the lecture.

"The third movement is axial nutation," the professor continues.

"It's a rocking motion that changes the angle of the planet's tilt in relation to the sun. The adjustments are diminutive—a matter of meters—but enough to move the location of the primary circles of latitude annually. The earth would appear to be nodding if it were animated and sped up."

"You're talking about natural attributes," Lloyd says. "How are they associated with the tumble?"

"The density of the displacement has diverted the external gravitational forces that should pass through the core to slice across the axis at an angle of thirty degrees and traverse the planet at two hundred forty-three point two degrees. It has created a new center of gravity, and to correct its alignment, the planet is twisting daily by point nine eight nine degrees. The resultant torque is causing the obliquity to the ecliptic to slide along the fortieth meridian at a steady point two one oh six degrees every twenty-four hours. The axial rotation is curbing the rate of travel, which has harmonized itself to the planet's orbital velocity around the sun."

President Sinclair listens attentively to the professor's elucidation, but it's left him confused. "I'm sorry, Mr. Bailey, but I'm lost."

The professor falls silent, and it's clear by his expression that he's trying to come up with a better way to illustrate his explanation. "To better explicate my point in layman's terms, the Northern Hemisphere is turning into the face of the sun. The most significant effect it'll have will be the extermination of eight point seven million species of animal, insect, marine, and plant life."

The professor has just opened Pandora's box. Unprepared for the blunt statement, Lloyd goes into a brain crash, and gawps in stupefaction at the academic. The tension-filled silence seems to go on forever, but Dr. Bailey hasn't finished yet.

"That includes seven point three billion humans."

Brian breaks the spell hanging over the small group, and the incredulous tone in his voice matches the expression on his face. "Isn't that the world population?"

"Yes."

Lloyd continues to stare at the professor, uncertain whether to believe his asseveration. The academic is too calm, which means he either has an innate ability to control his emotions or he's exaggerating. Lloyd is almost too afraid to speak. "You're proclaiming the extinction of mankind."

"We're facing the most unpropitious mass extinction since the Great Dying two hundred fifty-two million years ago," Jack replies. "It formed the boundary between the Paleozoic and Mesozoic eras, eradicating eighty-three percent of all genera. So much biodiversity was lost that vertebrates, and life in general, took thirty million years to recover. It's the only known mass extinction of insects."

"The Great Dying ... isn't that when the dinosaurs were killed off?" Robert asks.

"No, that happened sixty-five million years ago," the professor replies.

"Let's say you're right and the tumble induces a mass extinction event. What percentage of genera do you think the earth will lose this time?"

The professor's blunt response startles the president. "It will be the worst extinction event in the history of this planet. The survival rate will be between two and four percent at best—mainly insects that may well move on to be the dominant species of the future."

"Are you serious?" Robert asks disbelievingly.

The doctor shrugs. "Reptiles. Humans. Why not insects next time around?"

While Lloyd is cynical of Dr. Bailey's prediction, his sobriety gives him cause to be hesitant. "Please forgive me, but I'm having difficulty in grasping the concept that the human race is teetering on the precipice of extinction."

Jack sits back and crosses his legs. "I'd feel insulted if you didn't, Mr. Sinclair, but it's gone beyond teetering. It's real. The satellite failures and the record-breaking climate in the Northern and Southern Hemispheres are attestations to the fact. There's more to come; trust me."

"What will be our death knell, doctor? Famine? Disease?"

"No famine. No disease," Dr. Bailey replies. "You do understand what caused the weather satellites to start failing, don't you?"

"Only by what Jaeger claimed in his report," Lloyd answers.

"The report is accurate," the professor says grimly. "The North Pole is turning directly into the face of the sun. The daylight period in the Northern Hemisphere is extending in daily increments dependent on location. Close to the equator, it's between one and two minutes, but farther north—Alaska, for example—the augmentation is five to six minutes. The final result will be twenty-four-hour sunlight. The shift in the axial inclination will bring the North Pole closer to the sun, and as it does, the surface temperature will increase. You must remember that the earth's tilt is responsible for the seasons and influences our fragile bionetwork. Any change to the ecosystem is an impingement on evolutionary development, and the habitats of life forms within them."

Robert smiles. "How bad can *that* be? We'll have longer summers and shorter winters."

The professor casts a mordant glance in the secretary's direction. "The Northern Hemisphere has already seen its last winter. The longest, hottest summer in history has begun, and it's not going to end."

President Sinclair is astounded by the professor's proclamation. This isn't what he expected to hear when he sat down for the briefing. "Are you saying that the tumble isn't going to stop?"

"I've already told you that it'll stop when the internal displacement reaches equilibrium with the external forces in the cosmos, which will be when the obliquity to the ecliptic reaches ninety point two degrees. At that angle, the hottest place will be inside the Arctic Circle. The icecap will disappear fast, and without anything to reflect the heat back into space, it will get trapped within the earth's atmosphere."

"When you say 'trapped' ..." Terry starts, but he trails off.

"The upper atmosphere will act like insulation," Dr. Bailey says, anticipating the vice president's unfinished question. "The temperature in the Northern Hemisphere will increase exponentially, going well beyond the endurance threshold of any living organism on the planet. At the North Pole, the sun will be in the center of the sky, and it'll never move. Here in DC, it'll be somewhere over here"—the professor stretches his right arm up at an approximate angle of thirty-eight degrees and draws a circle around his head with a finger—"and move in a constant loop. Close to the equator, it will sit on the horizon and travel counterclockwise without setting. Ever."

The doctor extracts a sheet of paper from the documents in his folder and offers it to Lloyd over the table. "This is a crude chart I produced to help calculate the average temperature expected at any given latitude north of the equator. You can keep it for reference."

Lloyd takes it and holds it in such a position that General Morgan and Terry can look at it with him. The heading reads

"Mean Temperature," and his mouth drops open in bewilderment at the first entry. "North Pole, six hundred degrees minimum to eight hundred degrees Fahrenheit?"

"That relates to anywhere within the Arctic Circle," Dr. Bailey answers calmly.

Lloyd continues reading from the chart. "New York, three hundred forty-eight point eight degrees? Washington, DC, will be three hundred fourteen point two degrees? Los Angeles at two hundred forty-five degrees? Is this a worst-case scenario?"

"The margin of error is three percent," the professor replies, "and it's the *best* you can expect."

Lloyd is cautious of the professor's allegations. "Nothing can live in those kinds of temperatures. We'll all bake to death."

"What have I been trying to tell you?" Jack says.

Terry rests his forearms across his knees. "Is there any place where life will still be able to exist?"

The academic hesitates before responding. "Temperatures might remain stable at life-sustainable levels between the fourteenth and twenty-seventh parallels. I've called it the twilight zone because the sun will hang on, or just above, the horizon there. Crop cultivation may be possible between the twenty-first and twenty-fifth parallels, but you'll need to consult an agriculturist to know what will flourish."

"Why should I believe that all of this will happen as you say, Dr. Bailey?"

The professor throws his head back and laughs. "I'm not asking you to believe me, Mr. Sinclair. You're the one who solicited me for an overview." Jack's expression becomes serious again. He sits back in the couch and folds his arms. "It's important to remember that the total expanse encompassed within the safe region is ten percent of the earth's surface, but you mustn't forget that seventy-two percent of that ten is ocean. It leaves an area not exceeding two point eight percent for habitation by creatures great and small."

Robert's eyes widen in astonishment. "Are you saying that seven point three billion people will have to migrate into the twilight zone?"

The professor smiles acerbically. "Mr. Klaus, what would you tell me if I asked you to transfer every drop of water from a fifty-five-gallon barrel into a one-pint jug without overflowing?"

"It can't be done."

"Right, and that's analogous to seven billion inhabitants trying to occupy a space large enough to support one hundred million."

"It'll be the biggest exodus ever," Brian remarks.

The president is pensive. If true, the twilight zone could become a giant gladiatorial arena, and a horrifying bloodbath is going to be inevitable. Mankind's final demise could well be at his own hands.

General Morgan's voice invades his musings. "Mr. Bailey, I assume there'll be a similar zone in the Southern Hemisphere, too?"

"Newton's third law of motion," the professor mutters in a tired voice. "The South Pole is turning away from the sun, and when the obliquity to the ecliptic reaches ninety degrees, the entire hemisphere will be in a permanent state of night. The temperature drop from the equatorial line to Antarctica will be as dramatic as the rise in the north. The southern half of the planet is about to become a vast frozen tundra. I haven't had the opportunity to calculate how bitter it will get, but it'll be somewhere between minus six hundred degrees and minus eight hundred degrees Fahrenheit. It will be cold enough for natural lakes of liquid nitrogen to form."

President Sinclair studies the professor's demeanor with a sullen expression on his face. He's trying to figure out how much of the doctor's prescience can be trusted, and he comes to two conclusions. He's either a damn good actor or he's confident that his conjectures are written in stone.

"Are there other surprises we should prepare for?" Terry asks.

Dr. Bailey sifts through the notes in his file. "Far more than I can anticipate. The planet needs to adapt to a changed environment, and the new internal stress will result in major geological transformations. Seismic upheavals on, or greater than, the scale of the Andaman Event are going to be commonplace."

President Sinclair fidgets. "Isn't that only an assumption, doctor?"

"No. Any geologist will tell you that the internal structure needs to regulate itself to the impositions introduced by the tumble. What do you think has generated the extreme weather we've been getting over the past couple of weeks?"

"Global warming … carbon dioxide emissions," Terry replies hesitantly.

Dr. Bailey shakes his head. "The changes are attributed to the collapsing ecoinfrastructure, and it's just getting started."

The general sits forward. "So that freak tornado that hit a suburb of Sydney in Australia a few days ago and the massive sandstorm that swept across North Africa yesterday were caused by the tumble?"

Lloyd gives the secretary of state a sharp glance. "I never heard about a sandstorm."

"I haven't either," the professor complains bitterly. "I've been in my laboratory and unlawfully isolated from the outside world since yesterday morning."

Lloyd ignores the doctor's grievance and continues to address Brian. "Why have I not been briefed about it?"

"A report from the National Hurricane Center is on my desk, but I got caught up with the satellite problem. The storm originated in the south of Egypt and northern Sudan and cut a five-hundred-mile swath across eight countries, destroying everything in its path. Fine granules that were carried high into the atmosphere rained on the Canary Islands. However, it's now mutated into a hurricane, which is predicted to develop into a category-five superstorm over the next twenty-four hours. The NHC issued an advanced alert for the Carolinas this morning, but it'll be another week before it reaches the US mainland."

President Sinclair doesn't respond. He's struggling with Dr. Bailey's credibility. The professor made clear by his own admission that he holds him in low esteem, so Sinclair is wondering whether this could be a sick hoax. The sound of Barry's voice pulls him out of the reverie.

"Can we figure out the original location of the displaced mass?"

"That may already be known, General" Jack replies. "I confer regularly with Dr. Robert Andrews and a Russian astrophysicist, Dr. Boris Medvedev, but you've prevented me from communicating with anyone since yesterday."

Robert cuts in. "The constraints are for reasons of security, Mr. Bailey."

Jack snorts, and his voice is full of contempt. "I don't see why this is shrouded in so much secrecy. It won't take long for other scientists to figure it out."

President Sinclair stretches his legs out and crosses them at the ankles. "I agree, Dr. Bailey, but the longer we keep the tumble suppressed, the more time we'll get to decide how to manage the problems it'll create."

The doctor's voice is cold. "I'm not sure what you intend to manage,

Mr. Sinclair. Global panic and worldwide anarchy are predictable manifestations, and American citizens will be vying for a place in the twilight zone along with seven point three billion hopefuls."

The president's facial muscles tighten up. "I accept that something extraordinary is going on, but I'm not sure if I can believe your postulations about a mass extinction."

"I've been sincere, Mr. Sinclair, but what you do with the information is your prerogative."

"My priority is to ensure the safety of our citizens," Lloyd replies softly, "but before I can make any plans, I need to see where the twilight zone boundaries are on a map." He pauses. "How many years do I have before this thing really kicks in?"

"*Years?* Have you not been listening? You don't *have* years. *We* don't have years. The existence of mankind will cease in a matter of weeks, and there's nothing you can do to stop it."

Lloyd's frustration is growing. "So I should ignore it? Is that the best advice you can give?"

"I'm not advising *anything*, Mr. Sinclair," the professor fires back. The calm demeanor he's kept throughout the interview is starting to crack. "I'm only pointing out how vain your efforts will be. I admit capitulation is not programmed into our genes, and the impulse to resist when threatened is an instinctive trait, even in the face of the futility. This is our destiny as a race, and it's a nonnegotiable issue with Mother Nature."

General Morgan intervenes. "We're getting away from my initial inquiry, doctor. If your associates abroad know where this mass was dislodged from, and where it is now, my question is this: would it be possible to blast it back into its original position with the strategic placement of thermonuclear devices?"

Dr. Bailey leans forward. "The use of nukes to counteract a

geological event is a misconception. I know it's only fiction, but I wish authors and screenwriters would give a little more thought to their stories. It's misleading, and it irks me."

"It's never been tried, so how do you know it won't work?" the general asks.

"The effective depth at which the device would need to be detonated is unattainable. It would need to be at least a thousand miles deep, and even if there were a way to overcome the extreme pressure and high temperatures that far down, the simultaneous detonation of every nuclear device on the planet would generate less than one percent of the energy required. You'd have to duplicate the exact mechanics of the Andaman Event for any chance of success, and that's something we don't know."

A gloomy silence descends over the group. President Sinclair is now convinced that the axial shift is the reason for the satellite failures, but he's at a fork in the road. Does he accept Dr. Bailey's presumptions as accurate or refute them in totality?

"Mother Nature is sanitizing the earth of everything unnatural," Jack murmurs.

President Sinclair smiles weakly. "In that case, we humans should be safe."

"Whatever gives you *that* idea?" Jack asks.

"You just said yourself she's cleaning out stuff that isn't natural."

"And you think mankind falls into that category?"

"Don't you?"

"We're probably the most *unnatural* of all the species on this planet, and certainly the most disrespectful to the milieu."

"Mankind is a resilient race," the president counters. "I have no doubt that people are going to die, but we can adapt to new environments and evolve as they develop."

"Evolution is a process that plays out over thousands of years," the academic replies. "We're in a technological era that's going to disappear overnight, and it'll have catastrophic psychological consequences on those who do survive."

Lloyd uncrosses his legs and leans forward with a solemn expression on his face. "Dr. Bailey, whatever your perception is of me, I'm not a quitter. I *will* uphold the oath I swore to the people of the United States when I took office."

The professor drops his voice. "What's your ultimate goal, Mr. Sinclair?"

Lloyd ponders the question for nearly fifteen seconds before answering. "To ensure the survival of the human race."

"*If* your aim to save the human race from annihilation isn't mendacious, why don't you relocate some of the wild tribal communities native to the jungles and rainforests of New Guinea and Amazonia into the twilight zone? They're best adapted to endure the traumatic transformations without relying on modern technologies."

President Sinclair's response is vociferous. "I *will* save mankind, and I'll do so with intelligent Americans, not some uneducated culture from the Third World."

Jack raises his eyebrows. "When we plunge back a million years or so, these 'uneducated' ethnicities will have superiority over your intellects by far, trust me."

"Thank you for the input, Dr. Bailey, but while I'm commander in chief, it will be done my way."

"That's your privilege, Mr. Sinclair, and I wish you luck. You'll be assured of a place in the history books if you succeed." A broad smile appears on his face. "Why, I might even get to like you a little."

The professor has given them more than enough to chew on, and Lloyd decides to bring the meeting to a conclusion. "Mr. Bailey, you will stay at the White House tonight. You'll want equipment to continue the research, so draw up a list of what you need and give it to Mr. Klaus. He'll make sure you get everything."

"And on the morrow?"

"You'll be flown to a secret underground facility in Nevada. This is where some of the nation's top scientists are engaged in classified research-and-development projects. You'll have your own laboratory and a spacious family unit at the Nora Hartley Center."

"Who's Nora Hartley?" Jack asks. "It's not a name I'm familiar with."

"She's a five-year-old girl from Las Vegas who disappeared in 1931. A shallow grave was uncovered on the first day of construction back in 1993. DNA tests on the bones and samples from living relatives confirmed it was the missing child, so they named it in her memory."

"That was thoughtful," Jack remarks. "How have you kept it a secret for so long?"

The president grins. "Sequestrations and executions."

"And in that order, probably," the professor replies, yawning.

"Mr. Bentley of Infinity is already there, and I'm hoping you'll have use for the data gleaned by his weather satellites," Lloyd says. "I think you'll find him affable. I've heard that he has misgivings about me that are similar to yours."

"I presume he's an unwilling participant too." When Lloyd doesn't answer, the academic chuckles and adds, "Make sure you keep some ice packs on hand. Your ears are going to burn hotter than firebricks in hell."

The president studies the professor's demeanor. For more than an hour he's talked about the imminent demise of mankind with the same casualness as one would discuss the weather on a nice day. "Why are you so calm, Dr. Bailey? Are you not afraid that death will catch up with you and your family in the coming weeks?"

"Mr. Sinclair, I'm scared. I'm probably more terrified than all of you put together"—he stifles a yawn—"but my fear is dulled by fatigue. It's been more than thirty-two hours since I last slept."

Lloyd isn't satisfied with the reply, but for now he'll accept it. He stands up. "I'll show you where the guest rooms are. Diane is preparing dinner. I hope you'll join us in the dining room after you've freshened up."

Dr. Bailey closes the bulky folder and slides it into the briefcase, and the six men leave the Oval Office together.

40

Arland Avenue
South San Gabriel, California
Coordinates: 34° 02' 51.0" N, 118° 05' 38.2" W
Saturday, June 27, 2020, 1647h

Harvey is a die-hard fan of the Oakland Raiders, and today they are playing a special charity challenge match against the San Diego Chargers. It promises to be a good game, and the athletic, six-foot-tall twenty-nine-year-old went to great expense to secure his freedom for the afternoon. His wife had wanted to squander the day with him in a shopping mall, but because her plans conflicted with the football game, he persuaded her to take his mother-in-law in his place. Anita was greatly vexed until he sweetened the deal with $1,000 for her to spend on herself.

The outdoor temperature is in the triple digits, and even though the thermostat is set at seventy two degrees, it feels much warmer. Dressed in a pair of shorts, he stretched out on the couch to watch the pregame show at one thirty, but even the best-laid plans can go awry. Ten minutes into the program, the station cut in with breaking news of a double plane crash at LAX, which quickly took precedence. The infringement annoyed him, but he works as a meteorologist at the airport, and the horrific scenes caught his interest. Earlier in the day, he had watched his former place of employment burn to the ground, and the news that a couple of technicians were killed in the explosion upset him. Worried that Danny was a victim, he made several calls to him, but they all went straight to voice mail.

Harvey was staggered when President Sinclair declared his longtime pal as a terror suspect, and he's certain that there's been a mistake. He knows how much Danny abhors violence, and something in his head won't allow him to believe the allegations. The station rejoined the game at halftime, but his well-organized afternoon has already crumbled into ruins. The news about his friend plays on his mind too much for him to concentrate on the game. Every commercial break commences with a bulletin that denounces Danny as a dangerous fugitive, and his picture, details of his car, and the offer of a huge reward for information leading to his capture are flashed across the screen.

Close to five o'clock, the chime of the doorbell echoes through the house. Harvey deliberates whether to answer it when the bell rings several times in frantic succession. He gets up from the couch, slips his feet into a pair of sandals, and shuffles across to the front door. His eyes open wide in astonishment.

"Danny! What the …?" He leans his head forward and casts a furtive glance along the road in each direction before pointing to a blue Toyota parked in the street. "Is that your car?"

"Yes."

Harvey reaches into the room to pick up a set of keys lying on top of a console table beside the door and presses two buttons on a small remote. The garage doors and a wrought-iron gate at the end of a short driveway begin to open.

"Pull your car into the garage after I move mine out," he says demandingly.

"Why?"

"I'll explain once we're in the house."

Danny is perplexed by Harvey's strange behavior, and his eyes follow the meteorologist as he heads for the garage. "Where are you going to park your car?"

Harvey disappears into the garage without replying, and moments later, a black BMW reverses onto the street. Still mystified at the reaction his unannounced arrival seems to have stirred, he gets into the Corolla and drives it into the garage. By the time he climbs out, the German-built car is already back on the driveway.

"Quick, man, get into the house."

Danny obeys and steps into the living room with Harvey close behind. "Hey, that's rather a melodramatic greeting, bud," he says, turning around to face his longtime pal. He's caught by surprise as the African American takes a fierce grip on his upper arms.

"Are you carrying a gun?"

The meteorologist's fervent behavior scares him. "N-no ... of *course* not," he stammers. "You *know* I don't carry weapons. What the hell is going on?"

Harvey releases his grasp on Danny's arms. "I guess you weren't listening to the car radio?"

"No."

"The feds are after you—*big* time. I'm tired of seeing your ugly visage plastered on my TV screen every ten minutes."

Danny is astounded. "What for?"

"Terrorism, murder, industrial espionage—you name it. You've been declared armed and dangerous, and they say you shouldn't be approached."

The young technician takes a step back and stares at his friend in astonishment. This confirms the suspicions that have cast a shadow over him all day, and the blood drains from his face at the acknowledgment. Numbed, he slumps into an armchair.

Harvey's voice continues to penetrate his head. "The first allegations were made by President Sinclair on national television. He identified you as the person who wrote and introduced the Chameleon virus into the satellite networks."

"He's a fucking liar," Danny explodes. "The president *knows* why the satellites are going offline, and it has nothing to do with a virus."

"Are you able to prove that? Because you're also accused of Steve's assassination, the bomb that destroyed Infinity headquarters, and eighteen thousand plus counts of homicide."

Danny's eyes open wide in bewilderment. "Murder?"

"The Chameleon spread into the GPS satellites today causing dozens of airliners to crash. They're holding you responsible for the deaths of the passengers and crews."

Danny stares at the ceiling in desolation. There's something wrong with the picture, and it suddenly hits him. He sits forward in the chair. "It's not possible."

Harvey frowns. "What isn't?"

"*Think*, man. Even if there was a virus, it's impossible to infect other networks. They're all isolated from one another."

Harvey mutes the television before speaking again. "So where are the nukes? In the trunk of your car?"

Danny frowns. "What *are* you on about?"

The meteorologist doesn't answer the question. "Listen, I think you should turn yourself in. The burden of proof is on them, and if you didn't do it ..."

"*No*," he snaps, cutting his friend off in midsentence. "They don't want to arrest me. They intend to *kill* me."

"You're getting paranoid."

Tears well up in the corners of Danny's eyes. "They've already killed Steve, Bill, Jim, and Nancy," he blurts, almost choking on the words. "Brad has disappeared, and apart from the president, I'm the only one left who knows why the satellites are failing."

Harvey's jaw drops open. "Nancy ... Steve's secretary?"

The technician nods a silent affirmation with despair-filled eyes. "Why is he lying? What is the president trying to hide?"

"You have no idea where BB is?"

"He's supposed to be at the White House, but I don't even know if he's still alive. Our satellite situation revealed an unusual phenomenon and it's become clear to me that they're trying to stop me from talking about it."

"You know something that ..." He vacillates. "You've got to level with me, man. I want to help you, but I can't if you hold out on me."

Danny contemplates on the possible ramifications to his friend before replying. "I don't want to put you in danger. If I'd been listening to the radio, I would never have come here."

"Well, now that you're here, let's figure this thing out."

With no strength left to resist, he submits to the debilitating effects of stress. "BB told me some dubious shit, but if he's right, a lot of people are going to die."

"When you say a *lot* of people, do you mean dozens? Hundreds?"

"No. He was talking about millions. He even implied that humans are at risk of extinction."

Harvey stares back in astonishment. "*How?*"

Danny starts to give a blow-by-blow account of his week.

Harvey is hooked, and he absorbs Danny's detailed story in fascination, but skepticism starts to kick in when he recounts BB's conception of an ecological disaster on such an epic scale. He doesn't speak until his friend has finished. "What you've said is pretty wild, man, but let's assume for one moment that Brad is right. As crazy as it sounds, it's making sense."

"It does?"

"I think the president turned Brad's file over to someone who is qualified to analyze the data and discovered more is going on than the satellites turned up." Harvey cogitates for a moment. "The answer to just one question will fill in the blank."

"Yeah—why?" Danny responds bitterly.

"No—what? If we can find out *what* they found, I think the *why* will fall into place." He smiles. "There's a way you can get him to repudiate the accusations he's made against you."

The technician inclines his head with curiosity. "I'm all ears."

"For some reason, Sinclair is trying to prevent you from talking to the media, so that's what you need to do."

Danny gives a harsh, bitter laugh. "Like *that's* going to work when I have nothing to support my story. The explosion at Infinity was so huge it's probably destroyed every scrap of evidence."

"That was probably the intention behind a blast that big." He takes a moment to ponder. "You can sleep in the spare room tonight. We need to figure out how to get this to the media without endangering you, but you'll have to stay out of sight for now. The feds suspected you were coming to Los Angeles, and that means every mother and her bitch has an eye open for you. They'll all want a cut of the bounty."

"Bounty?"

"Yeah, they've put two hundred fifty grand on your ass, so you'd better think yourself lucky I'm not broke."

"How did they know I came here?"

"I'm not sure, man. The last news bulletin before you rang the doorbell said you were seen at Gustine on route 152 and that you may have gotten on the I-5 after that."

"I stopped there to refuel, but how the hell did they know that? I dumped my iPhone back in Palo Alto so they couldn't triangulate my ... *Damn!* The waitress at the diner."

Harvey ponders. "How did you pay for the gas and food?"

"I used my credit card ..." He trails off and scowls. "They're tracking my fucking transactions." He gets to his feet. "Hey, man, I appreciate your offer, but I can't stay here. You and Anita could be in danger while I'm in the house, and I'm not going to let that happen."

"Shut up and sit back down," Harvey snaps. "You're not going anywhere."

"But—"

"You are *not* leaving—end of argument. Neither of us needs a crystal ball to know you won't get far. We have to get some evidence and then reach out to someone who'll believe you. We've got to expose the president for the asshole he is."

Danny sits down again, and after a long silence, he turns his head to look at Harvey. "Where's Anita?"

"She's out shopping with her mother. She should be back at any time." A smile flits across his lips. "Man, she'll be happy to see you. It's been a couple of years."

"Yeah, and perhaps she may *not* be as joyful as you think."

"She won't be a problem; I assure you. She's known you

long enough, and she'll believe you over Sinclair *any* day." The meteorologist bites his lip contemplatively. "Her mother might be a different matter, though."

"Why? I met her at your wedding, and she was really nice."

"She is, but you'll see the dollar signs spin in her eyes when she knows you're here. Let's face it, you've only met her once, and that was two years ago. She doesn't have a bond with you, so she won't have a problem turning you over for the reward."

"Then perhaps I should leave."

"You'll do no such thing. When she gets here, stay out of sight in the spare room until she leaves." He hesitates and smiles. "You'll get to meet Grace."

"Grace?"

"Our daughter! She's five months old."

"Oh, *man!* Congratulations! I had no idea."

Harvey's eyes gleam brightly with the pride of a new father. "Anita intended to write you a letter tonight, but now that you're here …" He breaks off with another smile.

Danny is looking at him with curiosity. "Now that I'm here … *what?*"

"We'd be honored if you'll be Grace's godfather."

41

The President's Private Study
The White House, Washington, DC
Coordinates: 38° 53' 50.6" N, 77° 02' 15.1" W
Saturday, June 27, 2020, 1812h

President Sinclair stares across the top of his desk at Terry with a heavy frown, and contemplation in his eyes. "How accurate do you think Dr. Bailey's assessment is?"

The vice president weighs the question before answering. "It disturbs me. I want to believe him because it's his field of expertise, and yet I feel cynical. His revelations are inconceivable, but neither of us are qualified to dispute his skill, knowledge, or proficiency."

"What if it's a sophisticated hoax intended to undermine my credibility? This *is* an election year, and he'd be hailed a hero in certain quarters if I reacted irrationally."

Terry purses his lips ponderingly. "I think the professor deems his evaluation as bona fide. I watched him carefully throughout the interview, and at no time did his demeanor suggest disingenuousness. He's a respected scholar, and he'd be undercutting his own integrity. He's far too intelligent to take the chance."

"Hoax or not, his exit will be a hell of a lot easier than mine. He makes no bones about his dislike for me."

"It's a double-edged sword for sure," the vice president murmurs. "The decision you make could be your legacy."

"I'm unhappy with the time line, though. I'm being rushed into a decision without the opportunity to validate its authenticity. This is one time I'd sell my soul for a glimpse into the future."

"What kind of action *can* we take if Dr. Bailey's evaluation is right?"

Lloyd gets up, walks around to the front of the desk, and begins to pace back and forth with his hands thrust into his pockets. "We've got to determine whether he *is* right first."

"We can't prevaricate for too long," Terry warns. "I suggest we seek a second opinion but construct a foundation so we have something ready to implement if we can corroborate the professor's assessment."

"A reevaluation means more people will get involved, and that comes with a greater risk of a leak."

The two men fall silent, and the only sound in the study is the muffled padding of the president's feet on the carpet as he continues to pace. Two minutes pass before he speaks again. "This is too absurd for words. What's the latest from the airlines?"

"The last update from the FAA and ICOA isn't encouraging. The GPS is moving out of alignment by one hundred sixty eight feet per minute. That's one point nine miles an hour."

Lloyd stops pacing and perches himself on the front of his desk. "I have no doubt that the earth is tumbling, but I'm not convinced that we're on course for a disaster on the scale predicted by Dr. Bailey. That's *too* surreal."

"It took Infinity several days to stumble on the cause for the satellite failures. The false allegation you made to the press may redirect their focus for now, but I think you've only bought a day or two before the truth is revealed."

Lloyd grunts. "You didn't like it when I used the Chameleon as an excuse."

"You said a *lot* I didn't like," Terry fires back. "I don't like the way you made false allegations against an innocent man, not forgetting all the crap that spilled out of your mouth about WMDs and mobilizing the military. What the hell was on your mind?"

The president is nonchalant. "I think troop mobilization might be a good idea under the circumstances. All hell will break loose once the news gets out, and they'll be needed to maintain civil order."

There's a glint of anxiousness in the vice president's eyes. "It has the potential to backfire. You committed perjury on national television, and if you're impeached, you could be charged with terrorism."

President Sinclair glares at Terry. "How?"

"Because you proclaimed a threat knowing it doesn't exist. You have no evidence that Walker is a terrorist or that a nuclear attack is imminent, and once the intelligence agencies reveal that reports don't subsist, you're going to be in deep shit."

The president is obdurate. "That's a gamble I'll have to take." Lloyd walks around the desk to his seat, picks up a pen, and begins to doodle absently on a notepad. The vice president twiddles his thumbs in sullen silence with his eyes cast to the floor, but it gives a little time for their tempers to cool off.

Two minutes later, Terry speaks without looking up. "Are you going to consult with our allies?"

"Absolutely not."

Terry raises his eyes. "How they respond might help us make the right decision."

"Morally it's the correct thing to do, but they'll find out by themselves soon enough. We have an advantage, and I intend to use it to get ahead of everyone else."

"Good *God*, Lloyd. Have you lost all honorability, even to our closest friends?"

Lloyd's eyes flash in anger. "Sharing the information will cripple our chances to get American citizens into the twilight zone if we have to. God forbid, even our own allies will conspire against us, and it would be foolish to imagine otherwise. Do you think the Brits are going to say, 'Okay, mate, you go ahead, and we'll squeeze in behind you if there's any room left'?" He pauses to let off a derisive snort. "It'll be 'Bloody tallyho, lads, and don't stop to smell the roses.'" The president can tell that Terry is conflicted, but ethics and principles won't keep him alive. He waves an arm towards the north wall. "I want an atlas pinned up here so we can all see where the twilight zone is."

"I'll call across to the Eisenhower office and get someone to bring a world map over post-haste," Terry replies.

Lloyd takes a moment to contemplate. "Earlier I looked it up on the Internet. Based on the latitudes given by Dr. Bailey, the northernmost limit starts in Central Mexico and extends to the Guatemalan southern border. Belize is the only other country within the two parallels."

"That leaves *us* out in the cold then, doesn't it?"

The president sits back in the chair with a tiny smile on his lips, but before he can say what his intentions are, they are interrupted by a sharp rap on the door.

"Come in."

General Morgan steps into the office and hesitates at the sight of Terry. "I'm sorry, Mr. President, I didn't realize you had company. I can come back later."

"Come in and close the door," Lloyd replies. "We're holding a preliminary discussion on the professor's evaluation, and I think another opinion is appropriate."

"I had a chat with Dr. Bailey," he tells them as he walks across the floor toward the reading table. He pulls a chair out and sits down.

"He's still up? I thought he'd be fast asleep by now," Terry remarks.

"He's *just* gone to bed, so I decided to drop by before I turn in too."

"Did he add anything to what he's told us?" the president asks.

"I probed him a bit. He went into deeper detail on the effects but never deviated from his original review. I'm not happy one iota."

"How much of his summarization do you believe?"

Barry deliberates before answering. "The data from Infinity, along with today's failures of satellite TV and GPS, leaves no doubt in my mind that the angle of the earth's axis is changing. The outcome will be an ecological disaster, but what will happen and how bad it will be ..." He shrugs. "The professor is adamant that a mass extinction event is in progress, but I'm not in a position to dispute that claim."

Lloyd stares at the general with a forlorn expression in his eyes. "You sound like a doomsday prophet." He pauses for a moment. "Do you think the professor might have misconceptions in regard to the extent of the adversity?"

The general frowns. "That's a loaded question, Mr. President. He's the only person among us with the credentials to make these evaluations, and we don't have the criteria to refute the accuracy of his assessment."

The president scowls. Today has been a mental drain, and fatigue is affecting his ability to formulate. "General, there are *two* ways we can go with this. I can choose to ignore the professor's warning or I can pin my faith on his every word, but whatever decision I make, it *can't be wrong.*"

"That gives you a fifty percent chance of getting it right."

"*Christ*, you *are* a lot of help, Barry," the president responds coldly. "A word of encouragement from someone would be nice once in a while."

General Morgan waves an open palm in a gesture of rejection. "Oh, you can preclude me from entering that field, sir. My job is to advise you on military strategies."

"My intention is to ensure the survival of American blood. We *will* come up with the best way to achieve these goals together."

The general inclines his head. "It sounds like you've already made your mind up on a subconscious level but you're afraid to pursue it without an endorsement."

"Are you suggesting that my leadership is faltering?"

"No, sir, but I do advise that you don't procrastinate."

"There's nothing like pushing a condemned man one step closer to the gallows," Lloyd mutters.

General Morgan drums his fingers on the table. "Dr. Bailey confessed that his interest in your political aspirations is nonexistent, but he also said that he isn't trying to manipulate an erroneous decision. He's more concerned about the future *he* has left than about yours."

"Cheeky bastard," Lloyd mumbles. In contradiction to his earlier perspicacity, the fear of a hoax has faded, but the big question still nags at him. *The professor believes, but is he right?*

"The truth is, Dr. Bailey doesn't expect you to do anything," the general adds. "He genuinely feels that nothing can stop the gears from turning and that the savior of mankind will be chance, luck, and God."

Lloyd leans back with an exasperated expression on his face. "The professor has thrown a gauntlet down in front of me." He throws his hands up in surrender.

"He hasn't challenged you to *anything*," the general responds. "You're the one putting demands on yourself."

Lloyd's eyes grow icy. "Perhaps you are right, General. I've challenged myself to do what *I* think is the right thing to do. My resolution is *para*mount, and the stakes have never been higher, but we owe *not*hing to anyone." His eyes turn to Terry. "Empathy is a sign of weakness, and allowing it to cloud our judgment for a single nanosecond could be our demise. If Dr. Bailey is to be believed, time is running out, and we shouldn't squander a single moment that God grants us." The president hesitates, and his shoulders slump wearily. "Okay, time-out. Terry, will you call Brian and Robert back in. We'll reconvene at 2100 hours."

"So we should prepare for a long night?" Terry asks.

Lloyd is indifferent. "Hell, no. An early night is my preference, but it'll depend on how long everyone keeps it going. I only want to present a couple of thoughts for everyone to sleep on."

"Do you want the professor here, too?"

"No, let him sleep, but it's time to bring Andrew Johnson into the circle."

The vice president leaves the study, and General Morgan chortles. "Diane's got an amazing feast laid out in the dining room."

"She loves to entertain, and she's doing plenty of that today," Lloyd says. "Let's go over there and discuss the North Korean crisis over dessert and coffee."

42

Arland Avenue
South San Gabriel, California
Coordinates: 34° 02' 51.0" N, 118° 05' 38.2" W
Saturday, June 27, 2020, 1903h

Anita walks into the house carrying Grace. Harvey leaps up from the couch to relieve her of the infant. As he nestles the baby in his arms, he contorts his face and turns it to one side with a gasp.

"*Jeee*-zus!"

His wife bursts out laughing. "She's brought you her first gift back from the mall. We had to open the car windows on the way home."

Rosalyn Lambert comes in through the front door with a load of shopping bags and sets them on the floor. Anita is her only child. She's been divorced for twenty years, all of which she devoted solely to her daughter, but now she's looking for a man to share her twilight years. She smiles at Harvey. "How's my favorite boy?"

"I'm fine, Mom. What about you?"

"I'm just peachy. We bought new clothes for Gracie, and I even splurged out on a sexy evening gown for myself."

"She's happy because she has a hot date tonight," Anita explains.

"Yes, and I think I've found the right man at last."

"Is he taking you somewhere special?" Harvey asks.

"Dinner and dancing." She looks at her daughter. "Let me get the baby stroller from the trunk."

"Thanks, Mom. I need to take Grace upstairs and clean her stinky ass."

A wave of panic sweeps through Harvey. Danny is in the shower, and he doesn't want her walking in on him when she has no idea he's in the house. "It's okay, honey, I'll change her." He tries to hide his reluctance behind a weak smile. The thought of exposing the contents of the diaper is far from appealing.

Her eyes open wide in astonishment. "You *will?*"

Harvey nods and walks toward the staircase trying not to inhale too deeply.

"Oh, did you hear the *news?*"

He stops with one foot on the first step. "The plane crashes at LAX?"

"Danny's a *terrorist*," she says excitedly.

"He never did any of the things they are saying."

She looks at her husband in surprise. "How do *you* know? Have you been talking to him."

"I'll tell you later," he says, lowering his voice.

She places her hands on her hips defiantly. "No you won't. You'll tell me now."

Harvey hesitates. "He's upstairs in the shower."

She stares at her husband in disbelief. "Are you fucking insane?"

Surprised by his wife's reaction, he pleads with her. "Give him a chance to tell you his side of the story before you make an unfair judgment."

Anita's response is sharp and emphatic. "If he's innocent, then he needs to turn himself in and explain it to the cops."

"Honey, it's more complicated than that. There are people in prominent positions who want him gone—as in ..." He slices the edge of an open palm across his throat. "He's desperate for our help."

She looks at him warily. "I don't want guns around Grace."

"He doesn't have a weapon. All that crap that he's armed and dangerous is a lie."

Anita hesitates. Her eyes are full of suspicion, but she relents. "Okay, I'll listen to what he has to say, but if I don't believe him, I *will* call the police."

"Thank you, honey. Just don't tell mother."

A bustle at the door interrupts the conversation. Rosalyn enters the house dragging the folded baby stroller in one hand and props it against the wall. "Did you hear the news about your best man, Harvey?"

"Yes, Mom."

"I can't believe he's done all those awful things. He seemed like such a pleasant young man when I met him at your wedding. Oh well." She gives her daughter a hug. "I'll call you tomorrow and let you know how my date went. Bye for now, my dears."

As her mother leaves, Anita walks over to her husband. "*Now* I know why you wanted to change Grace. Give her to me; I'll do it."

"It's okay, honey, I'll bathe her. I want Danny to explain to you why he's here."

Anita is a good listener. For the next thirty minutes, she pays attention without interruption. He seems to be the same Danny that she's familiar with and doesn't perceive any change in his personality, except it's clear he's scared half to death. However, it's not an easy story to swallow, and she can't decide whether to believe it. Intuition tells her that he's innocently caught up in an event beyond his control, and because she's known him for a long time, Anita decides to give him the benefit of the doubt—at least for now.

Harvey comes back downstairs. "I've put Grace to bed. She's still sleeping."

"Show Danny up to the spare room, hon."

"You believe him then?"

Anita glances at the technician. "Kind of. It's hard to wrap my head around this mass extinction stuff, but I don't think he's a dangerous terrorist or has carried out any of the alleged crimes."

"I knew you'd give him a chance once you heard his story," Harvey says. "Come on, bud, I'll show you where your room is."

Twenty-five minutes later, Anita is working in the kitchen. The kettle on the stove starts to boil, and she lifts it away from the heat with one hand while turning the gas off with the other. Danny appears in the doorway.

"I'm making a pot of tea, but I can brew some coffee if you prefer."

"Tea will be fine," the technician replies. "I feel guilty for placing you guys in such an awkward position, but I'm relieved that you believe me."

"I didn't say I believed you. I just know you're not a terrorist. I'm still up in the air over that other stuff, though." Anita walks over to the windows and closes the venetian blinds. "There's a house at the back," she explains. "I don't want anyone looking in as they walk past. If they've been watching television, they'll recognize you in a flash."

"Where's Harvey?"

"He's gone out to pick up a couple of pizzas. There's a wonderful little Italian place around the corner." She gestures with a hand toward the table, inviting him to sit down. "He'll be back any moment."

The young woman places a mug in front of him, and as she pours the tea, they hear the front door closing. "Ahh, here he is," she mutters, drying her hands on a towel.

Harvey walks into the kitchen with two large pizza boxes and places them on the table. "One Hawaiian with mushrooms, and a bell pepper, onion, and italian sausage. Eat and enjoy."

"Mmm. Deep pan as well," Danny mumbles.

Harvey glances at his wife. "Is Grace still sleeping?"

Anita hands a plate to their guest as she answers her husband. "Yep, a day at the mall has knocked her out."

He laughs, and turns his eyes to his friend. "Would you like a beer?"

"No, thanks. Tea is fine. I think it's a good idea to stay alcohol-free until I figure out what to do next."

"I have to work tomorrow," Harvey says. "Is there any information I can download from the satellite that might help you?"

Danny appears surprised. "Is it still in operation?"

"It was still working when I left the office at six o'clock last night."

The technician chews slowly as he contemplates the question. "Your access to information is limited and may not even be useful. Now, if you can get into the temporary files where the sunrise and sunset data are stored …" He trails off, and a dark scowl settles on his face. "*Crap!* That won't work. If the satellite's still operational, it means that the differentiation is less than forty-five seconds, and it's not going to be of any use. If I could use a communicator, I might be able to access more data with my password."

"You could give me your code," Harvey suggests. "You'll need to tell me what I'm looking for, though."

"Call me once you're in, and I'll walk you through the process verbally."

Anita cuts in. "Why don't you hook a video link between your tablet and the home PC? I'm sure it would help if Danny could look at it too."

Harvey smiles at the technician. "Now you know why I married her."

Anita looks at her husband with a sparkle in her eye, but her response is interrupted by the chime of the doorbell. Harvey pauses with a half-eaten slice of pizza poised in front of his mouth.

"Who the hell can *that* be?"

His wife gives a nonchalant shrug. "It'll be one of your friends. I'm not expecting anybody."

Harvey places the pizza back on the plate, gets to his feet, and walks out of the kitchen to see who's at the front door. The two well-dressed men on the doorstep exude an air of officialdom, and taken by surprise, Harvey feels an uncomfortable jitter bubble up in his stomach.

"Are you Mr. Worrell … Mr. Harvey Worrell?" one of them asks. The second man raises himself on his toes and stretches his neck in an attempt to gawk over Harvey's shoulder into the room beyond.

"Yes, I am."

The man holds an identity badge out for him to inspect. "FBI. My name is Bobby King, and this is my partner, David Emery. May we come in?"

"I'm in the middle of dinner. Can you come back later?"

"We only have a couple of quick questions; then we'll be on our way."

Harvey is nervous, and he fakes chewing on the remnants of a mouthful of food to buy a few precious seconds. If he refuses, they might think he has something to hide and come back with a search warrant. Danny is in the kitchen, but he knows they don't have the right to wander through the house without a court order. He opens the door wider. "Uh … sure, come in."

The agents take up an intimidating stance in the center of the room just as Anita appears in the kitchen door.

"These men are from the FBI," he explains.

Her demeanor is calm, and she greets them with a polite smile. "Would you like a cup of tea, coffee, or a soda?" Both men decline, shaking their heads. "Then give me a moment to slip our dinner into the oven to keep warm."

Anita disappears, and Harvey invites the agents to sit down, but neither man accepts the offer. David is craning his neck to get a surreptitious peek into the kitchen, which unnerves Harvey until his wife returns. He's beginning to wonder how she can look so relaxed and confident because he's close to sweating bullets.

"I apologize for the bad timing," Bobby says. "I expect you've seen the news bulletins about your friend Danny Walker?"

Harvey is cautious with his response. "He was my colleague when I worked at Infinity, but I quit in 2017 and moved down here when I got married."

"You do keep in touch with him, don't you?"

"From time to time. I haven't seen him in eighteen months, though."

"What was the reason for the reunion?"

"He was best man at our wedding."

"What about phone calls, e-mails, and such?"

Harvey ponders for a moment. "The last time I heard from him was six months ago. He called us on Christmas Day." He can sense that the agent is getting irritated at his failure to volunteer information.

"Mr. Walker was seen on the I-5 earlier today, and because of your friendship, we thought he might be coming here."

Harvey's response is snippy. "You thought wrong then, didn't you?"

An angry blush colors the agents cheeks. "I didn't come here to play games, Mr. Worrell. Walker is a dangerous man, and if you've heard from him, or know where he is, you need to tell us."

"I've already told you, the last time we spoke was on Christmas Day."

Bobby pauses. "You'd help a good friend, though, wouldn't you? After all, that's what friends do."

Harvey's annoyance increases as the agent's questions become more aggressive. "Let's be clear, Mr. King. I have a five-month-old daughter, and I will *not* put her in danger for anyone—not even a good friend."

Bobby's reply is cold. "I'm not convinced that you'll break your camaraderie so easily without demanding an explanation from him first."

"That's irrelevant. He has not called. He has not turned up on our doorstep."

"Then where do you think he went?"

"San Diego sounds like a good destination to me."

"Why San Diego?"

Harvey's eyes open wide in surprise. "I expect he's in Mexico by now. Isn't that where fugitives head for?"

"Sometimes," Bobby replies. He reaches into a pocket and pulls out a business card. "You can reach me at this number if you hear anything from him." The agent glances at his partner. "Come on, David; we'll let these people get back to their meal."

Harvey follows them to the door. Anita comes up behind her husband and peers around his body. David steps outside and stops, and his eyes wander over the BMW. "These are nice cars, but they're expensive to maintain," David remarks.

"Something nice always comes with a price tag," Harvey responds.

The agent nods. "Which is why I'm wondering why it's parked in the driveway when you have a garage."

Harvey isn't prepared for a question of this nature and falters, but Anita is quick to cover him. "I don't think that's *any* of your business," she fires back indignantly.

"I was asking your husband, Mrs. Worrell."

"*My* car is in there," she snaps.

David inclines his head. "Oh ... you have a car, Mrs. Worrell?"

"Why? Do you think women aren't capable of driving?"

His eyes bore into hers without wavering.

"Actually, it isn't registered to me," she admits sheepishly. "It belongs to my mother. She's loaned it to me in case there's an emergency with the baby while Harvey's at work."

"What does your mother do when *she* needs a car?"

"Her boyfriend drives her around most of the time."

Bobby intervenes. "I'm sorry to have bothered you, Mrs. Worrell." He nudges his partner with an elbow and the agents retreat down the garden path. Harvey closes the door with a sigh of relief.

Anita has a concerned expression in her eyes. "Those aren't FBI agents."

He walks toward the kitchen. "They showed me their badges."

"Were they real or fake?"

"Well …" he stammers.

"You couldn't tell, could you?"

"Then who are they?"

"I don't know, but they're not FBI."

Harvey steps into the kitchen and stops. "Where's Danny?"

Anita pushes past him and opens the oven to take the pizza out. "He's in the broom closet."

43

The President's Private Study
The White House, Washington DC
Coordinates: 38° 53' 50.6" N, 77° 02' 15.1" W
Saturday, June 27, 2020, 2101h

President Sinclair waits in silence as the five staffers shuffle into the private study and take a seat at the reading table.

The newcomer is Andrew Johnson. Lloyd wants a clear verdict on Dr. Bailey's averment and hopes that an input from the Secretary of Health and Human Services will help him make some crucial decisions.

"Mr. Johnson, you weren't at the meeting with Dr. Bailey. Did anyone explain to you what's going on and why we are here?"

Andrew smiles at the president. He's an intelligent, soft-spoken man who isn't afraid to speak his mind. "Terry briefed me on the basics, but it's pretty hard to swallow."

"What part was tough to ingest? The shifting axis or Dr. Bailey's predictions?"

"Both. They're in direct contradiction to the Chameleon virus and terrorist threat you announced on national television this afternoon."

"That was an intentional distraction," Lloyd confesses. "I needed to buy some time so I could get things into context."

"And have you? Gotten it into context, I mean."

"Not yet."

"You only need to ask yourself whether the axis is shifting or not. There should be no question as to whether Dr. Bailey's assessment lacks verisimilitude if the answer is yes."

General Morgan joins the discussion. "The data supports that a shift is occurring, but we only have the doctor's word on *how* it's moving and the effects it will have."

"If the axis *is* changing, then it gives credence to the doctor's evaluation," Andrew replies. "The repercussions will be ca*lam*itous to life, even if the temperature doesn't reach the extremes he forecasts."

Terry leans toward the Health and Human Services secretary. "I know you're a strong adversary of greenhouse emissions, but this isn't a man-made catastrophe. We have to disassociate ourselves from the global warming phenomenon, per se."

Andrew shrugs. "I guess the *real* question is, what are we going to do about it?"

"We've covered that avenue with the professor," Lloyd replies. "He's promised a spectacular eradication of life that will culminate in the demise of mankind. The planet is going to be transformed into a nearly lifeless orb, with the exception of a narrow band around the planet's girth. I want to formulate a plan that can be swiftly implemented if necessary. I've brought you in so we can figure out how many people can safely inhabit the twilight zone, and to advise on any health issues we might encounter."

"I guess this is the defining moment of my career," Andrew replies.

Lloyd smiles before responding. "I don't think anyone is in disagreement that the earth is tumbling. It appears that you already trust the professor's evaluation, but the rest of us are conflicted because he hasn't produced evidence to support his theory. He told us that the tumble will continue until March 3 next year, but how do I know we won't wake up tomorrow morning to find out it stopped while we were asleep?"

Andrew returns the smile. "I wouldn't hedge my bets, sir. Astrophysicists are a unique breed who live on their own plateau. You'd be amazed at how they can make predictions with incredible accuracy."

It's never easy to ruffle Andrew's feathers, and his calm, almost blunt, demeanor irritates the president. "I like the rationale you've applied to make your decision, but I need more than that." Lloyd gets to his feet and walks across the study to stand in front a world map that Terry pinned to the wall thirty minutes earlier. Two parallel lines drawn in by a red marking pen signify the boundaries of the twilight zone. "If Dr. Bailey is correct, the safe region is between Central Mexico and Guatemala's southern border."

"What about Panama?" Robert asks.

"Dr. Bailey told me it will be the new Siberia," General Morgan replies.

Andrew nods in agreement. "Yes, it's too far south, and the sun will be below the horizon. I was on the Internet earlier, and the headlines coming out of South America reports a massive snowstorm is sweeping across Argentina and Chile. Winds in excess of two hundred miles an hour and temperatures below minus forty degrees are largely unconfirmed because of a communications blackout, but it's expected to rage on for at least seven days."

Brian emits a low whistle. "That's some storm."

President Sinclair picks up a wooden pointer to indicate key elements on the map as he brings the focus back to the twilight zone. "Other countries who get a division are parts of North Africa, Saudi Arabia, Central India, and small portions of the southern Asian continent, including sections of Thailand, Laos, Vietnam, Bangladesh, Myanmar, and about fifteen percent of South China." He hesitates and then drags the pointer down to the southeastern corner of the USA. "Our share is in southern Florida."

General Morgan shakes his head. "The polar ice cap is thawing. The subsequent rise in sea level will submerge the Floridian peninsula." He sweeps an arm toward the map. "Countries like Myanmar and Bangladesh that don't have enough elevation will disappear, and that means a significant reduction of valuable land space within the twilight zone."

Lloyd cogitates as he walks back to rejoin the group at the table. "General, let's assume for one minute that Dr. Bailey *is* right. How long would it take for a military operation to secure the twilight zone?"

Brian lurches forward and signals a time-out with his hands. "Hold on! Hold on! That's a dangerous ideation to contemplate. Mexico is a sovereign country, and what you're suggesting will contravene every act and treaty we have in place."

President Sinclair snorts. "Treaties will be worthless scraps of paper once the tumble goes public."

Terry leaps to his feet. "Come *on*, Mr. President. Do you honestly believe we can plan and execute an invasion of Central America *and* be victorious in less than … what … two weeks? One month?"

Lloyd's eyes blaze angrily. "My question was specifically directed at General Morgan."

The cacophony dissipates into silence, and five pairs of eyes turn to Barry. "We need to approach this with commonsensical rationality. A military incursion into, and successful occupation of, the twilight zone cannot be achieved."

The president scowls. "We have the greatest military power in the world!"

"That might be so, but it doesn't do any good when eighty percent of our servicemen and women are spread out across the Korean peninsula and the Middle East. The Mexican, Belizean, and Guatemalan governments will form a coalition, and it will be impossible to dislodge them from an incumbent position in the short time we have to plan, secure, and open a safe channel for our citizens to travel to the region. It would be foolish to think otherwise. There will be an unholy bloodbath for nothing. Those who don't die in battle will perish from the heat. You would do better to explore a strategic diplomatic solution."

Lloyd strokes his chin as he takes several seconds to ruminate. Although he doesn't see an immediate avenue where diplomacy could be a way forward, the general has restored some acuity to the discussion. "I'll give it some overnight consideration."

Andrew raises a hand. "Is it your intention to relocate three hundred forty million US citizens into the twilight zone?"

"Yes."

"You can't afford to overpopulate the region, sir," the Secretary for Health and Human Services advises. "A proportionate balance with adequate acreage per habitant needs to be maintained—not only for agronomical produce but for livestock too. Self-sufficiency will be the main ingredient for survival. There will be no foreign commerce, and the daily luxuries we take for granted are going to vanish overnight."

"Christ, who invited *him* on the team?" Robert mutters.

Lloyd throws a cautioning glance in the direction of the Homeland Security secretary. Andrew is the only one who seems to have an insight of Dr. Bailey's assessment, and the president has taken an interest in what he has to say. "You've captured my attention, Mr. Johnson. Please, continue."

"I'm only going by the notes Terry gave me, but when Dr. Bailey told you that just two point eight percent of the world will be habitable, don't make the mistake of thinking it's all across the border to our south. The combined area of the twilight zone in Mexico, Belize, and Guatemala is about twenty-seven hundredths of a percent of the earth's topography. If we reserve land within the temperate region suitable for agriculture, the habitable expanse is reduced to eighteen hundredths of a percent. I'm not an agriculturist, so it might be a good idea to seek the advice of Bernard Lehman in this area, but much of the land within the temperate zone is infertile desert. Toil and patience will be required to work the earth into malleable farmland. By my estimation, the maximum population in the twilight zone can't exceed two hundred four point four million."

The vice president frowns. "Are you *sure* about that number?"

"It's a pretty close approximation. Is that less than you anticipated?"

Terry flicks through a couple of pages in his notebook. "Yes, but here's the real problem. One hundred forty million people are distributed between these three countries who have every right to be there. If a migration becomes necessary, I hoped we could transfer at *least* one hundred twenty million US citizens into the twilight zone, but your calculation cuts that figure down to sixty-four point four million."

The news devastates Lloyd, and he groans. "I can't accept that, I simply *can't*. We're going to move one hundred twenty million. I will *not* go for anything less."

Andrew's expression remains placid. "Fair enough. We can make that our target, but we're still responsible for another two hundred twenty million Americans who won't be included in the exodus."

A heavy, uncomfortable silence descends over the group as the stark reality hits home. All eyes turn to Lloyd. When Dr. Bailey made a similar declaration at the afternoon meeting, there was so much skepticism that it came across as superficial and insignificant. The president's voice grows cold. "Unless we can come up with an alternative plan, we may have to sacrifice two thirds of our nation to ensure the survivability of the other third."

Loud gasps resound around the table. With the exception of General Morgan, who remains expressionless, they stare at the president in horror and disbelief. Lloyd squirms uncomfortably in his seat at the response.

Andrew is the first to react. "You *can't* abandon our citizens to such an ugly, grotesque fate."

President Sinclair's demeanor hardens, and the muscles along his jaw tighten as he clenches his teeth. He keeps his voice low but firm and resolute. "I didn't say I would desert them, but it is a realism we might have to face if we can't come up with a plan."

General Morgan gets up, walks over to the map, and studies it for several minutes. "We could put them on ships and send them across the Atlantic. Western Sahara or Mauritania could be viable destinations. These are underpopulated regions, and mostly desert, but they will be in the twilight zone."

Lloyd pulls his chair closer to the desk. "They'll be the likely destinations for Europeans too."

The general saunters back to the table. "Perhaps, but I don't think so."

"Eh?"

"North Africa won't be a popular destination. The desert is uninviting at best, and most will make the mistake of setting off for India and places across Asia instead."

President Sinclair stares down at the carpet with a morose expression in his eyes. "What's the latest update on the GPS satellites?"

Robert volunteers an answer. "I called the FAA after dinner. They've verified that their systems are still in failure mode. Tests confirm that specified coordinates are steadily moving out of position toward southwest by west."

Lloyd curses beneath his breath. "We *must* get our aircraft back into the skies." He looks at the general. "Can they revert to radio beacons like they used to?"

"The last commercial beacon was phased out two years ago after the law requiring all aircraft to be equipped with GPS navigational systems as standard became effective. The few that are still in operation were kept for strategic military functions, but there aren't enough left to be practical for commercial airlines."

"Can't they be reintroduced?" Terry asks.

"They can," Barry replies dubiously, "but it's going to take far longer than Mother Nature is willing to give us."

The president frowns and folds his arms across his chest. "We're all exhausted and need to rest. Perhaps I'll have an epiphany overnight, or if I'm lucky, I'll get a visitation from God and he'll offer some sound advice. Just in case that doesn't happen …" He finishes the sentence with a shrug.

"I'm in favor of a second opinion before we go any further," Terry says.

"I have a close friend at NASA whose qualifications are equal to Dr. Bailey's." General Morgan tells them.

Robert intervenes. "That poses a new problem unless you're prepared to have him sequestered too. Containment will be impossible once we draw NASA's attention to the tumble."

"It's okay; I can be discreet."

Lloyd ponders the general's suggestion. "How long will it take to get him to respond?"

"I'll have an answer by tomorrow morning," Barry replies with reassurance.

"If you can do it without raising red flags, then go ahead," the president says. "I intend to make a decision one way or another on the morrow. We'll reconvene at 0800."

"You have a rally in Ohio tomorrow," Terry reminds him.

"Postpone it."

"I don't think that's a good plan."

"I'm in accordance but unfortunately, it's the only one I have," Lloyd replies brusquely.

President Sinclair remains in his seat while the five staffers file out of the study, and he heaves a heavy sigh as the door closes behind the last person. Whatever decision he makes tomorrow needs to be the right one. There will be no second chance.

Continued in book two: *Tumble: The Golden Capricorn*

Acknowledgments

I would like to acknowledge the following people for their input, help, and advice:

- David Zwiefelhofer of www.findlatitudeandlongitude.com, who unselfishly shared his expertise so readers of the e-book version could have an option to bring up an interactive map with a single click at the start of each chapter
- Sarah Disbrow, for her candid evaluation and invaluable advice
- Teresa Parry, Rock Berntsen, Ralph Gilbert, and Scott Shaw, for proofreading and pointing out occasional factual errors
- Margit Elland Schmitt, who promptly pointed me in the right direction when I was faced with a dilemma; I wish you luck with your own projects
- Pete King, who offered technical support with Microsoft Word when I put out a cry for help

Finally, I want to give special mention to Don and Karen Gabel, whom I have never met but who took the time and effort to send me handwritten letters—the first true fan mail I ever received.

Thank you!